Tikiri

Copyright

This is a work of fiction. Names, characters, businesses, places, events and incidents are either the products of the author's imagination or used in a fictitious manner. Any resemblance to actual persons, living or dead, or actual events, situations, and customs is purely coincidental.

All rights reserved.

The use of any part of this publication, reproduced, transmitted in any form or by any means electronic, mechanical, photocopying, recording, or otherwise or stored in a retrieval system without prior written consent of the publisher—or in the case of photocopying or other reprographic copying, a license from the Canadian Copyright Licensing Agency—is an infringement of the copyright law.

. . . .

THE GIRL WHO MADE THEM Pay
The Red Heeled Rebels Series
Book Two
All rights reserved.
Copyright ©2020 Tikiri Herath
Edition: 2020
www.RedHeeledRebels.com[1]

. . . .

LIBRARY & ARCHIVES Canada Cataloging in Publication
ISBN: 978 1 989232 25 5

. . . .

AUTHOR: TIKIRI HERATH
Publisher: Nefertiti Press
Copy Editor: Stephanie Parent
Cover Design: Angela Oltmann
Back Cover Headshot: Aura McKay

---

1.   http://www.RedHeeledRebels.com

The Girl Who Made Them Pay

Book Two
Red Heeled Rebels Series

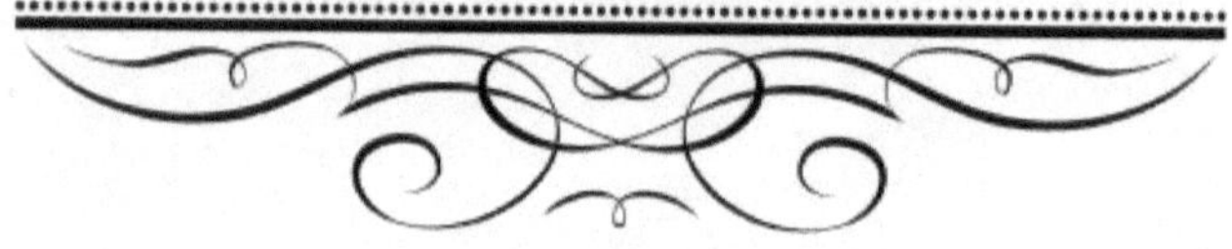

• • • •

Previously titled ABDUCTED.
This is the second book in the Red Heeled Rebels series. This can be read as a standalone novel, but you'll enjoy it more if you've read the previous book.
You can learn about the full series here.
www.RedHeeledRebels.com[2]

HAVE YOU READ THE PREQUEL story to the Red Heeled Rebels yet?

Here's a small gift for you for picking up this book!
Get your copy of **The Girl Who Crossed the Line** here. Download link is at the back of this book.

Other Titles by Author

• • • •

The Red Heeled Rebels Novels[1]
The Girl Who Crossed the Line
The Girl Who Ran Away
The Girl Who Made Them Pay
The Girl Who Fought to Kill
The Girl Who Broke Free
The Girl Who Knew Their Names
The Girl Who Never Forgot

• • • •

The Accidental Traveler
An anthology of short stories based on the author's sojourns around the world.

• • • •

The Rebel Diva Nonfiction Series[2]
Your Rebel Dreams: 60 Days to discover your purpose and passions and power up your life.
Your Rebel Plans: 30 Days to create a masterplan for your career and life change.
Your Rebel Life: 100 habit hacks to transform the ten most important pillars of your life.
Bust Your Fears: 3 easy tools to conquer your fears and upgrade your career and life.

• • • •

1. http://www.RedHeeledRebels.com

2. http://www.RebelDivas.com

Collaborations

The Boss Chick's Bodacious Destiny Nonfiction Bundle
Dark Shadows 2: Voodoo and Black Magic of New Orleans

The going from a world we know
To one a wonder still
Is like the child's adversity
Whose vista is a hill,
Behind the hill is sorcery
And everything unknown,
But will the secret compensate
For climbing it alone?
Emily Dickinson

T he man in the black suit pushed Katy toward the airport doors.

"Hey!" I hollered.

He ignored me. She didn't even look my way.

"Let her go!" I yelled louder.

Two smartly dressed businesswomen walking into the executive lounge in the terminal, glared at me as they passed by.

Why can't they see what's happening?

"I said, stop!" I shouted, waving my arms.

I wasn't watching where I was going and hit a trolley piled with luggage. The handle bar whacked into my stomach and I doubled over.

The trolley rolled toward a man reading the flight display screens, but I didn't stop. I couldn't.

I straightened up and kept running. I dodged a bunch of kids with their noses stuck to their phones. They didn't move aside an inch. They didn't even look up.

"Stop!" I shouted again, my voice getting hoarse.

Who's this guy? Where's he taking her?

From the corner of my eyes, I saw the vague shape of a man in a blue uniform at the other end of the corridor.

For half a second, I thought of turning around and sprinting that way to ask for help, but the brief distraction cost me. My heel buckled and I tripped. I caught myself before I hit the floor and looked up to see the man in the suit pull my best friend outside.

Why isn't she fighting back?

Ignoring the searing pain in my ankle, I crashed through the main doors, just as he pushed Katy into a black London cab.

"Katy! Come back!"

The cab door banged shut, catching Katy's bright red scarf on the door well. The man jumped in front and the car pulled out.

"No-ooo!" I screamed. Everyone turned to look. "Stop that car! Help!" I spluttered, pointing.

A group of businessmen waiting in the limousine line looked over with smirks on their faces. Others turned away as if embarrassed by the spectacle. I didn't care. I dashed across the road.

With a sinking feeling in my stomach, I watched as the cab gathered speed. Katy's red scarf fluttered from the door well like it was giving me the finger.

"Katy!" I screamed as the car turned the corner and disappeared from view.

Chapter Two

None of this would have happened if Katy had followed me inside the café.

But a fancy shoe store had distracted her and shoes for Katy were like crack for addicts. She didn't make a lot of money at Dick's Next Day Catering Company back in Toronto, but she'd rather starve than forgo a pair of sexy new heels even when the world was crashing around us.

Only a day earlier, four men had chased us across the city of Toronto to the airport, where we'd hunkered down in a women's washroom overnight. We'd barely evaded them on our way to the boarding gate.

On the plane, I tried to forget our worries while Katy switched on the little screen to get lost in the movies. But I never relaxed, and I saw Katy's eyes flit from the screen to the aisle and back again as if she was afraid the men would somehow appear in midair. When the plane finally touched down at London's Heathrow Airport, we stumbled out, burnt-out and nerve-racked.

My hastily packed backpack weighed me down and the wheels on Katy's fake Louis Vuitton suitcase made a racket to wake the dead. It was a relief to find our departure gate to Goa, but that was when Katy spotted the flashing red sign over Air India's check-in counter.

"Oh, no!" she cried out.

We'd been so desperate to get out of Toronto, we'd taken the only seats available, which were standby. This meant everyone else had first dibs and the airline could bump us as they wished.

I ran up to the desk. I hated these high service counters because they made me feel even smaller than my five feet. I got on my tiptoes. "We've got boarding passes, but they're standby. Could you find seats for us, please?" I asked, with a smile on my lips and hope in my heart.

The attendant didn't even touch my ticket. She wrinkled her nose like it smelled of bad cheese. "Do you not see the sign?" she said, pointing up. "The flight's full." Her tone was crisp. Final.

"Is there any way you can squeeze us in?" I asked, unbeaten. "It's just two of us."

"We'd fit anywhere. We're on the smaller side," I heard Katy say from behind me.

The attendant didn't look amused.

"It's an emergency," I said. That wasn't a lie. Dick and Jose, who owned the bakery in Toronto where I baked cakes and Katy kept the books, had plans to sell us like we were nothing more than lemon tarts or plum pies. I had no idea how far their reach was, but I didn't want to hang around to find out. "It's really, really urgent," I said to the attendant.

She sighed and snapped her fingers. "All right, passports and boarding passes please." Her fingers flew across the keyboard while we stood by, our own crossed tightly.

"Sorry," she said, turning to us. "There are absolutely no seats on this one. But—" She stopped to squint at the screen. We waited, holding our breath.

"I see a couple of seats in the next flight departing to Delhi. You won't be sitting together and I can't promise anything because you're on standby. That flight's tomorrow at thirteen hundred hours."

"Tomorrow?" I said. That would give Dick and Jose ample time to figure out where we'd run off to and catch up.

"Don't you have anything today?" Katy asked, in a plaintive voice.

"Booked passengers get priority," the ground attendant said. "Here are your new boarding passes, and ladies, don't be late tomorrow."

I took back our papers with shaking hands.

"If you need a place to stay the night, the airport Sheraton's right up—" She paused and looked us over. Our wrinkled, hand-me-down clothes were a dead giveaway. Lowering her voice, she said, almost sympathetically, "Girls, there are quiet lounges in Terminal Three if you need some rest for the night."

She glanced at the line that had formed behind us and snapped her fingers. "Next, please."

Katy and I stumbled to the closest waiting area and collapsed.

I swung my feet out and leaned against the back of the seat, my right foot clinking as I shifted. My ankle bracelet had been a gift from my cousin Preeti, a gift for my wedding day three years ago, back in Goa, the day I made the biggest escape of my life. That was also the last time I saw Preeti.

"What're we gonna do now?" Katy asked.

Dark circles ringed her bloodshot eyes, making her look years older than nineteen. I was only six months younger than her but I must have the same ragged look, I thought.

I pulled my bag off my back and rubbed my eyes. "Find a place to sleep, maybe?"

"Way too stressed for that."

"We could go hide out in the washroom again," I said with a weak smile.

"Don't even think about it," Katy said.

We sat silently on the stiff bench seats for an hour, leaning against each other, not sure of what to do or what to say.

Around us, businesswomen and men in sharp suits marched up and down, pulling their laptop bags behind them. Families hurried by with fussy kids in tow, toward departure gates. Couples with arms intertwined walked by on their way to honeymoons or romantic destinations. Occasionally, a harried soul stumbled by looking as jet-lagged and beat as we were, but they were few, and they seemed to know where they were heading, unlike Katy and I who felt totally lost and alone.

We must have looked a strange pair.

She was a sinewy redhead in a miniskirt and her signature three-inch red stilettos, all found in a consignment store, but as good as new. She'd dressed for a date with Jose, a date that never took place. And never will, now she's found out what he really wanted to do with her.

I sat next to her, a petite half-Indian girl in a hand-me-down miniskirt and more sensible red pumps. I couldn't afford to wear high heels like Katy, because while she sat at her desk in the book-keeping anteroom most of the day making client calls, I spent most of mine bustling between the bakery's kitchen counter and oven.

Right now, my skirt was streaked with white because I'd had only enough time to throw off my apron before running out of the bakery. After that, more important worries had crowded my mind than flour on my skirt or icing sugar in my hair.

Katy let out a loud sigh. She looked like she was asleep, but I could see her scan the crowd from under half-closed eyelids.

"Hey." I nudged her gently on the elbow.

"Hmm?" She stirred and opened her eyes. Her face looked pale and drawn and I could see visible lines on her forehead.

"We can't lounge here all day."

"I can."

"They've probably got a shoe sale over there."

"I'm tired, Asha."

"For *shoe sales*?"

She sat still for a minute, surveying the surrounding area. People were pushing trolleys, pulling suitcases, heads lost in phone conversations. Announcements blared from the loudspeakers: pre-boarding calls, boarding calls, final calls, final-final calls. It seemed like this airport never stopped.

Katy sat up. "I'm beginning to spot Jose and Dick everywhere."

"Me too," I said. "But I don't think they'll come here."

"Why not?"

"Because—" I paused to find the right words. I'd been ruminating over this for the past few hours. "They only picked on us because we were right there in their store. They won't spend a fortune flying all the way here after us."

Katy raised an eyebrow.

"We were convenient," I said. "Plus, you and me have nobody to call for help. They knew no one's gonna notice if anything happens to us."

"You think so?"

"Who'd we call for help?"

Katy looked down at her hands and shook her head.

"We're not worth the trouble. They probably already found other girls to make money off of."

"What a bunch of basta—"

A loud bang resonated inside the terminal. We both jumped.

A gunshot?

But it was only a suitcase that had dropped from a luggage trolley to the floor. Katy and I sighed in relief.

I sat up. We had to find something to do, a distraction, *any* distraction, or this paranoia would overtake us both.

I touched her shoulder. "Hey, let's get out of here. Come on."

With another sigh, Katy unraveled her legs and stood up slowly.

We spent the next two hours strolling the length of the airport. We had time on our hands now. We stopped for a sandwich and tea at a takeaway booth and walked through the terminals, mindlessly window-shopping.

Very soon, we'd left the airport's security zone and stepped into the shopping plaza to gawk at the high-end clothing stores, luggage shops, and shoe boutiques that carried gorgeous things we couldn't afford even if we worked a lifetime. But looking at them helped us to forget our worries if only for a little while.

We'd just stepped out of one of these luxury shops when I spotted the café.

I grabbed Katy's arm. "Look!"

Chapter Three

"What?" Katy whipped her head around. "Are they here?"

"Over there." I pointed at the red-and-white striped awning of the bistro in front of us.

She looked confused. "You still hungry?"

"No, but—"

I paused. I'd seen photos of Chef Pierre's cafés in the glossy magazines at Mrs. Rao's upscale, suburban house in Toronto.

Her home was where I first landed after I ran away from India. I wasn't the first girl to become a slave housekeeper and cook to Mrs. Rao who'd promised my wages would be sent back to my family in Goa. She'd known how to keep me under her thumb. Experimenting with the recipes in Chef Pierre's magazines had been my only escape from that hell.

But I never dreamed to see his cafés in real life.

The lettering on the window was unmistakable. Inside, pastries of all kinds weighed down glass shelves that extended the length of the store. Golden croissants, colorful fruit tarts, shiny sugar buns, mousse cakes, cheesecakes, caramels, and éclairs sat side by side looking rich and pompous. The heavenly smell of oven-fresh baked things wafted my way. I took a deep breath in and closed my eyes.

It was my mother who came to my dreams every night, bringing memories of us baking together on lazy Sunday afternoons in Tanzania a long time ago. She'd been in my life for only a short time, but I never forgot her captivating smile, her contagious laughter, and those sweet cakes she loved to make.

When I was confined to Mrs. Rao's house and later, when I was stuck at Dick's bakery, it was Chef Pierre's recipes I immersed myself in. I could get lost in his cookbooks and foodie magazines for hours. He'd kept me company on days when I felt like the whole world was against me. Everything I learned about the art of baking after my mother died, I learned from him. And it was this skill that had saved my skin every single time.

"What's so special about this place?" Katy asked, walking over and pressing her face against the window.

I stepped up next to her. "It's Chef Pierre's café."

"Who?"

"He's famous. I used his recipes at Dick's place."

Katy pulled her face from the window and gave me a dubious look. "Six euros for a ping pong-sized sugar ball? Seriously?"

"They're good. You liked them."

"Don't remember," she said, frowning at the cakes on display. If Katy could go through life without eating so she could preserve her skinny thighs, she would, so I forgave her for saying that.

I peered inside. "Wish I could work here. I'd wash their floor if they'd let me in."

"Who needs all this sugar and fat?"

"All our clients loved them, remember?"

She made a face. "I'm gonna gain ten pounds just by looking at these. How you stay so small with the sweets you stuff yourself with, I don't know." She sniffed as two thin European women walked into the café. "You and those French girls."

"Small portions," I said with a smile. Katy always complained about her hips, her thighs, and her waist, which was ironic because she'd been the prettiest girl at our Toronto high school. She was almost selected by a modeling agency and all the boys would have given an arm and a leg to date her. I worried on those days when she locked herself up in the toilet after supper. If I pressed my ears to the door, I'd hear her retching, but I never knew how to bring the topic up.

"Yeah, right." She turned away from the coffee shop. "Oh my god, look!" Her eyes flashed. She'd caught sight of the shoe store next door. "Jimmy Choo!"

It was her turn to grab me and pull me away. She marched inside and toward a pair of four-inch black boots studded with Swarovski crystals. They had a sticker price that could have bought a used car.

"Can I try these on?" she asked the store attendant, who barely acknowledged us. Katy didn't seem to care. She plopped down on the nearest bench with the boots in her hands and let out a happy sigh. This was her heaven. Mine was next door.

"Hey, Katy," I said, "I'm going to check out some of the pastries, okay?"

"Join you soon as I'm done," she said, but she was already lost among the crystals and plastic.

I felt goose bumps on my arms as I crossed the threshold of the café.

Chefs in Europe are like royalty. They usually come from regal lineages with noble blood and even nobler connections. They grace the covers of flashy magazines and hang out with fashion moguls and film stars. Chef Pierre, though, was an anomaly. He was the son of a coal miner from the south of Belgium who'd fought his way to the top, armed with his grandmother's recipes, a whipping whisk, and a big dream.

His story had a happy ending when he finally made it big and married his true love, Andre from the Netherlands, in the biggest, fattest, gayest wedding of the century. In those snazzy magazine photos, handsome and buff Andre looked like he'd just stepped out of *GQ*. Next to him, plump Chef Pierre looked like a village boy, out of place in any high society club.

Like him, I was different. I didn't fit anywhere. I was born in Africa but wasn't truly African. My parents were from Asia, but I wasn't truly Asian. I'd lived in Canada for the past three years, but I wasn't really Canadian. I was a strange, mixed-up girl who'd been everywhere but belonged nowhere. And just like Chef Pierre, all I carried with me were a whipping whisk and a big dream.

I dreamed of the day when my cousin Preeti, Katy, and I would set up our own bakery in Goa near the beach among the waving coconut trees. With the first money I'd make, I'd return to Tanzania and visit my parents' graves. That was my plan.

At the back of every Chef Pierre's coffee shop was a rack that showcased his foodie magazines. I walked over to it and picked up the latest edition. Following in the tradition of Oprah, Chef Pierre's magazine covers featured only him in his signature hat and apron, holding the pastry of the month. This month's cover had him showing off a beautiful soufflé. The side caption read, "Perfect dessert for the perfect royal party."

I picked up a copy and stepped up to the shelves. My mouth watered as I wondered which to try first. The éclair covered with dark melted chocolate or the cheesecake with fresh raspberries on top?

I'd been so preoccupied I hadn't noticed the tall man in the black suit sidle up to Katy in the shoe shop next door.

Chapter Four

It was only after I paid for my order and sat down at a table near the window that I remembered. When I peeked into the shoe store, Katy wasn't inside anymore.

I squinted through the café window. *Where is she?*

There. I saw her. Katy was near a recess in the corridor, standing with a man—a tall man with dark skin and a curly, scruffy beard. He was wearing a black suit and dangling a cigarette butt from his lips.

Who's he?

For as long as I'd known Katy, she'd been a big flirt. While all the boys at school wanted to date her, she had eyes only for men. "Real men," she'd told me. And no man was out of bounds: our teachers, the head of security, even the principal.

This thing she had for older men got her into hot water more than once and was one reason we were running away from Toronto. I watched Katy with this man now, their heads close like they were in deep conversation. The man's hand was on the small of her back. *He looks creepy. What's she doing with him? She doesn't even like beards.*

With a start, I remembered she had the stolen money packet on her. Twenty thousand dollars minus an airline ticket. *Blood money,* Katy had called it.

I watched them with a frown on my face, recalling what happened minutes before leaving Toronto. We'd been waiting in the plane for it to take off when Katy's phone rang. It should have been turned off and she shouldn't have picked it up, but she did.

Dick's voice came through loud, clear, and furious.

"You think you can get away with this?"

Katy's face went white. My heart sank.

I reached for the phone, but she pulled away, giving me an I-got-this look.

"Oh hi, Dick." Her voice was uncharacteristically calm. "How're ya doing?"

I leaned in to hear.

"You frigging bitches!"

I glanced around, my heart beating a tad faster. A passenger in the aisle across from us had noticed Katy turn on the phone and was frowning at her, but no flight attendant rushed over to shut us down.

"I know you took my money, you little shits!" Dick's greasy voice flew through the airwaves.

"I've no idea what you're talking about," Katy said, her voice dripping with honey.

"I'll call the police, you hear? Your fingerprints are gonna be all over it. They'll catch you, you goddamned—"

I signaled to Katy to hang up. She ignored me.

"You've got bigger problems, Dick. I don't believe you'll call anyone." she turned on the same voice she used on our most difficult clients at the bakery. "It was really nice to chat. You have a wonderful day now."

"You damn bi—,"

Katy hung up and looked at me, her lips tight and thin. She looked vaguely satisfied. I could just imagine Dick on the other end, red-faced, swearing at the phone with the blood vessels on his neck about to pop. He wasn't going to have a wonderful day.

The jet engine roared and the PA system crackled. "Cabin crew, please take your seats for takeoff and prepare for departure."

I sighed with relief. Thank goodness we were leaving this city and this part of my life for good.

"We should throw that phone out," I whispered.

Katy leaned in and whispered back, "I wanted to know how mad he'd get, knowing there's nothing he can do about it."

"You know this is dirty money, right?"

It had taken me more than a year to save up for my air ticket to Goa. I'd need more to pay off Preeti's nasty husband and the marriage broker to let her go free, but when we dashed out of the bakery, I had to also think of Katy. Our two standby tickets to India had cost over two thousand dollars. The money we'd taken from Dick's safe had already come in handy.

"This is back pay," I heard Katy say, more to herself than me. "He owes us."

Dick had gotten away with a lot, paying us next to nothing while we slaved away so he could visit strip clubs and gambling dens. Katy had seen this money packet go back and forth across the Canadian-American border many times. She'd thought it was to pay for legitimate supplies. It was only later she'd learned what it was really used for. Contraband. This was how Dick and Jose smuggled their money and their drugs.

How that packet got through the airport X-ray machine was a mystery. The only thing I knew was the last place Katy and I wanted to end up in was jail.

"*Voilà, mademoiselle.*"

I looked up, startled to see a server at my table. She placed a dessert plate embossed with Chef Pierre's gold logo in front of me. On it sat a wafer-thin crêpe topped with cream and strawberries.

"*Merci,*" I said and picked up my fork, but my mind was elsewhere.

I looked back at Katy and the man in the shadows of the corridor. It was hard to see, but it looked like she was burying her face in his chest. I dropped my fork on the plate. Something wasn't right. Katy was a flirt, but not that easy.

That was when I saw her move her shoulders like she was trying to wriggle out. I scraped back my chair, barely remembering to pick up my bag before I crashed through the café doors and ran out.

I could see them better now. Katy was trying to push the man away, but he kept pulling her in. He was using a handkerchief to wipe Katy's face. Very strange.

"Katy!"

The man looked up and scowled. He pulled Katy away from the wall, and with that, her suitcase fell down with a clatter. I broke into a sprint.

"Hey! What's going on?"

In half a second, the man had wrapped his arms around Katy's shoulders and pulled her away. She hung, limp like a rag doll, and didn't even look my way.

"Katy!" I was screeching now.

A few people shot me disapproving looks, but no one said or did anything. My heart was pounding. *Do I call for help? Can someone get the police?* Something stirred in the back of my mind reminding me of the stolen money and my fake visa.

The man in the suit tore out of the main airport doors, dragging Katy behind him. Whoever he was, he was fast and strong. Within seconds, the sliding doors closed and they were gone.

"Hey, come back!"

I ran outside, hollering my lungs out. I sprang across the road when a blue sports car zoomed by, missing me by two inches. Before I could react, a hand dug into my shoulder and pulled me to the curb. I looked up to the scowling face of an airport security guard.

"You wanna get killed?" he said.

"My friend...that taxi," I spluttered, pointing to the disappearing car.

"The line's over there. You'll have to wait for a taxi like the rest of 'em, miss."

"No!" I shook his hand off my shoulder. "It's my friend. You've got to do something!"

"Just because someone jumped in line and stole a taxi doesn't mean you get to do that too. I'm tired of people cutting in line."

"I'm not cutting in line. That's my friend, I tell you! He took her!"

"I don't have time for games, okay?"

I felt my throat tighten. "But that man. I saw him. He, he kidnapped...."

The guard wasn't listening anymore. A handful of college girls had just burst through the sliding doors. "Please get in line like everyone else, miss," he said in a gruff voice before stepping toward the girls. "Taxi, ladies? The line's over there."

I looked helplessly at the road where the cab had disappeared, my legs weak and my breath shallow. *What just happened? Who's that man? Where's he taking Katy? What do I...*

Just then, a taxi screeched to a stop right in front of me. A man got out, threw money on the front seat and sprinted toward the airport doors, clutching his briefcase. Without a second thought, I jumped into the backseat and slammed the door shut.

"Oi!" I heard the security guard yell behind me.

"Go!" I yelled at the driver. "Follow that cab!"

Chapter Five

"What's the rush, ma'am?"

The taxi hadn't budged. The back door clicked open. I looked up to see an agent in blue, like the one I'd spotted walking along the terminal corridor earlier. He was towering over me now. The first things I noticed were the UK border agency insignia on his uniform and the black gun strapped to his belt.

My brain kicked in.

"Help me! A man took my friend!" I yelled, pointing at the road. "We need to catch him. They went in a cab. Do someth—"

"Ma'am, I'd like you to lower your voice." He gave me a look that said he didn't have much patience.

"But...but..." I stammered. "He took Katy. That man..."

"Your passport?" It was like he hadn't even heard me. I stared at him open-mouthed.

He put out a hand. "Now, please."

With trembling hands, I pulled my passport out of my bag and gave it to him.

"Hmmm," the agent said, flipping through the booklet. I waited silently, but I could hear my pulse pounding. *Didn't he hear me? Will he do something?* I noticed the taxi driver up front watching me through the rearview mirror. He winked when he saw me notice him. I looked away.

"Step out of the car, ma'am."

"But...."

The agent moved a hand toward his gun belt. "This is not a request."

I got out, my legs feeling like jelly.

"Follow me, please," he said, signaling with his hand. "This way."

From the corner of my eye, I saw the security guard watching with a self-satisfied sneer on his face.

I turned to the agent as soon as we were inside the terminal, away from the mocking eyes of the guard and the taxi lineup.

"Excuse me, Officer. I really need to talk to you."

He looked at me, hands on his hips, his face impassive.

I cleared my throat and spoke in a low voice. "I need your help. My friend was taken."

"Taken?" He raised an eyebrow.

"Yes, this man took her. I saw him push her into a cab. He *kidnapped* her."

"Is that right?" The eyebrow remained raised.

"Yes. Everyone saw it happening, even the taxi guard outside."

"Hmmm..." He hesitated, surveying me from top to toe. "Let's go into our offices and we'll see what we can do about that, shall we?"

Without another word, he turned around and marched into the main thoroughfare.

I stared at him. If I ran out now, I wouldn't get too far. I had no choice. I followed him, trying to keep up with his strides. A handful of people glanced my way curiously. I didn't have handcuffs on, but I might as well have. I walked with my head down, wishing I could disappear through the floor.

We walked into a part of the airport I hadn't seen before. The insignia on the agent's uniform was plastered everywhere here, including on a poster about smuggling, which featured a photo of a woman in a solitary cell, her head buried in handcuffed hands.

The agent opened a door. "Step inside, please."

I stepped cautiously into a stark room with fluorescent lighting and just enough space for a desk and two uncomfortable-looking chairs. It looked like one of those interrogation rooms in the movies where they browbeat you before they send you to the back to get strapped down and tortured.

I sat down with my bag on my lap. The agent closed the door halfway and pulled out a chair for himself. My throat felt dry and a nervous tick had started on my right eyelid.

He flipped through my passport again. "Hmmm," he said as he found my Canadian immigration papers inside. He removed the staple, unfolded the document, and held it up to the light.

My heart sank. Mrs. Rao in Toronto had given me these papers, papers I'd later learned were fake. *What do they do to people with fake immigration documents? Is it worse than smuggling thousands of stolen dollars?*

"You don't have the proper visa to enter the United Kingdom, you do realize that?"

I gulped. "I guess so." I wiped my palms on my skirt.

"Yet, you were ready to depart the airport and head into town." He gave me a piercing look.

"I was trying to follow my friend. I told you, she was taken. We need to find her!" I felt my face go warm.

Ignoring me, he pulled out a yellow legal pad and pen from a drawer and started scribbling.

"What's your final destination?"

"Goa."

"So this is a layover?" he asked, scanning my ticket and boarding pass.

"Yes."

"Are you traveling alone?"

"No, with Katy."

"And Katy is?"

"My best friend," I almost snapped.

"Does she have a family name?"

"McCafferty."

"She's going all the way to Goa as well?"

"Yes!"

The agent didn't look twenty-five. *He must be new. Otherwise, why is he wasting all this time, instead of hurrying up and trying to find Katy?*

"Where's she now?"

I felt a hot flash in my chest. "I've been trying to tell you she got kidnapped just now!" I snapped fully this time.

He gave me a long stare, enough to make me wither in my seat.

I swallowed and mustered up my calmest voice. "It was a man in a black suit. He took her from the shoe store inside the airport, next to Chef Pierre's café. That's why I got in that cab. I've no idea where she is. I've no idea who that man was or why he took her but she's in trouble, and you need to *do* something about it. *Please.*"

The agent sat back and stared at me for five full seconds. I looked nervously back.

"I've got some important questions to ask you," he said, finally. "I need you to answer truthfully, okay?"

I swallowed.

"Okay?" he asked, with force in his voice this time.

I nodded quickly.

"What's your profession?"

"Er, I don't have one."

"What do you do for a living? Are you a student?"

"No." I shook my head. "I'm a baker."

"*Baker?*" Raised eyebrow again. "And where's your bakery?"

I hesitated. He waited, pen raised over the notepad. "Toronto." My mind raced. *Did Dick call the police? Will they find out about the money?*

"Where's your family? In Toronto?"

I looked down at my hands. I hated that question.

"Are they back in India?"

"No." I paused. "I don't have...my parents died when I was twelve."

"Do you have any other family?" His voice had softened.

How do I tell him Aunty Shilpa died of her sickness, Grandma died from heartbreak, and Preeti's now stuck in a deranged marriage, all because of me?

"I have a cousin. Her name is Preeti. She's in Goa."

"Is anyone paying you to go on this trip?"

I looked at him in surprise. "No."

"Is anyone forcing you to make this trip?"

"No," I said, shaking my head vigorously.

"Is anyone waiting for you at the airport in Delhi?"

"No." *Where's he going with all this?*

"Why is your friend, this Katy McCafferty, going to India?"

"She's coming with me because, because..." I hesitated. *Why is Katy coming with me?* It was because she had nowhere else to go. I was the only family she had now. Though we were worlds apart by bloodline, it felt like we were not just BFFs, but sisters. "She's my best friend and wants to come with me," I said, in a lame voice.

"Do you have any pictures of this friend of yours?"

I scrambled to open my bag, pulled out my phone and turned it on. I felt a slight sense of relief like we were going somewhere serious now. I shook the phone, silently urging the screen to wake up quickly.

The agent scraped back his chair to get up. "Find those pictures and wait for me here, okay?" He scooped the papers off the table and marched out.

It took me a few seconds to realize he'd dropped something. My airline ticket, my boarding pass, and the immigration document were all gone. My smaller and heavier passport booklet had dropped back onto the table. I stared at it motionless for half a minute. With shaking hands, I reached out and pulled it toward me. After a quick glance at the door, I slipped it inside my jacket pocket.

I sat back in my chair, my heart pounding. The door was fully open. Outside, a photocopy machine was whirring. I pushed my chair back quietly, tiptoed to the door and strained to listen. I could hear mumbling of voices nearby. I peeked out. About twenty-five feet away was a door to a large office. In the doorway was the agent, talking to someone. From where I was I could hear snatches of their conversation.

"Unauthorized entry...," said a man's voice from inside the office. From his sonorous tone and the way the agent was standing, I gathered this was the boss.

"...a song and dance about a kidnapping, sir," the agent replied. I froze. *He doesn't believe me?*

"...always have a good story, don't they?"

"...not a threat...."

More mumbling.

"Captain needs to approve...."

"...hold her...."

"Cell four is available...."

Cell four?

I stood shocked for a second.

There was no way I was going to get locked up. Not with Katy in danger too. I bent down, removed my heels and thrust them in my bag as quietly as I could. Then, in my bare feet and my bag on my back, I stepped out of the room. The agent was still standing inside the office, his back to me.

With my heart in my mouth, I tiptoed along the wall.

No one was in sight. Ten steps from the interrogation room were two corridors. The one on the left would take me to the main terminal, which was tempting. But if I took the one on the right, I'd go deeper into a labyrinth of offices, a place they'd never expect me to go. With a pounding heart and trembling legs, I stepped into the corridor on the right.

I moved fast, turning from corridor to corridor until I became hopelessly lost. Other than a man in construction overalls who rushed by, and three cleaners walking along the corridor with their wash buckets in hand, I didn't bump into anyone else. One of the cleaning women noticed my bare feet and gave me a dirty look. I ignored her and kept walking.

I had no idea where I was, but if I kept going, I'd come to an end, I was sure. And I did. At the far end of one corridor, I noticed a red "Exit" sign. I dashed toward it.

The sign on the exit door said "Restricted. Employees only." *Is it alarmed?* I wondered as I shakily reached for the handle. Just as I did, the door banged open, and a man stepped inside, right on my foot, crushing my toes.

"Ow!"

"Sorry 'bout that! Stepped right on you there, didn't I?"

I scrunched my face in pain.

It was a pudgy man who stood in front of me. He wore a white shirt with a silver name badge that said "Airport Lost & Found," and he reeked of cigarette smoke.

"Here." He flung the door wide open. "Next time I'll check before I barrel in like that, luv."

I looked at him and then at the opened door.

He gave a friendly smile. "Righto now. Sorry again."

Before he could ask any questions, I stepped through the door and into a pile of warm cigarette butts.

Click.

I turned around and grabbed the handle. The door had locked behind me.

Chapter Six

It was chilly. I zipped up my jacket.

My toes were still throbbing, but it felt so much better to be outside. I was standing next to the concrete wall of the airport building. In front of me was a twelve-foot steel fence with a gate that led to a sparse parking lot.

The parking lot was also fenced in, reinforced with barbed wire on top, and at the far end was a security gate and a guard shed. No one was in sight. Except for three large transportation trucks parked in a corner of the lot, the area looked deserted.

What do I do now?

As I surveyed the scene, I heard an engine start.

I slipped through the gate and walked toward the vehicles, my bare feet not even feeling the cold concrete pavement. Exhaust smoke was coming out of one of the tailpipes. I glanced behind quickly to make sure an army of border agents weren't storming out with guns in their hands and walked toward the truck.

A man appeared from behind and walked toward the driver's door. I stood and watched him silently. He was a short, brawny, Indian-looking man, sporting a full beard, and a faded, cut-out T-shirt. It was one of those tops the always impeccably dressed Jose back in Toronto called "a wife-beater shirt."

The man was at the driver's door when he noticed me. He gave a surprised start. And stared.

I stared back.

"Hi," I said, finally finding my voice. "I need a ride."

He glared. It wasn't encouraging, but I wasn't going to back down now.

"I need a ride to town."

"Take bus," he said.

"It's an emergency."

"Always emergency." He gave me a mocking look and opened the door.

"I can pay."

That stopped him.

He turned and squinted at me while I shifted from foot to foot. His eyes traveled down to my feet, and I wished I'd put my shoes on before coming out.

"Ahmed's girl?" he asked, looking interested now.

I nodded quickly and crossed my fingers. I was surprised the border guards hadn't already come out, but they may have thought I'd disappeared into the main terminal.

"Hindu?" the man said.

I shook my head.

"Nepali?"

I shook my head again.

"Filipino?"

I desperately glanced behind me. *I don't have time for this.*

"Sure," I said.

"Aah." His eyes cleared. He nodded. "You talk like American." He jerked his thumb toward the front of the truck. "Go inside."

I ran to the other side, opened the door and jumped in. Without a word, the man got in and revved the engine. He'd just changed gears when I heard the yelling.

"Oi!"

I instantly crouched in my seat. The driver gave me a curious look.

"Check behind the shed!"

"To your right!"

The voices were coming from behind us.

"Nothing here!"

"Over there!"

The commotion was getting closer. I dropped further in my seat and felt sweat streaming down my back.

The driver grunted.

"Go there," he said, pointing to the backseat. I didn't wait to be asked twice. I crawled into the footwell in the back. Without any warning, he threw a heavy burlap sack that smelled of diesel fuel on me. I balled up tightly underneath it and tried not to breathe.

To my surprise, the driver chuckled softly to himself up front. I heard a click of the radio and Bollywood music flooded the truck.

"Ahoy there!"

My heart jumped.

"Good afternoon, sar," the truck driver said, turning down the volume.

"May I see your papers?" It was a crisp British accent.

"Yes sar, I have clearance sar." I heard paper being rustled. Then silence.

"All good," said the other man. "Have you seen a young woman come this way a few minutes ago?"

Every nerve in my body trembled.

"No, sar. No girls, sar."

"Petite, Indian origin." The voice was close, very close. I could imagine an agent in blue, sticking his head through the window to survey inside.

"No, sar. I'm sorry sar."

"Would you open the back for us please?"

"Yes, sar." The trucker shut the engine off and got out. I heard the back of the truck being rolled open. Someone jumped in and walked around. I stayed hunkered down, not daring to move. After several seconds, the person jumped out and the door was rolled shut.

"If you see her, you must report to us immediately."

"Absolutely, will do, sar."

"Okay, you may leave now."

And with that, the driver got back in, shut the door and the truck started to move. I stayed where I was. We had not moved even fifty feet when I heard someone call out again.

"Stop!"

Oh no.

The truck stopped, but the engine remained on.

Someone spoke in a language I didn't understand, but I guessed it as an Indian dialect. The truck driver replied in the same language. They talked for a while, interrupting each other, laughing. It was like two friends chatting at a coffee shop. Their conversation lasted not more than two minutes, but under that diesel-soaked sack, it felt like an eternity.

To my relief, the truck began to move again. I stayed in the footwell for ten minutes at least, trying to think above the music blaring from the speakers.

Suddenly, the driver dialed down the music and called out, "You! Come here."

Is he talking to me?

"You come here. They all go now."

I pulled the sack off my back and unscrunched myself.

"Come." The man patted the front seat.

I peeked out the window. We were on a highway somewhere. I crawled to the front seat and fished my shoes out of my bag. As I was putting them on, I felt the driver look my way.

"I protect you, you know."

"Thank you."

"You owe me."

I kept quiet. I didn't like the sound of that, but there was nothing I could do now.

"Coke?" he said.

"No, thank you."

The man threw his head back and laughed. "No, you have drug? Coke?"

"No!" I shook my head.

"Oh." He sounded disappointed.

"You work for Ahmed?"

I had no clue who that was, but he was giving me a ride on that pretense. I looked straight ahead, my mind racing. *What do I say?*

"You not have to lie. I know operation well," he said, with a wide grin.

I cleared my throat. "I...er...I'm looking for my friend."

"Your friend? She pretty like you?"

I ignored that. "Someone took her," I said quietly.

"Took her, eh?" He sounded less surprised than the agent.

"I need to find her."

"Only place they take girls is South Hill Square."

"South Hill Square?"

"Sure as pudding. I take girls for Ahmed and Bob when they pay me extra. They always make me very happy." He grinned.

"Can you take me there?"

"That is exactly what I am doing." He gave me another creepy grin.

I inched closer to the door, my mind whirring. *Can I trust him? How does he know where Katy was taken? Will the guards catch me? Will they put me in jail?*

I felt the driver's eyes running over my thighs. I moved my bag onto my lap so it covered my legs, then, as discreetly as I could, I pulled down my skirt as much as I could.

We drove in silence for about half an hour. We were going at a fairly steady speed, the music now blaring, and the driver humming and tapping the steering wheel. I sat as far away as I could, glad he wasn't trying to take the conversation further.

I looked out of the window, seeing London for the first time, catching glimpses of the red Underground signs and the quintessential telephone booths I'd seen in Mrs. Rao's travel magazines.

We drove by century-old brick buildings with beautiful stained-glass windows. Then, we'd turn a corner, and get thrust between towering glass skyscrapers that grazed the sky, making me feel like I was in Toronto again. When we'd take another corner, I'd glance at a quiet, green park with bronze fountains. If Goa had been a claustrophobe's nightmare and Toronto a neophiliac's dream, London was somewhere right in between.

The driver slowed down and turned onto a smaller road. I peered at the signs but they didn't tell me anything. We could be anywhere in the city. From Mrs. Rao's fancy magazines, I'd expected to see only steel bridges and high rises in London, so it was a surprise when we drove through this grungier part of town.

Here, graffiti decorated the walls, garbage littered the streets and potholes pitted the roads. Rows of run-down attached houses lined the street, with clotheslines hung out in front. Boys played on the streets while the girls and women with head veils sat on benches outside their homes with unsmiling looks on their faces.

"Is this South Hill?" I asked.

The truck driver merely grunted.

We kept winding through streets, sometimes so narrow we'd have been in trouble if a vehicle had come from the other direction. After several minutes of twisting and turning, we stopped at a work yard strewn with construction material. Lumber and metal rods lay haphazardly all over the place, and at the back was a small warehouse-like structure.

This doesn't seem right. "Where are we?" I asked.

The driver didn't say a word. He shut the engine off and stepped out, still humming to himself. My mind was on full alert. I clutched my bag close and watched him from the rearview mirror. I felt a shiver go through my spine as he walked to my side. *What's he doing?* Before I could say anything, he yanked open the door and pulled me out of the truck.

I stumbled to the ground in shock, my bag tumbling down on me. I tried to get up but the man pinned me down by my shoulders.

"Hey! What are you doing?" I tried to jerk his arm off me. "Let me go!"

He curled his arm around my neck and pulled me to my feet.

"Stop!"

He tightened his grip around my neck, constricting my breathing. I thrashed madly, dug my heels into the ground, and hit whatever I could, trying not to get suffocated.

"You want South Hill Square, huh?" he said. "You need to pay for that!" I heard him laugh, a coarse laugh. "You know how I take payment? You want to know?"

"Stop it!" I got enough air to yell out. I scratched the man's arms and screamed, "Help!"

"Shut up, whore. What wrong with you? Other girls know how to behave. Ahmed not teach you anything?"

I pulled on his arms. "Help!" I croaked.

His grip tightened even further. I choked, half-coughing, half-spluttering.

"You shout and I will kill you."

I felt his foul breath on my neck. He kept dragging me. I kept digging my heels in and didn't stop struggling.

This was not the first time I'd had to fight my way out of a bad situation, and if there was one thing I knew, it was if I stopped fighting, I'd be dead. Only one thought went through my head: *Keep on fighting. Keep on fighting. Keep on fighting.*

We were at the warehouse doorway now. That was when I remembered something important from the self-defense class I took a long time ago in my international school.

I stopped struggling and slackened by body. He loosened his grip, thinking I'd given up the fight. I didn't wait one second. I thrust my hands between my throat and the crook of his elbow, squeezed my chin and gasped for air. In the next second, I stomped on his foot with my right heel and let out a blood-curdling scream.

I ground my heel into his canvas shoe, right where his toes were.

The man let go, more in surprise than in hurt.

I didn't hesitate.

I scrambled out and ran like mad.

Part TWO

Though you may see me holler,
And you may see me cry,
I'll be dogged sweet baby,
If you're gonna see me die.
Langston Hughes

Chapter Seven

I was in a red-light district somewhere in London.

Half-broken signs glowed on top of shops, buzzing on and off like insects caught in electric lights. The signs flashed: "Two for one," "Nude Girls," "Live Girls." *Live girls? Like animals at a zoo?* I shuddered.

It had taken me two hours to walk to South Hill Square. I'd only stopped for half a second to grab my bag from near the truck before I'd raced out of the work yard. Now, my bag and my beautiful red shoes had become dirty, dusty, and a burden. I'd damaged my right heel so much it was close to coming off.

I'd tried to call Katy but my phone kept giving me a "roaming not activated" message and a blinking red alert that said the battery was almost dead. So I slogged on, not knowing how close or how far I was. All I had was the name of a square and a general idea it was due south.

Every little while, I'd stopped to ask for directions. Most people averted their eyes before I could even approach them. Others took a wide berth to avoid me. One woman pointed vaguely and rushed off.

But I kept asking and I kept walking. Because if I stopped, that would mean I'd given up on Katy and that was one thing I wasn't going to do. The image of her hanging limp in that man's arms never left my mind. With every step, I prayed she was fine.

The horrid incident with the truck driver felt like an ugly monsoon rain that had thundered in without warning, drenched me to the bone and vanished in seconds. I didn't have time to digest what had just happened. I had scratches on my arms and a bruise on my thigh, but I didn't want to think about that right now.

It had taken half an hour to calm myself, to stop looking over my shoulder every few seconds, and to realize the trucker wouldn't come after me in the middle of a busy street. So I put one foot in front of the other, on a road I'd never been on, in a city that seemed stranger every minute, in a country I wasn't even supposed to be in.

My anklet clinked with every step I took. I wondered how my cousin Preeti was doing. I was responsible for what had happened to her, my sweet, innocent cousin who'd been forced to marry the alcoholic in our village who'd been arranged to marry me. The image of that man's red bulbous face flitted into my mind. The memory of him trying to force himself on me while I was still in my school uniform rushed in like a raging wildfire.

I'd escaped that attack, but I still remembered the wave of unspeakable terror and nausea that had overcome me that day—much like I'd felt only a couple of hours earlier. *Oh my god, what have I done to you, Preeti? Will you ever forgive me?* I choked back my tears and kept moving.

Hours later, when I wobbled into South Hill Square, I felt like I'd time-traveled three hundred years back.

In one lonely corner of this cobblestone square stood a dilapidated clock tower. Next to it was a chipped brass fountain, which looked like it hadn't worked for decades, maybe centuries. Remnants of trash and newspapers scattered in the wind.

The perimeter was made of a row of two-story buildings, lopsided, decayed, and sad like they were watching a funeral in the middle of the square. At one point in time they must have been stately, but now, with their dusty windows, crooked doors, and twisted chimney tops, they made the square look like a Charles Dickens novel had come to life.

I began by knocking on every door. My feet were sore and my back hurt but I walked into every shop, even those with neon lights in the shape of naked women. I had only one question to ask anyone who answered the door: "Did you see a redheaded girl come here today?"

Most just shrugged or shook their heads and looked away before I could say anything more. One man kicked the door shut and another swore and told me to get out. One man said, "Sorry, luv, but I'd love to invite you inside 'ere wi' me." I quickly stepped away.

In half an hour, I'd knocked on every door in the square, and all of them had opened except for one, even after I'd pummeled on it. I leaned against the crumbling brick wall of the clock tower to gather my thoughts, keeping one keen eye on the square.

Katy has to be here, somewhere. Though the last person I could trust was the truck driver, something in my bones told me I was close to her.

My head was spinning from exhaustion and hunger, and I no longer cared about border guards or police. If they came to take me, I'd have gone willingly. Part of me felt guilty for not having tried harder to convince them about Katy's disappearance. Maybe, if I'd explained everything clearly and calmly, they'd have understood. Instead, I ran out like a criminal. *But I am a criminal. Stealing money, even from crooks, is still a crime, isn't it?*

Nearby, someone coughed. I turned around. A man in a grubby coat lay in the gutter, passed out, clenching a bottle wrapped in a filthy brown bag. Flies swarmed around his coat and a foul stench rose from him. He coughed again.

Something buzzed over my head, and I looked up. One by one, the cast-iron light posts along the square were flickering on. Blobs of yellow light appeared from the windows of the homes and shops. I watched as the evening scene unfolded around me, wondering, worrying, still uncertain of what to do next. The place was deserted now. It was getting cool and the sky was getting dark.

What do I do now?

A chilly breeze rustled my hair. I shivered. I hadn't slept or eaten much in the last twenty-four hours. I was beginning to feel weak, too weary to think. I slipped to the ground and leaned against my bag, hugging myself to stay warm.

Is it Dick who got Katy kidnapped? How did he know we're in London? Or was it Jose? He's the big shot with cars, cash, and connections. Maybe his reach is bigger than we thought. But why did they take only Katy? She's the sweetest person in the world, the one who gave Jose everything he asked for. She had her moments, and she knew how to fight back, but I was the rebel. All this couldn't have been just a coincidence, could it?

I'd been sure Dick and Jose would never come after us here but I hadn't bargained for them having connections here.

It was getting dark now and almost impossible to see. I hugged myself tighter.

I'd come thousands of miles across the Atlantic with only one idea in mind: to get on that flight to India. But now, I'd gone and lost my best friend in a foreign country to horrors I didn't even want to even think about. What surprised me was why Katy hadn't struggled. She had a fire in her belly as red as her hair, and I'd seen what happened when someone crossed her.

I put my head in my hands. I didn't know if Katy was safe or hurt. I didn't know if I'd end up in jail. I didn't know if I'd ever get back to Goa and see Preeti again. I felt more lost and alone than I'd ever been in my life.

A loud cough from the drunk man in the gutter interrupted my worries. My bum felt numb from sitting on the cold, hard pavement and my limbs had gone to sleep.

Maybe it's time to call the police.

As far as I knew, there were no charges to dial 911 and it worked all the time, at least in Toronto. I wondered if it would be the same in London. *Does 911 work here too?*

Chapter Eight

I jumped.

Something had woken me up.

Bang!

I swiveled my head around to see a wooden door swing on its hinges. Boisterous male laughter erupted through the open doorway, the noise spilling onto the quiet street.

A man in a pair of dirty corduroy pants and a construction hat stood at the top of the steps and lit a cigarette. He stepped down to the pavement and flicked the match in my direction. I flinched as the burning stick fell two inches from my feet. He didn't even notice me.

I rubbed my eyes. *Where am I?* A light breeze was blowing and the air was cool. Up above me, the sky was a pale gray.

My head felt heavy and swollen like it was filled with water. My face was rubbery and my legs were stiff. I still held my phone tightly in one hand.

I looked around me. I was sitting cross-legged on the corner of a cobblestone street, in an unkempt square lined with run-down buildings. A clock tower pealed its bell above me, making me jump again.

I counted seven chimes.

Someone coughed. It took a minute to clear the haze in my brain. I was still in South Hill Square. I'd fallen asleep on the pavement next to the drunk, homeless man. He was still there, smellier than before, snoring into his grimy jacket.

I looked up at the door that had just banged open. There were no neon signs of nude girls here. The sign was so inconspicuous I had to squint to find it. Above the handle, in small letters, were the words "Night Day Café."

After staring at it for a minute, I decided to get up. I stretched my legs painfully, my bones cracking like they were a hundred years old. I dusted my skirt, picked up my bag, and heaved it back on my shoulders.

I made my way up the steps slowly and peeked through the door. It was hard to see. I inched the door open and a haze of smoke welcomed me.

Inside, a TV was tuned to a football match. A dozen men sat in front of it drinking coffee, all eyes glued to the game. In one corner, an old man lay on a rug with cushions, smoking a hookah pipe. A poster with curly Arabic lettering on a green background hung on the wall behind him. Except for the oversized flat television screen, I felt like I'd walked into a scene from the *One Thousand and One Arabian Nights*.

I stood at the doorway trying to figure out what to do. The smell of coffee and food made my stomach rumble. I hadn't eaten for days now.

"Oui?"

I looked up to see a tall, thin waiter with short, curly black hair and a sliver of a mustache, wearing a long apron. His face clearly said he disapproved of this apparition in front of him.

"Good morning," I said and cleared my throat.

He drew back slightly and looked me over. "Americaine?"

I could see I'd risen a bit in his eyes.

"Canadian," I said.

I'd spent my formative years in international schools in Africa where people came from all over the world, then went to a public school in India for three years, so my accent was as fusion as the cakes I baked. But having spent the past three years in Canada meant I'd added a distinctly North American drawl to the mix.

The man merely shrugged. "How might I help?" he asked.

"I'd like to use a phone, please."

"Use of phone is only for customers," he said in a tart voice, his mouth curling in disapproval again.

"Okay, then I'd like a coffee and a bun, please."

With a slight turn of his head, he indicated a table at the back of the shop, next to a sign that said "Toilets." I stepped in and walked toward it. There was already a dirty cup on it. Next to my table sat four Middle Eastern looking men deep in discussion. I looked back at the waiter but he'd disappeared as silently as he'd appeared.

I pushed the dirty cup away and sat down.

With shaking hands, I put my phone on the table and turned the on-and-off switch five times. Nothing. I held it high and shook it in the air to catch a magic-battery-charging wave or something, but the screen remained silent. Not even a flicker of life. It hadn't worked the night before and it wasn't going to work today. I stared at it, thinking I'd do anything to hear Katy's voice again.

From where I sat, I could see part of the square outside. *Is she out there somewhere? Does she know I'm looking for her? Is she okay?*

A bony hand slid an espresso and a brioche on my table.

"Two quid."

The waiter stood beside my table but was pointedly looking at the TV. I fished out two one-pound coins from my purse, thankful I'd exchanged my dollars at the airport to buy lunch. I looked at them wistfully before handing them over. After paying for my air ticket, my purse was empty. These were my last coins.

"Excuse me." I looked up at the waiter. "I'm looking for someone. Can you help me?"

He gave me a look that was something in between a sneer and a leer. He snatched the money from my hand and took off without a word, leaving me staring at his back as he vanished through the kitchen door.

The men at the next table seemed to have taken an interest now.

One of them leaned toward me. "American?"

"Yes." It was getting easier to lie.

"What you doing here?" another asked.

I looked at my phone and back at the men. "I'm looking for a friend."

"Me too," one of them said, and this time there was no doubt it was a leer.

I ignored him. "My friend came to this square in a black taxi yesterday."

They stared at me, blankly.

"She's tall, about five foot seven, in a red skirt. She was with a man in a black suit. Did you see someone like that?"

Silence. One by one, they turned their eyes back to their coffee cups.

"Did any of you see anything?" I asked louder and slower, thinking I'd spoken too fast or they hadn't heard me over the TV.

"We not see anything," one of them said, not looking up.

"Yeah, we see nothing every time," said another man with a smirk to his tablemates.

Someone chuckled. "No black girls here."

"She's not black," I said, shaking my head. "She's a redhead, Irish Canadian."

"Check the bedrooms then."

Those words hit me like a punch to the stomach. I stared at him.

"White girls go to the bedroom," he said giving me an ugly smile. "Dark girls go to kitchen."

Someone guffawed.

Another slapped him on his back.

With a scowl, I scraped my chair back and got up. It was time to find the waiter and ask for the phone. I'd paid for my coffee and was a customer now.

Just as I picked up my bag, a deafening howl filled the room. I fell back on my chair, my heart pumping wildly.

Chapter Nine

The men craned their necks to look outside.

It took me two seconds to realize the sound I'd heard was a siren, a police siren, coming from the square.

I got up and walked toward the main door.

Three police vans came screeching to a halt outside, their sirens still blaring. Half a dozen officers with batons in hands spilled out of the vehicles. They lined up in front of the house directly across from the coffee shop. Then at the sound of an ear-piercing whistle, they charged inside, crashing down the door, hollering, "Police!"

The café had fallen silent.

The waiter was standing by his cash register, scowling. Someone had switched off the television. All eyes were on the scene unfolding outside.

The house under siege was one I'd walked into last night, the one with the sign that said "Live Nude Girls," where the sleazy man had invited me in. Right now, a scuffle was breaking out in front of it.

Police yelled. People shouted.

A group of men bolted out of the house and scuttled all over the square like crabs at a beach. One tried to put on his shirt as he ran out, and another stopped to put on a shoe and was promptly apprehended. I watched, my heart beating crazily, with an uneasy feeling this had something to do with Katy's disappearance.

Out came a burly officer pushing a well-dressed man in front of him. It was a man in a black suit with a cigarette hanging from his mouth.

I did a double take. My mouth went dry. Feeling like I was moving through molasses, I stepped out of the café and onto the steps. The man in the suit was pushing and pulling like a steer at a rodeo, trying to break the officer's grip. He thrashed around until a second officer ran up to help the first. Between the two, they pinned him against the van and put him in handcuffs.

Is this the man who took Katy?

I took an unsteady step down. *Is it him?* That was when I noticed the stubble on his chin and his graying hair. This man was older, paunchier and shorter than the man I'd seen at the airport. *He could have shaved, but he couldn't have gone gray and shrunk overnight.* No, it wasn't him, but the resemblance was eerie.

A thought struck me. I hadn't seen the man who took Katy that clearly. He'd looked taller, but it had all been a blur.

I stood on the steps of the café, unsure if I was making a mistake, unsure how to approach the police even if I knew he was the right man. Before I could do anything, the officers shoved him in the back of the vehicle, already crammed to the hilt with the other men, and slammed the doors shut. Within seconds, the van tore out of the square, tires screeching on the cobblestones.

A cry made me spin the other way.

A stream of girls was now pouring out of the house. I watched as they shuffled out, heads hung low, trying to hide their faces, faces so pale they looked like they hadn't seen sunlight in a long time. They weren't handcuffed but they all looked shell-shocked. Most were teens, others much younger.

Feeling numb and with my heart in my mouth, I scrutinized every one of them. *Is Katy here?*

One young girl, a skinny blonde wearing only her panties, was clearly in distress. She sobbed loudly as she walked out, her arms hugging her naked chest. Seeing her broke my heart. I looked on with a lump in my throat as an officer threw a blanket over her shoulders and helped her into the van.

"That's the lot," another officer yelled. "We're done."

Wait. Where's Katy?

I was just about to dash toward the van when from across the square I saw someone I recognized.

In those two seconds I stood gaping, the police got into their vans, shut the doors, and took off, lights blazing and sirens blaring.

The square fell suddenly silent, a deathly silence like everything had frozen in place.

A burst of harsh laughter broke the spell. I swiveled around to see the men inside chuckle among themselves. Some picked up the hookah pipes they'd mislaid during the excitement, others signaled the waiter for more coffee, and another grabbed the remote to turn the soccer game on again.

I turned around and looked back at the square.

There. She was still there. Walking away from me.

I jumped down the steps and ran.

"Katy!" I yelled.

Chapter Ten

"Katy!"

She didn't look back. But it had to be her. A redhead in a short skirt, walking toward the other end of the square. I was so busy looking at her, I barely noticed the ghostly figure next to her.

I dashed across the square, waving frantically.

"Katy!"

I was getting closer now. It looked like either Katy had grown a tad taller or her skirt had shrunk.

"Hey! It's me!" I yelled and almost tripped over a cobblestone, but I kept running.

Why isn't she turning around?

I caught up to her as she came to the steps of a ramshackle house in the far corner of the square. It was the one place that hadn't opened its doors, even when I'd banged on it.

"Katy!"

I grabbed her by the elbow and pulled her around. I looked at her in shock and my mouth dried up. *This is not Katy.*

This was a girl with a mane of red hair and freckles on her nose just like my friend, but also nothing like my friend. She was taller and had packed her face with more makeup and knock-'em-dead red lipstick than Katy would wear in a lifetime. She had on a bright red leather miniskirt, a short leather jacket, and the highest stilettos I'd ever seen. She looked taut and cold, and her face said *back off*.

I let go of her arm. *How could I have made such a big mistake? Katy doesn't even wear leather skirts.*

"What do you want?" the redhead said, her green eyes boring into mine.

I drew back in surprise. Her accent sounded Russian or East European of sorts. Her voice was a raspy drawl like she'd been up all night drinking. Despite the heavy makeup, she looked washed out, like the old buildings around us.

"I'm sorry," I stammered. "I thought you were my friend."

She gave me a sullen smile.

"From far away, you look just like her," I mumbled, feeling lame. "I didn't realize...."

"She not here."

I looked around, startled.

That's when I noticed the figure next to her. I peered at the short, shrouded shape. I'd seen women dress like this back in India. They wore their midnight black body veils, hidden to the rest of the world from the tops of their heads to the tips of their toes. A tiny slit in her facial covering gave an impression of her eyes, but other than that, I could see nothing. Not her mouth, not her face, not her arms or even her feet.

"S-sorry?" I said.

"Your friend not here." One side of the robe shifted. It could have been the lift of an arm or a flick of a wrist, I couldn't say. Two fiery black eyes glared through the slit. "No one here for you." It was a strange guttural voice, a strong accent I couldn't place.

"Oh?" I said. "How do you know?"

"Go away." She sounded angry now. "I said go!"

"But, but—" I stammered, trying to find my words, "How do you know my friend's not here? Have you seen her?"

The woman glared but said nothing.

"Zero's always trying to find redheads," the redhead said, popping a wad of bubble gum. "There's always a huge demand, especially from the Arabs. But it's just me here. I'd know if there were others because—"

"I said she not here. You go now," the robed woman interrupted. "Go!" The robe jerked my way. I took a step back.

"Why are you always in a rush, Bibi? Relax, will you?" the redhead said, but a flicker in her eyes made me wonder if she feared the other woman.

The redhead turned to me with a curious look in her eyes. "Hey, are you American by any chance?"

"Canadian," I said. "And Indian," I paused. "But I was born in Kenya."

She raised her eyebrows.

"Tell me," I said, looking at her and ignoring the impatient robed woman beside us. "Do you know a businessman called Dick from Toronto?"

The redhead shook her head.

"What about Jose from Detroit? Ever heard of that name?"

"No. Why I should know these people?"

"Because I think they took my friend."

The redhead laughed. I looked at her in shock. *How can she laugh about something so serious?*

Then, a worried look came over her face. "Wait a minute. This friend of yours. Am I going to have competition?"

Competition? My stomach heaved thinking of where Katy might have ended up. "No!" I shook my head. "Oh, my god, of course not! I lost her at the airport. She's supposed to come with me to India. Not here."

"Come!" The robed woman had had enough. She tugged at the redhead's elbow and motioned her to come with her.

The redhead didn't budge. "Hey, Bibi. I said frigging relax, will you?"

"No time!" The robe had become more animated now. "No time. Come! Now!"

I couldn't see the woman's face, but I could feel fear emanating from underneath that cloth. The woman grabbed the redhead by the elbow again. With a curse, the redhead pushed the woman's hand away and sashayed up the stairs like she was born in those stilettos. She banged the door open and disappeared inside.

The robed woman was still standing in front of me. I didn't know what to say. Without a warning and with a twist of her wrist, the woman slid off her face veil.

I gasped.

It was a strange face that looked back at me, one with beautiful lips and dark eyes rimmed with long eyelashes, but her entire left side was a grotesque pink scar like her skin had been scalded by boiling water.

I looked at her in horror.

"Wha…are you ok?" I whispered.

"Same thing happen if you ask too many questions," she whispered hoarsely.

Without another word, she pulled down her veil, scurried up the steps, and walked inside the doorway.

The door slammed shut.

Chapter Eleven

I stood in front of this strange house wondering if I was in the middle of a crazy nightmare.

I pinched my left arm. No, I felt that. I was fully awake.

The sound of a car's honk made me turn around.

A black London cab was inching its way through a narrow alleyway on the side of the square, a path made to fit a medieval horse, not a modern-day car. A troupe of young boys who'd been playing football at that end picked up their ball and moved to let the car pass.

The cab was just like the one that took Katy from the airport. I knew it was one among a thousand but my heart beat faster.

I stepped to the side of the building and flattened myself against the brick wall. There was a small window just above me. I crouched below the ledge and peeked around the corner, hoping to spot Katy.

From my hiding spot, I watched as the car stopped twenty feet from the house.

The back door opened and out stepped a beautiful Chinese girl in super-high black heels and a micro-skirt that barely covered anything. She looked fourteen at most. A tattoo of Chinese characters circled its way up her slender thighs. Her hair was cut in a sharp bob style and her lips were smeared with the same blood-red lipstick as the redhead had worn.

She stood next to the opened cab door as if uncertain of her surroundings. Then, wobbling in those heels like a newly born doe, she took her first step.

A man jumped out of the cab from behind her and grabbed her by the shoulder. He was tall and thin and wore a black suit. I gasped out loud. He looked exactly like the man who'd pulled Katy from the airport. He wore the same badly fitted black suit. He had the same heavy beard that made it look like he was hiding something.

The girl stepped over the cobblestones, swaying dangerously. The man steered her roughly toward the main door, the same door the redhead and the robed woman had walked into, moments earlier. Neither the girl nor the man noticed me in the shadows.

The cab pulled away in reverse. The man and the girl were now at the top of the stairs. That was when I noticed a change in the girl's behavior. One second she was barely holding up. The next, her body jerked up as if she'd just woken up. As if she'd realized where she was.

She stopped and turned back toward the square. A strange look crossed her face like her mind cleared for a moment. The man grabbed her arm to push her inside. She slapped him away and took a step down. The man's face turned red. The girl took another step down, but it was too late.

He whipped out his hand and walloped her on the head, making her crumble to her knees. She grabbed on to the railing but couldn't hang on. I watched in horror as she tumbled down the concrete steps like a broken doll. My hands flew to my mouth to stifle a scream.

The man bolted down the steps. I covered my eyes. *I can't see this. I can't see this.* I forced my hands away to see him raise his foot to kick her. Once. Twice.

And something in me snapped.

"Oi! Stop!" I ran out of my hiding spot screaming at the top of my lungs. "Stop that! You're gonna kill her!" I waved my arms like mad. "Help! Police! Stop this! I said *stop* it now!"

The man jumped back, startled. I wasn't sure if it was the sudden sight of someone, anyone, dashing out, or if it was someone yelling in English, calling for the police no less. But that did it. He bolted up the steps and slammed the door shut.

I looked at the girl lying motionless on the ground. I fell to my knees and bent over her.

"Hey, are you okay?"

It was a pretty, petite face I was looking at. Her eyes were half-closed, but she was alive. Her chest was heaving. Her fingers groped at the air as if looking for something to hold on to. I gently put my hand in hers. She squeezed mine tightly.

"You'll be fine. Stay with me, okay?"

She blinked. Her eyes looked glassy like she wasn't fully there. I knelt all the way down and put my face close to hers. "I'm here to help you," I whispered to avoid frightening her any more than she already was. She gave me a vacant look and lowered her head back on the ground.

There was no one else in the square except for the kids playing a hundred feet away. They weren't paying attention or looking even slightly disturbed by what had happened. It was like they'd seen this sort of thing before. I looked around the ancient square with its ugly signs, its broken-down shops, and even more broken-down people. *Doesn't anyone care?*

"Arrrgh—"

The girl was trying to get up. She pulled in her legs, grimacing in pain. I reached out and touched her shoulder. She didn't pull back. "Take it easy now," I said, as I helped her sit up.

"Can you breathe okay?"

She nodded her head slowly.

Thank goodness, she understands.

I remembered my bag. I had two T-shirts and a bottle of water in there. I got up and ran to pick it up. I took the bottle out, pulled off the cap, and handed it to the girl who was still sitting unsteadily on the ground, looking dazed. I had to hold it as she drank because her hands were trembling too much. She chugged it down like she'd not had a drink of water all day.

"You'll be fine. You'll be just fine," I said, as she was drinking. "We'll get help for you soon. I'm going to call an ambulance and they'll take care of you."

She pushed the bottle away and gave me a wild look. "No!" Her voice was hoarse.

I looked at her, puzzled. "I think your ankle's broken. You're bleeding. Plus, we need to call the police."

She reached for my shoulder and tried to say something. I leaned in. Her hand tightened on me.

"No, no police," she whispered.

I didn't know what to say. I stared at her. She motioned for more water. I handed the nearly empty bottle back to her.

"Thanks," she said, when she was done.

She closed her eyes, and I felt her lean against me. I sat next to her, listening to her laborious breathing. We stayed at the bottom of the steps like this for several minutes in silence. I didn't know what to think or do. I needed to find Katy, but I couldn't leave this battered young girl by herself either.

"I'm Asha," I said.

She opened her eyes and gave me a blank look.

"My name is Asha," I repeated. "What's yours?"

She pointed at her chest.

I nodded.

"Win."

"What are you doing here, Win?"

Her eyes looked into the distance but she didn't say anything.

"I saw what happened to you," I said. "He hit you. He *kicked* you. We have to do something about it. This is serious."

"Nothing," she whispered, closing her eyes again.

"Nothing?"

A small shrug. Then, as if she'd remembered something, she opened her eyes and looked up at the door. She put a hand on my shoulder to steady herself, and holding on to me and the wall, got up painfully.

"Hey, where are you going?"

With one hand on the rail, she started to climb the stairs, dragging one foot behind her.

"Win!" I whispered as loudly as I dared. "You can't go back in there!"

She turned and put her finger to her lips. "Shhh—"

"But, that man. He's in there—"

She continued her walk up, with that twisted foot dragging over each step.

"Win!" I watched her helplessly. "Don't go in!"

She was at the top of the steps now. I vaulted up and landed next to her just before she pulled on the doorknob.

"Listen to me. Please. We need to tell the police what happened. This is crazy bad."

She opened the door, limped inside, and turned to me, while I looked at her desperately.

"It's okay," she said in a slight sing-song voice, "It's okay. This is my home."

Before I knew it, the door closed and the click of a key came from the other side.

Chapter Twelve

The morning breeze had turned into a blustery wind, blowing leaves over the square and strands of hair across my face.

I swept my hair back and looked up to the sky. Gray clouds were gathering above. A flash of lightning streaked the sky from afar. I could smell the rain coming.

The wind picked up newspaper shreds and empty plastic bags and swirled them across the cobblestones. The neon lights on top of the shops flashed on and off, buzzing intermittently like they knew a storm was on its way. No one was standing in the square chatting or smoking next to doorways anymore. The place was empty. Even strip joints had to get ready for a thunderstorm.

I stepped up to the door where everyone had disappeared through and rattled the ancient knob. The door may have been old, but the deadbolt was new and secure.

I surveyed the building and its facade of dirty brown brick. There weren't any windows on the first floor on this side of the house. There were two on the second floor covered by dark curtains, but they were high and barred like jail cells. My eyes wandered farther up. And I almost screamed.

On the third floor, tied to a black metal bar of a window was Katy's red scarf fluttering in the wind. I stared at it open-mouthed. This time, it wasn't mocking me. It was calling out to me.

"Katy!" I heard myself whisper. For a moment, I felt faint. I leaned against the railing to steady myself and swallowed hard.

Katy's here. Oh my god, Katy's here.

I felt my breath come fast and shallow. I looked up again. The window was too high for me to climb, or throw anything, even a stone.

How to get her attention? Think girl, think!

I walked down the steps and turned around the corner to where I'd hidden earlier. There. I thought I'd noticed a window under the shadows of the awning. I walked up to it, my heart beating fast now.

Like the rest of the building, this window was in need of repair. From where I stood, I saw a solitary black bar across the window and a ledge large enough to fit a pixie. The curtains were drawn. It was hard to see who or what was inside.

I glanced around to see if anyone was watching me, but there wasn't a soul outside. Up above, the sky looked heavier, darker and closer to the ground. I could hear the thunderclaps rolling closer. I peered at the window. If I used my bag as a footstool and pulled myself up using the iron bar, I'd be able to get on the ledge.

Before I made my next move, I checked my pockets to make sure I had my most important possessions on me in case I wouldn't be able to come this way again. This meant my passport and my little booklet of recipes. That booklet was as precious as my passport to me. Maybe even more. On its pages were my favorite recipes from my mother. Tucked between those pages was also the letter Preeti had sent me a year ago explaining what really happened after I left Goa.

Inserted in between the pages was also a thank you note from my VIP client back at the bakery in Toronto. I kept the letter from the Diplomatic Dragon Lady because it was a testament to my first baking gig, and because for the first time in my life, someone had taken me seriously.

I tucked the two booklets in my jacket pocket and zipped it up. Then, with a quick look around to see if anyone was watching, I placed my bag carefully at the foot of the wall, right under the window, and stepped on it. It gave me five inches of extra height. Getting on my tiptoes and using all the strength I could muster, I hooked my hands around the iron bar and pulled up onto the tiny ledge. For once, my small size worked to my advantage.

I leaned against the sill, to not fall out, and inspected the window. There was a latch at the bottom. With one hand holding on to the rusty bar for stability, I reached with my other and pulled the latch. To my surprise, it clicked open. This window must have been centuries old and may never have been locked. Or maybe, it had been unlocked recently by someone trying to get in. Or out.

I pushed the window. It slid open an inch. I tried it again, throwing all my weight against it. This time, the window slid open all the way, but the iron bar gave way. I gave a small cry before coming down with a resounding crash inside the house.

Oh, no!

I reeled from the pain of the fall, but looked up quickly and braced myself. I could just imagine the bearded man come roaring in to kick me senseless. But no one came.

It took a moment to orient myself. I'd fallen onto something rough but not too hard. I felt around me, trying to figure out where I was. *Is it a rug? A large sack?*

I bent down and felt my arms and legs to make sure nothing was broken. I rotated my ankles and wrists in slow circles. What hurt most was my head. It was throbbing on all sides. I sat still for several minutes to compose myself.

The sound of a door opening made me freeze.

Someone was on the other side of the room. I heard the sound of dishes and cutlery being picked up. Then, a chair being pushed back and noises of a spoon or a fork tinging on a plate. I waited, listening, not daring to breathe.

My eyes slowly adjusted to the darkness. It wasn't as pitch black as I'd thought at first. A faint yellow light came in from a streetlight outside, giving an eerie glow to the room.

I peered around me. This wasn't a room as much as a storage closet. There was a narrow wooden door ten feet from me, and on the other side of this door, someone was sitting and eating.

Along the walls of this room were sacks stacked on top of each other. There was a shelf in a corner, filled with tin cans and small plastic packets of flour, or something that looked like flour. It smelled musty in here, like a rice cellar, but with a trace of a chemical stink. At my feet was the rusty iron bar from the window which had fallen down with me. I reached down and picked it up.

I stood up to inspect the room better.

Near the shelf in the corner was a lone wooden chair. Draped casually over it was a black cloth, like a cloak or a super-sized towel.

It took me a few seconds to realize it was the midnight-black robe of the woman I'd seen in the square.

Chapter Thirteen

"**Y**ou took my cake?"

The voice was so loud, that for one frightening moment, I thought someone was inside the storage room with me.

It was a man's voice speaking in English. It was rough and guttural, an accent that came from somewhere in the Middle East, just like the woman in the black robe.

I tiptoed toward the corner shelf, making sure my anklet didn't jingle, and crouched between the chair and the shelf. It was the only place to hide if anyone walked in, not that I'd stay hidden for long behind that flimsy piece of furniture.

"Leave me alone, man. I'm hungry." It was the voice of another man, high-pitched. I imagined a tall and skinny man, with a taut face. "I work all day. What *you* do?" His accent sounded like the redhead's, from Eastern Europe or thereabouts.

"Me?" The first man sounded astonished. "What *I* do today?"

"Ya, you." The Eastern European man sounded amused.

"Who did important work today? Huh?" The first man sounded indignant. "Tell me that?"

"C'mon, picking new girls super easy," the second man said.

New girls? I sat up.

"Who went all way cross town, huh?" The first man asked. That was when I noticed how slurred his voice was. "Who risk life, huh? If police saw, I finished now. Cameras everywhere in airport. You t'ink I not work today? And now you took my cake, you moron."

Airport? He's talking about Katy!

"Calm the hell down, man. Look, more cake in fridge. Anyway, it's you who's working for American," the other man said. "This shit is dangerous."

American? Does he mean Jose?

"Bizness with Americans is always good money. I hate their guts, I tell you, but they good for bizness. You got no head, Vlad. We lucky to get dat call."

I heard a fridge door open and slam shut.

"Lucky?" the other man, Vlad, sniffed. "Jeez, you believe any shit."

"He pay good money."

"For two girls," the second man said. "Won't pay till you find second. Just see how much luck you have then. Haha!"

I felt the hair on my neck stand on end.

"You better appreciate I found one girl," the first man growled. "Second girl not interesting. Red hairs make lot more money than darkies."

A cold shiver ran through me.

"That redhead's enough trouble, I tell ya," Vlad said. "Why you agree to pick this old hag?"

Old hag? Maybe it's not Katy, then?

"American girls always trouble," Vlad continued. "Next time, try Asians. Thai, Burma, Laos. Get 'em young. Boom. Cash cows."

The first man grunted. The sounds of drawers opening and banging shut and dishes clanking came from the other room.

"Win was good idea," Vlad was saying. "She was ten. Perfect for job. I say go for twelve, tops. Easy to shut up and they stay quiet."

Oh god, they're talking about children.

"Wait till I get cash from American," the first man growled. "Then you see who's laughing."

"You just bought whole load of trouble," Vlad said. "Screeching and scratching like a dying cat, and no one even touch her."

I felt a huge relief wash over me. *If Katy's here somewhere, she's not hurt. Not yet, anyway.* I looked up at the ceiling and said silently, *Keep fighting, Katy. I'm going to find you soon.*

"You jus' don' know how to handle girls," the first man was saying. "Me, I know how to control. Beat till they forget their name. Dat's how."

"Right," Vlad said. "You done great job so far."

"You t'ink I went to all dat trouble so she work here?" the first man said. "I got brains, I tell you. I thought this hard. First, American pay me to find her. Then, I sell her for good profit. Ahmed always looking for girls. I make money both ways. Who's the smart guy now, huh?"

A door opened, silencing both men.

"Allo." A new voice. Someone younger. *A teen? A boy?*

"You early, Luc," Vlad said.

"Oooh, cake! Can I have some?"

"Look in fridge," Vlad said in an irritated voice.

"Where's Tetyana?" the young man asked.

"Upstairs, counting her money as usual, the mad witch," the second man said. "So you get what you look for?"

"*Oui.* It's been a good day for business today," the young man said. He sounded like one of my French teachers in the international schools of long ago, with the same nasal voice, and his words strung together quickly, one after the other. "Look what I got."

The first man clucked his tongue and Vlad oohed over whatever Luc was showing them.

"Latest version," the young man said, "not even out in the shops yet."

"How much?" the first man asked. "You waste good cash on stupid toys."

"C'mon, I deserve it," the young man said. "I work hard, and it was my birthday last week."

"Let boy keep it," Vlad said. "Hey, can you get for me too, Luc?"

"Sure," Luc said. "You want one too, Zero?"

"You buy this from selling your filth," the first man growled. "Don't want dat shit in my house."

"Shit?" the young man said, his voice rising a notch. "I make good money from this, I'll let you know. Enough to pay for your trucks. Talk about filth. You think this house is clean, man? You got girls coming in and out like a—"

"Shut your mouth or I slice it," the first man snapped. "Don't talk back to me, boy."

A shiver went through me.

"Don't listen to him," Vlad said. "Always saying he'll kill everybody. That's why fire is burning in Middle East all the time. Don't know how to keep their heads, these people."

"And you Polish are Russia's whores!" roared the first man, and promptly fell into a rough gagging-coughing fit.

"See what happens when you lose head," Vlad said, not seeming to take offense. "Boy got good point, you know. You know how much this business can bring us?"

"No!" The first man had found his voice again. "I only do girls. And boys when customer want, but I don't touch dis shit. Work of Satan. You end up in hell with dis!"

"And you won't?" Luc, the young man said. His tone was mocking. "I think you're only saying that so you can steal my stuff. I noticed some packets missing this morning."

"Do I look like thief, boy!" the first man yelled. *Bang!* I jumped. Someone had slammed a table or hit the wall.

I was only half listening to this cacophony. The other part of my brain was furiously trying to think of how to get upstairs and see where Katy was imprisoned. The front door was locked. The only way inside was through the small wooden door I was staring at, behind which a mad hatters' cake party was going on.

"What happens when they catch you, huh? Whatcha gonna do then?" the first man was saying.

"You got the same problem," the younger man pointed out. "Worse, actually."

"Not me," the first man said. "Belgium royals my best customers."

"You think that cover you?" Vlad asked. "You play with fire, I tell you. They'll fucking feed you with bullets. You and all of us, just to make point."

"*Merde*! The girls all hate you," Luc joined in. "You think they'll keep their mouths shut? They'll talk. Then you'll see."

"You born idiot, boy," the first man said. "My bitches do as I tell 'em or cops be pulling their bodies from river. And if you t'ink I help you when they catch you, you wrong. I put first bullet right through your goddammed head."

I clutched my iron bar tighter. Something in his voice told me these weren't empty threats.

Suddenly, there was a crash, as if someone banged open a door. Everyone stopped talking.

"What the hell happened!"

It was a woman's angry voice, a voice I'd heard before.

"Allo, Tetyana," the young man said. "What's up?"

"What's up? You want to know what's up?" she shouted. "What the frigging hell happened to Win?"

I gasped.

"Stop screaming, woman. My head hurt," Vlad said.

"Who did this to her? Tell me!" she demanded. "Zero, is this your dirty handiwork?"

I leaned in. I was sure now it was the redhead I'd met earlier.

"Not me. It was client," the first man said without a moment's hesitation. His voice was calm but slimy. "I try stop him, but he got real mad. He want more and she tired. But I save her, you know, and bought her home good. Hey, I did my job."

What?

"You said they won't get hurt!" The woman, Tetyana, sounded furious. "You promised me!"

"She not dead, right?" Vlad said, in a mocking voice. "You got lot to learn, woman. You know nothing about our business."

"I didn't sign up for this!" the woman said. "No one hits these girls! We had an agreement."

"Oh, no, we don't." It was the first man's voice, so low and dangerous, I wanted to take a step back. "I don't make agreement with any woman. She belong to me, not you."

"It is my business!" the woman shouted. "When you beat up a girl, it's my frigging business! How dare you lay your hands on her! She's just a child for god's sake!"

"Shut up, woman!" the first man shouted back, just as loudly.

A chair was scraped back.

"Enough!" the second man, Vlad, said. "You two keep pissing 'round." He laughed an ugly, chilling laugh. "Zero thinks I don't know to do my job, eh? I gonna show new girl how job is done. Ha-ha!"

Crash!

That sound came from inside the storage room. Vlad's ugly words had jerked me back and my elbow had pushed a small plastic packet off the shelf behind me. It had fallen with a thud but it was the tin cans next to it that had fallen to the tile floor, making a racket to wake the dead.

Silence in the next room.

I stopped breathing.

"What the heck that?" I heard Vlad say. "Where it come from?"

Please don't come in. Please.

"*Bordel de merde*," Luc said. "I saw a big rat outside today. Maybe it's inside the house now."

"You gotta be kidding," said Vlad. "I hate those little bastards."

"This is shit hole," the first man said.

"They give rabies," the young man said.

"We gotta do something!" the second man said, his voice rising even higher. "Luc, catch it, will you?"

I heard steps coming toward the door.

I looked around desperately, my heart beating wildly.

Chapter Fourteen

The storage room flooded with light.

Through an impossibly small opening, I gaped at a young man of about nineteen or twenty staring at me with one hand on the light switch. This must be Luc.

From what I'd overheard, I'd imagined a cocky teen in a hood, torn jeans and baseball cap worn backward. Instead, he was wearing a white shirt, a tie, and a smart bomber jacket—a mix of cute boy actor and bad boy biker. With his short brown hair, he looked like a charming model at a high-end department store, rather than a gangster on the street. I blinked twice.

The naked bulb hanging from the middle of the ceiling gave off a feeble light. But right then, it felt like stadium floodlights were on me.

Next to Luc stood a man with a razor-thin scar along one cheek, wearing a black leather jacket and army boots. He was short and hefty with biceps the size of a miniature horse. I noticed his left hand was missing. All he had was a stub where his hand should have been.

He was the kind of man you'd find in a gambling den at four in the morning, smoking cigarettes from the side of his mouth and groping waitresses if they were unlucky to get too close—a man you'd not want to meet in a dark alley in the middle of the night. Or anywhere, at anytime, for that matter. This must be Vlad. His squeaky voice had been deceiving.

The redhead, Tetyana, was standing next to Vlad. It was the same young woman I'd seen in the square earlier, but this time, she'd removed her leather skirt and jacket and was wearing nothing more than her heels, red lace panties and bra, and a see-through mini kimono. I averted my eyes.

"Where's the rat?" Vlad spat out.

I didn't say anything, not because I shouldn't speak but because I couldn't. I was paralyzed with fear.

He frowned, scanning the room. "Running loose in here?"

"Who dat?" Pushing his way through this raggedy crowd was the scariest man of them all, the man who'd kidnapped Katy and kicked Win outside. I swallowed hard. Closer now, his hairy face was even more intimidating. This must be Zero.

He frowned at me. "What you do here?" he snapped. "I told you go to mosque!" His eyes shone like the devil lived inside him. I was sure he could kill with just one look. I drew back but didn't say a word.

"What's wrong, you?" he glared. "Lose voice, stupid woman?"

A micro-second earlier, I'd done the only thing I could think of.

I'd grabbed the black robe, and without knowing which way was up or down, I'd pulled it over my head. In my rush, I'd put it on crooked so I could barely see, and only from one eye. With all the noise I'd been making, they must have wondered if an elephant had been rampaging in the storage room. I now stood perfectly still, half-blind, trying to calm the rising terror inside me, wondering what I must look like from the outside.

"What about damn rat?" Vlad's eyes darted anxiously around the room. "How I gonna sleep tonight with fat rat running around?"

Under the robe, I raised an arm deliberately and slowly and pointed to the furthest corner of the room. All three heads turned to look.

"It gone that way?" the man asked.

I nodded my head so they could see the movement. Underneath, a river of sweat was streaming down my back. My legs were trembling so hard, I was sure the world could hear my knees rattle.

"Jus' one?" Vlad asked.

I nodded again.

"Hey, are you okay, Bibi? *Ça va?*" Luc asked, his face puzzled. Three sets of eyes turned away from searching for the non-existent rat and back to me.

I was trying not to hyperventilate, feeling like a chicken in a wolves' den, knowing I could only keep up this charade for so long.

"Who the hell open window?" Zero asked, suddenly marching over to the small window I fell through. "Everyt'ing breaking here. Every time you find place, Vlad, it's a pisshole."

Vlad's face went red. "I bust my ass to find good place and you call it pisshole?"

"This is worse than house you got in Paris. Do better!" Zero snapped right back.

"First you say I don't know how to control girl. Then, you say I don't know how to find place?" Vlad shouted. "You know how hard is to find place where police don't—"

"Shut up, both of you!" Tetyana said.

"You leave, if you don't like!" Zero shouted at Vlad, ignoring the redhead.

"Boys!" Tetyana raised her voice. "Shut it, for frigging sake! Do you want to get attention? Do you want to attract the police here?"

The men stopped but glared at each other.

"Don't know what the big deal is," Luc said, leaning against the wall like this was just another Sunday afternoon conversation. "The front door can come down in seconds. One kick will do."

"It called psy-cho-lo-gy." Zero pronounced the word slowly, as if he'd just learned it. "Everyone know nobody can walk in like dat. Girls know they can't go out. They behave. We gotta show we're serious."

"You take their passports and beat 'em up. Isn't that enough psychology?" Luc said with a dry smirk.

"The plan was to make fast money, not attempt psychology," Tetyana said, in a quiet voice, shaking her head.

I looked at her. Even with that see-through kimono and undies, she didn't belong here. There was something strange about the way she held herself proudly and the fluency of her speech and language. She was nothing like the two goons here.

"What you doing here, anyway?" Zero asked, as if suddenly remembering my presence. He turned making me take an involuntary step back. "What you do in dark, huh?"

His frown deepened, darkening his already ugly face. He wasn't someone you wanted to get on the wrong side of. I kept silent, trying to stop the panic attack from overcoming me. My brain raced, trying to think of what to do next. *Run out? But where? Maybe a coughing fit? They'll know it's not her.*

"*I* know what you're up to." Luc said standing straight and giving me a dirty look. "There's no rats in here. I know what you're doing."

My heart skipped a beat. *Does he know who I am?*

He took a step forward and pointed an accusing finger at me. "It's you who's been stealing my stuff, isn't it?"

What?

"Then what's all my stuff doing on the floor?" He took a step forward, his eyes widening as he saw the full extent of the damaged package on the floor. "You've ruined my sacs, Bibi! *Merde!*"

I moved my arms sideways to say no, flapping the black robe like a monster-sized crow. I hoped he understood.

"I knew you were all double-crossing me," Luc wailed. "First Zero, and now you. How could you do this to me?"

"Jeezus, people," Vlad said, giving him a look of contempt.

Tetyana was watching me quietly. Something in her eyes bothered me.

Zero stepped closer to me. His step wavered, but his eyes looked deadly. Inside the robe, I squared my shoulders and balled my hands into fists, ready to defend myself. *I won't go down easily, Bibi or not Bibi*, I thought.

"Dis true, Bibi? You stealing this?" He asked. "You selling this filth to infidels?"

I stared at him, speechless.

"Oi!"

It was Tetyana. Everyone turned to look at her.

"Can't you all see she's just trying to pray?" she said.

Pray?

"Pray?" Luc said.

"Inside here?" Vlad said.

"You possessed, woman?" Zero gave me a strange look.

"Everyone out!" Tetyana clapped her hands. "Leave your sister alone, Zero. How can you interrupt when she's praying?"

Zero looked at her, confused.

"Don't you know that's bad luck? You'll go straight to hell if you don't watch it. No virgins for you!"

That did it. Zero walked out quickly, but not before throwing a bewildered glance my way.

Does Tetyana know I'm not Bibi? Or does she think she's saving Bibi?

"Jeezus," I heard Vlad say. "What wrong with you people today? So much drama. I need to nap. Dibs on TV," he said as he stepped back into the kitchen.

I sighed in relief. *Good. Watch the game, you brute, and leave Katy alone.*

"Out!" Tetyana ushered everyone outside.

Then she turned to me. I froze.

Giving me a strange look I couldn't make out, she stepped out and closed the door.

I was alone in the little storage room once again.

Chapter Fifteen

With a shaking hand, I reached for the knob.

I had mentally counted time and given myself five full minutes before stepping out of the storage room. I had no idea how long Bibi's prayers lasted, but that sounded sufficient, plus time wasn't on my side. It had been hard to focus because my brain was screaming to run and find Katy before anyone hurt her.

But I had to play smart. I had to outwit everyone to get out of here alive with Katy. One punch or kick from either Vlad or Zero and I'd probably go out like a light, but since neither sounded highly intelligent, from what I'd heard so far, I still had hope.

The voices on the other side of the room had died down. Footsteps above me told me someone or some people had retired upstairs. I opened the wooden door, not knowing what to expect, and took a step out to the grimiest kitchen I'd seen in my life.

Sitting at a dirty table was Tetyana, still in her racy getup, having a drink with the impeccably dressed Luc. Between them stood an open bottle of whiskey and two empty shot glasses. Both stopped talking when I walked out.

The kitchen counter was a mosaic of icky browns. It hadn't been wiped in ages. The sink was piled high with dried-out dirty dishes. A garbage bag in the corner was overflowing and smelled like something had crawled inside and died. The door of the fridge was slightly ajar as if someone had forgotten to shut it, and the floor squeaked with every step I took.

I stood still next to the door, trying to figure out what to do next. *Should have decided that before I came out*, I thought. *It's too late now.* That was when another thought struck me. *What if Bibi's in the house? What if I bump into her?* A chill went through me at the thought.

"What's the matter, hun?" Tetyana looked genuinely worried. "Everything okay?"

Under the robe, I crossed my fingers.

"Hey," Luc said with a sigh. "Look, I overreacted in there. I know you're not a thief. It's Zero who's always stealing from me, *tu sais?* Makes me paranoid."

I shrugged and spread my hands wide to say, "No hard feelings."

They stared back at me expectantly, waiting for me to speak. But I didn't have time to waste.

I gave a slight bow to both and looked for the exit. My bow didn't go unnoticed. I saw how both Luc's and Tetyana's eyebrows shot up. Note to self, I thought, Bibi doesn't bow or curtsy. I walked as calmly as I could toward the open doorway that looked like it led to the main part of the house.

"Something's wrong," I heard Luc whisper behind me.

"Snorted your frigging stuff, that's what," Tetyana whispered hoarsely back. "This is going to come back and haunt you."

I heard a chair being moved, then shuffling. *Are they following me?*

But I didn't look back. *Whatever happens, I've got to go ahead with this.* Trembling under the robe, I took one step forward, then another. I'd managed to straighten the robe while I pretend-prayed in the little room, but it was still hard to see through the veil. If there was any piece of clothing superbly designed to restrict a person's senses and movements, this had to be it. Bibi wasn't that much taller than me, so the robe fit, somewhat. Still, I stumbled forward, handicapped.

The kitchen doorway opened to a small foyer of sorts. It was dark here, but I could see the peeling yellow wallpaper and the stains on the orange carpet. The whole house smelled moldy like it had been left to decay for years, maybe even decades. Holding the robe up with both hands so as not to trip, I climbed up the wooden stairway.

I came up to an open landing. In front of me were two doors and another staircase in the corner that went up to the third floor. From one of the rooms, a TV blared. It was a football game being played out.

I tiptoed quietly over to the door where the television noise was coming from and peeked in. It was a small sitting room with a stained velour couch. Here, Vlad was sitting with his feet up on the coffee table, snoring loudly, dribbling spit from the corner of his mouth. One hand was holding a TV remote and the other a black handgun.

Where's Zero?

I turned around and walked toward the rickety stairway curling upward. *Katy's up there on the third floor. That's where the scarf was tied.*

Hanging on to the loose railing with one hand and holding up the robe with the other, I waddled up, making out each step through the narrow slit. *How does Bibi do this every day?*

It was a relief to get to the third landing without bumping into anyone. I had so little visibility, I had to turn around to see fully where I was. There were three rooms on this floor, and all were closed. I tried to remember which window Katy had tied her scarf to but after two minutes of trying, I realized my spatial abilities were as bad as a bat's in daylight. *I'll have to try all three rooms.*

Except for the TV noise from downstairs, there wasn't a sound in the house. I took a deep breath and reached for the first door. *If anyone other than Katy's in there, I'll pretend I'm Bibi. Act confused, close the door, and walk away.*

I turned the knob. It didn't budge. I tried it again. The door was locked.

I stepped up to the second door and turned the knob.

To my surprise, this door slid open. I squinted through the slit. The room was empty, apart from clothes, dirty plates, glasses and a used condom strewn around the floor. I shuddered in disgust. I peered at the window and I felt my heart leap. Katy's scarf was still tied to its bars.

Where is she? Did they take her someplace else?

I closed the door quietly and stepped up to the third room. This door was unlocked as well. I opened it and looked inside.

Win!

The girl was lying on an unmade bed, her face paler than before. *Is she sleeping? Is she alive?* I slipped inside, walked toward the bed and knelt down next to the bed.

"Win!" I whispered. "Win! Wake up!"

in didn't even open her eyes.

Her face was deathly pale like the blood had drained from her. I reached over and touched her arm. It was unusually cold. I put a hand on her neck to find a pulse. It was weak, but it was there. *Thank god.* She turned and whimpered.

"Win!" I whispered again.

A rustle nearby made me look up.

Other than the girl on the bed, I was alone in the room. There was barely enough space here to fit the bed and a chair. A funny feeling came over me, a feeling in my bones. *There's someone else in here.*

With my heart beating a little faster, I scanned the room with my eyes. There wasn't even a wardrobe where anyone could hide. There were no other doors than the one I came in through. I looked back at Win. She was still sleeping or unconscious.

Again, the rustle. I froze. It was closer this time.

I stood slowly and backed away from the bed, toward the door, glancing around the room as I did. The rustle again. *Is that coming from under the bed?* It was only when I had my back to the door that curiosity overcame fear. I bent down and peeked under Win's bed.

Two familiar green eyes glared at me from under the bed.

"Katy!" my muffled voice came through the veil.

I bounded toward the bed, but the robe got the better of me. I tripped and came crashing to the ground. I didn't have time to register the pain, but my head was now level with Katy's.

"Katy!" I said, trying to reach out to her, but she'd skedaddled to the other end of the bed and was staring at me with terror in her eyes. *Why isn't she—?* That was when I realized she wasn't seeing me.

I scrambled to my feet and pulled off the robe. Or tried to. It had not been easy to put this thing on, and it was harder to get it off. I twirled around trying to find an opening but instead shrouded myself like an Egyptian mummy. My anklet jingled madly as I tried to get out of the knot I'd tied myself into.

"Asha?"

Katy's voice. I stopped moving.

"That you?"

"Yes, it's me!" I mumbled desperately through the cloth. "It's me! Are you okay? Help me get out of this!"

I felt a hand on my shoulder.

"Shh," she said. "Don't move."

I stayed still while she pulled on the cloth, nudging gently this way and that, unraveling me from my mess. When she finally pulled the robe off, in front of me was the redhead I'd been searching for.

Katy stared at me in disbelief.

"What are you doing under that—"

I flung my arms around her. We hugged, half-sobbing, half-laughing.

"I spotted your scarf," I said finally, wiping my eyes.

"So it worked?"

I pointed at the scratch marks on her face. "Katy, did they—?" I couldn't get myself to finish the sentence.

She shook her head. "I screamed and kicked and yelled so much, he said he was going to get his gun so if I screamed again, he'd shoot me."

"Oh, my god."

"So I said, go right ahead. I'd rather be dead but I won't die quietly. That stopped him. He walked out yelling all the bad things he'd do and slammed the door. He forgot to lock it at least."

"Was it Vlad or Zero?"

"Who?"

"Is it the thug who took you from the airport? That's Zero."

"Yes, that's him. Tall, dark, crazy guy with a beard." She looked worried. "Are there more?"

"There are two of them and one has a gun," I said. "Plus there are two more. One's a girl a bit older than us, and there's this guy, but I don't know what they do here."

"How did you find me? How did you get in here?"

"Long story. Let's get out of here first, shall we?"

Win whimpered. We turned to look at her on the bed.

"Think she's been drugged," Katy said.

"Poor Win," I said, kneeling at the edge of the bed.

"You *know* her?"

The image of Win getting kicked was all too fresh in my mind. "He would have beat her proper if I hadn't come out screaming."

"Oh my god, this poor girl." Katy sat down on the bed and reached out to touch Win's hand. "She helped me."

"How?"

"After that man left, I slipped out of the room to find an escape route and got in here. She was here and told me to hide under her bed till night. Then she fainted."

I stared at the girl. *How old is Win?*

"We can't leave her here," I said.

"I don't wanna either. So what do we do?"

We sat quietly, trying to think of our next steps.

Something bothered me, and I had to ask. "Hey, Katy," I said, "why didn't you answer me when that man was pulling you away at the airport? Why didn't you try to get away? I was literally screaming at you."

"I dunno," Katy said, shaking her head. "I don't remember anything. I didn't even hear you. I was talking to this man one minute and the next minute, the world went black."

"Chlo-ro-form." Tetyana's voice was deadpan.

We spun around.

Tetyana and Luc were standing by the door. Katy and I had been so engrossed in our conversation, we hadn't heard them come in. The two were staring pointedly at us.

Oh my god, I forgot to lock the door.

"I told you she wasn't Bibi," Luc said, without taking his eyes off me.

"Who *are* you?" Tetyana asked, glowering at me.

I had to think fast. I looked at her. Her face was blank. *Does she work for those men?*

The more mysterious I made myself, the more leverage I'll have, I thought. I pulled my shoulders back and sat up straight.

"It doesn't matter who I am." My voice projected far more confidence than I felt. "But I'll tell you what really matters." I paused for effect.

Luc and Tetyana gave each other a quick glance.

"If you don't let us leave right now, the police will be here in an instant," I said.

My phone was still dead. I didn't know if Katy's was working, but maybe the threat alone would subdue them.

"You can call whomever you want," Tetyana replied, in her impassive voice. "Just be ready because Zero will shoot you first. Be careful what next step you take."

It was my turn to be surprised. "Does he know I'm not Bibi?" I asked.

Tetyana shook her head. "I don't think so. If he did, he'd already be here. And we won't be having this chit-chat, that's for sure."

"He's sleeping in his room now, but he can wake any minute," Luc said. "And he sleeps with his gun."

I looked at Luc. *Is he on their side too?* They were blocking our only way out, and neither looked like they planned on budging. It was time to try a different tactic.

"Will you help us get out of here quietly," I said, speaking slowly, "if we pay you?"

Tetyana didn't hesitate. "How much?"

"One thousand in cash."

Next to me, Katy drew her breath in. I hoped to god she still had the money packet in her jacket.

Tetyana threw her head back and laughed hoarsely.

"Shh," I said. "Do you want to wake up those thugs?"

"You want me to risk my life for one frigging grand?"

"Two thousand then," I said, keeping my gaze steady. "In dollars." There was no reason to specify we had only *Canadian* dollars on us. "And we take Win with us."

"That's not a lot of cash for a hell of a lot of work," Tetyana said, but she was no longer laughing. "This is not going to be easy."

"If you can guarantee our safety out and help us carry her out, I'm willing to consider adding more to that," I said.

Tetyana's eyes narrowed.

Luc spoke up. "Who do you work for?"

Before I could think of a smart answer, a loud bang erupted from below us. The noise reverberated throughout the house so loudly I felt the walls shake. Then, just as quickly, the house plummeted into an eerie, ominous silence.

No one moved. No one even breathed.

Tetyana's face had gone pale.

"Mon dieu," Luc said, his eyes wide with fear.

Part THREE

Bad is never good until worse happens.
Danish Proverb

Chapter Seventeen

I stared as Tetyana pulled a mini phone from her skimpy bra.

"What's going on?" I said.

"Put on Bibi's robe!" Tetyana commanded, not even looking up.

"I don't think...."

"You don't have time to think," she snapped, her eyes boring into mine. She pointed at the door. "That was a gunshot. Want to get into more trouble?"

Is she friend or foe? I couldn't figure it out, but I hesitated only a moment.

I took a deep breath and pulled the black cloth over my head with Katy's help. I couldn't see much, but I could smell the fear in the house. Whatever was going on, I thought, being disguised as the robed woman had its advantages.

Tetyana stepped toward the door, motioning to us.

"Follow me," she whispered. But before she could reach the doorknob, the door crashed open, hitting her on the head. She jumped back, with her hand on her forehead.

It was Vlad.

He stomped in, waving his handgun, looking like a demented zombie on the run. His bloodshot eyes flashed maniacally. It was hard to imagine that only a few minutes ago, I'd seen him sleeping in a La-Z-Boy, his feet up and with a football game on.

"They come!" Vlad's hands were shaking so badly he could barely hold on to the gun. I didn't know what was worse, a thug with a gun who had it all together or a thug with a gun who looked like he'd just lost it.

"Who fired that shot?" Tetyana demanded.

"You know what stupid son-of-ass Zero do?" Vlad spat out the words. Rivers of sweat was running down his puffed face. "You know what he do right now?"

"Tell me!" Tetyana said.

"This plainclothes cop was checking 'round. He ask questions. And you know what that idiot do? Pissed as hell, he shoots him. What the fuck was he thinking?" Vlad's face flushed a deep red.

"Zero shot a cop?" Luc asked, incredulous.

Katy and I looked at each other.

"Now, he in trouble. *I* in trouble. *You* in trouble. All screwed up!" Vlad shouted, waving his gun indiscriminately at the floor, the ceiling, the bed, and every one of us. A nerve on his neck was pulsing madly. No one budged. Everyone had their eyes on that wavering gun. Everywhere that gun pointed, our eyes followed.

"Where's he now?" Tetyana asked.

"Downstairs. Woke me up, that bastard. Still pissed. Couldn't walk straight. I help him put body in the basement."

"You brought the body into the house?" Tetyana's eyes widened. "Seriously? What were you thinking?"

"What the hell I supposed to do?" Vlad looked like he was about to explode. "Wait till somebody found dead bobby outside? Are you bonking crazy?"

He turned to Katy, who was huddled next to me near Win's bed.

"This your fault!" he hissed, raising his gun and pointing it at her. "You started this! All this trouble happen only after American called."

Katy recoiled and brought her hands to her chest as if to protect herself. It took me only a second to remember who I was now. I stepped forward, pushed Katy behind me, and spread my arms out, as if the black robe would stop a bullet. It would go through me first, then her. *But he won't shoot his own team, would he? Or would he?*

Vlad's face transformed from pink to a deep shade of purple. The gun in his hands shook even more.

"For frig sake, Vlad, calm down," Tetyana snapped.

"Calm down?" He spun to look at her. "Don't tell me to calm down, woman!" White froth was coming out of the corners of his mouth.

"Settle down," Tetyana said. "And put that thing away. I got this."

Either she had ovaries of titanium or she knew something we didn't.

"I said, I got this." He voice was firm, commanding even.

Vlad lowered the gun.

"We've got to get out before the police come," Luc said in a quiet voice.

Tetyana gave a knowing nod to Luc.

He straightened up. "I'll get the girls," he said, marching toward the door. Something told me they'd both gone through this routine before. Neither looked frightened as much as apprehensive.

"Okay, let's go," Tetyana said looking at us.

With an unhappy grunt, Vlad pulled a phone out of his pocket, cursing under his breath. His fingers shook as he dialed. Now that he was occupied with something other than us, Tetyana quietly motioned to us to follow her out. Katy and I tiptoed behind her.

"What about Win?" I said, as soon as we stepped out to the landing. "We can't leave her with that loose nut and his gun."

Tetyana gave me a funny look as if to say, *What do you care?*

"She'll be taken care of. They won't leave her here to talk to cops."

"What do you mean taken care of?" My voice rose. "Are they going to kill her?"

I made a move toward the room, but Tetyana grabbed me. She bent down, so her eyes were level with mine. "Those idiots just killed a cop. They won't touch her. Luc's gonna take care of Win. She won't get hurt. Promise."

I looked into her green eyes. They were wide open, still hiding something, but honest. I nodded. I had no choice. She let go of my arm.

"And please don't run down," she said, looking at Katy first, then me. "What's downstairs is going to be worse if you're not with me."

Katy and I stared as she sashayed over to the first door that was locked. She took a key from her bra, opened it and disappeared inside.

We huddled near the stairway, waiting for her. From where we stood, we could hear Vlad on the phone, shouting, cursing at someone. Snippets of words shot out every few seconds like bullets from an angry gun. *Pigs. Passports. Truck. Girls.* It was clear things weren't going well for him, which meant things weren't going to go well for us either.

When Tetyana came out, she'd dumped her red kimono for jeans and a T-shirt, and was carrying two knapsacks. She motioned to us to follow her down. We walked in single file, Tetyana up front, then Katy and myself at the back of the line.

There was a crowd huddled in the little kitchen when we got down.

There were four other girls I hadn't seen before, none older than seventeen, all anorexic-skinny and in varying stages of dress. One of them was smoking, her fingers trembling as she held the cigarette against her bright orange lips. There was a murmur of hushed, scared voices, but not one of them looked up as we walked in. A few glanced curiously at Katy, but they seemed mostly consumed with their own safety.

Tetyana marched straight to the back door of the kitchen, yanked it open and looked out. An Arctic wind streamed inside. Katy and the others pulled their shirts and jackets around them and huddled even closer. Even I felt a cold draft under Bibi's black robe.

"Everyone out," Tetyana said.

One by one, the girls stepped outside, unsteadily, warily.

I was the last one out. I stepped out of the house and surveyed the scene. We were in a back alley, behind the square. Nearby were two white cargo vans, parked and ready, their engines running.

It was raining outside now, the kind of rain that comes sideways and drenches you no matter how much you try to take cover. Though it was still late afternoon, the skies were dark, as if they knew what evil was going on below.

The girls climbed into the back of the first van, one by one. While I waited near the doorway for instructions from Tetyana, something in my brain began to whir. I tapped Katy on her shoulder.

"Hey," I said in a low whisper. "Let's make a run for it."

She didn't move.

"Now!" I whispered as loudly as I dared. "Now, Katy!"

She stood still like a statue. I followed her eyes. That was when I saw a shadow of a man near driver's door of the first van, watching us with a machine gun in his hands.

I felt something press against my back and push me forward. I turned around.

It was Zero scowling at me. He had a gun in his right hand and a small laptop cradled in his left hand. The gun was pointing right at me. He had a bloodshot crazy look on his face like he was drunk or drugged or both.

"Bibi!" Tetyana called out. "Time to go! Get in the van now!" It could have been my imagination but I thought I heard a hint of panic in her voice.

Zero motioned the gun toward the van, and like a zombie, Katy walked toward the second vehicle. Tetyana climbed into the back of the van and leaned out to help her in.

I stayed where I was. *Do I make a run for it? Call the police? Will Zero shoot me, his own sister? Will they shoot Katy after that?*

I looked at Katy's tear-stained, terrified face. She pulled her jacket around her shoulders as if to hug herself. *I can't leave her now.*

Whatever happens, I can't leave her. I stumbled toward the van and gripped the steel handle to pull myself up, without tripping on my robe.

Inside, the van was bare. There were no seats, no benches, just a bare floor. Separating the driver's seat up front and us was a long black panel of steel. Tetyana had pulled out scratchy army blankets from somewhere and was spreading them out in the back. The two bags she'd brought with her were lying in a corner.

That reminded me. Katy's suitcase was still at the airport, probably picked up by security now. My own backpack was lying outside the window on the street, just around the corner from here. *Thank god I've got my passport on me.* I wondered about Katy's, but this wasn't the time to ask.

Tetyana's speed and efficiency at arranging things gave me a dismal feeling she'd done this before. She pointed to where Katy and I should sit. I hunkered across the floor from Katy and waited for what was to happen next.

Tetyana reached over. I thought she was going to say something, so I leaned in. Instead of a whisper, I felt a prick on my arm.

"Hey, what're you doing?" I tried to pull away, but Tetyana was strong. I didn't struggle for long because my mind went fuzzy. *What's wrong with me?* I closed my eyes to stop the nausea, took a few deep breaths and leaned back.

Around me, I heard vague noises of people shuffling, men's gruff voices. Someone or something big and heavy was being put into the van, next to me. Then someone jumped out of the van, making it bounce up and down. I felt even more nauseous. *What's going on? Why do I feel so sick?*

In the distance came the sound of a police siren, an ear-splitting alarm I wished would stop. My head hurt as if it was being squeezed in a vice.

The van's doors slammed shut, plunging us into darkness.

Chapter Eighteen

My eyes opened to darkness.

It was pitch black inside, except for a yellow light that streaked across the floor every few seconds and just as quickly faded away.

It took several seconds for me to get my bearings.

I was moving. I was in the back of a car. No, I was on the floor of a van, a van with no seats. I stared into the dark space around me and saw only vague shapes. Silent gray shadows, looking like ghosts that had lost their edges. There were five, no, four. *Who're they?*

I reached down and felt around me. I was sitting on something cold and hard—a sheet of steel. I leaned back to stop the nausea. My head throbbed and I felt sore and weak like I was recovering from a fever. I took a deep breath and swallowed, trying to keep down whatever wanted to come up.

Where am I? Where am I going? What happened to Katy?

I looked up as the light fell across the van once again. Up above us was a narrow slit of a window. Every time we passed a streetlight, the inside of the van lit up for a half a second. I waited for the next light.

That was when I saw her. A woman crouched across from me, her head between her knees, her curly red hair cascading to the ground.

"Katy!" I said, sitting up. "Katy? Is that you?"

"Shh," someone said from a dark corner.

The redhead barely looked up, but I saw a twitch of her foot.

I waited for the next streetlight. A girl was lying on the floor of the van, her head resting on the lap of a third woman. *Who are these people?* I waited for the light again. I recognized the girl's short black hair falling across her pale forehead.

"Win!" I called out.

"Shh. Keep your voice down," the woman holding her said. It was a familiar rough voice. *Tetyana?*

"Who are you?"

Silence.

"Where are we?"

"On the road."

The girl stirred awake. "Hey," she said in a weak voice.

"Hi, hun," the woman said, stroking the girl's hair.

"Are we moving again?" the girl asked softly.

"Yes, hun."

The girl looked around. She seemed more alert than I was. I had a hard time focusing.

"Where's Bibi?" she asked.

Bibi. That rang a bell.

"She stayed back," the woman replied.

"Is she going to be okay?" That was a young man's voice.

Silence.

I rubbed my forehead. My headache was bad.

A distant dream was playing in the back of my mind, telling me I had to get somewhere urgently, a place I was supposed go to with Katy. I shook my head to clear the fog, but it felt like my mind was filled with mud. I squeezed my temples, but that only made things worse. My throat was parched and my stomach ached. I hadn't eaten for days. A vague memory of a cup of bitter black espresso at a seedy hookah bar crossed my mind.

The vehicle hit a pothole, throwing us up in the air a few inches. I landed back down hard. I steadied myself and leaned against the wall of the van, wincing from the pain. I put my head into my hands. It was throbbing like it was about to explode, but that jolt helped clear my mind.

I remembered everything.

The van changed gears. It was slowing down. I craned my neck to see through the high window, but all I could make out was darkness.

"Get everyone ready."

I was sure it was Tetyana this time. Her voice was low, signaling danger.

Peering in the direction of the voice, I saw her sitting with Win's head on her lap. Tetyana was trying to get everyone to move to my side of the van. She said something to Katy, then helped Win sit up. Win moaned but moved over. Katy followed her.

The van was traveling slowly in what seemed like a lit tunnel. The steady light was shining in now, enough to see the inside of the van.

I looked around with groggy eyes. Next to me, Katy was now leaning back, eyes closed. *Is she okay?* I leaned over and squeezed her hand. To my relief, she squeezed mine back. Win was leaning against her on the other side. Tetyana was busily building a fortress right down the middle of the van using the bags. *What's she up to?*

"Hey."

I turned to my left. It was Luc. His face was only five inches from mine.

"Put this on now," he whispered, shoving something on my lap—something big, black and billowy. I looked down. It was Bibi's robe. I pushed it away. I'd taken it off a few minutes into our ride, as it had made me feel claustrophobic.

"No," I said, shaking my head. "No way. I feel sick in that thing."

"*Zut!* You don't have a choice. Put it on."

"First tell me where we are." I spoke forcefully but it came out slurred.

"Do it!" Tetyana hissed at me, without even looking up from her task. "They'll open the doors soon."

"Who?" I demanded. "Tell me what's going on! And how come I feel so sick? What did you do to me?"

Luc shot Tetyana an exasperated look.

"Gave a double dose for the Americans," Tetyana said to him, rolling her eyes. "Too much trouble, as you can see."

"Double dose of *what*?" I asked.

Just then, the van stopped and something or someone scraped against the back doors.

"Are you trying to get us all shot?" Tetyana asked turning to me. I stared at her. She looked rattled. And that wasn't a good sign.

I reached for the robe. With Luc's help, I pulled the dreaded cloth over my head and adjusted the eye slit. My movements were sluggish like I was wading through a muddy pool.

"Where's your passport?"

I peeked out through the eye slits to see Tetyana still looking my way.

"Your *passport*," Tetyana whispered. "They don't know you're *you*. Give it to Luc."

"No way."

But Luc had already slipped his hand under the robe and was starting to root around.

"Get away from me," I said slapping at his hand, but he'd already pulled out my recipe booklet and my passport from my jacket pocket. He handed the recipe book back after a cursory glance and opened my passport.

"Asha," he read.

I glowered at him in reply.

"India?" he said, with a startled look on his face. "Thought you were American."

"Give that back," I said reaching for the booklet. But he pocketed it before I could grab it.

Tetyana squeezed in between Katy and me. I tucked my recipe booklet back in my jacket pocket and zipped it close.

We were now sitting with our backs to the front of the van, behind Tetyana's two-foot-tall fort construction. My fuzzy brain wondered how this flimsy wall of bags and blankets could stop anyone from shooting at us. Our heads were exposed. They'd get us easily.

"Down," Tetyana said. I felt Luc's hand on my head, pushing me down.

"What's going—"

"Shush," Luc said, pushing my head down.

The van rocked back and forth as if people were getting out. Doors slammed. Men yelled. I waited for whatever was to come. Everyone inside the van was breathing loud, fast, chest-heaving breaths, even Tetyana. I concentrated on trying not to throw up inside the robe.

The back doors screeched open and a bright white light blinded us.

I blinked, the screeching still ringing in my ears. The wall of bags was not high enough to hide us from them, or hide them from us. Even from my crouched position, I spotted the two strange men in khaki overalls prop the doors open. Without even a glance at us, they stepped away.

They saw us, didn't they?

I lifted my head slightly to look. From what I could see through the robe's eye slit, we were inside a large warehouse. Or an airport hangar.

Nearby were half a dozen white vans just like ours parked haphazardly. The two men in khaki overalls were now packing brown boxes into one. It could have been a scene from any warehouse, except for a beefy man standing in the shadows of a parked truck. On his face was a balaclava mask and in his arms, a machine gun. It made the handguns I'd seen so far look like toys. I felt a chill go through my spine.

I watched silently as the men worked methodically and rapidly, packing each van one by one. Then, a man I recognized came into view. It was Zero, smoking and talking in quiet tones to another unknown man.

Suddenly, a scream rocketed through the warehouse. "Nooo! Aiiiii!"

The van rocked as everyone startled at once. I craned my neck to look outside but couldn't see a thing. The shrieking started again. It was a woman's voice, desperate and frightened, and it wasn't too far from us.

"Noooo!" The woman's voice penetrated the air again.

The men in khaki kept working like they'd heard nothing. They might as well have been packing vegetable boxes into a grocery van. I trembled under my robe. The hair-raising shrieks went on for several minutes, but it seemed like everyone outside was pretending nothing was happening.

What in god's name is going on?

After a few minutes, Zero looked up with his signature scowl. It took only a casual flick of his hand for the man with the machine gun to stroll over to the van where the screaming was coming from. A hard knot formed in my stomach.

The man with the machine gun peeked inside the van, then climbed in. I held my breath.

The woman screamed again. "Aiii!"

Chapter Nineteen

I heard a sickening *thump* and the screaming ended.

A tremor of horror passed through me. I stopped breathing and strained to listen. *Did he hit her? Did he kill her? What's going on?*

Katy, Win, and Luc all had their heads down. I thought I heard a sob come from Katy. I noticed Tetyana, like me, was keeping an eye out. She didn't notice me, focused on what was happening in the warehouse.

Her face was contorted into something nasty, more furious than fearful, I thought.

The man with the machine gun emerged from the back of the van, holding his gun in one hand and pulling a girl with the other, his hand around her neck. To my surprise, Vlad came out behind them, pulling up the fly on his pants, a cocky look on his face.

I felt the bitter taste of bile in my mouth.

Vlad strolled over to Zero and his companion and dug out a cigarette.

I looked at the girl being pulled across the warehouse by her neck. She looked Hispanic, maybe fifteen or sixteen at most, wearing only a yellow blouse tied at the waist. I remembered her from before when we'd all waited in the kitchen in the house back in London.

The man threw her on the ground.

"What are they going to do to her?" I whispered in horror.

"Head down," Luc whispered and pulled at my robe. I didn't move.

"Hush." I heard Tetyana whisper.

If I'd felt nauseous before, but it was nothing like how I was feeling now, sick to the pit of my stomach.

I watched as the girl tried to pull away from the man. She got on her knees, trying to get up, but she didn't get far. The man gave her a swift kick, turning her body into a football that landed with a thud on the concrete floor.

Every nerve in my body cried out. I wanted to run out, grab her, and pull her away from these evil monsters. I twitched madly underneath the robe. I felt Tetyana reach over and put a hand on my shoulder. She squeezed it tightly and held on.

Even after that horrifying kick, the girl somehow regained enough strength to sit up again. This time, he hit her on her face. She fell on her back. I watched in horror as she fought to get back up, again and again. Each time, the man punched her. Again and again. She cried in agony with every blow.

I closed my eyes every time the man's fist came down and opened them every time the girl tried to get up. Tetyana's hand dug into my shoulder. I knew it was there as a reminder to stay quiet. But every time the girl cried out, her hand squeezed down tighter like she too felt that punch in her bones.

"Shut her up!" It was Zero.

The girl was convulsing on the floor now. *I can't watch this.*

The man with the machine gun stepped over her and lifted the butt of his gun high. My gut screamed. I wanted to throw up. I couldn't watch anymore. I couldn't move. Though Katy, Win, and Luc weren't watching, I felt the same frisson of unspeakable terror go through every one of us.

We clutched each other, like we were hanging on to our humanity, while out there unbelievable insanity raged. I closed my eyes, but I heard the dull thud.

It's over.

When I opened my eyes, the half-naked girl lay lifeless on the stark warehouse floor, her head open and bloodied, her yellow blouse splattered red, her legs crooked under her.

I sat frozen, staring at the girl's body. I wanted to scream. I wanted to sob. But I couldn't. Not because we weren't supposed to make a sound, but because I felt dead inside.

I'm sorry I didn't help you. I'm sorry I let this happen to you. I'm sorry I did nothing.

I wanted to scream, but nothing came out.

Zero and Vlad smoked another cigarette, taking puffs as if it was just another ordinary day.

The man with the machine gun threw a plastic sheet over the girl and joined them. Vlad offered a cigarette to him and a lighter.

Even seeing Zero kick Win hadn't prepared me for this. That had been horrifying, but I remembered how I'd thought these were small-minded, stupid criminals. *Who am I kidding?* These were ruthless men. *Men? Are they even human?*

My shock waned, and in its place came a surging rush of rage.

I remembered my grandmother telling us that when all else failed, we needed to put our trust in the gods. She should have known because she worshiped them all—from the christian gods, the hindu gods, the buddhist gods, the jewish gods, and even the islamic one, though she wasn't allowed in the mosques.

So where did all these good gods and prophets go to hide today? I wondered. *Where were those magnificent deities I'd seen in the temples of India, the shrines of Tanzania and the churches of Canada?*

Where were these omnipresent creators who are worshiped and on whom money is showered by the millions? Why didn't a single one of them come down from their precious heavens to stop this atrocity?

The world's mad, I concluded. Yes, the world's infuriatingly, infinitely mad, madder than ten thousand dogs with rabies.

Something stirred in me. Something raging, uncontrollable, insuppressible.

The image of the terrifying warrior Hindu goddess, Kali, sprang to mind. That purple-skinned woman with a necklace of dead men's heads, a sickle covered in blood in one hand and her ghastly red tongue hanging out. Back in Goa, Grandma had a picture of her taped over her mattress and a small shrine dedicated to her to ward off evil spirits. What a useless goddess, I thought. All talk and no action.

We, humans, were here alone, to take care of our own messes. The quicker we realized it, the better.

I knew then that before my stay was over on this continent, those men would pay for their sins. Every cell in my body wanted nothing but revenge now.

The two khaki-clad packers were now walking toward our van.

"Stay down." I heard Tetyana say.

I lowered my head, but not before I saw her tuck her mobile phone back into her T-shirt. She did it so quickly, I almost missed it. *What was she doing with it?* I wanted to ask but now was not the time. The men had come closer. I felt the tension rise in everyone next to me, even Tetyana.

The men got to work, without bothering to look our way. We could have been empty cardboard boxes for all they cared. Maybe that was all we were worth.

I now saw why Tetyana had rearranged the inside of the van. She had known this was going to happen. She'd created an area large enough for us to sit on the floor with our feet pointing forward. The bags were not a barricade as much as a demarcating line between us and the boxes being packed. The men started piling the boxes just behind the bags.

One by one, the boxes filled the van all the way to the top. They were building a wall, right in front of our eyes, locking us in. I wasn't sure if it was my imagination, but the air seemed to get thinner. I felt my chest constrict and I had to force myself to breathe. I felt Luc's hands squeezing mine.

"It's okay," he whispered in my ear. "It's only to hide us."

"From who?" I whispered back.

He didn't answer.

Chapter Twenty

"**S**he died for all of us," Tetyana said, quietly.

It wasn't the voice of the cocky, self-assured woman I'd met a few hours ago. Something had changed in her. In everyone. We were all broken now.

"I can't believe it happened," I said in a whisper. My stomach was whirling like a washing machine, but my mind had completely shut down. "I just can't believe it. I can't believe I saw that."

I heard Katy whimper next to me. She was rocking back and forth. I squeezed her hand and held it tightly.

"We knew this was coming," Luc said softly, staring at the floor. "We just pretended it wasn't. We pretended we were gonna make good money and get out."

"They're going to pay for this," Tetyana said, her eyes burning.

We sat in silence after that, each lost in our own nightmares.

The image of the girl's pretty yellow blouse splattered in blood was etched with fire on my mind. I couldn't get it out. The blouse was the least offensive thing I'd seen at the warehouse, but it was the only aspect my weakened mind could bear to remember without going insane. I vacillated between horror and guilt.

She had not been much older than Win. She'd probably been running away from something bad, seeking something good, like we all were. I could have been her. She could have been me. She could have been any one of us.

I wanted to hurt every one of those dastardly men. "Why didn't we do something?" I cried out, punching the floor. I heard the fury boiling in my own voice. "How could we let that happen right in front of us and do nothing?"

I tried to choke back the sobs threatening to surge out. But no one bothered to shush me now.

"We're no match for their weapons," Tetyana said finally.

I gave her a defiant look. I'd rather have died in a hail of bullets than live with that image forever branded into my brain. Knowing I sat and watched and did nothing would haunt me for the rest of my life.

"Why do you think they have a thug with a machine gun?" Luc asked in a soft voice.

"Does it even matter?" I snapped.

"It's a very efficient piece of equipment to mow down a rebellion from the vans," Tetyana said crisply. "Gets the job done in five seconds or less. A good pressure washer can clean it all up afterward."

I felt my blood chill.

"Do you really think they'd have killed all of us like that?" asked Katy, looking at Tetyana in horror.

"Yes," Luc said.

"In a heartbeat," Tetyana said.

"But the police?" I stammered. "You can't hide machine gun fire, can you? They'd hear it. And rescue us, wouldn't they? I mean, if we're still alive, that is...."

Tetyana laughed her coarse laughter. "Do you know how many graves there are in Europe with forgotten foreign girls, hun?"

I shook my head and looked away. Part of me didn't want to know.

"Sometimes, they find ten bodies in one spot. One time they found thirty. Do you think anyone cares?" Tetyana said. "They wash the blood off, pay the cops and it's back to business. No politician wants evidence of this happening under their watch, so they cover it up."

"Not in Europe," I said, not wanting to believe any of this. I'd seen the bad side of humanity by now, but this was different. This was on a spectrum of evil I hadn't even realized existed.

"Haven't you heard of white slavery?" Tetyana asked, looking at me pointedly, her green eyes glowing in the dark.

I shook my head.

"You better believe it happens."

"It's true," said a small voice, "but it's worse where I come from."

We looked over at Win, curled up into a ball, her head on Tetyana's shoulder. She'd been following the conversation without a word. She looked away when she saw us all turn her way.

Tetyana put a hand on Win's head and stroked her hair. "You know," she said finally, in a thoughtful voice. "I thought I had an agreement with those bastards."

Agreement? Is she profiting from all this?

"Tell me," I said, sitting up and looking at her directly. "Why are you here in the back of the van and not up front with them?"

I felt Luc give a start next to me.

Tetyana was silent for a second. "Because I'm not one of them."

"But," I said, pointing at her, "you seem to know a lot."

She took her time answering. "I do what I have to do because I have no choice."

"Why did you put me to sleep when we left?" I felt my voice rise. "Why did you prick me with that injection or whatever you did to me?"

"To keep you alive," she said.

Then, she looked away and refused to say another word. And that was the end of that conversation.

The van rocked us back and forth until one by one, we all dozed off. We'd been going through stop-and-go traffic for such a long time, I eventually got used to it, slipping in and out of consciousness, half-asleep, half-awake.

Next to me, Luc had fallen asleep, eyes closed, breathing deeply. I accidentally elbowed him but he didn't budge. Katy and Win had also dozed off, heads close together. I looked at Tetyana. Her eyes were half-closed like she was meditating, but her hands on her lap were clenching and unclenching. Clenching and unclenching.

She was still awake.

"Tetyana," I called out softly.

She opened her eyes.

Even through the darkness, I could see the weariness on her face. She looked decades older than when I first saw her at South Hill Square, and she'd looked terrible then. *How old is she? Twenty? Twenty-five? She couldn't be more than a couple of years older than any of us, could she?*

I looked down at the midnight-black robe we were now using as a makeshift blanket. "What happened to Bibi?"

Tetyana sighed before replying like it was too laborious an answer. "Probably ran away. Hiding somewhere out in the streets away from the cops."

Bibi was supposed to have been at the mosque when I fell through that window into the London house. I'd been lucky to get hold of one of her spare robes. I imagined her small figure shuffling through darkened alleyways, ducking into hidden nooks, peeking out fearfully through her eye slits as blue police lights flashed across the building.

"She must be really scared right now," I said.

"I don't think so," Tetyana said shaking her head. "I'd say she's happy."

"*Happy?* How?"

"Because she's far away from that madman."

Does she mean Zero? "Is she really Zero's sister?"

Tetyana didn't answer.

I remembered when Bibi showed me her face. It hadn't been a threat, but a warning. I remembered those fierce black eyes, that horrible, disfiguring scar on her cheek, that scar that gave me nightmares.

"Did Zero—" I swallowed. "Did he do that to her face?"

"You ask so many questions." Tetyana sighed.

I pointed at the robe on my lap. "I'm Bibi now, so I need to know these things."

"Good point," Tetyana said in a business-like manner. Then, she sat silent for five maddening minutes. I waited impatiently, not wanting to annoy her. The last thing I needed was for her to stop opening up to me.

I was nodding off when she began to speak again.

"It happened when they were back home."

I sat up and blinked.

"Where's that?" I asked.

"Pakistan."

"What happened?"

"She fell in love with the neighbor's son. They were fifteen or something, but she was supposed to be married off to a fifty-year-old man as wife number four."

"A fourth wife?"

"It's their tradition. The fourth wife is always a young girl, sometimes barely ten or twelve if she's lucky. Somehow Bibi had held off."

"Oh, my god."

"So Bibi ran off with her boyfriend," Tetyana continued. "But they didn't get too far. The village chief ordered Zero, he's the oldest brother, to find them. They found the two near the Indian border and brought them back to the village." She paused. "They whipped the boy till he bled to death, she said."

My mouth had gone dry. I stared at Tetyana wordlessly.

"Something about family honor, she said."

I felt cold goose bumps come all over me. Back in Goa, I'd heard about honor killings, read about it in the newspapers, but to know of someone who'd gone through that experience was chilling. It wasn't that I didn't believe it. I didn't *want* to believe it.

"That's what honor's all about in some places," Tetyana replied. "They torture and kill anyone who disobeys, and hey, presto!" She snapped her fingers. "Family honor's restored. Just like that."

"That's so twisted." I stopped myself. Like I hadn't seen enough nonsensical stuff in my life, I thought.

I remembered how Aunty Shilpa had been married off to an older man who beat her mercilessly. When he died of AIDS, they considered her "Untouchable" because she was a widow, and infected with HIV on top of that, a disease that took her life in the end. I remembered how my own grandmother had arranged for me to be married off to an alcoholic pervert when I was only fifteen. I'd escaped to Canada, where I thought I was going to work to pay off my debts to the immigration broker, only to discover he was the entry point for a human trafficking ring. A year after I fled, I learned how my cousin Preeti had been forced to marry that vile man in my place.

The world's a twisted place.

"Better believe it," Tetyana was saying. "Happens every day, and Bibi's family is not any different. The village chief made Bibi watch all this on her knees. She said her boyfriend cried like a dying animal with every lash. When they finished with him, the chief ordered Zero to throw hot oil on her face to punish her."

A shiver of horror went through me. Bibi's scarred face flashed to my mind. I choked. There was nothing I could say. I didn't want to hear anymore, but Tetyana wasn't done.

"You know that old man she was supposed to be married off to? He raped her while her own brother, Zero, and his friends held her down. In the middle of town while all the men watched."

"That's barbaric," I whispered, shaking my head.

"The chief wanted to whip her to death like her boyfriend too, but the imam of the village told him she was a slut because she lost her virginity in public. Regardless of how she lost it, mind you. This meant she lost all her honor, so according to the imam, that was a fate worse than death. They let her live to punish her."

"So inhuman," I said, my voice faltering. "Zero's an animal. How could he..."

I sat back, horrified, speechless. *What do you do when your own family hates you that much and hurts you that badly? Then blames you for it?* I pulled Bibi's robe up to my chest. I half-wished she was here, so I could give her a hug.

"How-how do you know all this?" I asked looking up at Tetyana.

"She told me."

"Just like that?"

"I found a strange bottle of pills in the back of the kitchen cabinet one day and asked her. She grabbed it and hid it under her robe, so I knew something was wrong. When I asked her what was going on, she told me it was her poison. She wanted to kill herself." She paused. "I don't blame her."

My stomach turned.

"She was scared because Zero had seen the pills before and told her she'd go straight to hell because their religion doesn't allow her to kill herself. He said if he saw those pills again, he'd slit her throat himself."

I clutched Bibi's robe even closer to my chest. *What a life she's had.*

It took me a minute to get my tongue working again. "So what happened?"

"I took the pills away and threw them down the toilet." Tetyana went quiet for a few seconds. "I thought I could help her somehow. Maybe she'd have been happier..." She stopped herself.

"Couldn't she have run away?"

"I asked her the same thing. Even said I'd help, but she said Zero would have hunted her down with the help of their community. They'd punish her even worse."

"How much worse can it get?"

Tetyana shrugged and let out a sigh. "She was trapped."

I tried to let this sink in.

"Do you know what rape is?"

I looked up at Tetyana, my brows furrowed. *Where's she going with this?*

"It's a weapon."

I stared at her.

"It's the most effective weapon to bring a human being to her knees. It's like bashing someone with a hammer, again and again, until they submit screaming, until they'd do anything you say. And then you shame them. It's a double whammy."

I was too numb to reply.

"At the mosque in London, men sit up front and the women always sit in the back. Dishonored girls like Bibi are relegated to the very back if they're let in at all, just like they don't allow girls with periods inside. Dirty and contaminated, I was told."

I sat back, closed my eyes and took a deep breath in. It was hard to digest all this. Why would any god punish a beaten up and raped little girl even more? What justified this harshness, this violence? What kind of people would treat a vulnerable child with so much venom and hostility?

I had no answers. But this was not a totally foreign concept to me.

I remembered when that vile alcoholic man had tried to attack me. I'd fought back and escaped, but Grandma had asked me to never bring it up and then pretended it never happened.

Even Preeti, my dear, sweet cousin Preeti, had thought it blasphemous to talk about the incident, saying I'd only bring dishonor to myself and my family. It was that man who'd tried to attack me, yet I was the one everyone had blamed.

Do they blame someone for getting robbed too? I wondered. *Or for getting beaten up by thugs on the streets?*

It was then I realized it wasn't the heinous act that mattered, but the victim. If you're a girl, whatever happens to you, you're the one to blame. I shook my head at the stupidity of this.

What happens to the people who do these terrible deeds, I wondered. *Aren't Zero and his gang the ones who are dirty and contaminated? Why don't they get sent to the very back of the mosque? Or straight to prison where they belong?*

"Bibi will be fine." Tetyana leaned back and closed her eyes. "She's free now."

Chapter Twenty-one

"**G**uys, I need to get out." Katy's voice woke us all up. She'd been unusually subdued, sleeping through so much of the trip I wondered if Tetyana had given her a double dose of whatever she'd given me as well.

"Are you okay?" I asked.

"Just need to pee," her strained voice came from the other end of the van. "Really badly."

"Hun, you have to hold," Tetyana said. "Toilets and food will come soon."

"How soon?"

"In a few hours."

"*Hours?*"

"*Voici,*" Luc said, passing an empty plastic water bottle to her. "Here, use this."

Katy took a long look at it and shook her head. "I'll wait," she said.

The thought of hiking up my skirt and peeing into a bottle while huddled so close to the others in the back of a moving van wasn't appealing. I was holding too. I knew from those long safari trips my parents and I took back in Africa a million years ago, the more you talked about peeing while on the road, the more you wanted to go. It was best to say nothing at all.

"Don't feel bad about pee in bottle," Win spoke up.

I looked at her. She'd regained some color from when I last saw her laid out on the bed, unconscious. While Win was sleeping, Luc told me she'd been drugged. That fall down the stairs and those nasty kicks from Zero would leave her with bruises, but she was going to be okay, he said.

As the most injured and the youngest, Win got most of the rations we had at hand. The "rations," which Tetyana carefully distributed among us through the trip, consisted of ten bottles of water and five Ziplock bags filled with nuts and dried fruit bars. This was what had been in the bags at our feet. One of the bags contained the injection kit Tetyana had used to put us to sleep earlier, but she kept that close and allowed no one to touch it. She obviously had prepared for this. Or had done this before.

"I peed in bottle for one month," Win was saying. "Easy to do after practice."

"One whole month?" Katy sounded shocked. "Why?"

"We were in a metal box."

"Metal box?" I said, in horror. "For a whole month?"

"You mean a container, right?" Luc asked. "Like a shipping container?"

"It was in a ship, yes," Win said with a nod.

"What were you doing in a shipping container?" Katy asked.

Win was silent.

"Win," I tried. "Can I ask where you are from?"

"My home is near Don Dhet in Laos." I detected a slight pride in her voice, a longing for a home far away.

"Why did you leave home?"

Her voice came soft and hesitant. "When I was ten, some Chinese men came in big jeeps and said we will get good jobs in Bangkok. My father said I was going to make a lot of money and took me out of school. I wanted to stay in school but I had to obey my father."

"Did he know where you were going to end up?" I asked, almost in a whisper.

"The Chinese men gave a big, flat television to my father. He was so happy. He said he was an important man in the village now. He said it was payment for me. My mother cried, but no one listened to her."

I heard a gasp from Katy on the other end. "Your dad sold you for a *TV*?"

I swallowed and wondered, not for the first time that day, how a family member could so easily betray their own daughters, their own sisters. *Did they matter so little?*

"What happened when you got to Bangkok?" Katy asked.

Win was quiet for a moment. "I was in a hotel," she said, her voice thin, expressionless. "I worked for men. Many men came every day, sometimes twenty in one day."

I felt nauseous again. Win's words had sucked any remaining air from the van.

"I'm sorry," I whispered. "I'm so sorry."

"It's okay," she said sweetly. "I wanted to go home, but they put chains on us when we weren't working."

I heard another gasp from Katy.

I felt like I'd seen and heard enough for one day, without going mad.

"See my tattoo," Win said, unfolding one leg. I couldn't see much from where I was sitting, but I remembered those Chinese characters curving up her thigh.

"This means I belong to that Chinese group. If they sell you to another group, they give you different tattoo. But Zero said he doesn't give tattoos. I'm happy because it hurt a lot when they put it."

That's not a tattoo, Win, I thought trying not to throw up. *They branded you like they brand cattle.* But I couldn't say this out loud.

Next to me, Luc put his head in his hands.

Tetyana was staring in front of her, her face stone cold.

Katy reached out, put her arm around Win, and pulled her close.

"One day, they told us they'll pay more if we work in a bigger city," Win continued, leaning her head against Katy's shoulder. "Supposed to be a better job. No more men, they said. They promised." It seemed like she wanted to let it all out, and in the confines of the dark van, she may have felt it safe to tell her story. No one stopped her.

"So, they took us to Pahang."

"Where's that, Win?" I asked softly.

"That in Malaysia, right?" Luc said.

"Uhuh. They put us on a boat and we went to Manila. That's where I saw the big ships. They were so huge, bigger than a building. It was at night and I don't remember going inside the ship, but they told me that's where we were going. I remember waking up in the dark and we were inside a big box with other girls from Thai and Laos."

"*Mon dieu,*" Luc whispered. "My god."

"How old were you?" I said.

"I was the oldest. I was ten."

I gave an involuntary shiver.

Tetyana was still silent, but I could see her clenching and unclenching her hands, faster and faster.

"I was lucky," Win said. "Four girls didn't make it. When the men came, they opened the doors to take them out."

Luc pulled his knees to his chest and buried his head in them like he didn't want to hear any more.

"We heard them splash into the water."

Oh my god, I whispered.

Then, there was silence. It seemed Win had worn herself out. She rested her head on Katy's shoulders and closed her eyes.

Everyone else seemed to have lost their voices.

I leaned back against the panel, trying to digest everything.

Something about Win's story stirred a memory from long ago. I was sitting in a classroom, reading a book I couldn't put down. It wasn't an ordinary book. Ms. Stacy from Canada, who taught grade six at the international school I'd attended then, assigned books beyond our classroom's mandatory list. Some had been hard to read because of their advanced language. Others had been hard to read because of their subject like the one I'd held in my hands that day.

It was a story about a boy who'd been captured in West Africa and sent on a ship with thousands of others to America, where they were sold off to become slaves in plantations. Instead of metal boxes, the boy and his companions were kept in the bottom of the ship.

Maybe they didn't have containers back then, I thought, but I understood one thing now. What happened hundreds of years ago, and what everybody claimed was a terrible thing, was still happening today. But no one wanted to talk about it anymore.

Everyone in the van had either lapsed into their personal nightmares or had fallen asleep.

All I could hear was the vehicle's steady hum. When we passed a streetlight, the inside of the van lit up for a split second, long enough for me to glance at the others. We looked like a bunch of discarded refugees who'd trekked through a lifetime of hell. I wanted to reach out and tell everyone that everything was going to be all right. That everything would get back to normal. *But what's normal? To them? To me?*

"Luc," I whispered, nudging him.

"Hmm...." He'd been resting his head against the van, eyes half-closed.

"What about you?"

"Pardon?"

What's your story?"

"What story?"

"How old are you?"

"Seventeen," he said. I felt my eyebrows lift involuntarily. I'd thought he was the same age as Katy and me. Or at least eighteen.

"How did you get here?"

Silence.

I prodded him. "How did you end up here?"

He sighed. "I've nowhere else to go." He paused. "I belong here."

"Here? With these monsters?" Those words came out before I could think.

"Better than where I was before."

"How can anything be worse than this?"

Luc shrugged. He turned his back to me and refused to say another word.

"Sorry," I muttered.

I took stock of my own situation. I hadn't been locked up in a trans-Pacific shipping container, or sold as a prostitute, or raped by a man while my own brother held me down. I'd had some close encounters, but for the most part, I'd gone unscathed. None of my worst experiences even came close to what any of the others here had gone through.

My curiosity got the better of me and I turned to Tetyana.

"Tetyana?"

I knew she wasn't asleep because she was still clenching and unclenching her hands. She didn't open her eyes for a whole minute, and when she did, she looked to me with raised eyebrows.

"It's strange you look so much like Katy from the back," I ventured.

"I'm nothing like her," she said quietly.

"It's not every day you find two redheads in one place," I said, trying to figure out how to get her to tell her story.

"You think this my real color?"

I stared at her.

"I only give what customers want."

I hesitated before asking my next question. "Why are you here?"

She looked away. "Because I choose to."

"Why would you choose something like this?"

She shook her head and closed her eyes again.

"Are you related to Vlad?"

"Absolutely not." That came out with force.

I'd met her only a day ago. I knew nothing about her, but I knew she knew this game. She knew the men up front, she knew everyone's backgrounds, she knew what to do, and most importantly, what not to do. There was something about her. Those hard green eyes, that grim red mouth. One thing was clear. Underneath that bravado and hard shell, Tetyana was hiding something.

"Hey—" I started, but I didn't get to finish.

The van screeched to a halt, throwing us all into a topsy-turvy heap against the wall of cardboard boxes.

"Watch out!" Luc yelled as the boxes came crashing down on us.

Chapter Twenty-two

Tetyana's and Luc's lightning-quick reactions saved us. They threw their bodies against the wall of boxes. I leaped up to help them and push the boxes back in place.

Win and Katy woke up in shock.

"What's going on?" Katy asked, her eyes widened.

Win's face was white.

Tetyana put a finger to her lips. Her self-assured look had returned.

"Halt!"

The van rocked as the men in front jumped off and slammed their doors. We could hear a mumble of voices outside.

"The stop sign's over there," said a commandeering voice. The voice didn't sound happy.

"Sorry sir, we not see it." I knew from the high-pitched voice it was Vlad.

"Passports and license papers, please." *Is that a border agent? A police officer?*

"Yes, sir," Zero and Vlad chorused. The front doors opened and shut again.

"Transport permits?"

More mumbling. It sounded like Zero and Vlad were on their very best behavior.

"Follow me," the voice said.

We heard the crunch of boots on gravel, walking away from us.

I sprang to my knees.

"Hey!" I shouted, startling everyone in the back of the van. I lunged forward with my fists, ready to beat the side panel. But before I could do anything, Tetyana grabbed me and clamped her hand over my mouth. I struggled, but Luc jumped in and held me down by my shoulders.

"Mmmmm." I tried to pull away from their grip, but they were both strong.

"*Allez au diable!* Stop it!" Luc said.

"Settle down, Asha," Tetyana said in a calm voice. "This is not the time for that."

I stopped struggling.

Tetyana's and Luc's grips softened, and I pulled away from them. Everyone was staring at me.

"If that's the police—" I began in an angry voice.

"It *is the* police," Tetyana snapped. "Local police."

"Then, we—"

She cut me off.

"You think it's that easy?" she said, with a look of scorn. "All we do is call 911 and everything will become all right? Is that what you think?"

"What's wrong with you?" I demanded, glaring back at her. "We did nothing when they killed that girl. Now we're not gonna do anything when the police are right here? Do you enjoy getting tortured?"

"Do you enjoy trying to get us killed?" Luc asked in a quiet voice.

"Asha," Tetyana said as if gathering all the patience she had in her. "The last thing we want to do is to walk into the hands of these men."

"Why?"

"Well." She paused. "How do you know they'll help us?"

"Because—" I looked at her helplessly. *We're not in India anymore, right?* "Because they're the police. That's why. How do you know they *won't* help us?"

When Tetyana replied, it was in a low, deliberate voice. "There are no border crossings in Europe anymore. At least in the EU." She paused. "Think about it."

"What do you mean?" A sudden chill went up my spine.

"When legitimate police forces set up traffic stops, they have teams in place who flag you down from afar. You see their lights and you hear them work. They don't have a single man holding a haphazard stop sign in the middle of an empty road."

I stared at her, confused.

"He heard you, all right," Tetyana said, her eyes boring into mine. "But he didn't come get us, did he?"

I felt like someone just punched me in the stomach.

The sound of boots crunching on the gravel came back. We instinctively hunched low, even though we were inside the van, behind the wall of boxes.

The back doors of the van screeched open. The wall of boxes didn't let much light in, but I could smell the fresh air from outside. I wanted nothing more than to take a deep, long breath in, but I didn't dare. The men were only a few feet away.

Someone was pulling out the boxes. I strained to listen with one hand tightly holding onto Luc's and the other clutching Tetyana's arm.

Someone was now opening the boxes up, inspecting them or taking something out, then closing them up again and throwing them back into the van. They were looking for something.

"This mine?" the officious voice asked.

"No sir, this for Belgium," I heard Zero say. He sounded confident, not the voice of an anxious man running away from the murder of a cop and trafficking five of us across borders.

"Where's mine?" asked the unknown man's voice.

"Here, right here, sir."

Another box was pulled out and cut open. More rustling of newspaper.

"Moroccan tea, sir. Very good for your heart," Zero said.

Vlad guffawed.

In the back of the van, Tetyana had spread her arms out, as if to keep us all back, to protect us. We sat quietly, just as we did at the warehouse a couple of hours ago.

"This also is for you, sir," Zero said. A box slid off the truck and was ripped open. "Especially for you."

A satisfied grunt from the officer.

"This is real?"

"Yes, sir. Always. We only work with real stuff."

More grunts. Silence from Vlad and Zero.

A car buzzed by, but other than that, it was quiet.

I tried to imagine the highways from London to Belgium. I knew Belgium was north of France, across the channel from England. *How did we get here? How many countries have we crossed? Where are we?* I regretted not paying more attention in my geography class.

"*Ça va.*" The officer sounded satisfied. "You can put these in my car."

I heard a grunt from Vlad, and the sound of boxes being pulled out of the van one by one and taken away. It took them several trips. I wasn't sure how many boxes they took from the back, but our wall remained intact.

"*Merci,*" the man's voice said. "*Bon journée.*" He sounded uncharacteristically friendly after all that commandeering.

The doors screeched shut again. The men got back into the van, slammed the front doors and started the engine.

"Ten thousand euro protection fee," I heard Luc say next to me. "Works every time."

Something bitter came to my throat.

Part FOUR

If they hadn't tried to break me down, I wouldn't have known I'm unbreakable.
Gabourey Sidibe

Chapter Twenty-three

It was early in the morning when we arrived at our destination.

After the first pit stop at the warehouse and the second one at the pseudo-checkpoint, the van stopped at four more places along the way. And Katy and I had gotten over the indignity of peeing in a bottle.

Sometimes, the van stopped for ten minutes, other times for an hour. Every time the van parked somewhere, I'd wondered if something nasty was going to happen. And every time I heard footsteps walk away from us and not return for a while, I'd wondered if they'd abandoned us to die, cramped behind this wall of boxes.

I wanted nothing more than to break through and run out, but Luc said it would be a waste of energy. "That's bulletproof glass and the doors can only open from the outside," he'd said shaking his head. "Trust me."

If Tetyana hadn't kept track of time and reminded us to breathe, I'd have gone stark raving mad.

When the doors of the van finally opened eight hours after our departure, we stumbled out like zombies. And I was back in Bibi's black robe.

The van was parked in a back alley next to a nondescript house with graffiti on its cracked walls and iron bars across its windows. It was a shabby, narrow three-story structure, one of those traditional European row houses that are taller than they are wide. This house looked like it had been built centuries ago and not been taken care of since, just like the one we'd left behind in London.

But we didn't have time to take in the fresh air or our surroundings. Vlad and Zero were grouchier than ever. They made us line up and move the remaining boxes into the house, one by one, while they watched with guns in their hands and dark frowns on their faces.

Once we were done, Vlad ordered us all inside. I was cold, hungry and afraid, but all I could think was, *At least we're alive.*

The inside of this house had the same peeling paint and musty smell as the previous place. Exposed electric wires hung from the ceiling. Someone had either taken out or stolen the light fixtures. One spot on the kitchen wall looked like someone had gone berserk on it with a carving knife. The dark maroon splatter was ominous. Luc examined it and nodded. "Dried blood," he said, matter-of-factly.

The only drinking water here trickled out of the kitchen tap. The remaining taps in the house drizzled a disgusting brown liquid we suspected was water, but couldn't say for sure.

Vlad ordered Katy, Win and I into a room on the second floor.

It held a simple desk and one bed, which occupied most of the space. A small bathroom was right outside this room. He pointed Tetyana and Luc to the room next to us, large enough to fit a bunk bed. Zero took the entire third floor of the house while Vlad took over the first floor where the living room was. He slept on the couch with his gun by his side, to "make sure no one get out," he said with an ugly curl of his lips.

We woke up the next morning to a surprise.

The police were everywhere, patrolling the streets with sniffer dogs, looking inside every parked car and watching every doorway. Five police vans were parked on the street right across from the house we were in. Luc was sure they were raiding the brothels in the neighborhood. Tetyana wondered if a sting operation was happening across Europe, especially since a police officer had been shot dead in a red-light district. A trigger to finally take action, she said with a wry look on her face.

Zero and Vlad were all nerves. This meant they had us on lockdown. No one was allowed out and no one was allowed in. And no one was allowed to make noise, except for when one of the men went on a rampage. While both men slept through most of the first day, worn out from the long drive, we remained alert, knowing our lives were at the mercy of their moods.

That first day, while the men were asleep, we spent most of our time trying to figure out how to escape this sick place. We quietly tried all the doors and windows, but nothing would budge open.

All we'd done was move from a prostitution house in London to another one very much like it in Brussels. It even smelled the same here, that stale, unwashed smell like the old house in South Hill Square.

Our most immediate problem was food. I'd hoped the boxes in the van contained something edible, but they were loosely packed with cheap clothing, T-shirts, pants, and skirts. That was one reason none of us got badly hurt when the boxes came tumbling down on us in the van. It was only later I learned that Zero and Vlad had hidden contraband cash wrapped inside the clothing—currency at rogue checkpoints.

The men found four bottles of evil-smelling alcohol in one box. They then bullied Luc into handing over a packet of his white stuff which he'd hidden in his jacket pocket.

By the end of the first day, Vlad and Zero had drunk up all the booze and sniffed part of Luc's stuff. Whatever it was, it was potent. Sharing a small house with two drugged-out, gun-toting nervous gangsters wasn't what I'd planned when I'd fled India, or when Katy and I had escaped from Toronto. We were now further off our original track than ever before.

The five of us huddled in our room after pushing the heavy desk against the door so neither man could come barging in. They seemed too preoccupied with what was going on outside to bother us, anyway. For the moment, at least.

We remained barricaded in our room until the second evening when Win swore she was ready to starve to death. Then, Katy said she was going to die of an exploding bladder. No one wanted to risk going outside the room. But we had to do something.

Very early the next morning, Tetyana and I opened the bedroom door and sneaked out, leaving Luc, Katy and Win behind. We had to take our chances with Zero and Vlad.

Chapter Twenty-four

S*lam!*
I ducked just in time, almost tripping on my robe.

I'd been scavenging for food in the kitchen. It was very early in the morning and I'd thought the men were still asleep. But I was wrong.

The kitchen door crashed open and a crack-filled raging bull roared in. The hair on the back of my neck sprang up. I spun around to see Zero's flushed face. His bulging red eyes looked like they were about to explode. He stomped toward me with his gun in one hand. He pushed his face three inches from mine and snarled.

"You useless piece of nothing!"

I turned my face away, but the stench of stale saliva marinated in drugs and alcohol was too strong. I tried not to gag.

Zero didn't believe in selling the stuff Luc sold, but he made a regular habit of snorting it. I was learning quickly what an unstable and walking contradiction he was. And when he was high, he became as dangerous as a stampeding rhino I'd once seen on safari.

I peered through the eye slit of my veil, my eyes darting across the room, looking for an escape. But I was trapped. Trapped between a hungry, boozed-up, drugged-out thug and the kitchen sink.

"Do your job, you stupid, lazy girl! Why you not make food for me?" His voice was a slur. His spit rocketed out and landed on the veil. I cringed in disgust, thankful for Bibi's robe.

I'd done a good job being Bibi so far, but there had been close calls. In the van coming over, Tetyana had said I'd be okay as long as I kept my mouth shut. Bibi supposedly didn't talk to men, any men. She cowered in the presence of males, a mute puppet who bent to their whims. I was glad I was impersonating a woman as voiceless as a street pole. This shouldn't be difficult to do, or so I'd thought then.

"Answer me, you idiot! Are you stupid and deaf?"

Zero swayed unsteadily to one side, then to the next. I wondered if he would crash and fall anytime now. My mind raced to think of a way out without giving myself away.

He jabbed a thick brown finger under my nose. "Remember, I own you! Your older brother. Respectable brother!" He drew back and gave me a disgusted look like I was a pile of rubbish.

Respectable?

"Should have burn you alive." He glared at me with those angry eyes. "Or sell you to gang master in London. Maybe I thrash you to death now!" He threw his gun down on the table and raised his hand.

I ducked. He missed and hit the countertop instead.

"Arrrgh!" He drew his hand back in pain.

I shuddered under the robe. There was no place to run. I stood silently, my heart pounding, watching, waiting to duck another incoming fist.

I remembered how mercilessly he kicked Win in London, and I couldn't get the image of that bloodied girl in the yellow blouse out of my mind. The self-defense classes I took at my international schools were like child's play now. I was no match against raging fists and deadly weapons.

He was frothing now. "You can't cook for me. You can't feed your own brother, but you can run in night like stupid female goat in heat. You shame me!"

What a madman.

I wondered how much of the white stuff he'd inhaled. I spread my arms innocently, shrugging as visibly as I could. I hoped that was a gesture Bibi did, that it would placate him somehow.

"You talking back to me?" His eyes looked like they were about to spurt blood.

Talk back?

"You whore!" His roar blew back my face veil. "That what! I saw you without niqab."

My blood froze. *Oh my god, he knows I'm not Bibi.* I looked away. Inside the robe, I was shaking like a leaf. *What do I do? If I make a run for it, where do I run?*

"I saw you talk to dat boy!" Zero's eyes were glowering. "You ruin my family's name again? That's it, ha?"

Ruin family's name?

My mind cleared. I understood now.

Win had woken up at three in the morning the night before, sick to her stomach. She'd woken up shaking and gagging and had wanted to use the bathroom. She had been in such a bad state, I hadn't had time to think. I'd jumped out of bed, moved the desk enough to squeeze through, and tiptoed with her to the bathroom outside, leaving Bibi's robe at the foot of the bed. A careless move.

As I'd waited for Win outside the bathroom, I'd seen Tetyana and Luc's door crack open. It was Luc coming out to see what was going on. He'd walked over, helped me clean the bathroom and take Win back to her bed. I hadn't thought anyone else had been up at that time.

"You dishonor me and my father!" Zero raised an index finger to the sky as if calling his gods. "My father, may he rest his soul, is turning in grave to have stupid daughter like you!"

Underneath the robe, I was trying to stay sane.

How is having an innocent chat with someone from the opposite sex worse than dealing in drugs, running a brothel, threatening to kill, kidnapping, murdering and inciting a man to rape his own sister? And doesn't he know what his sister looks like? Or was he too drugged last night to see clearly?

I straightened up. *If he thinks I'm going to sit here and get beaten up, he's wrong. I'm gonna fight,* I told myself. *I'm gonna fight like a tiger, claws, teeth, and all.* I glared at the man in front of me.

"If he here now, he twist your neck in half!" Zero loomed over me. "Maybe it's time I did Father duty and get honor back to family."

I glanced at the table that was at arm's reach from me. On it sat Zero's gun, glinting under the pale kitchen light. A few inches to the side and I'd be able to touch it. I lifted my arm slowly, so he wouldn't notice.

Bibi's robe felt heavier than leather sheeting and my whole body had broken into a sweat. But I hadn't forgotten all my self-defense lessons yet.

Zero opened his mouth to yell something about his father and god again when I raised my knee and slammed him, aiming right between his legs.

"Aaargh!" He doubled over screeching, more from shock than pain, I was sure. But I didn't wait to find out. I ducked around him and snagged the gun.

Zero straightened up and tried to grab me. "Get here, you slut!"

I pointed the gun at him with shaking hands.

He gave me a wild look. "What the hell you do? Give dat or I thrash you to pieces!"

I don't know what overcame me, but I felt a surge of electric strength travel from the hand that held the gun to my spine. I whipped the gun up, so it pointed directly at his face and took a confident step forward. Through that slit in the veil, I gave him a dark look.

His face went white.

That jelly feeling in my legs had disappeared and was being replaced by rage—rage from knowing what he had done to Bibi, from remembering how he had kidnapped Katy, how he had kicked Win, and how he had directed those soul-less men to torture and kill that young girl in the warehouse.

It all flashed across my mind like a fast-tracked video. I felt adrenaline course through me. My feet felt solid on the floor, my back strong and my arms tight. I peered through my slit to give him a penetrating look. The gun was steady in my hands. I was ready for blood.

"Are you possessed, woman?" Zero's eyes bulged. "Why you do this? I'm your brother." His voice faltered.

I took another step forward and with a quick flick of my wrist, cracked the gun against his nose.

Zero jumped back, cradling his nose, his face ashen. Now, he was the one stuck between an angry woman and the kitchen sink. How ironic. I hadn't even touched the trigger. I didn't even know where the trigger was, but that was enough for him. He threw up his arms.

"Aiiiee!" he cried.

I cracked the gun across his face again.

"Stop! God willing!"

His eyes glistened with water. His chest heaved and he started simpering in fear, unable to hold my gaze.

Guess it's hard to look at people you abuse, right?

I held my stance for a few seconds and thrust the gun right into Zero's pot belly. This time, I found the trigger. He whimpered. I jabbed again, deeper into his stomach cushion. He wheezed like a sick water buffalo, sweat streaming down his face.

Bullies are the biggest cowards, I thought.

I didn't want an easy death for this man. I wanted him to feel the pain of all the people he'd hurt over his lifetime.

"What the hell's going on?"

I snapped my head around.

That momentary distraction cost me. In a flash, Zero turned around and fled the kitchen.

Chapter Twenty-five

"Ash...I mean, Bibi!"

I spun around. It was Tetyana. Her cheeks were pink and she was panting.

"What the hell is goin..." Her eyes widened when she saw the gun in my hands. "How did you manage to get that?"

"Where were you?" I asked.

"There's a basement in the house," she said, in a low voice. "There's got to be a doorway out. Probably to a sewer, maybe an underground tunnel. There's a maze under Brussels, just like Kiev." She turned to leave. "Let's get everyone. And bring that gun."

"Stop that!"

The cry startled us, stopping us in our tracks.

"Help me!"

Oh my god. That's Katy.

Lifting up the robe, I rushed out of the kitchen with Tetyana at my heels.

A door slammed upstairs.

"Help!"

This time her voice was muffled. I ran up to the second landing, holding my gun in front, trying not to trip on the robe.

"Hey!" A shadow sprang aside.

"Luc?" I said, adjusting the eye slits to see better.

"What are you doing with that thing?" His eyes, wide with terror, were on the gun. I lowered the weapon.

"Where's Katy?"

"Zero took her."

"*What?*"

Behind him, the bedroom door opened and Win peeked out, her eyes fearful.

"Win! What happened?" Tetyana asked.

Win stepped out of the room like a frightened deer. "He got her when she came out of the toilet. She couldn't hold any longer," she whispered. "He pulled her up there." She pointed to the third floor.

Someone was stomping down the stairs.

We all looked up.

I lifted the gun and trained it in the direction of the sound, my feet solid, my hands steady.

"Jeezus!" Vlad jumped back when he spotted the weapon. "What the hell?"

I took two steps forward and pointed the gun squarely at his chest. He threw his hands up.

"My god, woman. What got to you?"

"Where's Katy?"

Vlad blinked.

"Bibi?" He leaned in slightly and peered at me, keeping a safe distance, hands still up in the air.

"I said, where's Katy?"

He inched backward, toward the stairs, both hands still up. "He's right. You possessed. Sweet bejeezus!" He slowly moved one hand to his chest and crossed himself, one wary eye still on me.

Then, without a warning, he spun around and clambered up the stairs like a frightened monkey.

Picking up my robe with one hand and brandishing my weapon with my other, I rushed up to the attic. Behind me, I heard the others troop up the stairs.

Vlad was at the attic door when I came up. He had the look of a cornered animal, searching frantically for an escape.

"Open up, you bastard!" Vlad screeched at the door. "Your sis gone stark raving berserk." He pounded on the door with so much vigor, I was surprised it didn't crash open. "Oi!" he yelled, giving me a scared sidelong glance as I came up. "Let me in, you godamned idiot!"

We heard someone speak from the other side of the door. Vlad stopped the pounding. I leaned in. It was Zero's voice, but I couldn't make out the words.

"What?" Vlad put his ear to the door to listen. Zero mumbled something.

"*Your* bloody sister. Not mine!"

"Get away—Bibi—gun—" It sounded like Zero was busy with something, his voice fading when he turned away and clearer when he faced the door. I strained to listen. There wasn't a sound from Katy.

"She possessed, I tell you!" Vlad's voice had risen several pitches higher. "Spooking me like hell."

"I told you!" Zero yelled from behind the door. "Crazy mad like cousin's wife!"

Vlad looked at me warily. I stared back at him and he seemed to shrink a little.

He was three times my size and could have easily overpowered me, but I realized then, just like Zero, he was a bully. And bullies don't do too well when they're surprised or cornered. Their power lay in the threat of their bullets. I held that power now.

It was time to raise the stakes. With deliberate movement, I lowered the gun, pointing directly at Vlad's groin area. He didn't have to see my face to know I was serious.

"I tell you this house is haunted." Vlad crossed himself.

"I come out only if Bibi not curse me." Zero's voice came clearly now as if he was standing just on the other side of the door now.

"*Curse you?*" A dark vein on Vlad's forehead was throbbing like an electric wire gone mad. "You talk about curse? She got bloody gun on my dick, you idiot!"

"Where your gun?" Zero asked.

"With you, baboon. You took it from me, remember?"

Silence.

"Help me, man!" Vlad screeched.

Zero's voice came plaintively through the door. "But my cousin die like this."

"Cousin?" Vlad spluttered, looking like he was about to implode. "I don't give crap about your bloody cousin! Your crazy sister's gonna riddle me with bullets and you talking about stupid cousin?"

"My cousin wife was possessed. Just like that. All nice and normal one day and he beat her when he want. But one day she turn into she-devil. Just like that. That night he choke on his blood. It was curse, I tell you. She a witch!"

Vlad looked disgusted. "Your dumb family affair is not my problem. Open goddamn door!"

I prayed that Katy was okay. *Why's she so quiet? How do I get her out safely?* Tetyana was standing beside me now, surveying the door. We exchanged a quick look.

Zero's voice through the door again. "I come out only if you tell her not curse on me, okay?"

Vlad seemed lost for words. He gave me a pleading look. I returned it with a venomous one.

"Please?" he squeaked. "Be nice, Bibi."

I didn't move my gun. It was getting the effect I needed and I wasn't going to change my tactic now.

"Okay, okay," Vlad said, crossing his chest once again. "Zero! She promise. No curse. No witching. She do anything you want."

"I want food," Zero said.

"Food?" Vlad's eyes widened.

"I hungry, man. Two days now. No one take care of me anymore," Zero moaned. "Stupid women don't cook for me."

"Okay, okay, what you want?" Vlad said as if talking to a child. "We give you anything you want. Anything."

"I want *chapli kebab, sajji* and *biriyani*. I want *shawarma* also."

Vlad took a deep breath. For a second, I worried I'd pushed him too far and he was about to snap. Instead, he looked at me, begging.

"Come on, Bibi, he's your only brother. He's family. All he want is to eat. Come on."

I glared at him. I knew exactly what kind of a brother he'd been to Bibi.

"I want burger too," Zero was saying from behind the door. "And don't forget chips."

"He's just hungry. He don't mean anything bad." Vlad sniveled. "Be good sis, will you? Put gun down. We can figure this out in a civilized way, you know, like family."

Civilized? Like killing Bibi's boyfriend? Like burning Bibi's face? Like kicking Win? Like raping and killing that girl in the warehouse?

"Also halva. I want sweets," Zero continued. "I want Indian sweets."

"Jeezuz. If I lose my balls, I kill you myself," Vlad muttered to the door. "Zero! Get out. You get everything you want. Even a boy."

I looked at him startled.

"*A boy?*" Zero's voice came clearly through the door. He seemed to have perked up.

"Yes," Vlad said. "Promise."

"*A boy?*" I asked.

I glanced at Tetyana. Her face was impassive, cold. Next to her, Luc was staring at the door. A look of pain crossed his face, but when he saw me looking, he turned away. *There's something else going on here I don't know about.*

I'd never held a gun in my hands before this day, nor did I know how to use it, but I was ready to shoot every bullet in that gun on both men.

I stepped forward.

Around me, I felt the room stop breathing.

"Tell him to come out, and he'd better not have laid a finger on her," I said in my most dangerous voice.

Vlad stared at me. "You speak English pretty good."

He cocked his head to the side. "Dunno what got into you." He paused and his eyes widened. "You not Bibi!"

I glared at him.

He looked me up and down and his eyes rested on my hand that held the gun. His mouth turned into an ugly smirk. "You don't shoot that thing. You don't know how."

Chapter Twenty-six

The door banged open. Everyone jumped back in surprise.

Before I knew it, Tetyana grabbed the gun from me and trained it on Zero.

"Get back!" she shouted.

Vlad flattened himself against the wall.

I peered inside the attic room. It was a mess inside like a hurricane had ravaged the room.

Katy was sitting on a wooden chair next to the bed, her feet bound by a rope to the chair legs, and her mouth gagged with a rag. From the broken lamp, an overturned table and Katy's frazzled red hair standing out like a lion's mane, I was sure she'd put up a fight. She didn't look as fearful as much as she looked angry. Her eyes flashed furiously at Zero.

Zero stood at the doorway, pointing his gun at her head. "The girl dead if you curse me," he said glaring at me. "You she-devil!"

The cut I'd given his nose with my pistol whipping was bigger than I thought. I noticed a new bloodied scratch just below his right eye. It must hurt because he kept blinking. *Good for you, Katy.*

If Zero had looked unhinged before in the kitchen, he looked like a lunatic now. His hair was askew and his face was puffier and redder. He spat on the ground. "You curse me, you will get vile death!"

Before anyone of us could make a move, he pulled the door hard and slammed it shut behind him.

"You want?" he said, shoving a rusty key in my face. "You do what I say."

It took me a second to realize he was pointing his gun at me. I stared down the barrel. No one breathed. Not even Vlad.

"One move and I'll blow your brains out," Tetyana said in a low voice. She still had her gun trained on Zero.

My mind whirled between panic and shock. *Is he going to shoot me? Is Tetyana going to shoot him first? What do I do?*

"And I blow her brains," Zero snarled back.

No one moved.

Without changing his aim, Zero took a step backward. Tetyana's took a step forward. Without a warning, Zero turned and bolted down the stairs.

Vlad had been standing against the wall with his mouth open. As soon as Zero disappeared, he stepped out to run after his partner, but Tetyana was faster. She whipped the gun around at him.

"Stay right there, asshole," she said.

With her back straight, her shoulders firm, and her legs rooted to the ground, she looked solid. She held the gun like it was the most natural thing in the world. She'd done this sort of thing before, I was sure now.

"You move one inch and I have only one decision to make," she said, "your head or your balls."

Vlad went white.

"On your knees!" she screamed.

He fell to his knees, hands in the air.

"That girl changed everything," Tetyana said in a hoarse whisper.

Which girl? The girl in the yellow blouse in the warehouse?

Vlad turned away, looking ashamed. Ashamed at being called out, not because of what he did, I was sure.

Tetyana moved a step closer.

Vlad shuffled back on his knees, watching her with panicked eyes. "Aw, c'mon. Can a man have fun? Was only...."

She took another step toward him. He shuffled back again.

"You call that fun?" Tetyana bellowed so loudly, it surprised even me.

Vlad looked at the floor. His arms, held up in the air, were now trembling.

"You rat bastard!" Tetyana cracked the gun across his head so fast, we all jumped. Vlad clutched his face. A gash appeared on his forehead and blood trickled out.

I looked over at Luc and Win.

Both were staring at Tetyana, faces pale. *Have they seen her like this before?* It was hard to tell. I glanced behind them anxiously. *Where's Zero?* He had the other gun. We couldn't have him come back up now.

"Please don't hit. What I done for you? I fix everything. I found Zero to help you," he sniveled.

"That crackpot?" Tetyana's face was firm. "Look what he's done now."

"Please, Tetyana." Vlad was whimpering. "I help you when those men after you. Don't kill me!" he howled.

Tetyana stepped back, breathing loudly, her gun hanging limp from her hand. "Oh, I don't plan to kill you," she said in the calmest voice that made me shiver under my robe.

"I the good guy. I'm like your brother..." He didn't get to finish.

Tetyana's face turned into a furious ball of fire. She raised her arm and gave another resounding whack to his head. The sound of the gun whip echoed through the house. Vlad keeled to the ground. She hit him again and again until his face was a bloodied mess. I wanted to look away, but couldn't.

Using her heel, Tetyana gave a powerful kick to his chest. He fell flat on his back with a cry. Not wasting a second, she stamped down on his groin and ground her heel, while he screamed to high heaven. He deserved what he was getting, but it was hard to watch. When she took her foot off him, Vlad was lying on the ground curled in fetal position, tears streaming down his bloodied face.

Tetyana looked at him, her nose wrinkled as if trying to block a vulgar smell. "Don't you *ever* compare yourself to my brother."

Vlad's life was on a very thin line. I didn't know whether to be impressed or terrified.

"Luc," Tetyana said, without turning her head. "Keep an eye on this man, will you?"

Luc stood to attention and almost saluted. "Will do," he said, marching over to take her place in front of Vlad, who didn't look like he could put up a fight now.

"We need rope," Tetyana said stepping toward the stairs. "Stay here all of you."

We watched as she stepped down the stairs, bracing ourselves. None of us wanted a gunfight, but that's what we were all expecting.

"Mmmm..."

I turned around. It was Katy's voice coming through the door.

"Katy!" I rattled the doorknob and gave a kick at it for good measure. It didn't budge. "Katy! I'm here!"

"Mmmm...."

"It's okay," I shouted. "We'll get you out soon. It's gonna be okay!"

I turned to Luc. "Can we shoot the door down?"

He shook his head. "She's right behind the door. It will hit her."

"There's no other way in?" I said, looking around desperately. "What about the window?" I asked, remembering how I broke into the house in London.

"We'll need a really high ladder or someone who can climb like a monkey. But the cops will see us then."

"All okay?" Tetyana was back, dragging two bedsheets behind her.

We nodded.

"Can you rip these up for me?" she asked.

After slashing the sheets into long pieces, Luc and I helped Tetyana gag and tie Vlad up. He was on his knees now, with his arms and legs twisted behind him in the most uncomfortable position.

If Tetyana had wanted to extend the pain in his groin, she couldn't have done a better job. When we were done, she kicked him swiftly between his legs once again with a sickening sound. His eyes rolled to the back of his head. I was sure he'd fainted.

Tetyana turned to us and said, "Too bad Zero doesn't care too much about him, or we could threaten to kill him if we don't get the key."

"Where's Zero?" I asked.

"Locked himself," she said. "In the bunk-bed room." She looked at Luc. "You plied him with too much coke."

Luc shrugged. "He asked for it. What am I supposed to do?"

"How do we get Katy out?" I said, trying to focus on the most important thing now.

"We don't have a choice," Tetyana said, with a sigh. "I can't go blazing into his room. Too risky. We need to distract Zero to get the keys."

"What about the police parked outside?" I now knew there were good officers and bad officers, but we had to take our chances. "Maybe they'll help us."

"Sure, if you want them to take us away," Tetyana said. "You'll never see your friend again for a very long time."

"But why? What did we do wrong?"

Luc and Tetyana looked at me like I was crazy.

"Honey, you don't know this business, do you?" Tetyana shook her head. "If they come, they'll take us all to the station and lock us up for months, no questions asked. Maybe years. Gangsters pay their way out before the girls get clemency, and I can't afford to get locked away like that. I've got to get back to Kiev. We're not calling the police, okay?"

I stared at her. *Locked up? For years?* The smuggling poster at Heathrow Airport, the one with the woman in handcuffs, flashed across my mind.

I nodded.

"Listen," Tetyana said. "You and Luc get something that smells a lot, like fish and chips or some curry, and come back quickly. That'll get him out of the room where I can corner him."

"I'm not leaving Katy."

"The police will stop Luc if he goes out by himself, but with you in that get-up with him, there's less of a chance for that happening. I'll hold fort here."

I guess I had no choice.

"Hey, Win." Tetyana wasn't done. "I need you to do one important job for us, okay?"

"Okay," Win said.

"I want to you to stay near the outside kitchen door and keep watch for us."

Win nodded. "I'll go now."

"Not yet!"

Win spun around and looked at her with big eyes.

"Go with Asha and Luc, just in case Zero comes out. We can't have a second hostage. Stay near the back door, got it?"

She nodded.

"If you hear Zero come down, or you hear a gunshot, or anything, I want you to run out to the street. Don't look back. Don't come up or stay in the house. Do you understand?"

"Yes."

"What about Katy?" I asked.

"I'll keep guard here. If Zero comes up, he'll have to deal with me." She looked at me squarely. "I won't let him get to her. I promise."

I took a deep breath. I was putting a lot of trust in these people I'd just met.

"Asha." She gave me a pointed look. "For everyone's safety, please don't do anything silly, okay? Just follow Luc's lead."

I opened my mouth, then closed it. *What does she mean, "silly"?*

She turned at Luc. "And get my usual prescription, will you? Make it fast. We don't have a lot of time."

Chapter Twenty-seven

I felt the fresh air even with the robe on.

Luc and I'd just stepped out the back door, our first foray to the outside world after two whole days of being cooped up inside. We were on a mission to find food and maybe a boy. *A boy?* I still wasn't sure I'd heard that last item correctly, but I wanted to get far from the house before I asked Luc.

We left behind a gagged and bleeding Vlad on the attic floor.

Tetyana had taken position on the top step of the third floor which gave her a good view of the rooms on the second floor and the attic room where Katy was locked up. She sat legs splayed out, gun in hand, and a look on her face that said she was ready to kill at a moment's notice.

Win had taken watch near the kitchen door, but I was sure it was a pretext to get her out of danger, out of the way if anything happened upstairs.

Zero had locked himself in Tetyana and Luc's bedroom. As we walked by the door, I heard him mutter to himself, chanting something, like he was praying.

We slipped passed the parked police vans, walking as casually as we could.

A slight breeze ruffled the robe. I wished I could throw it off and feel the sun on my skin again. Fresh-baked bread wafted our way as soon as we left the house. I'd barely eaten for two days, and the aroma was like a punch to the gut. I wanted to follow the smell, touch and taste the loaves, but this wasn't the time for any of that.

A police officer who'd been patrolling the street with his dog crossed our path.

He glared at Luc for a second and then at me. I felt like he could penetrate the black cloth and see right inside. His face said one word: contempt. Though I was already hidden behind Bibi's robe, that look made me want to crawl into a hole. Then, without a word, he marched off.

Luc and I kept walking in the opposite direction, but I couldn't help but feel the officer's eyes on my back. After ten yards, I glanced back to see him standing, frowning at us, a hand on his radio. He yanked the dog's chain and walked off, disappearing around the corner of our building.

We walked briskly toward the main street.

Luc was trying to remember the city from when he last came here. "We've got to find the immigrant market. That's where all Pakistani and Arab food stalls are. Zero will come out for sure when he smells that stuff."

I nodded, thankful he knew his way around here.

"Just remember when we talk to the Belgians, speak both Flemish and French, so you don't insult them, okay?"

Through my veil, I gave him a look. "But what if I don't speak Flemish?"

"Then use English. The Flemish don't mind that."

"Halt!"

We stopped and stared. Two smartly dressed police officers, a man and a woman, stood in front of us, radioed up, with guns and handcuffs neatly packed in their belts.

"*Bonjour, monsieur, madame,*" Luc said, with a polite nod of his head. "*Goedemorgen.*"

"Can we see your papers, please?" the female officer asked in English, looking me over.

My stomach fell. I'd left my passport at the house and Luc had done the same. For good reason. I didn't want anyone to know I was the girl who'd stolen money in Toronto and run away from border guards in London. I could only imagine what Luc didn't want the police to know.

Luc answered for both of us in a mixture of French and English. "We're on our way to the market to get groceries," he said. "We left everything back home in case of pickpockets, you see."

But the police didn't seem to see.

"Citizens of Belgium?" the male officer asked in English.

"*Français,*" Luc said. French.

The officers turned to me.

It felt hot inside the robe, and suddenly, I wasn't able to articulate in any language, English or otherwise.

"Pakistan," Luc said, quickly.

I gave a series of vigorous nods from under the robe.

The officers turned to each other and spoke rapidly in a language I hadn't heard before. This must be Flemish, I thought.

"Follow us, please. This way," the male officer said. They turned around and marched toward a police van parked on the edge of the street.

Luc and I looked at each other and followed them. We had no choice.

Are they going to arrest us? Is this the end? I squeezed Luc's hand and he squeezed it back.

When we got to the van, the male officer pulled Luc to the side. I followed the female officer inside the van. I looked back before I stepped in and saw Luc being patted down. The van's door closed, and the officer motioned for me to take off my robe.

I hesitated.

Using hand gestures, she asked me again to remove the robe.

I stood still, frozen partly out of fear, and partly because I didn't want her to see my face. For all I knew, it had been plastered across all airports with a caption that said, *Have you seen this thief?*

The officer's eyes narrowed. She picked up her radio hand piece and spoke in Flemish. Someone replied. The officer said one word,

"Fatima." Then, the radio went silent, and she leaned back, hands on her hips, watching me.

The heat inside the robe was reaching boiling point. An image of armed cops with machine guns storming through the door and stripping off my robe flashed to mind. With shaking hands, I pulled off the robe, struggling with it as usual. Though it felt good to be back in my own skin, I stood in front of the officer feeling utterly naked.

Looking relieved, and using hand gestures, she asked me to spread my arms and legs wide. I complied. She patted me down, and even went through my pockets, but found nothing. When she was done, she pointed at a bench seat in the back. I sat down with shaking legs. She pulled a chair and sat across from me.

"What's your name?" she asked in English.

I gave a weak smile. *Do I answer? Do I pretend I'm Bibi?*

I was saved by a knock. The van's door opened and in came a stout, Arabic-looking woman wearing civilian clothes.

"Ah, Fatima," the policewoman said looking relieved.

The two spoke briskly with each other. I heard the words "Pakistan" and "Urdu" bandied about. I watched them quietly, wondering what Luc was going through outside.

The second woman turned to me and said something at length. It sounded very much like Arabic, in an accent close to Bibi's or Zero's. She stopped speaking and the two women watched me expectantly as if waiting for an answer. I stared back quizzically.

With an exasperated sigh, the Arabic woman pointed at herself. "Fatima." She then pointed at me and asked in English, "And you?"

I couldn't keep up this pretense for too long. Feeling my cheeks burn, I said, "Bibi." I could barely look at their eyes. I could never lie well, not even a white lie, and here I was lying to the police, of all people.

But they looked happy I'd answered their first question.

"How-old-are-you?" The police officer spoke in English, articulating each word as if speaking to a child.

I hesitated.

"Eighteen." It felt good to tell the truth.

"Why-are-you-here?"

Do I answer that? I racked my brain.

"To eat."

"Eat?" The officer frowned.

"I, er, make, er, cakes," I drew out the words slowly, in an accent that was a cross between anything that came from south of the equator.

"Cakes?"

"I er, sell, er, cakes." I paused. "At market."

The women looked at each other with confused looks on their faces.

"*Refugie?*" The Arabic woman asked. Refugee?

I stared at her. I was digging this hole deeper and deeper.

The officer turned to me. "Where-are-you-from? Where-is-your home?"

"Pakistan." That was easy. Luc had already answered this.

"Who-are-you-with?" the police officer asked.

I peered at her as if I didn't understand, but I was sure my face was giving everything away.

"Who is that boy with you?" the officer tried again.

"Friend," I said.

"Is that correct?" She didn't sound convinced.

"Yes." I nodded.

Suddenly, the officer's radio crackled to life. This time, it was a man's voice. When she was done with the radio, the officer pointed at my robe and motioned me to put it back on.

I reached for the black robe, and Fatima, who seemed to know how this worked, reached out to help me. The officer talked to me while Fatima adjusted my eye slits.

"If you are ever in trouble, I want you to come here and call us." She tapped the metal badge on her shirt. "Any of us with this, do you understand? We're here to help."

Inside the veil, I nodded.

"If you are in any danger, you must tell us. Never hide." The officer hesitated and peered at me. "Do you understand?"

I nodded again. The image of Katy tied to a chair in the attic room swirled in my head. I bit my tongue.

The officer sighed and gave Fatima a look that said she didn't think I got it. Fatima pursed her lips and shrugged in response. The officer opened the door and stepped out. I followed them out to see Luc waiting outside. The male officer who'd been with him was no longer there.

Luc gave me an awkward smile.

I turned to the female officer, who now looked like she had more important things to do.

"You may go," she said, nodding.

"Thank you," I said, without thinking and felt my face go warm. *Did she hear my real accent?* I didn't wait to find out and didn't look back. I walked straight into Luc's arms.

He pulled me in close. *What's he doing?*

"You're my girlfriend," he whispered in my ear.

"What?" I looked at him, startled.

"You're just a poor Pakistani girl who got kicked out of her family because you fell in love with a white boy. That's what I told them."

Chapter Twenty-eight

"Come on," Luc said.

But, suddenly, I couldn't do this anymore. I picked up the skirts of the robe, ran to the end of the street and glanced around.

Nearby was a nondescript apartment building with laundry hanging in its balconies. I walked over to what looked like a forgotten alcove on the side of the building and struggled out of Bibi's robe. I felt Luc reach over to help me. I pulled the thing off with a swoosh.

The warm sun fell on my face and hair. I let the black cloth fall to the ground and pushed my arms to the sky, breathing in the fresh air, soaking in the sun, and feeling the wind on my face. I took another deep breath in.

Bibi's scarred face flashed to my mind. I remembered how she fearfully scurried across the square in London. I folded the robe carefully, wondering what it must be like to be condemned to a lifetime of something that robbed you of your personality, self-expression, and movement. Underneath that robe, I'd felt entombed. With it on, I was faceless, a person without a name, feelings, dreams or desires. I hoped Bibi was in a better place now. Happier and freer.

"We got one hour," Luc whispered.

I shoved the robe into a corner.

"Do you have any money?" I asked him.

"Money?" Luc shook his head and gave me a half-mocking look. "I thought *you* had tons. Didn't you say you had a shitload of cash? Or did you make that all up?"

My money had run out a long time ago. All I had was the drug money we stole from Dick's safe, which Katy kept on her, everywhere she went. She even slept with it under her pillow. That packet of money was now locked up with her in the attic. I didn't trust him to tell him all that yet, so I merely shrugged.

"Don't worry. I know how to make money," Luc said, with a smug look on his face. "You'll see."

I remembered the conversation I overheard in the pantry a few days ago, back in London. "But don't you make money selling—"

"Zero stole it from me just before we left Brussels," he said quietly. "They probably gave it all to the checkpoint police in France."

"How do we buy food?"

"We'll think of something," he said, taking my hand. "This is not the first time I've scrounged. I know some tricks." He winked at me.

We walked in quick steps toward the main road. I saw a sign on a street pole written in Arabic. Then another, and another. I pointed at them and said, "I thought we were in Belgium."

"It's the immigrant district."

It was a narrow street, crowded with smoke shops, dingy cafés, and trinket stands. At the end stood a mosque with a green minaret. As we walked toward it, it began to broadcast a call to prayer. A heavy and somber voice bounced off the stone walls and echoed through the alleyway.

This place was full of people from many countries, wearing multicolored robes and outfits I'd never seen before, not even in Goa's busy markets. I spotted many women who wore the same black robe as Bibi. They walked in pairs, threesomes, foursomes or with a man or two. Never alone.

I remembered Aunty Shilpa telling me a long time ago that a veiled woman is not allowed to walk by herself—something about having "a male guardian for honor," she said. These women had to follow strict rules, like walking three steps behind the men, behind even their own young sons.

I walked shoulder to shoulder with Luc, taking in the sights, keeping a sharp eye out for a Pakistani food stall where we'd find the things Zero had asked for.

I didn't realize we'd entered the market until we were halfway in. It was a market like I'd never seen before, a blend of West and East, of exoticism and quaintness. The markets I'd seen in Tanzania and India had been loud, dusty, rustic affairs that sold mostly food, animals, kitchen pots, and children's clothing, all laid out in rickety stalls or mats on the floor.

This market in Brussels sold everything from shoes to coffee beans, from books to antiques—all displayed on beautiful Persian rugs. It was a flea market made for kings if kings ever shopped at markets, that is.

We walked toward the food stalls in the back, meandering our way through the antique stands that showcased figurines, pottery, kitschy jewelry, record collections, books, and even old fine china. I marveled at the priceless items lying haphazardly on the floor rugs beneath the white tents.

"Stolen goods," Luc whispered when he saw me crane to look at one beautiful piece of art.

People popped in and out of these tents, talking to family and friends. A trio of men had congregated to drink coffee at a table that had been pulled out to the street. Kids ran across the street, disregarding honking cars and busses. If not for the European facades around me, I'd have felt like I'd entered one of Scheherazade's Arabian tales.

But Luc was steering me away from the stalls toward the edge of the market, where a group of young men was hanging out. If I'd been alone, I'd have crossed the street away from them, but Luc insisted.

A dozen rough-looking young men, wearing leather jackets and smoking cigarettes, had gathered around an old motorcycle. A couple of them looked up curiously as we walked by. Luc gave a polite nod and a slight salute. They saluted back. One of them leered at me. I looked away. These were exactly the sort of men Vlad would be friends with, I thought.

Behind them, a fast-food *shawarma* joint was selling its fare through an open window. The aroma of fresh-cut Belgian fries came sliding into my nose. *Shawarma and chips!* That would be perfect to get Zero out. I was about to point it out to Luc when I remembered. We had no money, not even to buy one chip.

We were at the edge of the market now, and Luc had slowed down. His brows were knotted as if contemplating something important. That was when I noticed something strange.

It was like an invisible line separated where we'd just passed and where we were standing now.

The immigrant district, with the market, the mosque, little trinket shops, and *shawarma* joints was messier, busier, and louder. On the other side of the street, the shops were well built, fancy, upscale, and the pavement was cleaner. I looked back and forth, surprised at the striking difference between the two areas. It was like I was standing between two continents, only ten feet away from each other.

That was when something familiar caught my eye. There. Down the street. The fluttering of an awning—a red-and-white striped awning. I took a sharp breath in. I let go of Luc's hand and stepped toward it.

It was as if a force was pulling me toward it. I walked over in a daze, my heart beating a tick faster with every step. The floor-to-ceiling glass window with curved gold lettering was unmistakable. It was a Chef Pierre café. And just outside the store was a sign that said, "Now Hiring."

I pressed my nose against the glass.

Laid like jewels on spotless glass shelves were the most delicate array of baked foods imaginable. From waffles to croissants, rolls to bagels, baguettes, whirly breads, honey buns, and sweet brioche, this was a baker's heaven. In the middle of the shelf, lay the crown jewel, a dark chocolate roll beautifully encased in white laced cloth, packed in a see-through container. I licked my lips. My stomach growled and my head hurt.

Inside, a girl, probably nine or so, took a seat at a table, her blonde ponytail swishing from side to side as she settled in her chair. The plate in front of her was stacked high with golden Belgian waffles. As I watched entranced, she slathered her waffles with butter and poured a generous amount of chocolate syrup. She broke off a chunk with a fork and put it into her mouth. As she licked the chocolate off her fingers, I could almost smell the waffles from where I was outside.

Maybe, I thought, maybe, if I get a job here, I can buy all of us out and get away from Zero and Vlad. I shook my head. *What are you thinking, girl? Katy's stuck in that room right now! You don't have time.* I couldn't linger. Katy's ransom was our return. We had to think of something fast.

"Luc?"

Where did he go now? I scanned the area.

Where is he?

"*Bonjour, mademoiselle!*"

I jumped and swiveled around.

Chapter Twenty-nine

"**O**h, hi," I said.

It was a man in a long, crisp apron embroidered with Chef Pierre's logo. I stared at it. *What would I do to wear that?*

With a friendly smile, he reached over to wipe a smudge of dust from the window.

"Sorry, I didn't see you," I stammered.

"Americaine?" He raised his eyebrows and smiled pleasantly.

"Yes," I said. I was now resigned to it. It was much easier than to correct them, anyway.

The man's eyes traveled down to my rumpled skirt. I quickly smoothed it out. I'd been living in this skirt for five days now. He raised an eyebrow but didn't comment. "I guessed correctly," he said in English.

I gave him a frozen smile.

"I saw you looking at my pastries. Would you like to come inside and take a look?" He opened the door and waved me in.

I hesitated.

"Window-shopping is great, but real shopping is even more delicious. I can promise you that. Haha!"

I smiled. I stopped for a second to see if I could spot Luc and then stepped inside. My brain had begun to whir again. *This could be a solution to our problems.*

The fragrance of fruit, spices and gourmet baking embraced me as I stepped in.

"So what would you desire, *mademoiselle Americaine*? Might I suggest our waffles? You must never leave Belgium without trying the waffle."

But something more important had caught my eyes.

"Can I take a look around first?" I asked, brightly.

"*Bien sur,* of course," he said, "Please, be my guest." With a slight bow, he turned around and went off to charm an old couple who were getting up to leave.

One of Chef Pierre's signature marks was the kitchen at the back, set behind a glass partition. I walked over to look.

The stainless-steel ovens, fridges, and mixers gleamed spotless. A stack of fresh-baked bread sat on a wooden table, calling out to be sliced and buttered. Bakers and sous chefs in white hats and aprons busied themselves like bees at a happy hive.

I watched them as they worked the mixers, kneaded the dough, poured the batter, slid trays of beautifully shaped dough into the industrial-sized ovens, then pulled out the final baked goods with thick white serviettes in their hands. They worked fast but unhurried. I breathed it all in, trying not to get lost in the warmth of it all.

This is my heaven. I imagined standing behind the bread counter with a tall white chef hat. *To be the queen of cakes and crumpets. If only they'd let me work here.* A man in the corner was rolling dough so quickly, his hand seemed to blur from where I stood. He saw me watching and winked in acknowledgment. I blushed and looked away. I wasn't just standing here for fun. A plan had been forming in the back of my mind.

I needed to buy time and blend in, so I strolled over to the newspaper rack. The same magazine I'd picked up at Heathrow in London was still out. I'd left my own copy in my jacket pocket back at the house.

I looked around. The store wasn't as busy as I'd like it to be yet.

I picked up the magazine and started flipping through the pages, scanning the photos and headlines, not really reading. But when I opened the centerfold, I almost dropped the magazine.

The photo spread was of an ancient stone castle on a hilly landscape. In front of this magnificent piece of architecture stood a shriveled-up woman, dripping in jewelry twice her weight, and cuddling two brown dachshunds.

If it weren't for her modern clothes and the vivid colors in the picture, I would have sworn the photo was from a bygone era, a time of knights and dragons. The caption read, "The indomitable Grande Baroness Agathe to host international party of the year."

But it was the picture inset that had grabbed my attention. In it, Chef Pierre beamed, looking his happy self, as usual. Leaning casually against his arm was a tall woman in a superb white Chanel suit. I did a double take. *The Diplomatic Dragon Lady?*

She looked exactly the same as when I'd met her in Toronto. Striking yet haughty. Beautiful yet venerable. It was this grand woman who'd chosen me, from all the professionals in town, to cater to her diplomatic parties in Toronto. I'd worked for her. I'd catered her parties. She was here, in Europe for a party hosted by this baroness in Luxembourg, no less.

Someone dropped a spoon nearby. The clatter as it hit the floor woke me up. *I can't stand here all day reading. I have work to do.*

There were six people in line at the counter now. Behind it was a young server in a red shirt and black skirt, and white gloves on her hands. She was rushing up and down the aisle with boxes and trays, packing cakes for a birthday, piling macarons for a tea party.

Everyone was busy. Even the man in the apron was immersed in a problem with the coffee grinder. No one noticed me. I'd faded into the background, exactly as planned. *Good.*

I returned the magazine to the rack and walked over to the glass shelf, then, after another quick glance, I picked up the dark chocolate roll. As casually as I could, I walked out the door, carrying my booty with me.

"Hey!"

I didn't look back. I hopped down the steps and ran.

"Arret!"

"Voleur!"

I broke into a sprint, running toward the *shawarma* joint, the only place I could get lost in the bustle of the market.

"Asha!"

I'd bumped into Luc head-on. I didn't even look at him. I grabbed him by the shirt and said, "Run! Now! No time to explain."

He held me by my arms. I struggled in panic. "They're after me."

"What the heck's going on?"

"I stole a chocolate roll," I said, breathlessly. "We gotta run!"

"No, we don't," he said, pointing at something down the street. "Look."

I turned to look.

The man in the apron was standing on his side of the street, waving an angry fist. That invisible line that separated the fancy stores from the immigrant district was like a force field. He didn't dare cross to this side.

I looked around. A crowd had gathered around us now. It was the gang of men who'd been admiring the motorcycle earlier. They stood casually, arms crossed, watching the scene. It dawned on me it was they who were keeping the man from the café away.

I couldn't look at him anymore. Even from this distance, I could see the hurt on his face, that shaking of his head. He'd welcomed me in with a smile to try his baked treats, and I'd rewarded him by stealing one of his most expensive pastries. A pang of guilt went through me but my desire to rescue Katy was far greater.

Someone jostled me. The crowd was inching closer, claustrophobic now.

"Who are these people?" I whispered to Luc.

A bearded man looked me over, his creepy eyes slithering down me. I inched closer to Luc.

"Your girl?" he said to Luc.

Luc grabbed me by the elbow. "Come," he said, pulling me out of the crowd. "Let's get out of here."

He didn't say anything until we were halfway inside the market, well away from the men.

"Why did you take off like that?" he said, half-angry. "I was looking for you".

"Look what I got," I said, showing him the luxurious chocolate roll. "This'll keep Zero busy and we can get the key."

"Asha," Luc said, giving me a piercing look with his bright blue eyes.

"What?"

He put his hands on my shoulders and squeezed them gently. "You didn't have to do that."

"How come?"

"I got enough cash now to buy a thousand chocolate rolls."

Part FIVE

I am strong, because I've been weak.
I am fearless, because I've been afraid.
I am wise, because I've been foolish.
Unknown

Chapter Thirty

"How's Katy?"

It was my first question when we got to the third floor. "You're back!" Tetyana jumped up when she saw us.

She was still holding the gun and had been leaning back against the railing when we'd tiptoed up. Vlad remained tied up and on his knees, his face lined with exhaustion. I noticed a couple more bruises on his face. He didn't even bother opening his eyes when we came up.

Win, who'd been waiting for us patiently in the kitchen, told us that Zero had been sound asleep for the past hour, having succumbed to the cocktail of drugs and alcohol he'd taken that morning. We heard his sonorous snores through the locked door as we walked up.

I had Bibi's robe back on now. On our return, we'd managed to sail past the police patrol outside. I wasn't sure if it was my imagination, but I detected a note of sympathy from them. One officer even nodded as we walked by her holding hands, trying hard not to hurry as if we were merely returning home from a casual trip to the market.

"So did you get some?" Tetyana asked Luc.

Digging into his trouser pockets, Luc produced a small yellow container of pills, like one you'd find in a drugstore.

"Not as strong as what I usually use, but it'll do," Tetyana said, inspecting the container. "You're resourceful, Luc. Don't know how you do it, but you always come through."

I pulled out the chocolate roll from under my robe with a flourish.

"Look what I got to get Zero out," I said, with a mixture of pride and guilt at my contribution. I looked up at Tetyana expecting a compliment for my hard work.

Her face fell. "That's it?"

That's it? A Chef Pierre luxury chocolate roll?

"We also got this," Luc said, showing her a plain brown paper bag of *shawarma* and fries.

"Oh good," she replied.

I looked down at my gourmet chocolate roll which would have cost thirty times the fast food we'd brought.

"There's more downstairs," Luc was saying. We'd picked up a container of cheap food from a Pakistani stall on our way back. We'd put it right outside the room Zero had barricaded himself in. "Once he smells it, he'll come out."

I could smell it too. My stomach rumbled, reminding me I hadn't eaten for more than two days now, but with Katy gagged and locked up and not knowing what our future held, I didn't feel much like eating at all.

"I'm starved," Win said, looking longingly down the stairs.

"Here," I said, handing the chocolate roll to Win. "It's really good." *Someone might as well enjoy it.*

Win opened the cover, swiped the icing with her fingers and licked them.

"We have to wake the man first. Go bang on the door or something," Tetyana said thoughtfully as she reached over to break a piece of the cake. "Then, we have to figure out how to take the key without him realizing. That's where the pills come in handy."

"What do they do?" I asked, looking at the container.

"Put him back to sleep," Tetyana said, with a wry smile. "He managed to do that all by himself, I know. But we need him out here, sleeping, so we can grab the gun and the keys and get out with minimum fuss. Without arousing the authorities outside."

"How do we get out?" I asked. "Through the passageway?"

"What passageway?" Luc asked.

"That won't work," Win said, looking slightly sheepish.

"How do you know?" I said.

She shot Tetyana an embarrassed look. "Sorry, I know you wanted me to watch the back door, but I went exploring a bit just in case."

Tetyana merely raised her eyebrows.

"So did you find anything?" I said.

Win shook her head. "There's a door in the basement, but it opens to a cellar. There's no way out there. Just found some stale food in the back."

"Food?" I looked at her in surprise. *We went on a wild goose chase for food when there was some right here?*

"Not much," Win said. "One small bag of old flour, a can of oil and a bag of moldy potatoes. There's also a loaf of bread, but it's gone hard. Must have been sitting there for ages. There's nothing to proper to eat or to get Zero out."

We were silent for a minute, everyone in deep thought.

A phone rang, startling all of us. With trembling fingers, Luc pulled a phone out of his pocket and turned it on.

"*Oui,*" he said to the mouthpiece.

I strained to listen. It was a man's voice on the other end.

"Just preparing the delivery right now," Luc said with a worried look his face.

We stared at him. He turned away from us, still focused on the phone, but we could still hear him.

"Sure," he was saying. "But can I get an extra hour?"

Tetyana gave me a quizzical look. I shrugged.

"The thing is," Luc stammered, "there's police everywhere. Can't rush it, man."

Silence.

"Come on man, give me a break, will—"

The phone line went dead.

"*Merde!*" Shit.

Luc stared at the phone for a few seconds before switching it off. Then, he turned around slowly to face us.

We watched him silently, warily.

He cleared his throat. "I er forgot to tell you something."

Tetyana's eyes narrowed. "Apparently."

"While you were away—er—procuring your chocolate roll, Asha," he said with a side glance at me, "I sold some of my packets to make some money."

"Who are these people? You know them from London?" Tetyana asked, her brow furrowed.

Luc nodded. "My crew in Paris knows these guys. There's always someone who knows someone, so I just had to connect the dots. It's a small world."

"How did you do that with the police around?"

"The cops never go to the immigrant district. They burn police cars there. They hate white people coming in. Same thing in Paris, Amsterdam, and Berlin. But I know these guys so it always works for me."

Luc reached into his pocket and pulled out a wad of cash.

We huddled closer to take a look.

"This is the deposit," he said. "They gave me two hundred, but I spent most of it on the pills." He looked down at the phone in his hand. "They gave me this to call for the pickup." He paused. "And to track me."

This was news to me. I looked at the phone.

"Why did you take such a risk?" I asked.

"How did you think I'd find money to buy the food and the pills?"

"Take it," I said, ignoring the guilty pang that went through me. "Like I did."

"You were lucky," Luc said. "You think we can go around stealing stuff and get away in the immigrant district? They'd beat me up in a heartbeat. And *you*, they'll do things to you, you'll never sleep for the rest of your life."

I shivered under the robe.

"You say one wrong word, they get offended and you're dead. You gotta negotiate with these people. That's how you survive."

"We didn't need all that food," I said. "The chocolate roll would have done the job."

"Zero doesn't even like chocolate!" Luc snapped.

"People, people," Tetyana said. "We're here now. Let's move on, okay?"

Luc shrugged. "I was trying my best."

"You both were," Tetyana said gently. "So when's the delivery?"

"In two hours," Luc said.

I looked at him aghast. "So we have to wake Zero up, get him outside, put him to sleep again, rescue Katy, run out and deliver drugs in two hours?"

"We'll find a way," Luc said looking away. "We always do."

"There's one big problem," Tetyana said. "How to get the packets out without those cops intercepting?"

"They didn't check us when we got back," I said.

"Don't let that fool you. They can stop you at any time. Again and again, if they feel like it, and if they take you away, I won't be able to help you."

"Can we just ignore them, these drug men? I mean, we have the police all around us, right? They're good protection."

"Cops won't be here forever," Tetyana replied. "They make a lot of fuss for a day or two, check everyone, then move to a new place."

"Why can't we get these drug men to come here, then?" Win asked. "Then, it will be their problem."

"Good thinking, Win, but that'd be too dangerous," Luc said, shaking his head. "The police probably know all of them. They won't want to come anywhere near here and show their faces."

"Recipe for a gun battle," Tetyana said, nodding. "And we'll be right in the crosshairs."

Recipe? My mind began to whir.

"We need a waterproof system. Those dogs smell everything," Luc said. "And the police know all the tricks."

"I know a woman in Bangkok who swallowed a package, and it burst in her tummy in the plane," Win said.

"Extreme," Luc said.

"She died," Win said.

"I know a Russian woman who hid packets in her implants," Tetyana said. "But they found her out pretty fast."

"Luc," I said, an idea solidifying in my mind. "Can you break your stuff into tiny packets? Say this size?" I showed a three-inch gap using my fingers.

"Should work."

"I think I know how to confuse the police dogs," I said. "And get your packets to those men."

"They're smarter than you think," Tetyana said. "The dogs, I mean."

"There's a risk, but there's always a risk," I said.

Tetyana gave me a long, thoughtful stare. "How long you need?"

"Thirty minutes tops."

Chapter Thirty-one

"Oh my god, he's so cute!"

"Take picture with me!"

I stared at the little boy peeing brazenly in front of everyone.

A throng of older Japanese women were giggling and jostling each other to take a picture of the two-foot bronze statue posing in all his naked glory, unabashedly urinating into a stone fountain. The statue was near a busy street full of lace shops, chocolatiers, and buzzing tourists.

"I used to do that all the time as a kid and they yelled at me," Luc said. "If I did that now, they'd arrest me or something."

We were walking toward Brussels' *Grand-Place* looking for his "partner," as Luc called the man from the market we were supposed to meet. Back at the house, we'd banged on the door, called out and made enough noise to wake the devil, but the real devil, Zero, had slept through it all. The plan now was for us to deliver the packets and return quickly to help Tetyana figure out her part of the mission.

It bothered me to leave her and Win alone to battle the madman. I was also worried sick about Katy. At least she knew we were working on a plan to get her out. After another huddle, we decided the delivery job had to be taken care of quickly, and it would be better for me to go with Luc to show the police what a lovely, sweet couple we were.

No one bothered us when we walked out. The police dog was nowhere to be seen and no one seemed to notice us. I ditched Bibi's robe in the same spot as before and walked freely in the streets of Brussels.

"Are you sure he said pissing girl?" I said. "Not pissing boy?"

"That's what he said." Luc furrowed his brow as he tried to recollect the instructions the man had barked at him through the phone.

"He said go three streets up to Delirium Café. But the GPS doesn't show any statues over there."

He stopped to fiddle with the map on his phone. It had taken us longer than we'd planned to get here, as we'd dived into side streets every time we saw anyone remotely resembling the authorities. By the time the GPS recalibrated and got us back on track again, we were late for our appointment.

While Luc fought with the GPS, cursing it in an impressive array of languages, I stood on the sidewalk gawking at the architecture around us. We were surrounded by thousand-year-old buildings, each adorned with intricate carvings and exquisite wrought-iron balconies. I'd seen these sights in Mrs. Rao's fancy travel magazines, but I'd never dreamed I'd be lucky enough to see them in real life.

I wasn't the only person mesmerized by what I saw. Every tourist had their camera trained on building facades, doorways, balconies, and statues. Despite everything that was going on, it felt good to be in this beautiful place, under the warm sun, taking in the happy sounds and smells around us.

"*Merde!* Why can't this stupid phone work?" Luc muttered. "Okay, let's cut across here to get to the other side." He ushered me through a cobblestone alleyway. "It's a shortcut, I think."

My jaw dropped as we walked into the shortcut.

If I'd thought the streets outside had been opulent, this place was magnificent beyond belief. It was an immense square we'd walked into, a majestic cobblestone space flanked by stately buildings, clustered so close together it was difficult to spot the passageways out. I looked around in awe. Surrounding this football field-sized square were medieval structures with beautifully preserved gilded roofs pointing to the sky. If the modern light fixtures and tourists disappeared, I could easily imagine having time-traveled to a royal court of the seventeenth century.

We started crossing the square. Jotted here and there were street artists and vendors selling everything from paintings to flowers to figurines. The square was teeming with tourists from every part of the world, taking pictures and buying waffles and ice cream.

But I couldn't afford to linger. We kept walking through the crowds, past the quaint lace boutiques, past the famous Belgian chocolate shops, past the outdoor cafés where people sat drinking coffee and beer and watching other people stroll by.

Luc checked his phone every few seconds to make sure we were heading the right way.

"Oh, no!" I said.

"What?"

I nudged him and nodded in the direction of two hefty men in uniform. They were walking through the crowd toward us and one of them had a hulking police dog on a leash.

"I guess this is going to be the sniff test," I whispered.

If we lose this, we're done.

"They're here to stop pickpocketing," Luc whispered.

"I'm worried about the dog," I said.

The officers were now twenty feet away from us, casually scanning the crowd. From where I stood, the dog looked like an overgrown monster. I could almost imagine its bared fangs ripping at my throat.

All of a sudden, I felt exposed, like the entire square knew what I was carrying. It was like I was emanating a neon radiation light that declared, "Here! Check these babies out."

I glanced around nervously, but no one was scrutinizing us, not even the cops. Yet they were our way, pulled by the Alsatian's nose. I felt Luc's hand squeeze mine. We slowed to a stroll and pretended to admire the chocolate shop nearby.

Should we slip inside?

The officers were only fifteen feet from us now. They were so close I could hear the dog panting as it pulled on the leash, its nose intensely on the ground.

I did the only thing I could think of. With a discreet twist of my hand, I pulled the dishcloth that had been covering the cupcakes I was carrying, and let it fall to the ground.

"Oh, no," I cried out, putting my hand on my mouth. "My cakes! My beautiful cakes!"

A gust of wind whipped the dishcloth right in the direction of the cops. Luc ran after it.

Oh, god.

"Stop!"

I looked up, startled. The police officer had yanked at the dog's chain so hard, it had almost flown back toward its master. The officer said something sharply to it. The second officer bent down, picked up the cloth and handed it to Luc.

"*Merci, monsieur!*" Luc said, giving his best smile to the men. "*Dank u wel!*" He came back with the dishcloth in hand, breathless, his cheeks bright pink.

I took my time covering the cakes. I wanted the world to see their fluffy swirls. With one woeful look at us, the dog followed its human colleagues. We watched with half-frozen smiles as the officers disappeared into the crowd.

I let out a breath. "Phew, that was close."

"Good thinking," Luc said. "Now how to get the hell out of here?"

"There can't be that many exits out of this place, can there?" I glanced around but it was hard to see between the crowds and the crowded rows of buildings.

Luc didn't answer. His nose was on his phone, trying to zoom into the map.

"Maybe we should ask someone?"

"No," Luc said, his fingers busily tapping on the map.

That was when I saw her right in front of us. It was a slightly hunched woman, with perfectly done-up white hair, a designer tote in one hand and a smart-looking umbrella in the other. She was alone, carried no camera, and was walking toward a chocolatier, using the umbrella as a walking stick.

"*Bonjour, madame*," I said, turning to her. "Good afternoon," I added, remembering Luc's language tip earlier.

She looked me over from head to toe and sniffed.

"*Excusez moi*," I said. "Are you from Brussels?"

"*Absolument*," she said, without a smile.

"We're looking for the pissing girl. Do you know where she is?"

"Pissing girl?" she said, giving me a look of severe disapproval.

"Er," I said, "I meant to say the girl version of the boy over there, going to the toilet. The one peeing, I mean urinating." I felt my face go warm.

"Ah, you mean the *Mannekin Pis*? He's our symbol."

"Yes, but we're looking for the girl."

"*Jeanneke Pis*!" the woman said, tapping her umbrella on the ground impatiently. "The brother is named *Mannekin Pis* and his sister is called *Jeanneke Pis*. Do you not know this?"

"No, sorry," I said. I felt like I'd touched a raw nerve.

"You have to get these things right, you know. And you must also refer to *Zinneke Pis*."

"*Zinneke*?"

"Asha," Luc said, in a warning voice. I felt his hand pull on my elbow.

"You did know there is a dog in the family, didn't you?" the woman said, now standing close to me. "Brussels is not all about beer, as you young people think. There is culture here! You need to learn about the places you travel to!"

"I'm so sorry. I didn't mean to...," I stammered, regretting starting the conversation.

"Well, you should be sorry." Her gray eyes drilled into mine. "When you go to London you see street puppet shows. When you go to Paris, you visit Montmartre, and when you go to Copenhagen you learn about the Little Mermaid, do you not?"

"Asha." Luc pulled at me again.

"Er...thanks so much, madame, but I think I have to go—"

The woman raised her umbrella and pointed to an alleyway we hadn't noticed earlier. "That way. Second exit. You will find your *pissing girl* there." She said those last few words with more venom in her voice than I thought necessary.

Merci beaucoup, madame." I almost curtsied. "*Un grand merci.*"

"Well, at least you speak some French." she said, looking slightly satisfied. "Foreigners." She shook her head and walked off, her umbrella clicking angrily on the cobblestones with every step.

"What are you doing?" Luc whispered in my ear as he pulled me away. "Talking to strangers!"

"She helped us, didn't she?"

"We can't go around talking to people with drugs in our hands."

Shh. Don't use that word." I still hadn't come to terms with what I was doing. It was one more thing to add to my growing rap sheet.

We hurried toward the alleyway the woman had pointed to. As soon as we stepped into the corridor, the air around us changed instantly.

We'd moved from the hustle and bustle of the large square full of tourists to a cooler, darker little street with almost no one around. A few pubs and small restaurants scattered the alleyway, but they were quiet, dark, brooding.

"There!" Luc said, pointing. "I see her!"

A roar of laughter startled us. We turned around to see three men shakily climb out of a narrow stairway coming from a sunken doorway. We were standing next to the entrance of an underground pub. The sign above the steps said, "Delirium, all five hundred Belgium beers on tap and more." The men stumbled down the alleyway, barely keeping upright.

I squinted to where Luc had pointed. He's right. She was here, in a secluded corner of the street, on a ledge in the wall, and secured behind a grill.

The "pissing girl" was a pigtailed three-year-old made of dark gray limestone, squatting naked on a high-placed mantel with a tiny stream of water flowing between her legs into the fountain. Her impish face looked up with an expression that said "What are you looking at?"

I smiled at her cheeky little face.

"She's cute," Luc said. "I like her better than the pissing boy."

"Me too," I said. "How come she's hidden over here while her brother's up there in front of all the tourists?"

"I don—"

"Bonjour Monsieur Luc," a deep voice said inches from our ears.

Luc and I looked up so quickly, we bumped our heads.

Chapter Thirty-two

He was a skinny, clean-shaven man in a pinstriped suit and a Panama hat, looking like he'd just stepped out of the 1920s. He was leaning casually against the wall, hands in his pockets, in the shadows next to the fountain with the girl.

He'd been there all along watching us, I thought.

Even in the dim light, I could see he was smart and sharp, not at all what I'd expect from a small-time drug dealer. There was no comparison between him and the thugs I'd seen on the street earlier with their torn leather jackets and scruffy jeans.

"You must be Monsieur Fred," Luc said, with a slight bow of his head.

"*C'est correct.*" The man beamed, showing tobacco-stained teeth. "*Bonjour mon ami.*"

"*Bonjour,*" Luc said, and softly nudged me. "This is Julie. I mentioned there'd be two of us."

"Yes, yes. We were looking forward to seeing you. It is indeed a great pleasure to meet you, Mademoiselle Julie."

"*Moi aussi,*" I stammered, trying to remember the high school French I'd learned back in Canada. "*Ravi de vous rencontrer.*" "Great to meet you too."

"*Americaine?*" he asked.

"Yes," I said. Even my French accent betrayed me.

Fred bowed his head and for the second time that day, I felt I should curtsy. While he looked a bit like Zero—dark olive skin, brooding eyes, and short, curly hair—his manners were exquisite, and nothing like the crazed man back at the house.

"Sorry about the delay," Luc said. "We've been walking all over the place looking for—" He cocked his head toward the little naked statue squatting behind the grille bar. "Looking for her."

"Have you seen her esteemed brother on the other side of *La Grand-Place*?" Fred asked.

We nodded.

"He is indeed popular with the tourists and is one of Belgium's national treasures." Fred flashed a big smile. "Did you know that statue is more than three hundred and fifty years old?"

"Wow," Luc and I said in unison.

"Legend tells us how Brussels was under attack and the enemy had set up a fire to burn the city down. But a little boy who saw the burning wick pulled down his pants, urinated on it and put the fire out. Imagine that."

Luc nodded with a grave expression on his face.

I looked at Fred and then at Luc closely. *Is all this code for something?*

"That statue was built in the memory of that brave young boy," Fred said, raising his arm so expansively, his jacket flapped open, showing the black gun on his belt. I looked at it startled. *That wasn't done accidentally.*

Fred gave me a genial smile. "I should know all this. You see, if I may say so humbly myself, I do have a doctorate in world history."

He bowed again.

"Bravo," Luc said.

Fred straightened up and cleared his throat like he was about to give us another history lecture. I was at a loss for words. We'd just met the most educated and polite drug dealer in all of Europe. But we didn't have time for this, not with Katy tied up in the attic.

I nudged Luc. "We need to get back home soon, no?"

"Monsieur Fred," Luc said, his worried face returning, "May we talk business now?"

"*Non! Absolument non!*"

Fred looked so appalled, I drew back in surprise.

"You must never rush business. Why, we just met. One must have a good mint tea first and inquire about each other's families at the least." He shook a long, skinny finger at Luc. "You've been hanging out with our dear American friends too long. Haha!" He laughed at his own joke.

"Sure. Tea's fine," Luc said uncertainly. He pointed at the tray I was carrying. "We did bring your merchandise. It's right in there."

I lifted the dishcloth daintily to show what was underneath.

"Cakes?" Fred said, beaming. "They look beautiful."

"Thank you," I said automatically.

"This is *The Delivery*," Luc explained, raising his eyebrows.

"Come now, *mes chers amis*," Fred said ignoring Luc's comment. He stepped out of the shadows. "I know of a very good coffeehouse where we may sit and enjoy some good Moroccan tea. I would be delighted to discuss your lovely cakes then."

He led the way up the street and we stepped behind him, perplexed.

"Are you sure he's the right guy?" I whispered to Luc. He shrugged.

"Monsieur Luc," Fred said, casually turning back to us.

"*Oui*, Monsieur Fred," Luc replied quickly.

"Your reputation from London precedes you, *mon cher monsieur Luc,* did you know that?"

Luc's face went slightly pale.

On our long walk to this rendezvous, Luc had explained how these gangs worked across Europe. He'd told me about the intricate but dangerous alliances they formed, arrangements you didn't want to mess with. They were stronger than the European police forces and INTERPOL combined, according to Luc, and they had their own free trade system, now that the borders were open within the EU. We had to tread carefully.

The three of us walked down the street, with me flanked by the two men. Luc remained silent, while Fred did all the talking.

"So you like sweets?" Fred asked. "Have you tried any Moroccan sweets yet, mademoiselle?"

"No," I said. "Never had any."

"Well then, we must certainly try some date cake today. It's from my homeland, Morocco," he said, spreading his hands out. "How lovely it is to introduce new friends to good foods they've never tried before!"

I forced a smile.

"Do you know what a date cake is?"

I shook my head.

"It is indeed an exceptional dessert," he said, kissing his fingertips. "Superb, but not difficult to make. I bake it for my mother's birthday every year. Dates are very healthy for you, you know, and it is the oldest cultivated fruit in the history of mankind."

I looked at Luc, puzzled. *Who is this man? A drug dealer, a world historian, a foodie, or a nutcase?*

Fred led us through the maze of cobblestone streets to a coffeehouse a few blocks from the pissing girl's fountain.

Walking in, my mind flashed back to the café I'd stumbled into almost four days ago in London. A haze of smoke from the hookah pipes hung in the air. Red and gold tasseled cushions were laid out haphazardly on beautiful Persian carpets. Like last time, there were only men inside. Luc stepped in, looking distinctly uncomfortable. I guessed he hadn't expected this. Neither had I.

Fred led us to a dark corner where a blue rug was strewn with piles of cushions.

"Please," Fred said, bowing deeply to me. I removed my shoes, stepped onto the rug, and kneeled down. I placed the cake tray in the middle of the carpet and gave Luc a look that said, *You take care of this. He's your problem.* We sat in a circle, fake smiles on our faces, nodding awkwardly at Fred's history anecdotes until a waiter came to take our order.

The waiter, dressed in embroidered pants and shirt, looked like he'd just been whisked out of Aladdin's magic lamp. On his head was a blue turban, and on his feet were Arabian slippers I'd seen before at the immigrant market. But what struck me most was the curved steel dagger on his belt.

Since when do waiters walk around with naked knives in their belts?

In a quiet voice to the side, Fred ordered mint tea and date cakes for everyone. He turned and flashed his grand smile at me again. "You will absolutely love the cake, I assure you, mademoiselle. They make it almost as good as I do. Haha! *Almost.*"

I smiled back politely. "I'm sure I will," I said, feeling my stomach constrict slightly.

"The trick is to keep the oven temperature low and leave the cake in longer. That is what makes it moist. And that is the most important thing, isn't it?"

I nodded noncommittally.

"So tell me, how do you keep your cakes moist?" Fred smiled in earnest. "Do tell."

I shot Luc a worried look. Was he talking about real cakes or the delivery we'd bought with us?

Luc gave a miserable shrug.

"Well," I said, turning back to Fred. "Using the best ingredients always helps, but when I make my island fruit cakes, I soak them in rum and let them marinate for a while. That makes them really moist."

I felt Luc gently squeeze my elbow. Fred fixed me with an unhappy expression.

What?

"That is a very interesting idea, indeed. A very interesting but foreign idea," Fred said, shaking his head. "You see, we do not endorse alcohol in baking, mademoiselle. Or in anything for that matter." He looked at me sadly.

"I'm sorry," I stammered. "I didn't mean any—"

Just then, the waiter came, carrying a bronze tray with a fancy teapot and cakes.

Fred made a grand gesture of serving us tea, and we drank in silence for a few minutes. The waiter, however, didn't leave. He stood silently behind us, like a mysterious jinn waiting for his master to call for him.

I tried not to look at Fred. I wanted to leave this place, and leave it fast. Tetyana's quick-thinking street smarts were all they had to rely on back at the house, but even she might not be able to tackle Zero, with or without Win's help.

Luc cleared his throat after a sip. "This is delicious tea, Monsieur Fred."

"We use the best in the world." Fred smiled happily again, all his teeth showing. Something about it made my body and mind go on full alert like I had to prepare to defend myself. From what exactly, I didn't know.

"This is the tea of the Berbers, the first settlers of Morocco," he said, turning to me. "Did you know the Berbers can be traced back to almost four thousand years ago? Four thousand years of North African history in this cup of tea. Imagine." He paused and looked at me. "Now, tell me, my dear friend from across the Atlantic, how old is the United States of America?"

I stared at him silently. *We don't have time for this.*

"Only two hundred and thirty odd years, I believe," he said, smiling prettily. "You're a very young nation indeed."

I gave him a frozen smile. *He calls himself a historian and he forgot all—*

"Well, of course, you must not forget to take into account the aboriginal cultures that survived well before that." He winked at me.

"Ahem." Luc cleared his throat, louder this time. "Is this a good time to get into business, Monsieur Fred?"

"Absolutely, we can discuss business at any time you desire, Monsieur Luc," Fred said, spreading his hands out as if he'd never suggested anything different.

"Okay, then." Luc lowered his voice and pointed discreetly at the cake tray in the middle of the rug. "The *merchandise* is secured inside there."

That was my cue. I pulled the dishcloth off with a swoosh, and my make-believe cakes beamed under the light, looking tantalizing and devilish, just like they were supposed to. Our job was over. It was time to go back.

"Ah!" Fred said, "How delightful. Are these your creations, mademoiselle?"

"Yes." I nodded. Despite their looks, the cakes smelled to high heaven. And for good reason. I wondered if Fred smelled them too.

After our group huddle near the attic with Tetyana, I'd followed Win to the basement. She was right. There was nothing edible in there. On top of what she'd already discovered, I found a gallon of petrol in a rusty can in a corner.

With Win's help, I picked up what I could use and walked into the kitchen. Within half an hour, I'd made a dozen barely risen, tasteless, toxic cake-like objects. Since I couldn't find any baking pans in the kitchen, I used leftover aluminum foil instead, just like I had for my very first batch of real cupcakes in Goa a long time ago.

Once the cakes were baked, I hollowed them out, inserted Luc's small packets snug into the holes and covered them back up. Then, as Luc and Win watched, fascinated, I used the smashed potatoes to make yellow swirls of topping on each cake.

"You must tell me the origins and name of these exotic sweets," Fred said, looking at me expectantly.

"Er," I gave Luc a side glance, "these are cupcakes."

"They look simply delicious," Fred said. "It would be a great honor for me to try your *Americaine* cupcakes."

His hand hovered over the cake tray and, before I could say anything, he plucked the biggest cake and bit into it.

Chapter Thirty-three

"**N**o!" Luc and I leaped up at the same time.

But it was too late.

Fred's face went red as he spat into his napkin. He doubled up, moaning. I watched horrified, my hand on my mouth. He didn't move for several seconds. The waiter stepped closer, hovering over Fred.

When he straightened up, Fred's face was a mix of confusion and disgust. Spitting out a delicacy brought by a guest was probably the most impolite thing he'd done that day. That was also probably the healthiest thing he'd done that day.

"I'm so sorry," I spluttered. "I didn't mean for you to eat it."

"They conceal the merchandise," Luc whispered, taking a second cake and splitting it open. The white packet jutting out of the pastry was unmistakable. He pulled the packet out, wiped it clean with his napkin, and deposited it on Fred's plate. "*Vous voyez?* You see now?"

Fred stared at the packet for five long seconds. Then put his half-chewed cake back on the tray like it was a live grenade.

"What, in god's name, did you put in that?" Fred said, turning to me. "Pray tell."

"Petrol."

He looked at me shocked and wiped his mouth, grimacing. "*Petrol?*" he whispered.

"So the dogs won't smell the other stuff," I said.

Fred stared at me for several seconds. A rivulet of sweat ran down my back. I thought of the dagger on the waiter's belt and the gun on Fred's. *They're going to finish me right here, right now. And do it so politely too.* I braced myself.

"Brilliant," Fred said finally. "*Absolument brillant.*" He paused. "And I thought the traffic fumes were particularly bad today."

I watched him warily. He was watching me too, his face intense.

"Mademoiselle Julie," he said, looking straight into my eyes.

I clenched my sweaty palms into fists. *I didn't come this far to go out quietly. I'm ready to fight if I have to.*

"Will you work for me?"

I looked at him in surprise.

"I may be just a *pied-noir*, but I can assure you, mademoiselle, that I pay better than anyone else in this business, even the local Belges."

It took me a few seconds to collect my thoughts. "I er—already work for someone."

"Would that be our dear Monsieur Luc here?" Fred said.

"No," I said. I couldn't get Luc into any more trouble. "Someone in London. Someone who won't let me go easily."

"I wouldn't either."

Fred surveyed me with curious eyes.

"Where are you really from, mademoiselle?"

"Many places," I said, looking directly back at him. I can play his game too, I thought.

"Is Julie your real name?"

"It is now," I said, not wavering in my gaze.

Fred was quiet for a minute, rubbing the white packet between his fingers thoughtfully.

I took a deep breath in. *We could stay here and play all day, but we don't have time.*

I was about to get up when he reached into his jacket pocket and pulled out a Swiss Army Knife. Next to me, Luc recoiled at the sight. Like he'd done this many times, Fred deftly snapped the knife open, sliced a corner of the plastic packet and shook a few drops of the powder onto his plate. He slid his finger over it, sniffed it, and put a trace of it on the tip of his tongue.

We waited. It seemed like Luc had stopped breathing at this point.

"According to your reputation, Monsieur Luc, you don't disappoint your clients," Fred said. He paused dramatically. "And that is indeed correct."

Luc let out his breath.

"Monsieur Fred," I spoke up. "If you're happy with the merchandise, we need to take our leave now."

Is it just me, or did the waiter move closer?

Fred, pretended to stretch, exposing his gun again.

"I would be happy to let you take your leave, mademoiselle et monsieur," he said. "If you would kindly promise one thing."

Luc and I glanced at each other. *What does he want?*

"Bring me more." Fred tapped the white packet.

Luc remained silent.

"I know you're a good-hearted, honest French boy." Fred's voice had turned slightly darker. "I've been watching your work for a while now. Maybe if I tell you I give a percentage of my profits to charity, that will motivate you?"

Luc wasn't even meeting Fred's eyes. I could feel him breathing fast.

"It's how I give back," Fred said with a chuckle. "I see nothing wrong in giving some of my profits to the famine charities back in Africa." His smile widened as he turned to me. "Here's a small history fact for you, my young American friend. When Algeria rebelled against their colonizers starting in nineteen fifty-four, the streets ran with the blood of one and a half million of my Maghreb brethren. Now, don't you think I'm a kind man to attempt some sort of reparation, mademoiselle?"

I gave him a blank stare.

He's mad. Totally insane. We don't have time for these games. I've got to get back to Katy.

"Shall we say midnight tonight, then?" Fred said with a confident smile, though Luc hadn't even responded. There was an evil glint in Fred's eyes. It had always been there, I thought, masked by all that fake civility.

Luc's face had gone slightly pink. I knew he'd only had time to grab a few of his packets when we ran from London and all that was now inside the cakes.

Fred settled himself comfortably into his cushions, still watching Luc intently. "You know, I heard some interesting news through the grapevine recently."

I felt like I was in the company of a cobra, its head spread out, swaying this way and that, toying with us before it moved in with lightning speed to sink its fangs in us.

"I heard a van full of girls crossed the border recently."

I gasped. If Fred had heard me, he didn't show it. His eyes remained firmly on Luc. He didn't even blink.

"Coincidently, Europol are searching for a murder suspect who supposedly fled a brothel in London, leaving behind the dead body of a young police officer."

How does he know all this?

"I understand you don't have many options, Monsieur Luc," Fred said, in a steely voice. "We can protect you. This can be lucrative for you and me. For all of us." He bowed slightly in my direction. "We will, however, need more batches than this. Many more. Can you do this?"

"It will be difficult," Luc mumbled.

"Nothing in life is easy, Monsieur Luc."

Luc fell silent.

"Do we have a deal?" Fred said, smiling a smile that could charm a snake.

The waiter was now right behind Luc and me, inches away.

Luc was cornered. He sighed and nodded.

Fred offered a clawlike hand across the rug. Luc looked at it for a few seconds before offering his own limp one. Fred beamed. He turned to me. Feeling like I was about to touch a slippery reptile, I gave my hand. Instead of shaking it, he took it and brought it to his lips.

I suppressed an urge to retch.

Chapter Thirty-four

When we returned to our street, we hardly recognized it.

The tinted police vans, the patrolling officers and the sniffing dogs had vanished. Except for the wooden barricades stacked on the side of the street to be picked up later, it was like they'd never been here.

It had taken us less time to return to the house, partly because we no longer needed to dodge into side alleys, and partly because we ran all the way back, nonstop. The only pit stop we made was to retrieve Bibi's robe from its hiding place at the neighboring building.

I was just about to crash through the back door of the house when Luc pulled me back.

He put a finger to his lips. I nodded and turned the knob quietly. We stepped into the kitchen and stopped. An eerie silence.

"Do you think they packed up and left?" I whispered to Luc.

Luc shook his head. "Van's still parked out."

We stood silently and listened. Though it was midafternoon, it was dark inside the house and no one had turned on the lights. I couldn't hear anything, but something in my gut said the house wasn't empty.

Not all was right.

Luc bent down and removed his shoes, taking care to not make a sound. I pulled my heels off as well and tucked them under one arm. Luc reached over and picked up the knife lying on the kitchen counter, the one I'd improvised to mix the cake batter earlier.

He motioned me to get behind him. We tiptoed to the second floor, Luc holding the knife and me holding up Bibi's robe so as to not trip or fall.

We weren't prepared for what lay on the second-floor landing.

Zero's door was flung open but he wasn't inside. No one was.

The meal container on the table had been ripped open and everything had been devoured, like a pack of dogs had attacked the food. There were fresh curry stains all over the table and crumbs of *naan* on the floor. On the corner of the table lay my beautiful chocolate roll, half-eaten, icing smeared all over the packaging.

Disgusting, I thought. *But where is everyone?*

That was when I heard a noise. I strained to listen. Something or someone was upstairs on the third floor.

Luc motioned that he'd go up first. I hiked up Bibi's robe, clutched my shoes tightly so they wouldn't fall, and followed him.

Halfway up, I heard slow, heavy breathing coming from the third floor. A few more steps up and Luc froze. I crept up next to him and nearly gasped. We could only see part of the third floor from where we were, but that was enough.

At the top of the stairway, with his back to us, was Zero holding a gun to Win's head. She looked pale. On the other end of the landing, we could see part of Tetyana, and she looked furious. She was looking straight at Zero, but her gun was pointed at someone or something else.

No one was talking.

Zero was breathing heavily, swaying from side to side. Tetyana's eyes flickered only for a semi-second as she caught sight of us, but her face remained still. The two of them stood in this silent standoff for half a minute.

Zero spoke first. "You know I kill everyone." His voice slurred and unsteady.

"One bullet in her is one bullet in him," Tetyana snapped.

"Do I care?" Zero said. "Shoot the dickhead."

"Right!" Tetyana barked. "If he didn't have the password for our account, you'd have shot him by now. Did you think I wouldn't figure that out?"

"You whore," Zero slurred. He swayed from side to side.

I watched him in alarm. He was still under the influence of the drugs. He buckled and leaned on Win for support. It was like watching a full-grown bull crush a slender young calf. Win pushed and tried to stand upright despite Zero's weight on her.

"Let her go!" Tetyana commanded.

Zero clutched Win by the neck. He was choking her now. She tried to wiggle out, but he had a death grip on her. She struggled, gasping for air.

"You're going to kill her, you bastard!" yelled Tetyana. "Let her go! Now!"

The image of Win lying on the ground at the London square flashed across my mind. My mind raged. The image of the bloodied yellow blouse of that girl in the warehouse came next. Something in me snapped.

"Aargh!"

Before I knew it, I bounded up the steps with a warrior cry I didn't know I had in me and slammed my shoe heel to the side of Zero's face. Once. Twice. Three times.

"Let her go! You bastard!" I screamed as I slammed him, aiming for his ears, his eyes, and his throat. Zero let go of Win in alarm. She folded to the ground.

Zero roared in fury. "You she-devil!"

He reeled back and stared at me stupefied. And that moment was all I needed. I raised my heel and aimed at his right eye. A direct hit.

Through my eye slit, I vaguely saw a hand come crashing down. I ducked just in time. With a surprised yell, Zero fell with a thud to the floor. Tetyana shouted something. I heard a holler from Luc.

Adrenaline was pumping in my red-hot blood now. I jumped on Zero's back and rained blows from my heel onto the back of his head. I dug my knees in, kicking him whenever he tried to get back up.

"This is for Bibi, you dick!" I screamed with every blow I gave. "This is for Katy!" "This is for Win!"

But that robe became my liability.

It severely limited my vision and movement. I wasn't ready when he twisted around and pulled on it with force. I felt myself come crashing to the ground on my back. I couldn't see anything but I kept hammering, screaming, fighting with every ounce of energy I had.

Zero's movements were sluggish but strong. He slammed a fist down but hit the floor instead. I kept punching, sometimes hitting flesh, other times air.

Suddenly, with a blood-curdling cry, Zero fell on me, squeezing the breath out of me. His hands went to my throat and tightened. I was trapped. I writhed under him, gasping for air.

Without a warning, a gunshot rang out, shaking the whole house.

Zero's hands softened. I could breathe again.

Silence.

Someone pushed Zero's body off me and pulled me up. I stood for a moment, trying to catch my breath. The robe felt claustrophobic like it was choking me too. I tugged at it and pulled it off with someone's help. I threw it on the ground and looked around.

Win was standing close to me, looking frightened to death, but alive. She must have helped me with my robe.

Tetyana and Luc pulled a lifeless Zero to the side. She gave him a swift kick before picking up his gun and tucking it in her boot. She still had hers in her hand. Luc wiped his knife on Zero's shirt. I noticed blood on it. *Where did that come from?*

Vlad was still gagged and bound in a corner, with bloody gashes on his face. He was looking at the scene with bulging, blood-stained eyes. It was the first time he'd seen me, and he clearly didn't know what to make of it all. I was just as confused. *Who shot the gun? Is Zero dead?*

Luc and Tetyana rooted urgently through Zero's pockets.

The key to get Katy out!

Instead, Tetyana pulled out a black tube. "Would have helped to have this a minute ago."

"What's that?" I asked.

"Silencer."

"Did you *kill* him?" Win whispered in a terrified voice.

"Just got his kneecap so he'll be crawling for the rest of his life," Tetyana said. "Got enough dead bodies to worry about. No need to add two more."

Enough dead bodies?

"Did you stab him?" I asked, pointing at the bloodied knife.

"Luc jumped on him when he was trying to choke you, but the man didn't even feel it. Too drugged out. That's why I shot him."

"Thanks," I stammered, "but, but...what if someone calls the police about the gunshot?"

"In this neighborhood?" Luc said with a raised eyebrow. "No one's gonna want any attention on them, I think."

"What about our fingerprints?" Win asked. "Won't the police come after us?"

"No one's going to believe a bunch of brothel girls did this," Tetyana said, surveying the room.

As if she'd done this a hundred times before, she fit the silencer tube onto her gun and stuck it on her belt. She ripped up the remaining piece of bedsheet and began to tie Zero up. With Luc's help, she worked fast and furiously, shifting his limbs into the most uncomfortable positions.

A low moan came from Zero. Her lips curled with scorn. He had only a second to whimper behind his gag before she gave him a thundering whack to the head with a gun. He collapsed forward.

"What a coward," she said. "You fought him well, Asha. But he's not dead. Not yet anyway."

"A cop killer's gonna get what he deserves," Luc said, with a hint of satisfaction in his voice.

Chapter Thirty-five

Luc rummaged through Zero's pockets.

With a yell, he held up a small bronze object. It took my bleary mind a second to realize what it was. I jumped on it.

I ran to the attic door, shouting, "Katy! We're gonna get you out!" With trembling hands, I slipped the key in the hole, swung the door open and sprang toward her.

She'd been tied up for half a day now, and looked it. With trembling hands, I began to untie her. Win came to help me.

While we'd been working to get Zero to open the attic door earlier, he'd done a good job tying Katy up really well. It took several tries to get her mouth gag undone and Win struggled with the knots on her ankle.

"You'll be fine, honey, you'll be okay," I kept saying over and over again as I tackled the twists in the cloth. When I finally removed the gag, I saw tears streaming down Katy's face.

"Oh my god, Katy. I'm so sorry."

She stood up shakily and reached out to me. I threw my arms around her and hugged her tightly. She started to sob on my shoulder.

"Hey, you're safe now. I'd never leave you behind."

"You'll be okay," said a small voice next to us. "Don't cry."

We pulled Win into the hug.

"Girls!"

We looked up to see Tetyana motion to us. Her voice was urgent, hurried. "We can do reunions later. We need to clean up and leave now."

We stepped out of the room and joined them on the landing.

Tetyana and Luc had rearranged the room.

Zero was on the floor with my batter mixing knife in his right hand. I noticed blood seeping near his knees. The mobile phone Fred and his gang had lent to Luc was placed strategically in his left hand. The screen was lit up.

"What about tonight's delivery?" I asked, suddenly remembering our other problem.

"They'll come straight here," Luc said. "No doubt about that."

"We'll let gangs take care of gangs," Tetyana said, with a smug smile.

I looked at the two unconscious men in their twisted positions on the ground. "I just want that girl in the warehouse to not have died in vain," I said.

"I can kill them both now," Tetyana said, with a deadly look on her face. "For that girl, I can do it."

We looked at her wide-eyed.

"But it will be far more interesting to let them live." She paused. "They'll learn what true pain is once the cops grab them and send them to jail to meet their kind."

With that, we quietly shuffled down the stairs to the second floor.

We should have felt elated to be escaping, to have got back at these evil men, but no one was smiling. No one said a word. It was like we were carrying a heavy burden on our shoulders—one that felt the suffering of all the girls these men had hurt for years.

Something in the back of my mind bothered me. It was a memory from not so long ago, niggling to come out.

"Hey, Tetyana," I said, "When we were at the warehouse, you had your phone out. What were you doing?"

"I recorded it," she said, "to blackmail the bastards."

"Why don't we send it to the cops?" I asked, feeling a smidgen of hope rise in me. "There must be good cops somewhere who'll do something if they see it."

Tetyana shook her head. "I keep things simple with one SIM card for voice and I throw it away every few days. Don't have WiFi or a data plan. No one can track my phone. Don't know how I can do that without anyone tracing it back to me."

"That's too bad," I said. "If we can put it online, the world will know what's really happening."

"I can do it."

We all turned to look at Win. She blushed at the attention.

"I can put the video online."

"You can do that?" Katy asked.

"I can transfer the video to Zero's laptop so they won't know it's coming from you."

We stared at her.

"Zero made me fix his laptop all the time. I know all his passwords," she added, with an embarrassed shrug.

"Wow," Luc said, staring at Win.

"Maybe we can tag Europol or INTERPOL or something," I said, feeling hopeful for the first time in a long time.

"I can send it anywhere you want, just tell me and I'll do it."

"How long will it take?" Tetyana asked.

"Ten minutes."

"Sounds like a plan." Tetyana dug her phone out of her pocket and handed it to Win. "Work your magic, hun."

Win stepped toward the stairway and disappeared downstairs to the first floor, presumably to find Zero's laptop.

We looked at each other.

"We can't hang around here for too long," Tetyana said, looking worried.

Luc nodded. "Fred's going be looking for me soon and there's no police to stop them anymore."

We gathered around Win on the living room sofa and watched her handiwork, fascinated. It took her five minutes to upload the video. Her fingers flew across the keyboard, lips pursed, face frowning in concentration.

"So this is going out under Zero's own name and account?" I asked.

She nodded. "He's the only one with the admin password to this forum." She had logged on to a private online forum, switched its status to public before posting the video under Zero's name.

We looked at each other with raised eyebrows.

"Wow," Luc said. "You're good."

"Genius," I said.

"How's he ever going to defend that?" Katy said.

"Wonder what else is on this computer," Tetyana said in a thoughtful voice.

While the video was being uploaded, Win began to poke around Zero's folders. "He's so stupid," she muttered, as she ran a password-unlocking tool to open a folder that had a series of x's in its name. "He doesn't even understand the basic stuff."

She opened the first document in the folder, a plain text file with clearly the addresses of transit warehouses and brothels. Their network spread as far east as Russia, and as far south as Tunisia.

"Oh, my god," Katy said as Win scrolled through the list.

"They're a small part of a bigger operation," said Tetyana peering into the screen.

The next document Win dug up troubled us all.

It was a list of women's names. Only first names. We listened silently, without breathing, as Win scrolled through them, reading name after name. She faltered for only a second when her own name popped up, but she kept moving. I felt a cold shiver go through me. *All these girls going through unimaginable torture.*

"Get rid of that," Tetyana snapped. "Permanently. Safer for the girls."

"Didn't realize how big this was," Luc said, his face slightly pale.

"How did they get away with all this?" Katy asked.

No one had an answer, not even Tetyana.

Win trashed the list and pulled up an app to clean the file for good. "Anyone can read files in the trash can, even after double deleting," she explained. "I have to run a cleanup code to remove it for good."

"Do what you have to, hun," Tetyana said. "How long will that take?"

"Ten minutes, not even," Win said, but she wasn't even looking up, absorbed in her task.

"You're amazing, you know that?" Luc said, giving Win a friendly nudge. Win blushed.

"You're a total whiz," Katy said.

Win's blush deepened. "Zero only used RSA. Anyone can break that." She pointed at a file with a long name of numbers and letters. "Can you believe how stupid that is?"

We shook our heads. I don't think any of us knew what she was even talking about.

"How did you learn all this?" I asked.

"He gave me work to do on his computer because he didn't know how to use it. But if I suggested something, he yelled at me and said, just do what I say. So his security is really bad. Not what I'd do."

"You learned all this by yourself?" I asked.

Win nodded, her head back in the computer now. "I used it every day and took my time. He didn't know I was trying new things. Also, he left me alone and didn't book clients when I worked."

Tetyana let out a big sigh.

The app was still running in the background when Win's eyes fell on another folder. "This one has a long password," she said. We waited patiently, trying not to breathe down her neck, as she tried to figure out how to open it.

I felt goose bumps as a spreadsheet sprang to life on the screen. Win scrolled through a list of names and telephone numbers.

"*Mon dieu!*" Luc said, bringing his hands to his head.

"Jackpot!" Tetyana said.

"What is it?" I asked.

"Look at those names," Luc said, pointing at the screen. I peered over his arm. Most were foreign names, names I didn't recognize. Win kept scrolling. The list was long.

"Minister Oaten," I read out loud. "Michel Patim, Martin Shkel, Tony Berluscono, Chand Deepak, Rodrigo Duter, Mohamed Il-Fayad, Bob Halt—"

"It's a list of Johns, isn't it?" Katy said. "Bob Halt's supposed to be the next James Bond. Wow."

Tetyana leaned back with a self-satisfied look on her face. "That list is going to be saved and go out to the world. Hit the upload button, Win!"

Win did so with a triumphant but shy smile on her face.

Something about that smile made me feel sad. This is what half a decade of physical violence and mental manipulation does to you, I thought. *Grooming*, Tetyana had explained to me earlier. It's when they take a very young girl, beat her and rape her into subjugation and allow no one else in her life. So she knows no other way of living. Mentally, she's trapped. Win could have easily called for help or alerted the police through a myriad of online forums and groups, but she hadn't. She hadn't known any better. *She's just a kid.*

"We gotta leave now, guys," Luc said, straightening up.

"Where are we going?" Katy asked.

"To the other end of the world," he said.

"Wonder what Fred's going to do when he gets here," I said.

"If the cops don't get here first," Tetyana said. "Win, make sure to alert Interpol only just before we're leaving, okay? By the time they call the right people in the right local department and they scramble their teams, we won't be here."

Win nodded.

"Time to go," Luc said.

We all got up to leave, except for Tetyana.

"Hey." I heard her speak softly to Win. "Can you check something real quick for me?"

"Sure," Win said, clicking open the laptop again.

"What you doing?" Luc asked, curiously.

Tetyana turned to the rest of us. "Go find our passports, will you?"

Part SIX

Hope is the thing with feathers that perches in the soul and sings the tune without the words and never stops at all.
Emily Dickinson

Chapter Thirty-six

We whizzed along the highway, passing a small Belgian town called Liege.

On my lap was a crumpled, torn map Luc had discovered in the glove compartment of the van. The word BENELUX was written on top, barely visible and every jolt of the van threatened to dismantle this old map. Though the passing streetlights were all I had to read by, I had managed to trace the fastest path out of Brussels.

When we stepped out of the house, leaving behind the two men tied-up, we had only one choice. There was no underground passageway as Tetyana had hoped, and we couldn't just walk into town, so we dug the car keys from Vlad's pocket, piled into the white cargo van and drove out as quickly as we could.

Luc was driving and Tetyana was sitting up in front next to him. Her gentle snores meant the past few days had finally caught up with her. She'd collapsed with fatigue.

Crammed in the backseat, big enough to hold a couple of big dogs, were Katy, Win and me. Katy and Win were fast asleep, heads nodding together. Both looked worn out. Behind us, in the back, was the open compartment in which we'd been smuggled into Belgium. It was empty with lots of space now, but no one wanted to get back in there.

I was drained too, but couldn't fall asleep. Now I had time to think, my mind buzzed, trying to make sense of everything.

So much had happened since I left Toronto five days ago that even the craziest things I'd experienced then seemed like a tea party in comparison. Bibi's scarred face, Win's fall down the stairs, and the bloodied yellow blouse of the girl in the warehouse kept playing in a loop in my head. I wondered if I'd have nightmares for the rest of my life.

In my pocket was the one thing that kept me sane: Preeti's letter from India connecting me to the only family I had.

I'd written to Preeti many times before that, but she'd never gotten my letters. I only found that out the day I discovered them intact, still in their envelopes, stashed away in Mrs. Rao's office. That was the day I learned she'd been working with Franky's human smuggling ring in India all along. Franky and Mrs. Rao were good at what they did—they even tracked me down at Dick and Jose's bakery in Toronto. I'd been so naive.

Through all this running, evading and hiding, I never forgot my mission. No matter what happened, I promised myself, I'd get on a plane to India. I no longer had our airline tickets. They weren't good anymore, anyway. All Katy and I had were the clothes on our backs, our passports and the packet of stolen cash.

But it wasn't going to be easy to get on an overseas flight. I wondered how much information the UK border guards shared with their European counterparts. I sat back with a sigh. My records weren't squeaky clean.

I took stock of all the crimes I'd committed in my life. It started the day I stole a pair of ruby red slippers at the market for Chanda, in my childhood home of Tanzania. My desire to see my best friend happy outweighed that theft. It was the same feeling I had when I took the packet of cash from Dick's safe to pay for Katy's air ticket. It was the same when I walked off with that chocolate roll from Chef Pierre's bakery. On one hand, I felt like I didn't have a choice. On the other, I knew I was wrong.

Weariness finally overtook me and I fell asleep, only to jerk awake when the van revved to pass a truck.

"Hey, Luc?" I spoke quietly, to not wake the others. "Not falling asleep or anything, are you?"

"Nope but you can sing to me if you want." He grinned through the rearview mirror.

"Let me know if you get tired and we can switch."

"I'm good. I like driving." His cheeky grin reappeared in the mirror. "Wish you were up here to tickle me or something though."

I gave him a look. "How far do we have to go?"

"Almost at the border. Saw a sign a minute ago."

I wiped my eyes and sat up. I smoothed the map to see where we were and traced the highway with my fingers.

"We'll get to Aachen first." My finger hovered over the small German town across the border. "Then what?"

"I say Frankfurt. It's a real fun city. Great place to take you out on a date."

"Luc, that ain't happening."

"Why not?"

"You're seventeen and I'm almost nineteen."

"So?"

"You're underage, aren't you?"

"That's age discrimination."

"It's illegal."

"You Americans are so stuck up."

It was Tetyana who said Germany was the best place to lie low. As far as Katy, Win, and I were concerned, we just wanted to get as far from Brussels and London as possible. Luc had suggested a long drive down to Sicily, where he had "good colleagues," but Tetyana ruled it out firmly, saying we didn't need to meet any more "Freds."

I looked down at the map, trying to learn this new world we were in.

To the west of us was the rest of Belgium. To the north were the flat lands of the Netherlands. To the south were France and Luxembourg. And to the east was Germany, where we'd be within minutes. The map, however, stopped at the border.

I unfolded the bottom half. If Belgium was shaped like a foot, Luxembourg was its big toe. It was a tiny country nestled between

Germany, France, and Belgium. *Luxembourg...why is that name so familiar?* Then, I remembered.

I reached into my jacket pocket and felt Chef Pierre's magazine still tucked inside. I was surprised it hadn't fallen off. I pulled it out and flipped to the centerfold with the picture of the castle in the Luxembourgian hills. That was where Chef Pierre and the Diplomatic Dragon Lady would be this weekend. I looked at her photo, wondering how in the world someone like me even got to meet her.

It was the Dragon Lady who'd singled me out from my more experienced competitors back in Toronto. She hadn't judged me by how I dressed, what I looked like or even by my experience. She'd only judged me by my work and handed me the most amazing catering contract in the country.

She'd been demanding, but fair. Plus, she'd passed my name to everyone else, so half the diplomatic community in town called me for their parties. While the recent, and more urgent, events had been occupying my brain, I couldn't ignore the guilt of running away without letting her or her team know, and just before an important charity ball at that. The Diplomatic Dragon Lady had probably fired me. In absentia.

"Hey, Luc? What do you know about Luxembourg?"

"Filled with snooty rich people."

"What about Germany? Even been there before?"

"Only once, to make a delivery."

"Has Tetyana been to Germany?"

"Don't think so. She spent a lot of time in Bucharest and Graz before heading off to London, when she was running away."

"Why was she running away?"

Luc was silent for a long minute. "You're gonna have to ask her yourself," he said, finally.

I pulled my attention back to the map, wishing we had a proper GPS instead. But Katy's phone and mine were tucked in our bags back in London. Win never had a personal phone in her life. Tetyana had one, but as soon as the video was uploaded online, she flushed the SIM card down the toilet and threw the phone out of the van into a giant wheat field, somewhere between Bierbeek and Hoegaarden.

"Would be much easier if I had a phone," I said out loud. "This map's so hard to read and there's nothing after Aachen."

"You can use mine," Luc said, digging into his pant pocket and slipping a shiny mobile between the front seats.

"You brought your phone?" I said, taking it. "Didn't Tetyana—"

"Shh. She's a bit paranoid. Thinks the whole world's out to get her. Besides, it's shut off."

"But if I turn it on, the police will know where we are, right?"

"It's brand new. Got it only a couple of days ago in London. It's not even out officially. Besides, no one has my number."

"Are you sure?" I said, staring at the bright Apple logo.

"Turn it on. It's got the coolest apps, you'll see."

"But does it have GPS?"

"Have you been living in a cave all these years?" Luc sounded insulted.

I switched the phone on. It rang as soon as I did.

I dropped it, startled.

The phone tumbled from my lap, bounced off my foot and landed with a dull thud on the floor.

"Allo!"

I froze. Somehow, the call feature had turned on.

"Allo, Monsieur Luc?"

Oh, my god. That's Fred.

"Merde!" I heard Luc swear up in front.

"What's going on?" It was Tetyana, waking up from the commotion.

I bent down and picked up the phone with two fingers, feeling like I was touching a live bomb. I clicked on the red phone icon, cutting Fred off in mid-sentence. Holding down the main on/off button, I switched it off for good.

"Shit!" Luc said, banging his palm on the steering wheel. "Shit, shit, shit!"

"What the hell?" Tetyana had turned around and was looking wide-eyed at the phone in my hand.

I gave her a guilty look.

Next to me, Win and Katy stirred awake.

"Stop the damn car!" Tetyana shouted.

"What's going on?" A sleepy Katy asked.

Luc pulled over to the shoulder, looking a little shaken. I glanced behind to see if anyone had been following us, but only one car zoomed by, not giving us a second glance.

"Who still has a phone?" Tetyana demanded. "Hand them over. Now!"

I passed her Luc's phone.

"Any more?" she snapped.

Katy and I looked at each other and shook our heads.

"Left mine in London," I said.

"Me too," Katy said. "Somewhere in the airport."

"Luc." Tetyana glared at him so hard, I could see daggers come out of her eyes. "You know better than this."

Luc put his face in his hands.

Tetyana opened the door and jumped out. We watched as she bent down in front of the van. Within seconds, she was back.

"Go forward," she commanded Luc. "Real slow."

Luc followed instructions.

She nodded. "Now, reverse."

The crunch was unmistakable.

"Again," she said. Luc complied.

Tetyana jumped out, picked up the broken pieces and flung them toward the empty field next to the road. She got back in and slammed the door shut, her face grim.

"They can trace you even when it's off." Her voice was controlled, but her face was a ball of fury.

No one spoke.

I peered through the windshield and saw the large green highway sign that announced Germany was only five kilometers ahead of us.

We're almost there.

"They know where we're going," Tetyana said. "They're going to call their goons as soon as we cross that border."

"Sorry," Luc choked, finally finding his voice. "I'm really, really sorry."

"What's done is done," Tetyana said with a huge sigh. "We've got to find a new route now."

"Do you want me to turn back?" Luc asked meekly.

"I don't wanna go back to Brussels," Katy spoke up, a note of panic in her voice.

"Me neither," Win piped up.

"Same here," I said.

"We can try Germany through the southern border," Tetyana said thoughtfully.

"Why don't we go to Luxembourg instead?" I asked, tapping my map.

"That's a two-hour drive south," Tetyana said.

"Wouldn't that still be better than driving into the hands of Fred's goons? Or the police?"

Luc looked at me via the mirror. "He'll never guess we're heading that way, that's for sure."

Tetyana contemplated this silently, while I wondered if she'd had any run-ins in Luxembourg. She was a mystery to me, one I was too afraid to inquire about because of what I might uncover. The less I knew, the better, I thought.

"Luc," she said in a quiet voice.

"Yes?" he replied timidly.

"Luxembourg."

Chapter Thirty-seven

We were driving into the land of fairy-tale princes and princesses.

Thousand-year-old castle towers soared above the ancient city, dark ominous shapes against the twilight sky. Visions of Sleeping Beauty lulled into a never-ending sleep by a vengeful sorceress flashed across my mind. Surrounded by fortifications on top of a sheer rocky cliff, Luxembourg looked forbidding the moment I glimpsed it.

We were ravenous and we needed to find a place to sleep for the night, but all we had was a total of fifty euros and seventy-three cents among us, remnants of the deposit from Fred.

Without Vlad and Zero, Tetyana no longer had access to the money she'd saved from her work with them. They'd put it all in a Swiss bank account which could only be accessed with three passwords, one held by Vlad, one by Zero and the third by her. She shrugged as she told us, but I could see defeat in her eyes. "Should have known better than to deal with thugs," she said in a flat voice.

I gave Katy a discreet look. She was guarding our packet of cash with her life, and wouldn't let anyone near it except me. We had no choice now but to dip into it.

I was surprised how demure Tetyana was in her thanks when I told her we'd take care of the expenses. She didn't even ask how much we had.

I knew she had two guns on her, one tucked in her right boot and another somewhere under her shirt. She had a knack for carrying concealed items in the strangest of places. Luc and Win merely looked relieved we could finally eat and find a place to shower and sleep.

A few minutes later, I was in line at a currency exchange booth with one thousand Canadian dollars of drug-tainted money in my purse. My palms were damp and my heart was beating faster than normal. I wondered if they'd hold the bills to the light, refuse to take them, call security, or even the police.

Tetyana came with me, for "security," she said, though I had a hard time imagining how we'd get away if they called the cops. A gun-fight wouldn't do anyone any good.

But things went better than I expected.

The woman behind the counter handed over the euro notes in a matter of minutes. I picked up the money with shaking hands and walked out quickly, with Tetyana two inches behind me, like a trained bodyguard. I half expected someone in uniform to jump out and shout "freeze," and I only started to breathe again once we got back in the van.

We stopped at the nearest shopping center to find toilets, freshen up, and get new clothes to change into. Plus, some food before the stores closed for the night.

Ever since she'd been kidnapped as a child, Win had been wearing hand-me-downs that had once belonged to an older prostitute. Or a dead one. She now walked through the H&M aisles as if in a dream, brushing her fingers on the clothes racks, not believing her eyes. This was no haute couture merchandise, but it might as well been for her.

"I can get anything I want?" she whispered for the third time. I nodded, "Anything you want, sweetie." I had enough money to buy ten rounds of tickets to Goa if I wanted, though it was in highly questionable cash. If a handful of new outfits made Win happy, it was perfectly fine with me.

I noticed she avoided the faux leather skirts and bawdy tops like the plague and went for jeans and T-shirts like any regular teen. She was especially keen to cover up the tattoo on her thigh.

The rest of us crowded into the couch near the fitting room and coaxed her out to show us her outfits. While Win seemed scared and shy, it was like watching her come alive. At that moment, as we sat shoulder to shoulder, cheering her on, it felt like our worries and paranoia had disappeared. It was like we were meant to be together, doing normal things like this.

Katy turned on her full shopping mode after that.

While the rest of us chose casual, comfortable gear, she picked a stack of party dresses. "You never know when you'll need a proper black dress," she said, pulling a petite off-the-shoulder piece from a rack. "Try it," she urged, pulling me toward the fitting rooms. When I resisted, she turned and hissed, *this is therapy*." With a sigh, I followed her in. I was anxious about throwing our money on frivolous things, but she was right. We all needed to do something fun to take our minds off everything we'd gone through.

When we were done with the clothes, Katy, without missing a beat, steered us to the shoe department. "We need new shoes," she declared, as she marched in front of us.

So we spent the next hour trying on new shoes—even Luc. Katy grabbed a red mid-heel that came with a fancy gold broach in front. To humor her, everyone tried on variations of red.

In the end, Win fell in love with a pair of red kitten heels, I ended up with comfortable red wedges, and Tetyana got herself a pair of new red boots. Then Luc dug out a pair of red canvas shoes from the bargain bin. They looked so comfortable we all bought a pair each. "Good for walking," Tetyana said. "And for running." We didn't know it then, but that was the smartest purchase we made that day.

We walked over to a café to eat after that, our first full meal in days. It was nearing closing time and the bistro had run out of most dishes, so we ordered everything still available and stuffed ourselves like we'd never had a proper meal in our lives. Katy devoured her food like the rest of us and I noticed she didn't even make her usual run to the bathroom afterward.

Before we got back into the grimy van, we walked around to stretch our legs.

We were in a high area of the city, at the edge of a steep cliff. From up here, we could see the city lights against the darkening skies. A placid river wound through the valley below us, looking like a silver velvet ribbon. A medieval church sat in this sunken gorge, serene and peaceful. Near the city's fortress, a thousand-year-old black tower, remnants of an abandoned castle turret, jutted out. From afar, it looked like an ugly black tooth in a witch's craggy mouth.

"*American Werewolf in Paris* was shot right here," Luc leaned over and whispered to me.

"I can believe it," I said. The stark hilly backdrop punctuated by the fortress was the perfect set location for a werewolf movie. The streets were almost empty now. I could easily imagine strange creatures soundlessly leaping among the frosty skyscrapers in the dead of the night.

"So where do we sleep tonight?" Katy asked, looking at me.

In the few hours since we'd run from Brussels, we'd each taken an unofficial role for the team. While Tetyana still kept a close eye on everything, she was clearly head of security, ready for anyone or anything that spelled trouble. Luc was our driver. He didn't mind the long-distance hauls and had refused to give up his seat for the two-hour drive to Luxembourg. Katy, the professional bookkeeper from Toronto, was now guardian of our cash, a job she carried out like her life depended on it. We all knew Win's whiz kid gifts now. And I, somehow, had morphed into a trip coordinator of sorts.

"I booked a room at a youth hostel," I replied. While Katy and Win had been busy at the purse department, I'd used a phone at the information center to reserve a room with two double bunk beds and a cot for Win.

"Oh good, I need sleep badly," Luc said, yawning.

"So what do you think?" I asked Tetyana. "Safe to stay here for the night?"

"Safe as anywhere," she said quietly, surveying the area. "We can stay a few days till things get quiet. Might be good to stop running for a bit."

"Oh, good," Katy said, her face relaxing. "I'd love to stay here. This is my first time in Europe. First time out of Toronto. First time on a *plane*."

"Nothing wrong with some sightseeing," Tetyana said with a shrug.

"Can we go see that?" Win asked, pointing at the magnificent castle towers nearby.

"Me too. I'd love to visit it," Katy said.

"I wanna see the dungeons," Luc said. "Saw them online. I always wanted to see them in real life."

"Whatever we do," Tetyana said in her low voice, "we've got to stick together. Don't go off alone without telling me, okay?"

In the last few hours, she had ditched her scowl and the scornful look she reserved for anyone who disagreed with her. It was a kinder, gentler Tetyana with us now.

Everyone nodded.

Win didn't need to be told though. She latched on to us like glue like she was scared someone might snatch her if any of us were more than three feet away.

The five of us stood silently in the growing darkness, watching the lights of this fairy-tale city, lost in our thoughts. I was among newfound friends and one old one. I tried not to think of the uncertainty of our future.

A light breeze drifted by, ruffling our hair.

This was probably the first time in a long time any of us had felt free. No one had to worry about being chased, kidnapped, raped, tossed around like a piece of furniture, or dragged off to be harmed by someone else. As for young Win, I imagined this was the first time in her entire short life she'd felt this way.

Huddled in the middle of this raggedy group, I felt like I'd found home. *Home.* What a nice ring that word had.

It dawned on me that home wasn't a place I'd been yearning to find all my life. It wasn't in Kenya, where I'd been born or Tanzania, where my parents lay buried. It wasn't in India, where my one and only remaining relative lived. It wasn't in Canada, where I grew into adulthood. It wasn't in London, Brussels or Luxembourg, places I'd only known in passing. Home was where I was surrounded by friends, friends I knew would have my back, as I'd have theirs.

"Hey," Luc said, shattering the silence. "Did you know Dracula's real name was Vlad?"

I think he expected a laugh, but then he saw Win shiver. We all did.

Tetyana spoke up. "I just realized what we left behind." Her voice was subdued, introspective. "I just didn't think it was going to get this bad. I didn't think I was going to go this far."

"Me too," Luc said, with a sigh. "Didn't plan for this either."

"But you were only twelve when Zero found you. He tricked you."

Luc looked down at his feet. His face was scrunched up like he was ready to burst into tears or punch someone. Maybe both.

"But me," Tetyana was saying, "I was twenty-one. I mean, I *am* twenty-one. Should have known better than to get involved with them." She turned to Win. "I allowed this to happen to you. I'll never forgive myself for as long as I live."

"But I was with them way before you came," Win said, reaching out to touch Tetyana's arm. "They bought me when I was ten. It wasn't you who did bad things to me."

Tetyana frowned.

She's angry, I thought, *she's furious at herself.*

"I could have saved you," Tetyana said, "got you out three months ago, instead of letting it all go on." She looked at Win and her eyes softened. "I'm not asking you to forgive me, Win. I want you to live a better life and I'll do everything I can to make that happen."

"It's easy to see things in hindsight," Katy said, but I didn't think she heard her.

"All I wanted was to keep my brother alive," Tetyana continued. "That's all I was thinking about. Nothing else. That's what I promised her just before she died." Her voice faded to such a whisper that if I hadn't been listening carefully, I wouldn't have heard.

"Promised who?" I said, my curiosity overcoming me.

"My mother."

Chapter Thirty-eight

We got three days in Luxembourg. Three blissful days. That was all.

During that time, Katy's rosy cheeks reappeared. Tetyana showed her more compassionate side, and to our surprise, an intellectual side we hadn't seen before. Luc grinned and joked around though he was slowly getting the hint I wasn't interested in a date.

He wasn't unattractive. But it was like having a cheeky brother around, one you cared for, but who annoyed you all the same. The perfect man for me, the one I daydreamed about, was older, wiser, with dreamy brown eyes and more buff. Yes, definitely more buff. *When I stop all this running, I'm going to meet him,* I told myself. *With almost four billion males on this planet, he's got to be out there, somewhere.*

Win had her ups and downs and remained reclusive, staying close but not saying much. One day, I caught her listening to a sparrow singing outside the window of our hostel room, with a soft smile on her face. How incredible it is, I thought as I watched her watch the bird, that someone can go through such an ordeal and still hang on to her humanity. It will take a long time for Win to open up, but that smile gave me hope. For her. For us all.

No one discussed what had happened in London or Brussels. No one stopped to glance at a newsstand, or dropped into an Internet café to find out if anything had come out of the information we'd posted online. Like me, everyone wanted to put it behind us. We simply decided to live in the moment, a luxury none of us ever had.

It was like we were on holiday. We explored the dungeons and the castle ruins. We tried new foods at outdoor stalls, picnicked on park benches and napped under the afternoon sun. But we always stayed on guard.

Tetyana took her security duties seriously and gave us rotating four-hour shifts at night. This was helpful because Win had a habit of waking from nightmares every night, so someone was always up to calm her until she drifted to sleep again.

Our van was parked under a tree at the back of the hostel lot, strategically placed so no one could read the license plate easily. And there it sat, remaining untouched. Renting cheap bicycles from the hostel was much more fun than driving, and made us look like student tourists. No one bothered us.

Until our third day.

We'd been lining up to enter the history and art museum that afternoon. It was an outing we'd all wanted to do, not because any of us were history buffs, but because we were eager to experience something completely different from our previous lives.

Luc had stepped out to visit the washroom but came back running within seconds. His face was white. Something was wrong.

Tetyana straightened up, her hand on her belt where I knew she had a gun. We stepped out of line.

"What's going on?" Tetyana asked.

"We gotta get outta here," Luc said, panting.

"Why?" I asked stepping out to survey the area.

He pulled me by the elbow. Motioning the others to follow, he ushered me into a quiet alcove near the toilets. Everyone gathered around him.

"I saw Busboy!" he said. I noticed his hands were shaking.

"Busboy?" Katy asked.

"Who's that?" I asked.

"Hired gun. He shoots at point blank. Even the thugs are scared of him!" Luc spluttered.

"Wait," Tetyana said. "Who is this man and why do you think he's after us?"

Luc threw his hands in the air. "Because he's with Staples, that's why! I just saw them!"

"Who's *Staples*?" Katy asked.

"Staples works for Fred. His job is to hunt people who don't pay up. Busboy's job is to shoot them down if they don't cooperate," Luc explained with a crazed look on his face.

"Hold on," I said. "We don't owe Fred anything. Okay, except for that small deposit, but he can always find another supplier. Why would he—"

"That's not the point!" Luc almost shrieked. "You don't make a promise to a drug king and run off like that. They think you're tryna' play them. It's not the money. It's his reputation!"

We stared at him.

"That's when they send Busboy. He cleans everything and brings Fred's reputation back."

"Shh," Tetyana said, as a tourist walked by. "Keep it down, okay?"

"You're sure he's coming for *us*?" Katy whispered.

"Why do you think they're here? In Luxembourg? Nobody comes here." Luc's eyes bulged. He looked like he was ready to tear his hair out. "Staples looked right through the window. I'm sure he saw me!"

We stood silently, trying to digest this.

"On the other hand, maybe he didn't see you," Tetyana said. "All the windows are tinted here." She paused. "But we need to move. Tell me, what does this Busboy look like?"

"Like King Daddy Tom."

"Who's that?" I asked.

"You're American and you don't even know?"

I shrugged.

"He's a rapper from the Bronx. Got the biggest album this—"

"Hey," Tetyana interrupted him. "Just give me his description."

It took a minute, but we finally got to learn about Busboy and Staples. With all his suave charm, Fred was part of a vicious international gang with a reach across Europe, and he wasn't someone you messed with. Or get involved with. But that was too late for us.

Tetyana sent Katy out to flag down a cab immediately and asked Luc and me to hide behind her and Win in the corridor. Fred had only met Luc and me. So far, anyway.

It took us ten minutes to get back to the hostel from the museum. We scooped up our clothes and bags, checked out within minutes and piled into our van, while Tetyana kept a sharp eye out. On the plus side, it would have been hard not to miss two young men with gold chains around their necks and oversized diamond rings, swaggering inside a student hostel in Europe.

We were on the road again, this time heading west, back toward Germany.

Luc stopped hyperventilating only after we left Luxembourg's suburbs, but he still looked pale. When Tetyana asked him if he was doing okay, his response was curt. "You've no idea what those guys can do." Then he lapsed into silence, focusing on the road.

Tetyana put her shades on and leaned back in her seat. She looked asleep, but I was sure she was as alert as any watchdog. Katy, Win and I settled in the rear, huddled together, mindlessly watching the green forest zoom by us. The lump in my stomach had returned. I tried not to dwell on our uncertain future, but it was hard not to feel lost again. The past three carefree days already felt like a forgotten dream.

Twenty minutes into the drive, Luc groaned, making us all sit up.

"We're running out of gas," he said slamming his palm on the steering wheel. "I completely forgot to refill. *Merde!*"

We had to find a gas station, so we stopped at a secluded rest stop off the highway.

While Luc was pumping petrol, we got out to stretch our legs and get hot drinks. Better than sitting restlessly in the van, I thought as I followed Katy out.

Next to the gas bar was a small roadside motel set at the edge of the forest line. Built with rustic wooden logs, this looked like a place you'd find in the back roads of Canada, not in the middle of Europe.

There was a café on the ground floor of the motel, doubling as a reception area. An open fireplace sat at the end of the room, with firewood piled around it. Next to it was a lone Internet station with a paper stuck to the monitor that said, "Free for coffee lovers only." A young woman with her hair in a blue kerchief sat next to the cash register with her nose in her phone.

It was mid-afternoon, just after the lunch rush and just before supper time, so the place was deserted. This place probably only attracted tourists and commuters, I thought.

We grabbed our teas and coffees and took a seat near the fireplace, as far away from the entrance and cash register as possible. Luc joined us soon after but refused to sit, his eyes peeled on the road.

"Hey!"

We turned around.

While we were hastily debating our next steps, Win had slipped over to the Internet station.

"You've got to see this," she said in a loud whisper, furiously pointing at the screen. Her cheeks were pink, from either excitement or fear.

We quickly gathered around her.

She had the *Guardian* open to the front page. The headline screamed, "International prostitution ring foiled!"

I felt a thrill go through me. The list of names and addresses we'd put out two days ago was broadcast for the world to see. *Thank god.*

"Good job," Tetyana said, giving Win a pat on her back. Katy smiled. Even Luc perked up and gave Win a high five.

"Smart work, genius," he said, making her blush.

"Hey, do you think they know it was us who leaked this?" I asked.

"Don't think the police would figure out that easily. They'll be too busy apprehending Zero and his gang." Tetyana shook her head as if thinking this through. "My only worry is if Fred got to Vlad and Zero before the police and they're now working together against us."

"And sent Busboy after us," Luc said, looking like he was about to have a panic attack again.

"We don't know for sure," Tetyana said. "Just thinking out loud, so let's not jump to conclusions."

"But how did they know we're in this country?" Katy asked.

"Maybe they checked all the cities around Brussels already," Luc said. "They had three days."

"Are we going to be safe anywhere?" Win asked.

Everyone turned silent.

"We need help," Katy said. "This is scary."

"This weekend," I said, as an idea whirled around in my head, "the Diplomatic Dragon Lady's coming to Luxembourg."

"The *who*?" Tetyana asked.

"She's part of the powerful diplomatic community," I said, "and she knows me. I worked for her. Maybe we can ask her to help us."

No one spoke.

"Here," I said, pulling Chef Pierre's magazine out of my pocket. "See this?"

Everyone slid up to peer over my shoulders. The photo of the castle in the centerfold still looked magnificent, but under the low lights of the café, it had taken a slightly menacing tone.

"Looks like Dracula's castle to me," Luc said.

"That's her," I said, tapping the photo of the tall woman in the white suit.

"She looks like a president," Win said in awe, taking the magazine from me to get a closer look.

"She almost is," I said. "So what do you all think?"

"Baroness Agathe....party of the year...," Tetyana read under her breath. "This Saturday? That's tomorrow."

"We don't have a lot of time," I said. "She'll probably fly back home on Sunday."

"Or go shopping in Milan," Katy quipped.

"How do we get to her?" Tetyana asked.

"We can find her at the castle," I said. "It'll be a party. There'll be tons of people so we can mix in."

"Mix in? Us?" Luc said. "At a posh party?"

Katy's face lit up. "I know. We can go as a catering company."

"That's not a bad idea," I said.

Tetyana and Luc still looked skeptical.

"Do you guys have a better idea?" I asked.

"Drive down to Sicily," Luc said. "That's what I keep saying."

"To your drug friends? And make it even easier for Fred to find us? No thanks," Tetyana said, giving him a look. She turned to me. "How can she help us?"

"I can explain what happened, how we exposed the ring, and ask her to talk to the police. She should support us, won't she, after all we did? And if we're with her maybe we can get immunity."

"Immunity?"

"So the police won't lock us up. So they can protect us from Fred and his gang, and maybe even help us to get to the airport, or wherever we want to go. We won't have to keep running like this."

Everyone was looking at me thoughtfully, except for Win. She was busy tapping at the keyboard, the magazine on her lap, her head deep in something, oblivious to the rest of the world.

"How do you know she'll want to help us?" Tetyana asked, her brows furrowed.

"I don't," I said with a sigh. "I just know she's the most important person I know in the world. She really liked my work. She chose me over all the other bakers in town and even gave me a security pass to the Foreign Department building. She's here now. That's all I know."

"So it's a risk," Tetyana said.

"I didn't say it was a perfect idea."

"It could make things worse for us," Tetyana said and paused. "Then again, it could turn out well for us too."

"Fred's gonna catch up with us one day," Luc said. "We can only hide for so long."

"The bigger the risk, the bigger the reward," Katy said. "Worth a try."

Tetyana nodded. "So how do we get inside the castle then?"

"I can put us on their list," Win said.

We looked at her.

"What are you doing, Win?" Katy asked.

"Finding a way to get inside. Isn't that what you want?"

We peered at the computer.

She pointed to a page with lots of letters and numbers on it, all of which looked like gibberish to me. Seeing the puzzled look on our faces, she flipped quickly through more pages and stopped on one that said, "Baroness Agathe to host event of the year."

At the top of the page was a list of distinguished invitees including the Diplomatic Dragon Lady. At the bottom of the screen was a short list of companies catering to the event, including the local butcher, grocer, florist, chocolatier and produce delivery company. Win pointed her mouse to this list.

"I can add our name right here. Just need to fix the back end codes."

We looked at each other.

"So what name do you want me to put?" Win asked, looking up at us innocently.

"You mean…?" Katy paused. "Like a catering company name?"

Win nodded.

"Er, Better Batter Bakers?" I blurted.

"Really?" Luc said, rolling his eyes. "How about Rebel Bakers?"

"Sounds like a bunch of terrorists," Katy said. "We're supposed to sound posh if we're going in there."

"No," Tetyana said. "We need to sound avant-garde, edgy. European royals like that these days."

Everyone looked at her in surprise. For someone good at handling guns and bringing bad guys to their knees, she said the strangest things.

"Red-Heeled Bakers?" I asked, pointing at Katy's heels.

"That'll leave Luc out," Katy pointed out.

"I'm cool with that," Luc said, with a shrug. "And for the record, I'm all for girl power."

"I know!" Win said.

"What's your grand idea?" Luc asked.

"Red-Heeled Rebels," she said. "That's like a really cool secret club."

"Sounds good to me," I said.

Everyone nodded.

Tetyana shrugged.

Win turned back to the computer with the serious focused look on her face again. She typed quickly, clicked save and refreshed. "How do you like this?" she asked when the page came up again.

"Wow," Luc said.

"Nice job!" Katy said.

Tetyana merely raised her brows.

"It's great," I said, a little shocked to see our phantom catering company show up on the castle's official website in a matter of seconds.

"I feel better already." Luc blew a raspberry. "Even Staples and Busboy won't guess that's us."

"I love it," Katy said. "Just wish it was real."

I sighed. My mission was to get back to India, to Preeti. I'd already spent too much time running around Europe. I closed the magazine and tucked it in my pocket. "We've got work to do, guys," I said.

"Hey, Win," Tetyana said, leaning over Win's shoulder. "Would you mind checking that site for me again, real quick?"

While we watched, Win brought up a page and scrolled down a chat forum, looking up to Tetyana from time to time.

"What are you looking for, Tetyana?" I asked.

"A name," she said, her eyes focused on the screen. "A name." When she got to the end of the forum, she shook her head and straightened up. "Can you clear the browser for me, hun?"

Win pecked at the keyboard for a few seconds, then looked up. "Done."

We glanced at each other. *Now what?*

Tetyana looked at me. "You're right, we've got work to do."

"All right, Red-Heeled Rebels!" Luc said with a grin. "Let's move it!"

He grabbed Win by the hand, pulled her out of the chair and waltzed her around the café.

Part SEVEN

These woods are lovely, dark and deep,
But I have promises to keep,
And miles to go before I sleep,
And miles to go before I sleep.
Robert Frost

Chapter Thirty-nine

The next day dawned sunny but chilly.

We were back on the road. The sky above was a pale blue and speckled with tufts of white clouds. The imperial trees of Luxembourg's forests stood at attention along the highway as if shepherding us toward Baroness Agathe's castle.

It had been easy to find a map to the castle in a brochure of historic sites at the motel.

After showers and breakfast, we piled into the van. We were now headed north, driving along a winding road that cut its way through the dark, green-forested hills. Once in a while, we glimpsed a forgotten castle up on a hill, making me feel once again like we were traveling through the land of Sleeping Beauty. We drove in silence, admiring the magical landscape.

The day before, we'd booked ourselves into the motel for the night. The party at the castle didn't start until Saturday evening and it was only an hour's drive from where we were, but we didn't want to go too early and give anyone the time to uncover our disguise. It also gave us ample time to rest before plunging into what might solve all our problems, or put us into deeper trouble.

The motel didn't have a room large enough for all of us, so we doubled up. Tetyana and I took one room with two single beds, Win and Katy took another, and Luc had the luxury of having a room all to himself.

"Does she know you're here?" I heard Tetyana say from her bed, as I tucked into mine on the other side of the room.

"Who?" I asked.

"This dragon woman."

"She doesn't."

I wondered if they'd managed to find a substitute caterer for the charity ball. I'd left Toronto only a week ago, but it felt like an eternity had passed. *Maybe they've blacklisted me now.*

"To tell the truth," I said, swallowing my worries, "she may not be too happy with me right now."

"Is that right?" Tetyana's voice had turned slightly cold.

"I left without telling her or her team. But I think she'll understand after I tell her what happened."

"Why did you leave? With a nice package of cash, too."

"We worked for a bakery." I paused. There was so much more to the story than I could tell her in one night. "At least we thought we did. But the owners were drug dealers, crooks."

Tetyana was quiet.

"On my last day there, we learned they were planning to sell Katy and me off to a trafficker to make extra money."

"To a brothel?" She hadn't sound surprised by what I said, merely curious.

"This Indian man wanted to come to Canada, and I was supposed to be his bride so he'd get a marriage visa." I shivered as these words left my mouth.

Tetyana didn't respond for a while. I wondered if she'd fallen asleep.

"So we ran away," I said. "That money is our money. Katy's worked for them for years and I worked hard that year and brought a lot of clients. We ran that bakery and did all the work, but they barely paid us. They used us to cover their dirty work."

"Thieves," I heard Tetyana say from her bed, "thieves and murderers everywhere."

I had to agree. I wanted to feel angry, even rage, at everything that had happened to me and some days I did. But most of the time, I just wished I had wings to fly across the ocean back to Goa to find Preeti.

"Hey, do they take Ukrainians in Canada?" Tetyana asked.

What an odd question. I turned her way. "I think Canada takes everyone. They're really open."

"Everyone?"

"Well, except maybe dictators, rapists, murderers, and con artists." I stopped, wondering how true this was. Mrs. Rao, Franky, and Jose belonged to most of these categories, but they'd easily got into the country and did well for themselves. Very well. And they didn't seem too worried about getting caught for helping others like them to get in. *Maybe Canadians are okay with these sort of people coming in. Maybe they didn't want to see the bad things happening right under their noses. Maybe they just didn't care.*

"Are there any Ukrainians over there?" Tetyana asked, interrupting my thoughts.

I had to think about that for a moment. "Perogies are really popular."

"*Ukrainian perogies?*" Tetyana sat up in her bed. "In Canada?"

"It's a national food, like maple syrup and beaver tails. It's popular in the prairies and not that difficult to make, either." I remembered the time I'd found a recipe in a local newspaper and made a batch to the delight of Mrs. Rao's guests. *Food.* Now that was a topic I knew something about.

"Wow. Sounds like a dream place," Tetyana said. "Do you think I can talk to this Dragon diplomat about going there with my brother?"

"We can ask her," I said. "I'm sure she can tell you how to go about it."

I had no idea how these things worked. I had got in illegally—smuggled in by a lying Franky to work as a slave for Mrs. Rao. This was partly why I was always checking over my shoulder. I didn't know how many laws I'd broken without even knowing. How many years would they put me away, if they knew everything I'd gone through?

I looked over at Tetyana. She was lying back now, eyes closed, her face so soft and relaxed that I hardly recognized her.

I switched the bedside light off and sank my head into the pillow.

• • • •

AFTER AN HOUR ON THE freeway, Luc turned the van into a narrow road that curved through a thicket of woods. We drove for about five minutes until we hit a dead end. I looked at my map. We'd arrived at our destination.

Luc switched off the engine and we peered through the windows.

I felt like I was in the middle of a Brothers Grimm fairy tale. In front of us loomed the stone castle, even more awe-inspiring in real life. From where we were, we could see the castle doors, large enough to allow a horse and a rider through. An ancient tower with a spiked black roof rose imposingly from the center. The turrets on either side looked like the perfect place for guardsmen to sit, waiting to lob arrows at intruders. Surrounding the grounds was a fortress of green trees.

Barring the road in front of us was an immense iron gate. Beyond this black gate lay a cobblestone driveway lined with old-fashioned lampposts, leading to the castle about five hundred meters ahead. This place was shrouded in magic—of the dark kind. I could feel it in my bones.

"Are you sure we want to do this?" Katy whispered.

"Who knows, we might even meet Count Dracula," Tetyana said, with a wry smile.

"Perfect place for werewolves to hide," Luc said, pointing to the woods in the back.

"What do we do now?" Win whispered.

I frowned at my map. *Yes, what do we do now?*

Everyone was depending on me for this part. *Did I really think we could brazenly walk up to a castle? Let alone up to an important guest at a semi-royal party? Even if I do, what am I going to say? "Sorry I skipped out on your charity ball. Can you please help me get back to India, and while you're at it, help my friends escape an evil gang, the one that's in the news right now?"*

In retrospect, and in broad daylight, my plan sounded positively moronic.

"Toot!"

We all jumped.

A delivery truck had just arrived behind us and was honking impatiently.

Luc started the van and backed us out of the driveway to let it through. The delivery truck moved closer to the gate and tooted loudly again. It took a few long honks from the truck driver for anything to happen. We watched in silence as the gates glided open, operated from someone inside the castle. The truck waited for the gates to open fully before rumbling in. I watched it drive in, my heart in my mouth.

"Luc!" I shouted, "Now!"

Luc swerved sharply behind the truck, and we all swung against the door. I sighed in relief as we got through and the gates began to glide shut behind us.

"Follow the truck," I whispered.

The truck rattled along the driveway, crossing in front of the castle and its palatial doors. Parked in the cul-de-sac in front were two limousines and a luxury black Mercedes SUV. We passed these and turned into the back of the building.

Here, two trucks just like the one we were following were parked. The truck we'd followed pulled into the end of the line and stopped. Luc parked right next to it and we waited.

Now what?

We were at the back of the castle. The service entrance wasn't as beautiful as the doors up front, but it was busier back here. The back doors had been thrown open, and delivery men were bustling in and out.

A girl, about twelve years old, was playing hopscotch by herself near the doors. If I had to imagine what Alice in Wonderland might have looked like, it would have been her. With her sky-blue dress and petticoat, flat blue shoes, and a white band on her shoulder-length hair, she made the perfect Alice. It was midsummer so school must be out. She looked bored, I thought.

Two young men got out of the truck we'd just followed and began to unload sacks of potatoes. They didn't seem to think it odd that a white cargo van filled with people had followed them. They went about their work quickly, only occasionally calling out to each other about something or the other.

One of the first trucks started its engine and drove out. Then, the second truck pulled out.

I had to think fast.

Very soon, once their work was done, all the trucks would leave and we'd be left alone, conspicuous, for anyone to see.

I was racking my brain when a young blonde woman marched out. She wore smart dress pants and a crisp white shirt and had her hair tied back in a ponytail. She marched over to the two men in the truck beside us and handed them an envelope. One of them took it with a slight bow. She nodded.

She was just about to return to the castle, when she noticed us. She frowned.

Oh no.

"She saw us!" Katy whispered.

"What do we do?" Luc asked.

"Act natural, everyone," Tetyana said in a low voice.

The woman began to walk toward us, her brows furrowed.

I pulled down the window and leaned out.

"Hi!" I said, giving her my most brilliant smile. "How ya doin'?" I said, in my best American drawl.

Chapter Forty

"*Vous êtes Americains?*"

"Yes," I nodded. For once, I was glad for the mistake. "Yes, Americans here."

"Are you lost?" she asked in perfect English.

"No, we're here to cater to the party this weekend." I felt my face go warm and hoped she didn't notice.

"Oh?" She looked baffled. Her eyes scanned our van and her face said, *You came in that?*

"We're the dessert caterer for tonight," I said. I was still smiling, but inside, I felt my stomach roll.

She shielded her eyes to get a better look at us. "But Monsieur Wilmar is already taking care of that."

"We were invited privately by Ambassador Bouchard's wife to cater for her afternoon tea."

"Madame Bouchard?" She stood straighter. "I didn't realize she had done that." She pulled a phone from her pocket.

"The embassy made the preparations in advance. Did they not inform you?"

She swiped through her phone, her brows knitted, then shook her head. "No, I do not see anything, I'm afraid. What is the name of your company, please?"

"The Red-Heeled Rebels," I said, trying not to stumble over the words.

"Red-Heeled—?" her frown deepened.

"Incorporated," I added, quickly.

She looked down at her phone, muttering to herself. She looked back at me after a few tries and said, "I don't see it in my schedule."

"You'll find it on your catering list. It's on your website."

She went back to her phone and gave a start as she saw it. I watched, my heart in my mouth. This was it. She was either going to let us in or call the police.

"They did not inform me of this." She sounded annoyed. "But isn't Madame Bouchard from the *Canadian* Embassy?"

My heart skipped a beat. "Yes, she is."

"And you're *American*?"

I gulped. *She's sharp.* "We work very closely. It's a new arrangement to cut costs. We help each other where needed, like in Luxembourg, Monaco, Liechtenstein—" I tried to recall the names of the smallest European countries but my memory had dried up.

Suddenly, I remembered the letter I carried with me. I pulled out my mini recipe book and plucked out the thank you note from the Diplomatic Dragon Lady printed on the Foreign Department's official letterhead. I leaned out of the window and handed it to her.

"Here's my reference letter," I said. "I cater to all her parties in Toronto."

She scrutinized the paper.

"You can also ask Madame Bouchard about me."

She looked at me with a frown. "One does not just walk up to a guest with questions like that." She sounded astounded I'd even propose such a thing.

"She's nice. Doesn't bite."

She didn't smile. "I presume you are Mademoiselle Asha?"

"Yes, that would be me." *Please don't ask me for my passport.*

"Thank you," she said, handing the letter back to me. "Well then, please come inside. I'll introduce you to Monsieur Wilmar."

"Thank you," I said, and pulled my head back in the van.

"*Merci,*" Luc whispered from the driver's seat. "In French!"

I popped my head out again. "*Merci,* madame!"

The woman gave a slight nod of her head in acknowledgment and almost smiled. She turned around and strode crisply back toward the castle doors.

I let out a breath and wiped my sweaty palms on my skirt.

"Okay, let's go inside and see if we can find the Diplomatic Drago....I mean Madame Bouchard." *Better not make that mistake again.*

"Wait," Luc said. "Are we all supposed to be American?" He pointed at his chest. "My accent doesn't lie."

"Me, too." Win looked worried. "Maybe I'll stay in the van with Luc."

"No," Tetyana said firmly. "We're going to stick together, no matter what."

"Just don't say anything and you'll be fine," Katy said to Win.

"Katy and Asha," Tetyana said. "You take the reins here, okay?"

I nodded. "I'll be head chef. Katy's my deputy chef, and the rest of you are helpers."

"Great," Luc said, with a smirk. "We're cheap labor now?"

"Sous chefs," I said.

"Best not to talk at all, you and me," Tetyana said to Luc. "The girls can handle this."

"I have a funny feeling this is not going to end well," Luc said.

Ignoring him, Tetyana turned to me. "Some ground rules before we go in."

"Sure."

"First, everyone carry their passports at all times so if we have to leave, we make it out fast."

"Will do," I said.

"Yes," Win said.

"I do that anyway," Katy said.

Luc nodded.

Tetyana looked at Katy. "Second, be sure that money packet is safe at all times."

Katy nodded, patting her breast pocket. "I watch it like a hawk."

"Good."

"Third." Tetyana flipped open her jacket to show us the gun tucked into her belt. Then, she pulled up her right pant leg to show the second gun tucked into her brand-new boots. "If anyone needs help, I'll be happy to use these. But you've got to stay close and listen to my instructions because that's the only way I can guarantee your safety. Got it?"

We all nodded.

The security briefing now over, it was time to enter the castle.

"Okay then," I said, opening the door and taking a deep breath to steady myself. "Shall we proceed, my merry band of American bakers?"

We climbed out of the van, smoothed our crumpled shirts and pants, and straightened each other's collars. The little girl who looked like Alice in Wonderland stopped her game to stare at us with her mouth open.

Once we felt like everyone looked reasonably professional, we crossed the parking lot toward the castle doors. Katy and I walked up front, Luc and Win were in the middle, and Tetyana took the rear. Behind her, I caught a glimpse of the little girl trailing us. We walked through the doorway and stepped into a medieval corridor, lit with soft lighting. I smelled the warm comfort of the castle's kitchen before we saw it.

At the end of the corridor was an enormous entranceway and in front of this stood a rotund, middle-aged man with a red nose and a mammoth mustache. On his head was a starch white chef hat, and on his face, an austere look. The blonde woman was standing next to him. The man looked us over like we were something the cat had dragged in, and gave the woman a look as if to say, *Really?*

The woman spoke first. She stretched her arm toward the man and said, "Monsieur Wilmar, executive chef of the castle."

"It's a pleasure to meet you, Monsieur Wilmar," I said, with a wide smile. "Hi, I'm Asha from New York."

Without a change in his expression, Monsieur Wilmar extended a bear-size paw toward me. I gave him my hand and immediately regretted it. "Ow!" I said, before I could stop myself, and pulled back my throbbing hand. I noticed a slight flicker in his eyes like he was pleased at my reaction.

"I am Chloe Schmidt, the head administrator here." The woman gave me her hand. I extended mine gingerly, hoping she wasn't a crusher too. "You may call me Chloe," she said, "American style." A trace of a smile appeared on her face for just a moment.

"It's very nice to meet you, Chloe," I said, subdued by Monsieur Wilmar's presence.

I introduced the team one by one, trying to remember titles from what I'd read in Chef Pierre's magazines. *Mademoiselle Katy, chef patissier et sous chef. Mademoiselle Tetyana, chef de partie. Mademoiselle Win, commis chef. Monsieur Luc, sommelier.*

Neither Chloe nor Monsieur Wilmar blinked. Everyone shook everyone else's hands with the most formal looks on their faces, like we were about to embark on international diplomatic negotiations. Then, we followed the head chef into his kitchen.

I gaped as we walked in. This was no ordinary kitchen. This was a massive hall, the size and height of a basketball court, with flat stone slabs for walls that must have been built in the fifteenth century.

In one corner of the room stood a ten-foot grandfather clock. Next to it, an immense stone fire pit burned bright. I could just imagine long-ago cooks sitting around this, plucking geese, stirring cauldrons and preparing feasts for kings. The gigantic fire roared, casting a warm glow throughout the hall. Piled next to the fireplace were the largest cast-iron pots I'd ever seen. I could fit whole into one of these, I thought with a shudder.

Halfway up the room were rows of wooden counters piled with vegetables and uncooked meats, all waiting for attention from the cooks. Up above, thick wooden beams were suspended from the ceiling, from which hung legs of smoked ham, sausage, and meats of all kinds.

On the wall across from us was the most modern feature of this kitchen: a large flat-screen TV that was projecting a series of culinary images. Photos of racks of lamb, whole roasted pig, beef steak, and veal scallops flashed by as we watched. But it was what hung next to the screen that made my mouth open. The head of a large boar, tusks still intact, stared out from its pedestal. On the other side of the screen hung the head of a large deer, its antlers rising a meter high.

"Wow," I said. "Impressive."

Monsieur Wilmar smiled a crooked but satisfied smile.

"This is my, er, *mon bureau*—how do you say it—my office," he said, his chin up in pride. "You do not have *this* in America, do you?"

I shook my head, speechless. *Not in Canada either. Nor in Tanzania or India.*

Monsieur Wilmar walked ahead proudly. We followed.

Past the wooden counters lay a dining table that comfortably seated twelve. A dozen staff, dressed in immaculate white kitchen uniforms, occupied this table, having lunch. Next to them, at a smaller table, was a trio of wrinkled men who looked as old as the castle itself. They were smoking pipes and playing cards. Tumblers full of a golden drink sat by their sides. No one smiled. Everyone had stopped talking when they saw us come in.

"Madame Bouchard's private catering team," Chloe said to the group as we walked up to them.

"Hi, there," Katy said.

"Morning y'all," I said.

"Bonjour," someone replied.

"*Gudden Nometteg,*" said another.

From the corner of my eyes, I noticed Luc and Tetyana give two polite bows.

Chloe leaned to the table of the old men and whispered, *"Les Americains."*

"Aah," the men said, nodding their heads.

Monsieur Wilmar turned to us, his hand on his belly. "You have your own equipment, am I correct?"

"No, sorry." I shifted my feet. "It was, er, rather difficult to bring everything over. We don't need much space though, just, um, a small station to make cakes."

He stood silently, rubbing his belly, his face a mixture of disdain and unhappiness.

"What about the kitchenette, Monsieur Wilmar?" Chloe said, pointing toward the far wall. "You hardly use it. We can offer it to them, can we not?"

With a dour look on his face, Monsieur Wilmar marched toward where she was pointing. He yanked a knob and opened the door. We trooped in after him, while Chloe stayed back in the main kitchen with the others.

I blinked. We'd crossed a magical threshold between the medieval castle and a futuristic starship. In front of us was an enclosed kitchenette, but what a kitchenette it was. Spotless, shiny, and ultra-modern. I gave my head a shake to make sure I wasn't dreaming.

Around us, stainless steel kitchen appliances gleamed. The island countertop, made of white marble, shimmered under the bright fluorescent lights. On it was a basket full of fruit. Peaches, bananas, apples, pears, even a pineapple. Next to this was a sleek silver appliance. Was that a blender or a cake mixer? Or a teakettle from the future? A refrigerator, much smaller than the double-door ones in the kitchen outside, stood regally in one corner, looking like something you'd find on *Star Trek*.

I looked around in wonder. I'd died and gone to kitchen-nirvana, I was sure.

"Mademoiselle," Monsieur Wilmar said, breaking the spell. He glanced over his shoulder as if to make sure no one was listening and stooped over me. His gray eyes pierced mine. I could smell the rich cigar smoke on his breath.

"I have only one request," he said in a voice so bristly, it was almost a growl. Close up, his face resembled an angry bear more than a castle chef.

"All I ask is that you do not, under any circumstances, come into my kitchen or interfere with my staff. Do you understand?"

I felt my face go warm. I nodded.

"I do not care what special arrangements you have made with Madame Schmidt or any of our guests. I do not want to see you or your ragtag team. I do not want any one of you to even open this door. Is that clear?"

"I didn't mean to intrude, monsieur...."

But Monsieur Wilmar had stomped out, banging the door behind him.

I stood frozen, staring at the door.

"Quel salaud!" Luc swore. "What a bastard."

The door opened and in came Chloe.

"Do you have everything you need?" she said in a business voice. "High tea will be served shortly, so there is not much time."

I collected my thoughts. "Where can I find ingredients?"

"You need to talk to Monsieur Wilmar about that. I am sure he would be more than pleased to assist you."

Oh, I don't think so, I thought. "I know he's busy. I don't want to bother him. Maybe you have a pantry we could use?"

Chloe pointed at a small wooden door in a corner, no higher than three feet. We hadn't noticed it before. "That leads to the castle cellar. But you must talk to Monsieur Wilmar before taking anything. He manages everything on this floor."

Luc walked over and opened the door. It didn't open to any room, but a darkened stairwell going down.

"Now, we need to discuss menu items," Chloe said, opening a small notebook. "I can't seem to find any correspondence from the embassy, I'm afraid. So I have no idea what you will be serving."

"All Madame Bouchard wants are cupcakes," I said.

"Cup cakes?"

From the corner of my eyes, I saw Luc roll his eyes.

"Petite cakes in a variety of flavors and intricate decorations," I explained. Making it all up as I went along wasn't as easy as I'd thought. I crossed my fingers. "I know exactly what she likes. One thing she enjoys is Rémy Martin Black Pearl Grande in my black forest chocolate cake," I blabbed.

"Black Pearl Grande Cognac?" Chloe looked startled.

I nodded, trying to look as stately as I could. She looked me over. The change in her face was obvious.

"I'm impressed," she said, finally. "I believe both Madame Bouchard and the Grande Baroness will be delighted."

"Thank you," I said, with a slight bow, like the one she'd given me in the parking lot.

"Afternoon tea is served at exactly fifteen thirty hours," she said, snapping her book shut. "You have two hours to get prepared."

Chapter Forty-one

"Now what?" Tetyana asked.

I took a deep breath in. "We bake."

"Bake?" Win sounded surprised.

"We gonna play cook?" Luc said.

"We can't just go barging upstairs, can we?" I said. "We have to work our way in."

I looked at my team of involuntary sous chefs.

"Look, if you've got a better plan, let me know."

Silence.

"Okay then, here's what we need. We need to check the cellar to see what's in there. We need to look for cake trays, a flour sifter, mixing spoons, serving trays, and all that. And we need to find milk, butter, and eggs. Maybe that's all in the fridge. Also, we need a menu for Chloe, which I'll do right now."

"I'll look for pans and things," Katy spoke first.

"I'll check the fridge," Win said.

"And I'll check the cellar," Tetyana said, walking toward the wooden door.

"I'll come with you," Luc said, getting up.

"Make it quick," I called out, as they stepped down into the darkness.

Ok, now for the menu. I spotted a pen and paper pad with the castle's logo on the counter. I pulled out one of the high stools, took a seat, and put together a menu the Diplomatic Dragon Lady wouldn't be able to resist. While I wrote down the ingredients list, Katy and Win rooted through the fridge and cupboards and spent the next ten minutes getting things ready.

"It's dusty down there."

We looked up. It was Tetyana popping her head out of the cellar door.

"I need your ingredient list," she said.

"Where's Luc?" Win asked.

"Poking around the dungeons. Well? Do you have your wish list?"

I walked over and handed it to her.

"There's a wine cellar down there but I couldn't get it opened," she said, her eyes running down my list. "Hey, but I don't see that Black Pearl stuff here."

"You won't find it in a cellar anyone can walk into," I said. "One bottle's worth twenty thousand dollars."

She stared at me. "Twenty grand? You're ready to waste twenty-thousand-dollars' worth of good alcohol on *cooking*?"

"I used it only once, and only when the Dragon Lady sent a bottle with her chauffeur to make a special plate."

"For an elite diplomatic gathering," added Katy, "I remember that."

"So—" Tetyana looked confused.

"So I just wanted Chloe to believe me, that I was the real deal," I explained. "Anyway, I'll have to have to substitute now. Maybe with Armagnac. Worst case, brandy. It'll taste a bit funny, but it'll get us in the door."

"Look," Tetyana, said with an exasperated sigh. "All I know is vodka. If you want a fancy bottle, you better come down yourself." She turned and ducked back into the stairwell. I put my finished menu aside and followed her.

"You guys coming too?" I asked hearing Katy and Win behind me.

"I want to see this cellar," Katy said.

"I'm not staying in the kitchen by myself," Win said.

We climbed down the steep, narrow steps. The ceiling was so low even Win and I had to stoop to avoid hitting our heads.

At the bottom was a cool cavern cut into the rock. Along the walls of this cave hung a string of naked bulbs that emanated a low light, enough to see our surroundings and each other. I'd had many firsts these past few days, but this was definitely a worthy first.

We were in a luxury underground pantry the size of a two-bedroom apartment.

To our immediate left stood two temperature-controlled wine fridges with clear glass doors in front. In the first fridge, I counted at least a hundred bottles of white wine, all lying on their sides. The second fridge was filled with various sizes and shapes of liquor bottles. I walked up, peered through the glass, and gasped.

There's a bottle of Black Pearl in there! I yanked the door handle, but it didn't move.

"Keypad," Tetyana said. "It's very well secured. No one can break into that."

Win stepped up to the fridge and started to play with the buttons.

I scanned the rest of the cave.

The back wall was lined with sturdy wooden barrels, from floor to the ceiling. I stepped closer. On each barrel, written in a black stencil, was a fill date and the word *"vin."* Wine. Red wine. One of the barrels was dated more than a hundred years earlier. I did a double take and touched it. *Is this for real?* I rubbed the ink but the black lettering stayed and instead I got a century's worth of castle dust on my fingers.

In the corner of the cavern stood one solitary rack that held three smaller barrels. The markings on these said "port." Peering through the soft light, I saw that while the wine barrels had a fine coating of dust all over, it was fingerprints that covered these barrels.

A small shooter glass sat on the floor, next to this rack. I bent down to pick it up and held it to the light.

"A taster glass?" I said.

"There's still a few drops left," Katy said. "Someone's just used it."

"Maybe the fat chef comes here for a drink between jobs," Tetyana said.

I put the glass back down gingerly, hoping Monsieur Wilmar wouldn't come barreling into the cellar.

Along the side walls of the cave were ancient wooden shelves filled to the rafters with bins, tin cans, and wooden caskets. Everything was neatly packed, organized, and labeled with the same stencil as on the wine barrels. I opened a bin and peeked inside. White flour. Then, another. Wild black rice. Coffee beans. Dark chocolate slabs. *What an underground heaven. Monsieur Wilmar's the luckiest chef in the world*, I thought. *No wonder he's not happy another cook's here to share this with him.*

"Is this German?" I asked, pointing at the labels on the bins.

"I think so," Katy said, stooping to get a better look.

We both looked at Tetyana. She shook her head. "Don't look at me. I can help if it's Russian. You need Luc."

"Where is he?" I asked.

"Said he was going to explore. I gave him a gun, just in case." She scanned the cavern with a frown. "Now, where did he get to?"

The place was empty except for us.

"I only see one door out," Katy said, pointing to the large double door near the wine fridges where Win was still playing with the keypad, her head down, in total concentration.

"That must go to the main kitchen," I said.

Tetyana walked over, slipped it open an inch, and closed it just as quickly. "You're right," she said, turning around. "Our fat angry chef is out there."

"Guys!"

We jumped. The sound had come from the corner of the cave where the port barrel shelf stood. To our surprise, it moved sideways and opened. A shadowy figure emerged from behind the port barrels.

"Luc!" I said.

"How did you get back there?" Katy asked.

"Where the frig have you been?" Tetyana demanded. "I said explore, not disappear."

"You won't believe what I found," Luc said, motioning to us. "Come see."

We walked over to where he was standing. The shelf with the port barrels was a stealth door, and behind it was a gaping black entrance going into the belly of the castle. Luc shone a torch down the shaft, lighting a flight of rough steps leading into darkness.

"Where does it go?" Win asked in a whisper.

"Dungeons!" Luc said, using a fake scary voice.

"How did you find this?" I asked.

"I was looking for that Black Pearl stuff for you," he said, looking at me. "Couldn't get that fridge to open, so I checked out the wine barrels. Cognac, old wine, what's the difference, I thought."

How can he even compare? But I didn't say anything.

"I pulled out one of the stoppers to see if the wine was any good."

"You *opened* a wine barrel?" I asked.

"Wanted to see what hundred-year-old wine tasted like," he said giving me a defensive look. "Come on. I'm French."

"Was it any good?" Katy asked.

He shrugged. "Acceptable. Tasted like good table wine to me."

"Might as well drink vodka," Tetyana said more to herself than us.

"I saw these barrels that said *port*," Luc continued. "I pulled out the stopper of this one to try a bit but the whole thing came apart. Just like that. Thought it was gonna fall on top of me, but it opened out like this." He waved at the doorway in front of us. "And I found the torch right here."

"And there's nothing to drink in here," Luc said, tapping one of the port barrels and getting a hollow sound.

"A secret castle door," I said, examining the port barrels.

"Impressive," Katy said.

"Scary," Win said.

"Maybe," Tetyana said, looking thoughtfully at the doorway. "Maybe, we can find a way to the upper floors from there. Then, we can cut out all these middlemen and talk to the Dragon Diplomat directly."

"But this goes down, not up," Katy pointed out.

Luc was staring at Tetyana. "You know, you could be right," he said. "Old castles had hidden tunnels from the bedrooms upstairs to the cellars below, so the nobles could escape enemy attacks."

Tetyana nodded. "Faster than trying to fight these kitchen bureaucrats."

They both looked at me.

"Sure, let's check it out," I said. "Whatever works to get us closer to her."

"Is it safe though?" Win asked, peering down the shaft.

"As sturdy as a rock," Luc said, tapping the wall. "Must have stayed like this for centuries. You get right behind me, Win, and you'll be safer than anyone else alive."

Following Luc's torchlight, one by one we clambered down a short stairway to a landing, one much smaller than Chef Wilmar's pantry.

"This way," Luc said, stepping into another corridor, the only way out.

All around us was naked rock. The only light we had was Luc's little torch. My only comfort was we were all together, and Tetyana and Luc each had a gun. Though that did little to help the claustrophobia rising in me.

We followed Luc silently, huddling as close together as we could without tripping over each other. The passageway gradually became narrower and steeper. I shivered. We climbed down another slippery stairway, holding on to a rough iron railing that must have been installed eons ago.

After a minute, we came to a fork. One tunnel went dead straight ahead, darkness swallowing the end. The second tunnel twisted steeply into a dark abyss below. Neither looked appealing.

"That's a dead end," Luc said, pointing to the tunnel going straight. "We're going down. Get in single file, it's a bit narrow here." With that, he stepped into the darkness.

Visions of strange subterranean monsters sprung to mind. *Why would anyone do this for fun?* I thought, remembering the tourist brochures for dungeons and castle tunnels back at Luxembourg's city hostel. It was so quiet down here, I could hear everyone breathing. *Who knows what creatures lurk down here? Ones that prey on humans,* I thought with a shudder. *They can probably smell my sweaty fear from a mile away.*

We finally reached the bottom of the stairwell. We were now in a large and open space. Latched on one wall was a thick wooden door. A pale yellow beam of sunlight seeped in through the cracks of the doorway, allowing us to see each other better, a welcome relief from the darkness of the tunnels we'd trekked through.

"Where does this go to?" Tetyana asked, surveying the door closely.

"Opens to the bottom of the parking lot," Luc said. "This is the perfect place to dig an escape tunnel from upstairs. I didn't have time to explore because I knew you guys would get worried. I think there's a doorway to the upper floors somewhere here."

"Wouldn't it be obvious?" I said. "Like staring-in-our-face obvious?"

"No," he said. "Should be a secret door, so the slaves and servants couldn't find their way upstairs. One passageway for the kitchen staff and another to the main rooms upstairs."

He stepped up to the nearest wall and started to tap it.

We watched him work on the wall for a few seconds, then the rest of us joined in, tapping here and there, poking into holes between rocks and pushing anything that jutted out. It was Win who found the entrance.

Next to what looked like a large crack in the wall was a simple wooden doorknob, the same color as the rock. She gave a cry as she discovered it. We all gathered around her.

It took several tries to open the door with all of us heaving in unison. It hadn't been used in decades, maybe centuries.

Luc shone his torch into the pitch-black darkness.

"That's not going to the bedrooms," Tetyana said, shaking her head in disappointment.

We were staring at another staircase going down, this one going all the way to the middle of the earth, it seemed.

"The catacombs," Luc whispered. A few steps below us, lit up by his torch, lay a human skull.

Chapter Forty-two

Luc shut the door and looked at us grimly.

"What now?" Katy asked.

"Back to Plan A," Tetyana said, giving me a slight nod.

"Better get moving then," I said.

Luc led us back up the narrow staircase, through the tunnel, and to the pantry chamber. When we got there, he pushed open the port barrel shelf and peeked in to double-check if anyone was in the cellar. But the cave was empty.

We got to work, gathering our supplies, including pastry flour, baker's chocolate slabs, baking powder, and icing sugar. I asked Luc to find a decanter to pour half a liter of the hundred-year-old wine to substitute for the cognac. It wasn't at all ideal, but I had to invent.

"How come you don't want to use this?" Win asked.

I whirled around to see her holding the shiny black bottle of Rémy Martin Black Pearl Grande. Behind her, the fridge door was wide open.

"How...?" I stared at her.

"Did you just open that?" Katy asked.

Win nodded. Like it was the most perfectly normal thing to do, she walked over and handed me the bottle of the twenty-thousand-dollar Cognac.

I cradled it in my arms. "Tha-thanks," I stammered.

"Wow," Luc said, staring at her. "You're really good."

Win looked away demurely and went back to close the fridge door. "It was easy," she said.

"You're a whiz," I said, finding my voice. "I'm so glad you're with us. Thank you, Win!"

"Good job, hun," Tetyana said, patting Win on her back. "And my plan was to shoot that lock if I had to. Imagine."

Carrying our supplies, we walked up the steps in single file, back to the kitchenette. It was Katy, at the front of the line, who made the discovery.

"Door's locked," I heard her say.

"Lemme try," Luc, who was right behind her, said. I heard rattling, banging, then swearing in French.

"What's wrong with this damn door?" More rattling. "Someone's locked it!"

"Does anyone have the key?" I called out from the back.

A chorus of "no's" came from the stairway.

"Maybe it locks automatically when you close it," Katy said.

"No," Tetyana said. "Remember, I opened it from the cellar side when I came up to get the list?"

Luc was banging on the door. "Oi! Anyone there? Open up! *Ovrez la porte vite!*"

Nothing.

"Are we stuck?" I heard Win's panicked voice.

"No," Tetyana said. "There's the door to the main kitchen. Let's go back."

We turned around and climbed down. Tetyana who was now in front of the line marched to the main door and yanked at the doorknob. She fell back.

"What the hell?" she said staring at the door.

"Locked?" Katy asked in shock. She walked up and tried the door as well, but it didn't move.

"Lemme try," Luc said. He put the supplies he was carrying on a nearby shelf, rolled up his sleeves and pulled on the handle with all his might. Nothing. No amount of pushing, pulling, jiggling or banging worked.

That was when I realized what had happened. "He locked us in," I said. "That man actually locked us in."

"Monsieur Wilmar?" Katy asked.

I nodded. "Probably laughing at us right behind that door."

"Bastard," Tetyana said, banging on the door.

"I told you, these people are mad," Luc said. "*C'est des conneries!*" he yelled, shaking his fist at the door.

I had to agree. This was bull.

"Are we going to be stuck here forever?" Win asked, her face slightly pale.

"We'll find a way out," I said, not feeling as confident as my words. "Don't worry."

"Won't die of starvation, that's for sure," Luc said wryly.

"Come here, Win," Katy said, holding an arm out. "It's a huge cave with lots of tunnels below. There's plenty of air for us. Breathe now. That's it."

While I was trying to think of what to do, I caught a glint of steel from the corner of my eye. I looked up to see Tetyana pointing her gun at the lock.

"What are you doing?" I asked, shocked.

"Unlocking the damn door," she said, in that quiet voice she used whenever she was about to do something dangerous. "Stand back everyone."

"We can't go around shooting at things!"

"I don't plan to stay stuck here forever."

"What if they call the police?"

She hesitated.

"How are you going to even have a chat about immigration with the Dragon Lady?"

Tetyana lowered her weapon slowly.

"So we wait till they return to replenish their royal supplies?" she snarled, glaring at the door.

"Guys!" Luc called out.

I turned to look. He was fiddling near those port barrels again.

"There's another way out."

"What other way?" Katy asked.

"Back down. Remember that door to the parking lot?"

"Maybe that's locked too," Katy said.

"Nope, I tried it. There's a dried crust around the frame, but I think I can open it."

We looked at each other.

Tetyana tucked her gun inside her jacket and said with a sigh, "Well, not much of a choice, is there?"

"Worst-case scenario, you can shoot that door down," I said. "It'll be less of a scene there, than inside the building."

"You're worried about making a scene?" Tetyana said, her mouth curling into that old sneer of hers. "I'd like to make a scene on the idiots who frigging locked us in."

"We have to use diplomacy, not violence here," I said. "I'm trying to get someone important here to help us."

Ignoring me, she marched toward the port barrel shelf door, which Luc was now holding open for us.

Our trip down took longer than the first time because we were laden with supplies now. Also, Tetyana was in a bad mood, Win was on the verge of a panic attack, and I was trying to keep my claustrophobic fears from flaring up again.

It was a relief to get to the end chamber with the crusty door to the parking lot.

Luc was correct. The door was rusty and heavy but it was working. We stumbled out of the cave at the edge of the castle's parking lot.

Our van was exactly where we'd left it. No one else was around and all the delivery trucks had left. We walked toward the castle's service entrance, which thankfully, remained wide open.

I stopped before we walked in.

"We're going to walk in with our heads held high. We will be graceful." I glanced over at Tetyana. "That will be the best revenge."

She muttered something under her breath. I turned and walked in the door.

It was Monsieur Wilmar who saw us first.

He was busy cutting meat at the main counter with a butcher knife when we walked in. His eyes widened as he saw us enter. I gave him a quick nod and a noncommittal smile and kept walking. The entire kitchen had fallen silent. No one in my group said a word either.

We strode through the kitchen hall, heads held high, carrying our bins, bags, and trays of supplies toward the kitchenette. Someone had locked this door too. From the outside. I unlocked it, took the key out and pocketed it. Everyone trooped in after me. Tetyana came in last and made a point of slamming the door behind her.

"Phew!" I said, putting the baking soda and chocolate containers on the kitchen counter.

I looked at my team.

"Wanna help me bake some cakes?" I asked cheerfully.

No one smiled.

Win had found a stack of white aprons in a drawer when she'd been rummaging for supplies. I took one and tied it around me. Win and Katy followed suit, and to my surprise, so did Luc. Win discovered a chef's hat at the bottom of the pile and plonked it in front of me. I put it on and got to work.

It took us an hour to mix the batter, bake the cakes, and decorate them using whatever I could find in the fridge.

Luc seemed to have forgotten his skepticism. He joined in his sous chef duties, swirling chocolate icing on top of the mini-cakes like I showed him, working intently and even egging others to a competition of who could ice the fastest. He took to his tasks so naturally that I thought, *If I ever have a bakery one day, I'm hiring him.*

Tetyana helped as well, but not as happily. "I'm a fighter, not a damn baker," she snapped at one point, looking angrily at an icing glob that had fallen on the floor with a splat.

By the time we were done, my team looked like legitimate kitchen help, with icing sugar smeared on their aprons and their faces.

On the flour-stained countertop now sat a three-tier platter of fifty black forest chocolate mini-cakes made from a Chef Pierre's gourmet recipe plus that one outrageously exorbitant ingredient. I looked at the clock. Three twenty-five. We were just on time.

Someone knocked on the door. Before anyone could get to it, Chloe strode in.

"Bonjour," she said, with a curt nod.

"Bonjour," all except Tetyana greeted her.

"Are you ready?"

"Yes," I said, feeling like I needed to salute her or something.

"Oh!" She'd noticed the cakes.

She stood still, staring at the display.

"This recipe was a special favorite of Madame Bouchard," I said. "And Chef Pierre," I added, remembering his picture in the magazine.

"Chef Pierre?" Chloe looked at me, surprised. "You know him?"

"With my compliments," I said, not really answering her question.

Chloe walked around the platter inspecting the cakes from all angles.

"May I try one?"

"With pleasure," I said, picking one and handing it to her.

She gave me an odd look. "Do you not have plates?"

Win passed a small saucer to me from the glass cabinet. I placed the cake gently on it and handed it to Chloe.

She didn't touch it. "And the cutlery, mademoiselle?" she said, giving Win a stern look.

From the corner of my eyes, I saw Luc roll his eyes. Win reached for the top drawer, brought out a fork and knife and placed them next to Chloe's plate. Chloe's mouth curled down at the corners. Katy jerked open the drawer again, searched for a matching pair and switched the pieces.

But Chloe wasn't done. "What about a serviette?"

We stared at her.

"It's a friggin' cupcake," Tetyana said, forgetting she wasn't supposed to talk.

Chloe stared at Tetyana. She glared back, unblinking.

"Unlike in America," Chloe said, pronouncing every syllable, her eyes firmly on Tetyana's, "we prefer not to use our fingers to eat."

Tetyana's face went red. I wasn't sure if it was because she'd been mistaken for an American or because she'd been dismissed so contemptuously. Maybe both. I saw her hand go to her side, the side where she kept her gun.

"Katy!" I yelled, jumping in front of Tetyana. "Get a serviette!"

Katy slammed open a drawer, pulled out a crisp white serviette and threw it next to the cake saucer. Chloe stared at us, eyebrows raised like we'd gone mad.

I smiled my best frozen smile at her. *"Bon appétit,* madame," I said, with a low bow.

As we all stood around the counter and watched, Chloe daintily cut the cupcake with her gold cutlery and took a bite. She showed the most sophisticated table manners I'd ever seen. She seemed to eat with even more ceremony than the Diplomatic Dragon Lady herself.

"Does it meet your expectations?" I asked, once she'd had a bite. She nodded. *"Bon."*

Good? Just good?

Before I could say anything, she tapped her phone once. The door opened and in walked two men.

I felt Win move close and clutch my hand. I squeezed hers back.

With their black bow ties, red waistcoats and crisp white shirts, these men looked like a cross between palace guards and waiters in a five-star hotel. Their faces were as impassive as wax figures and their demeanor as impeccable as anyone who routinely served royalty. I watched as they glided across the floor and picked my cake tray up.

"You may take leave now," Chloe said nodding to me. She turned to the two men. "To the drawing room, please."

With that, she marched out. The men followed, carrying my cupcake tray high above their shoulders.

Chapter Forty-three

"**P**hew, I thought she was going to eat me," Win said.

"*Quelle pute pompeuse!*" Luc said. "What a pompous woman."

"How is that going to help us get to the Dragon Diplomat?" Tetyana asked.

I whipped off my apron, threw it on the counter, and stepped toward the door.

"Hey, what are you doing?" Katy asked.

"Find out where they're going," I said, opening the door.

I stepped out.

Chloe and the two men-in-waiting were walking past the staff table toward the other end of the kitchen.

Everyone in the main kitchen had stopped their work and was staring at the cake tray passing by. I caught sight of Monsieur Wilmar glaring from the meat station, the fat cleaver still in his hands. "Back to work!" he shouted at his team, startling me.

I closed the door behind me and started my walk across the hall, my back tingling, wondering if I was going to feel that cleaver between my shoulder blades any moment.

Halfway through the hall, I heard a loud smash from behind. I turned to see Monsieur Wilmar thrash a piece of meat on the cutting board. He was hitting it so hard, I was surprised it hadn't gone through the board. For all I knew, it had. Everyone had gathered as far away from him as possible.

In those few seconds of distraction, I'd lost sight of Chloe and the two servers. They'd vanished.

Where did they go?

I walked faster toward the end of the kitchen. There were two doors on the far wall. I opened the first only to find a set of bare concrete steps going down. *That can't be it.* Chloe had said they were going up to the drawing room. I looked at the second door but it didn't have a handle. I poked around, pushing and prodding until I noticed a modern panel of buttons next to the door frame. I punched a button and the doors slid open.

An elevator!

I looked behind me. No one was watching me anymore. The sous chefs were busy over their pots and pans. Monsieur Wilmar was inspecting something on the stove and the old men were engrossed in their card game. I stepped into the elevator and the doors slid shut.

Where to now? There was only one floor up. I pressed the button. The elevator whirred up obediently.

When the doors opened, I was sure I'd traveled to another world.

I stood gaping until the elevator doors started to slide shut on me. I slammed my arm between them and jumped out.

I found myself standing in the ritziest foyer I'd ever seen.

My feet sank into the luxurious royal red carpet. Gold trimmings adorned the walls and beautiful motifs of flowers covered every inch of the ceiling. Wrought-iron chandeliers dripped down from above, and along the walls, red candles burned in copper candelabras, bathing the room in an opulent glow. I'd never seen anything like this before in my life. I turned around and around to soak it all in.

I couldn't linger though.

There were three doorways from this foyer. I stood still for a minute and listened. A faint hum was coming from the doorway on the far right. I walked toward it. I could hear voices, soft voices. I stepped through, treading softly on the carpet, and came to another grand foyer with an immense doorway in front of me. Straddling this entranceway were two guardsmen dressed exactly like the two who'd come to get my cakes, moments earlier.

They saw me as soon as I stepped onto the landing. There was no place to hide and I couldn't run now.

Act natural.

I straightened my back, leveled my shoulders, clasped my hands behind me, and walked up to them as casually as I could. I couldn't stop my legs from shaking but I noticed they were looking my way with more curiosity than hostility. One of them glanced at something above my head. That was when I realized I still wore my chef's hat.

"May we help you?"

It was one of the guards.

"I am here to see Madame Chloe Schmidt," I said, with a small bow. "She asked me to come up."

To my surprise, he nodded and indicated a side door. I bowed again to say thank you and pushed the door open with trembling hands.

No one noticed me enter the room and slip into the shadows.

Near the side door was an alcove with a long buffet table piled with three-tier food trays. They overflowed with lavish finger foods, sandwiches, and savories of all kinds. I stared at the spread. There were shortbreads, and scones, biscuits of all kinds, mini cheese plates on beautiful bone china, cucumber and salmon sandwiches, and little white containers filled with jams and creams and butters of all types. Whatever I thought of Monsieur Wilmar, he sure could put a good tea party together.

Then, right in the center of the table, I saw my platter of cakes.

I took a sharp breath in, forgetting for a moment why I was here. They looked every bit as grand as the other royal dishes. There was only one other full dessert on the table—a dark fruit pie of sorts, and that was sitting to the side. I stood a little straighter and held my head a little higher to see my fairy cakes so prominently displayed in this sumptuous drawing room of this Luxembourg castle. *My mother would have been so proud*, was all I could think of. I smiled to myself.

It took several seconds to tear my eyes away from the buffet table and remind myself why I'd come up here.

Set neatly across the drawing room were about fifty tables for six, draped in white tablecloths. Beautiful flower arrangements sat in the middle of each table and crystal chandeliers hung from the ceiling. The guests were seated, smiling and talking in soft voices. It was exactly how you'd expect a castle tea party to look.

The men wore linen shirts and jackets, but it was the women who struck me the most. They wore extravagant summer dresses in all styles and colors, decorated with ruffles, cowls, feathers, and jewels. Strands of pearls adorned their necks and feathery fascinators perched precariously on their beautifully coiffed heads. Everyone was immersed in their meal, laughing occasionally, golden forks and knives clinking happily on the china.

Young waiters treaded quietly in between the tables, filling water glasses and pouring tea. They traveled back and forth between the buffet table and the diners, absorbed in their tasks. As long as I drew back into the alcove when they came to the buffet table, I remained hidden.

From my hiding spot, I had only a partial view of the guests and had to peek around the corner to see the room in its entirety. During a lull when all the waiters were away from the buffet table, attending to the guests, I stuck my head out and scanned the room.

There. There she was. Hard to miss.

Tall and exquisite in her chic white Chanel pantsuit and pearl choker, the Diplomatic Dragon Lady looked as elegant as I'd remembered.

She was the only woman in the room not wearing a dress. I was now sure the Europeans gave slack on etiquette and protocol to North Americans, just like Chloe had tolerated our arrival in a white cargo van with no supplies. A European baker would have never got away with as much as I had. She'd expected us to be different, irreverently so.

My eyes traveled around the table to the Diplomatic Dragon Lady's companions. I nearly choked to see plump Chef Pierre sitting across from her. Two of my favorite people at the same place. I couldn't believe it.

My mind raced. *Maybe I can get his autograph? Ask him about his recipes?*

I suddenly remembered my foray into his café in Brussels and felt my neck go warm. *Maybe he knows I stole the chocolate roll from his Brussels café.* I shook my head. *Of course, he doesn't. He's the CEO of an international company. People steal stuff every day. It's the store manager's job to deal with these things.* I felt something heavy in my chest. *I can't believe I did that. I'm not a thief!* I shook my head to rid myself of the guilt and took a few deep breaths in to steady my nerves.

I waited a full minute before peeking out again. This time, I looked for the one person I didn't want to see. Chloe was standing against the far wall, next to a tall man with white hair. He was dressed in the same uniform as the servers, but with more buttons and trimmings on his coat. *Must be the head waiter,* I thought.

The two of them stood silently, scanning the room from side to side, their focus on the guests, making sure no needs went unmet. This meant there was no way I could walk up to a table unnoticed. I watched them with my fingers crossed, waiting to see if they'd leave the room.

Polite laughter and chatter continued at the tea party tables, while servers moved like silent ghosts in between them.

Should I wave at the Dragon Lady? Will she see me? Will she wave back? Or will she get angry at the interruption? Maybe I should wait for everyone to finish and then walk to her table. Chloe won't see me in the midst of everyone getting up and moving around. Or will she? She's sharper than a fox. Maybe I'll wait for the Dragon Lady to go to the washroom and get her attention in the corridor.

One server walked toward the buffet table, and I quickly drew back into the shadows. To my delight, he picked up my cake tray and walked to the closest table. Using a long silver tong, he daintily picked up a cupcake and deposited it on a guest's plate with a small bow. *So that's what Chloe had expected me to do.*

I watched the waiter work his way through the room until he reached the Dragon Lady's table. She was in the middle of speaking to Chef Pierre and picked up her dessert fork without glancing at her plate. When she did look down, she stopped talking, her mouth dropping slightly open. I watched without breathing. *Does she recognize my work?*

The server placed a cake on Chef Pierre's plate next. My mouth dried up.

What if he hates it? What if he spits it out? I watched as he sliced a tiny piece off the cake with his fork and brought it to his mouth. He chewed and swallowed it. I think I stopped breathing. I saw him take a second bite. This time, he chewed it thoughtfully before swallowing. He sliced another piece, then another, until the little cake was gone. He stared at his plate with a funny expression.

"Mademoiselle!"

I jumped.

"May I help you?"

My heart thumped. "Hello, Chloe. I was—er—I came to see if everything was okay."

"Everything is perfectly fine," she snapped. "You, however, must not be here."

"I just wanted to, er, make sure everyone's happy with the cakes. Checking on, er, customer satisfaction, you know?"

"Mademoiselle, this is highly unusual."

"I need to get a feel for my audience," I babbled. "Find out how they eat, how they smell, how they taste. I need to know what they're like, so I can make a better batch for tomorrow's—"

"There's absolutely no need for all that. If a chef's creations are not acceptable for our diners, they will be told to leave. Immediately. It is that simple."

"But how do I know what to make tomorrow then?"

"We will inform you." She moved a step closer. She didn't look intimidating, but the message was clear.

"Will you ask Chef Pierre what he thinks, at least?" I said, before turning to leave.

A shadow fell on us. The head server had walked up to us.

"Everything all right, Madame Schmidt?" he asked.

Chloe straightened her jacket without taking her eyes off me. "Chef Asha was just leaving."

I opened the door. Just as I stepped across the threshold, I heard her voice. "Why must Americans be so maddeningly boorish?"

She wanted me to hear that.

Chapter Forty-four

Iclosed the door behind me and managed a smile for the two guards. They didn't return the gesture.

Feeling their curious eyes on my back, I walked out as casually as I'd walked in. Once I got to the elevator foyer, I let out a big breath and pressed the button with shaking fingers.

Now what?

I'd failed my mission. I could have one more chance the next day, but only if Chloe didn't kick us out and if everyone else agreed to try again. *Maybe they've all had enough and got back in the van.* I stepped out of the elevator and into the main kitchen. Monsieur Wilmar was nowhere to be seen and the staff had thinned. I walked up to the kitchenette and yanked the door open.

To my relief, everyone was still there, sitting on the high chairs around the island countertop.

Luc had his head down on the counter. Win was curled up in her chair, looking half-asleep. Katy was flipping through a recipe magazine, and Tetyana was cleaning her guns with a kitchen cloth, naked bullets scattered around her. My first thought was *I put food on that table, you know.* But this wasn't the time to fuss about kitchen hygiene.

"Well?" Tetyana asked, looking up.

Luc and Win stirred awake. Katy put down her magazine.

I closed the door behind me.

"How did it go?" Luc asked.

"The Dragon Lady's here."

"That's good news," Katy said.

"Did you talk to her?" Tetyana asked.

I shook my head. "Tomorrow," I said, summoning my most confident voice. "This was the first step. Now she's tried my cakes and knows I'm here, she'll want to talk to me."

Tetyana scrunched up her eyes and stared at me for a couple seconds before going back to cleaning her guns.

A knock on the door made us look up. I braced myself. *Is it Chloe and her guards?*

Luc opened the door and in came the young Alice-in-Wonderland look-alike.

"Hallo, mäin numm ass Greta," she said prettily to Luc.

"Hallo, Greta," Luc said, waving her in with a bow.

Chloe had asked Greta to take us to our lodgings. Greta didn't speak much, but from the cautious way she regarded me, I was sure I was in Chloe's black books. At least she hadn't thrown us out of the castle, I thought. Not yet, anyway.

We followed the little girl through the main kitchen. She led us to the far end and opened the door next to the elevator.

We climbed down to the servants' quarters in the basement. There were no luxurious wall trimmings here or lush carpets or chandeliers. On both sides of the stark corridor were small rooms, each with two beds and tiny windows that opened to the parking lot on one side, and the forest on the other. Prison rooms were nicer than these, I thought.

After Greta opened the first room to us, she tipped her head to the side, tucked her hands underneath it and closed her eyes. She then opened one eye to see if we understood.

"We sleep here tonight," I said, nodding, "Thank you, Greta."

"Villmols merci," Luc translated with a smile.

Greta nodded and pointed at the door through which we'd just come down. She wagged a finger at it.

"What does that mean?" Katy asked.

Luc bent down to get to her level. *"So mir, Greta – ech versti."* You can speak to me, Greta, I understand.

"*Et ass verbueden fir an d'Kichen zréckzegoen,*" the girl said in a sweet voice. "*Dir musst héi bleiwen, bis den Här Wilmar iech rifft fir d'Owendiessen.*"

"She's saying we can't go back to the kitchen," Luc explained. "Not till Monsieur Wilmar calls us up for supper."

"Oh, really?" I said. *How generous.*

"So he doesn't want us wandering around?" Katy asked.

"I'm sure that's it," Luc said, straightening up.

The girl pointed at a small door nearby and another one at the end of the corridor. "*Dës Dier geet an den Keller an dës um Enn op de Parking.*"

"*Merci.*" Luc nodded and turned to us. "That door is to the cellar, and that one on the end is to the parking lot where our van is."

The girl stepped away with a shy wave. Win and Luc waved back while the rest of us stared at the disappearing fairy-tale-like figure.

"I guess we'll be spending the night here," I said.

We walked over to our van and got our knapsacks filled with the clothes, shoes, and toiletries we'd gotten in Luxembourg City. I wanted to explore the castle grounds to see if I could find another way to get to the Dragon Lady, but Luc pointed discreetly at the two foot guards having a smoke break near the back door.

"Don't think that's smart right now," he said.

So we returned to our rooms. Tetyana took a room with Win. Katy and I picked a room together, and Luc had the smallest room with a cot to himself. We took advantage of the communal showers in the servants' quarters and got ready for whatever was to come next.

An hour and a half later, Greta came down to escort us to the kitchen for dinner.

The lines had clearly been drawn.

The kitchen staff sat at the main table with Monsieur Wilmar at its head. Our crew had been relegated to a much smaller table in the back, ten feet away from theirs.

No one looked at us or spoke to us. It was like we were at the loser table in high school where I'd eaten most of my school lunches when only Katy would come and sit with me.

"At least they're feeding us," I whispered to Tetyana.

"Geneva Convention," she said, with a grim smile. "You must always feed prisoners of war."

I don't think anyone slept well that night.

The rooms were cold and the beds were hard. The stone walls didn't allow any heat to remain inside, and there didn't seem to be any electrical heating on this floor. It hadn't helped that a howling wind whipped at the windows most of the night and Luc had talked about werewolves throughout supper. I tossed and turned for hours and was glad when the morning light streamed through the small window.

I'd just woken up when I heard a knock on the door.

"*Gudde Moien,*" Greta said brightly. She was wearing the same outfit as the day before. Does she have several Alice in Wonderland costumes, I wondered.

"Good morning, Greta," I replied.

She handed me a yellow envelope and left with a wave. I stared at her back, unsure if I was still asleep and dreaming. I rubbed my eyes.

"What is it?"

I turned around to see Katy sitting up. Closing the door, I walked over to sit at the edge of her bed and pulled out a beautifully handwritten note from the envelope. My heart skipped a beat. *A letter from the Dragon Lady?* No, it was a menu, the menu for this afternoon's tea party. I drew my breath in.

Katy peered over my shoulders. "Wow," she said. "We'll be baking all day."

"Where do we find these ingredients?" I said, running through the list.

Chloe wanted three hundred and fifty cakes, in several flavors. "Lemon meringue, black forest, tiramisu, candied hazelnut, hummingbird, chrysanthemum cheesecake, marzipan fruit. Oh my god, where do we even start?"

I tried to remember what I'd seen in the cellar and the fridge in our kitchenette.

"Impossible," Katy said, shaking her head. "We won't even have time to bake."

I looked over the list again and nodded gloomily.

A second knock made us sit up.

"Come in!" Katy called out.

Win and Luc stumbled in, with Tetyana behind them.

"Sleep okay?" she asked.

Everyone shook their heads.

"So?" Tetyana said, "What's the plan for today?"

I waved the menu. "Chloe just sent her commands."

She took the list and let out a whistle. "You have to make all this?"

"By eighteen hundred, thirty hours," Luc said, reading over her shoulder.

"They want the cakes for after dinner," Katy said, turning to me with an encouraging smile. "This means they really liked what we did yesterday."

"But I can't do this," I said, shaking my head. "They probably have all this stuff in the main kitchen, but Monsieur Wilmar will kill us before he lets us touch it."

"So what do we do?" Win asked.

"Maybe it's time to find another way out of our mess," I said glumly. "I guess we'll have to take our chances with Fred and the police."

Someone rapped on the door.

"Fruhstuck in einer halben Stunde!" Greta shouted from outside.

"Breakfast in half an hour," Luc translated.

"Let's have something to eat first and figure this out," Tetyana said.

We took half an hour to shower, dress and climb upstairs to the main kitchen.

Everyone else was at their designated spot and had already started on their homemade croissants and pastries with jams and fruit. They'd set a place for us at the small side table again and all we had was dry bread and butter to go with our coffee. Other than desultory replies to our good mornings, everyone kept to themselves.

The chatter at the large table was subdued, everyone occupied with their food, or too intimidated by Monsieur Wilmar. Greta was all smiles and sunshine, though. She sat at the edge of her table, closest to us, and once in a while slipped Luc jam jars and pastries from her table.

I moved my half-eaten bread around my plate, brooding. There was no way I was going to find all the right ingredients and even if I did, I wouldn't find enough of them to make that many cakes by six thirty in the afternoon.

Chloe had set me up for failure. I'd never be able to talk to the Dragon Lady, and I'd never get to meet Chef Pierre. *Maybe it's time to leave.* I stared forlornly at my coffee cup.

"You received your menu, I presume." It was the sonorous voice of Monsieur Wilmar.

I looked up. He was looking at me with a glint in his eyes.

I nodded.

"I wish you lots of luck today." His voice dripped sarcasm. I didn't answer. He gave a satisfied grunt and went back to his coffee.

I stared at him. *Is he the one who convinced Chloe to make this menu?*

"Monsieur Wilmar."

I turned to look at Tetyana.

What's she doing?

Everybody had turned silent.

"Ja Fraulein," Monsieur Wilmar replied, looking at her from across his table, arms crossed.

"Are those yours?" Tetyana pointed at the stuffed boar and deer heads on the wall.

The chef straightened up and cleared his throat. "Indeed. That is my work."

"Very impressive."

"Danke." Monsieur Wilmar uncrossed his arms and looked at his prized possessions, his chest puffed ever so slightly.

"When did you get them?"

"The boar was in 2000 and the deer in 2010. Only one shot each. Clean and fast."

"Point three-o-eight caliber?"

He raised an eyebrow. "That is correct. You know your ammunition. You hunt as well, I presume, Fraulein?"

"Only with this," Tetyana said, flipping her right jacket flap open. The handgun, fully polished after all that cleaning the day before, gleamed in the light. Tetyana's eyes, intense and strong, stared straight at Monsieur Wilmar.

I heard a collective gasp.

What's she trying to prove? I wanted to shake her but was rooted in my chair.

Monsieur Wilmar's face turned a light purple. Without a word, he poured himself another cup of coffee, studiously avoiding eye contact with anyone. It took a full minute for everyone else to start eating again, and when they did, all eyes were on their plates.

I gave Tetyana a *what-are-you-doing* look. She winked in return.

With an angry grunt, Monsieur Wilmar scraped back his chair and got up to leave. In that same moment, Tetyana pulled her chair back and stood up too.

Everyone froze. The only sound in the room was the tick-tock of the grandfather clock in the corner.

"Monsieur Wilmar, Chef Asha needs special ingredients for this afternoon's menu," Tetyana said in her most polite voice. "We would greatly appreciate it if someone from your kitchen would assist her today."

Three tense seconds ticked by before Monsieur Wilmar responded.

"Greta!" he yelled. *"Zeig ihnen die speisekammer!"*

He threw his napkin on the table and stomped out of the kitchen.

Chapter Forty-five

We took all day. But it was worth it.

I stepped back to look at what we'd created. On the countertop stood a four-foot-tall, multi-level cupcake tower.

I hadn't had to worry about ingredients, serving platters or cake holders, because Monsieur Wilmar's kitchen was equipped to serve a king. But I'd also noticed most of his cake pans and serving plates were as good as new.

"He only serves *Quetschentaart* for dessert," Greta said when Luc asked about this.

"What's a *kwetshentart*?" I asked.

"Open pie made with plums," Luc explained. "It's very popular here. The baroness probably grew up with it."

"I think I saw one," I said, remembering the fruit pie on the side of the buffet table the day before.

Greta pulled on Luc's arm and said something. We waited.

"Supposedly," Luc translated, "Monsieur Wilmar is famous in this region for his pie. That's all the baroness normally has for dessert."

I nodded. *And he hates me now for having overturned his comfortable dessert tradition,* I thought.

I looked with pride at my cake tower.

The multi-tiered silver platters made the tower look formidable, royal even. I'd met Chloe's requests and more. On the bottom tier were the Dragon Lady's favorite black forest cakes interspersed with several of Chloe's requests. In the middle tier, I added half a dozen peach and cream cakes to the mix, and on the top plate, I arranged a dozen pineapple cheesecake bites. It was an exotic combination of cakes that the Dragon Lady always loved.

Everyone had chipped in to build the cake tower, even Greta, who seemed to enjoy hanging out with us. I guessed it gave her a diversion from the everyday and the satisfaction that she was, in effect, in formal charge of the foreign baking team. But that didn't stop her from giggling as she swirled strawberry icing on a cupcake under Luc's watchful eye.

Luc proved to be well on his way to mastering the art of cake decorating, coming up with ideas that made Katy gasp and Tetyana roll her eyes. But they worked like a charm. He seemed to have a hidden artist in him, so I let him experiment to his heart's content.

Everyone had found a job they wanted to do or could tolerate, at least, and we'd created a fully functioning assembly line in the kitchen.

Tetyana took charge of bringing ingredients and pans from the main kitchen and putting dirty pans and bowls into the dishwasher once done. Katy measured the ingredients and helped me bake the cakes. Luc and Win worked on the icing and decorations while Greta inserted herself wherever she could, ending up with flour on her hair and icing sugar on her nose. *My team,* I thought as I watched everyone bustle around, doing their bit.

I now had access to all the ingredients I needed, including the liquor fridge downstairs, and used the Black Pearl Cognac in my cakes liberally. I remembered the Diplomatic Dragon Lady's face when she'd tasted my cakes for the first time back in Toronto, a year ago. I wanted her to bite into these cakes and know instantly they were mine. I was sure there'd be no way she wouldn't agree to help us after that.

A loud rap came on the door.

Before anyone could say *"Entrez,"* the door opened and in marched Chloe. Following behind her was a rotund man with a cheery face.

My jaw dropped.

Chef Pierre? Oh my god, it's Chef Pierre! He looked exactly like he did in the magazines. Even in his tuxedo, he looked friendly and kind.

"Are we—?" Chloe stopped in mid-stride as she saw the tower. She stared at it.

"Impressive," she said. "You created this?"

I nodded, dumbfounded at seeing my idol in real life.

"Extraordinaire," Chef Pierre said, stepping up to the tower and inspecting it with a keen eye. He then turned and looked at each of us, appraising us. "Might I know who the chef is?"

My mouth had dried up.

Katy nudged me from one side and Tetyana from the other.

"I...er...I....," was all I could say. The image of the chocolate roll I'd stolen from his café in Brussels sprang to mind and I felt my face burn.

"Ah, Chloe mentioned you," Chef Pierre said, looking at me and stroking his chin. "Chef Asha, is it not?

He knows my name!

"So you're the nonconformist baker? The one who threatens to use Black Pearl to make edible fêtes?"

I nodded wordlessly.

"I liked what you did yesterday."

I straightened up. "Really?" I said, my voice squeaking. I cleared my throat. "Did you like it? I mean, really?"

"Why do you think I've come down here?" he said, spreading his hands expansively. "To meet the talented chef who baked yesterday's cakes."

"Tha..thank you," I said.

He dropped his voice. "To be frank, I was getting tired of the plum pies every time I visit the baroness."

I didn't know what to say.

"May I try one?"

His hand went to the side plate which contained the leftover cakes that didn't fit in the tower. His hand hovered over the chocolate cake, then the raspberry cream one. "What a delightful dilemma," he said to himself. He was just about to pick the pineapple cream cheesecake when I remembered.

"Wait!" I said, finding my voice.

He looked up, startled.

"Katy, please get a dessert plate. Win, a white napkin, please. And utensils." I opened a drawer to find a pair of silver tongs, like the ones they had in the drawing room for tea.

Chef Pierre looked at me strangely.

"Chef Asha, I do not drive my Maserati to the corner store when I can walk," he said. "I will use my fingers," he paused to pick up the chocolate cake, "if that does not offend anyone."

We all shook our heads. No one looked at Chloe, but from the corner of my eyes, I thought a slight pink tone had come over her face.

"That's based on one of your own recipes, Chef Pierre," I said.

He stopped and stared at me. "You've baked my recipes?"

"All of them."

"I didn't think my work was known across the Atlantic."

"I had access to your magazines and cookbooks." I paused. I wasn't going to tell him where or how. "Baked everything from scratch," I added.

He nodded thoughtfully and turned his attention back to the cake. I watched as he brought the cake to his mouth and took a bite. I swallowed involuntarily and wiped my sweaty palms on my apron.

Chef Pierre chewed slowly before he swallowed. I looked warily at the yellow crumbs on his cheek and felt a stream of sweat trickle down my back.

He stared at the ceiling silently for the next few seconds, as if ruminating over the taste. I think I stopped breathing.

"Interesting combination," he said, after what seemed like the longest five seconds of my life. "I've never had anything like this before. It is....fascinating. Delightful."

I let out a breath.

"Ladies and gentlemen," Chloe spoke up. "This conversation is riveting. However, I must take this upstairs now. I'll summon the footmen." She whipped her phone out.

"No!" I almost shouted.

Chloe turned to me with a frown.

"No need to bother them. I'll take the cakes up myself. Save you some trouble."

"*You?*" She looked at me.

"Yes."

"But that is not customary."

Tetyana spoke up, forgetting she wasn't supposed to. "But she did all the work."

"Excellent point," Chef Pierre said.

"We must follow protocol," Chloe said, looking at us in surprise.

"But we don't follow this protocol in America," I said.

"Well, we do so here, mademoiselle!"

I thought I heard a snicker from Chef Pierre. He was leaning against the counter now with a marzipan cupcake in his hands watching the debate with an amused smile on his face.

"The Diplo—" I caught myself. "Madame Bouchard would be interested to know we have come all the way to create this for her." I waved my hand grandly at the tower. "Americans like to know who made their meals and how, and you know, have a chat."

"*A chat?*" Chloe looked like she'd blow a blood vessel.

"I like *les Americains*," Chef Pierre quipped from the side.

"Well." Chloe seemed lost for words. "This goes against all tradition."

Chef Pierre cleared his throat. "Madame," he said, turning to Chloe, "if you would permit me, may I say I have to agree with this young chef. The time for cooks to be relegated to the back of the kitchen is long gone. Would you not agree?"

"With all due respect, monsieur, I do not mean to be disagreeable with an esteemed guest; however," she paused, "tradition is tradition."

I felt bad for her. She was only doing her job.

"I understand what you mean, madame," Chef Pierre said with a charming smile. "Perhaps it's time to change some of these customs, do you not think?"

"This is highly unusual." Chloe was spluttering. "You must understand. What will the baroness say?"

"She will be delighted, I am sure," Chef Pierre said, with another smile.

Silence.

"I will permit this," Chloe finally said, her face flushed. "But only if you change into fresh aprons and caps." Her eyes traveled down my wrinkled skirt, which was dusted in flour. "And follow all my instructions fully."

"I promise," I said.

Win was already opening the top drawer to dig out fresh aprons.

Chef Pierre turned to me. "I hope to continue our conversation, Chef Asha. I hope this is not the last time we meet."

I watched him step out of the kitchen with a half-eaten cake in his hands, wanting to pinch myself.

Chapter Forty-six

Just before we left, Tetyana slid up to me and pretended to check the tie on my clean apron. She leaned in and whispered, "Put in a good word for me and my brother with this Dragon Diplomat, will you?"

I nodded. "I'll do my best."

Katy and I were both freshly aproned and hatted, and we had on the black dresses Katy had picked up in Luxembourg City. "I told you, you can't go wrong with the little black dress," she said, with a smug smile. Chloe seemed relieved to see us change into more formal attire.

We followed her out wheeling the cake tower, with Greta skipping at our heels.

With a pompous grunt, Monsieur Wilmar turned his back to us as we came out of the kitchenette. His team stared at the tower hypnotized, mouths open. Katy and I smiled back and waved goodbye to Greta as we got on the elevator.

The elevator opened on the second floor and Katy and I followed Chloe out to the same foyer I'd visited the day before. This time, Chloe marched through the larger middle doorway, her nose firmly stuck to her phone as she walked.

We followed, looking around us in awe. This corridor was even more lavish than the one I'd seen the day before. It was impossible not to get distracted by the luxury.

The trolley dug into the lush carpet, slowing us down, but Chloe didn't seem to care much when it did. She stopped to glance back only once to say with a slight huff, "This is why we have footmen in the castle." We ignored her, retracted the wheels, and kept rolling.

We stepped into a mezzanine and passed an immense flight of stairs that looked exactly like the ones Cinderella might have run down as the clock struck midnight. Still absorbed in her phone, Chloe walked toward the entrance of a palatial ballroom at the end.

We could hear the hum of conversation and the smell of good wine as we got closer. Chloe nodded at the two guards in starched tunics standing stiff and somber next to the ballroom doorway. Their gaze didn't waver as we rolled the high cake tower right by their noses.

Chloe motioned us toward the service door.

When we got close, unseen hands opened the doors. Two footmen were holding the doors for us. *Chloe runs this place like clockwork*, I thought. We rolled our cake tower carefully into the room.

I'd thought the drawing room had been magnificent, but I was unprepared for the staggering opulence of the ballroom.

This room was three times the size of the main kitchen downstairs and had a domed ceiling carved in intricate occidental designs. Five elegant crystal chandeliers, each the size of a small car, hung from the high ceiling, blinding me when I looked up. A single piece of medieval tapestry covered an entire wall of the room. It was nothing like I'd seen before.

A massive dining table occupied the breadth of the room, draped with a white cloth embroidered in gold and silver. On this was sparkling china, imprinted with the castle insignia. Engraved golden forks and knives glittered beneath the chandelier lights. In between the dinner settings were extravagant flower arrangements in tall gold-colored vases. Standing behind each chair was a uniformed server in white gloves. They stood like soldiers at attention, expressionless, waiting to pull the chairs out at a moment's notice.

Chloe pointed at an alcove where she wanted us to roll our cake trolley until it was to be served. We nodded and squeezed ourselves and the trolley into the small space.

Everybody was milling about in the open area at the other end of the ballroom where a trio of musicians played soft chamber music.

The men, with glasses of red sherry in their hands, looked superb in their black tuxedos. The women floated around in stately gowns, dripping in rubies and sapphires. From where I stood, they looked like a flock of beautiful tropical birds. A handful of foreign dignitaries were scattered among the crowd, mostly men, and mostly in long Arab clothing. I wondered where their womenfolk were.

Katy nudged me. "Can you believe this?" she whispered.

"Amazing," I whispered back.

"Look at all these famous people. Like we're in a movie."

"Our best catering gig ever. And we didn't even have to sign a contract."

Katy suppressed a giggle. "Hey!" She pointed discreetly at a man in his thirties ten feet away from us. "Is that Bob Halt over there? And Anne Tuppence too! Oh, my god!"

Bob Halt? Why did that name ring a bell? I recognized a few famous faces here and there, but it was Katy who followed the celebrities.

Just like the day before, a buffet table had been placed next to the side entrance. But tonight, there were no open platters or trays, no sandwiches or finger foods, but a lineup of fancy plates covered in silver domes. This must be the first course, a salad or paté of some sort, I thought. The rest of the dishes were probably being kept warm somewhere nearby by Monsieur Wilmar's team.

We'd just settled into our alcove when a clock chimed nearby.

Like magic, everyone stopped talking and turned toward the woman in the center. I craned to look. I hadn't seen her when I'd first walked in and she hadn't been at the tea party the day before, but I recognized her from the magazine photo. *Grande Baroness Agathe.* She was sitting on a plush red chair, set on a small platform. She looked like a queen on a throne, with two dachshunds by her feet. The guests gathered in a circle around her.

The grande baroness got up from her throne slowly. Someone held out his hand to help her, but she ignored it.

When she stood, I realized she didn't come to more than five feet, almost as tall as I was, but she stood regally on that platform, her back straight, her head held high. Her white hair was cropped boyishly but stylishly short. She wore a full-length black gown with a high neck and long sleeves. It looked simple, but I was sure it came from a discerning designer house that catered to the world's über-wealthy. The glittering stones on her fingers and the diamond necklace left no doubt she was one of the highest of high society—that and her castle.

In a baritone voice as deep and rich as the stones on her fingers, she spoke. "I hope everyone is present now. One must never be late for dinner," she said, speaking in perfect Queen's English. A polite murmur went through the crowd. The baroness panned the room, making everyone bow and curtsy lightly as her eyes passed over them.

"Härzlëch wëllkom," she said and paused. We waited. Then, she embarked on a fifteen-minute formal speech in German, or so I assumed, as it sounded exactly like the language Greta spoke.

While she talked, I peered around discreetly.

Where's the Dragon Lady?

I felt eyes on me and swiveled my head around. It was Chef Pierre. He saw me looking and winked. I gave him a quick nod back. That was when I noticed. Five feet from him, looking majestic in a long white evening dress, stood the infallible Madame Bouchard.

On her hands were long black gloves, and around her neck a three-strand pearl necklace. Dropping from her ears were beautiful pearl droplets. She seemed to be listening intently to the baroness, one hand holding a sherry glass and the other a sparkling white purse. *I didn't know she spoke German.* I wondered if all the foreign guests just pretended to understand these formal speeches.

I looked around to see where Chloe was. She was standing in the shadows of the wall next to the same old man as the day before, both pretending to be invisible, scanning the room as usual.

I looked back at the Dragon Lady. Now I was this close, my plan sounded ridiculous. *What am I going to say to her? How am I going to even approach her?* I looked over at Chef Pierre, who was intently listening to the baroness. I wanted to talk to him so badly, ask him about his recipes, tell him about my baking life, and share my aspirations.

Everyone clapped politely. The baroness bowed her head slightly in acknowledgment, and a man who looked very much like a white-haired Prince Phillip walked up and offered his arm. She took it, and the two stepped elegantly over to the dining table. The rest of the crowd got in line, two by two, behind the hostess and her escort. The servers pulled back the chairs at the dining table and waited for everyone to come to their places. It seemed no one could sit before the baroness did.

The Diplomatic Dragon Lady sat right across from the baroness, with Chef Pierre to her left. The servers got to work silently. It was like watching a ballet come alive. They had choreographed everything.

They picked up the covered plates from the table next to us and took them to the guests. When everyone was served, on silent cue, the servers leaned over in sync and swiftly removed the silver domes. I almost gasped. The plates had been meticulously arranged, like pieces of edible artwork.

The dinner went off without a hitch. The baroness held court, leading the conversation from where she sat. Others nodded and replied in hushed tones. Empty trays and plates were whisked away, as course after course went by.

A canvas of gourmet art passed under my nose that evening. All the food and cutlery on the table that night could have fed the entire state of Goa where I grew up. I'd now seen it all. The grim poverty of my parents' childhood, the comforts of Mrs. Rao's house, which had seemed luxurious until now, and the unparalleled sumptuousness of this castle.

"Mademoiselle?"

I looked up to see Chloe and instinctively straightened my chef hat.

"It's time to serve your cakes."

Chapter Forty-seven

"Good evening, Madame Bouchard."

Using long silver tongs, I placed the most sumptuous strawberry and cream cupcake on her plate. I'd made it with cinnamon and nutmeg, a combination I knew she loved. I'd decorated this cake myself. It was the most beautiful edible thing on earth, or so I thought.

She didn't seem to hear me.

The room hummed with conversation. In the far background, I heard something wail, a siren of sorts, but I was so focused on trying to get the Diplomatic Dragon Lady's attention I didn't take much note of it.

I bent down. "Hello, Madame Bouchard."

She gave a start and looked up, her white pearl earrings swinging from her earlobes. She frowned.

"I hope you're having a great evening," I said, with a smile.

She looked me up and down as if to ask who had dared interrupt her meal. I swallowed and tried again.

"This is one of your favorite cakes," I said. "It's got cinnamon and nutmeg in it."

The siren outside had got louder now.

She looked at the cake on her plate and wrinkled her nose like it smelled bad.

A server came toward the table carrying a water carafe and nudged me aside with an *"Excusez-moi."* He filled her glass and left. I leaned in again.

"Madame Bouchard," I said in a low voice. "I'm really sorry I left without telling anyone. It was an emergency, a really bad one."

She didn't even look up this time.

"I hope your charity ball went well and you found another caterer. I truly apologize. I only came here today to ask for your help."

I thought I heard a dismissive sniff but couldn't say for sure. She reached for her glass of wine with her gloved hand and took a sip. It was like I wasn't even there. From the corner of my eyes, I saw Chloe move closer. I could feel her eyes boring into my back.

"Does this young lady work for you, Madame Bouchard?"

I looked up, startled. The chairs were close enough and Chef Pierre seemed to have the ears of a fox.

The Diplomatic Dragon Lady replied in a crisp tone. "Many work for me around the world, monsieur. I do not recall every one of them."

I felt a breeze of Arctic air from somewhere and a shiver went through me.

"Well, this young lady has a special talent, I can tell you. I might steal her from you, madame, if you don't watch out." He gave a hearty belly laugh.

"I am not the least bit concerned, monsieur," she said, putting her glass down with a gesture of finality. "I prefer help who know their place." She paused. "Especially at official foreign functions."

A hand slammed down on my shoulder, and I was pulled away. It was Chloe.

"Mademoiselle!" She turned me around violently. "Please return to your station," she said in a sharp whisper. "Now!"

"But—"

"I've tolerated enough!" she hissed.

Bang!

The room fell silent. Chloe's hand dropped from my shoulder. Everyone whipped around in their seats. A worried murmur rippled through the crowd.

The two foot guards who'd been standing like statues at the doorway rushed toward the baroness. One of them whispered something in her ear and helped her out of her chair. Within seconds, she was whisked away through the doors.

Bang!

Again. This time, it was clearly a gunshot.

Inside the dining room, chaos erupted.

"Oh, my god!"

"What's going on?"

"Terrorists!"

"Someone do something!"

"Don't panic!" someone yelled with a distinct note of panic in his voice.

Chloe tried to take charge. She walked over to the baroness's empty chair and waved her arms. "Mesdames et messieurs, please take your seats. *S'il vous plait.* Security has been called. Please. We must stay calm."

But no one was listening to her. Half the people were getting up. Some walked over to the windows and peered out. A smattering of guests had decided to walk out of the room altogether, and a few sat frozen in their seats, looking like zombies. The Diplomatic Dragon Lady was on her phone, talking urgently, maybe to her security detail. Chef Pierre was fanning a purple-haired woman next to him who'd just fainted.

Where's Katy?

I dropped my tongs and tray and dashed out to the mezzanine, dodging an elderly couple scurrying out of the ballroom. Two guardsmen ran into the room, almost bumping into me. Katy was standing at the top of the Cinderella stairway, holding on to the railing, peering down with a troubled look on her face.

"What's going on?" I asked when I caught up to her.

"Don't know," she said. "But I heard it from downstairs."

We looked at each other.

"Do you think—?" She stopped, her face pale.

Tetyana's gun flashed to mind. A sinking feeling in my stomach said this had something to do with her. With us.

"Let's go find them," I said. "This way." I ran down the stairs.

Katy scrambled after me. We got to the bottom of the landing, just as a small figure ran up to us.

"Greta!" Katy and I called out at the same time.

The girl's face was flushed. She pulled at our elbows and said something urgently in German.

"What is it, Greta?" Katy asked. "What's going on?"

The girl spoke rapidly, gesturing madly toward the castle kitchens. The only word I made out was *police*.

"Hold it, Greta," I said. "Tetyana? Okay?"

She shook her head.

Oh no.

"Luc, okay?"

She shook her head again.

Katy and I looked at each other.

"Win? okay?"

She shook her head again.

I felt sick to my stomach. The sound of men hollering came from the other end of the corridor. She grabbed us and pulled us into the shadows under the stairway. And there we remained quietly as a group of men stampeded up the stairs, shouting, *Police!*

They're after us! What have they done with the others?

When the men reached the top floor, Greta pointed at a corridor nearby and pulled on our arms urgently. I threw down my chef hat and undid my apron. Katy followed quickly. We tiptoed out from under the stairway and turned into the corridor, following our young guide. It seemed like a commotion was happening upstairs now. A woman screamed. A man shouted.

What in god's name is going on?

Glancing nervously behind us, Katy and I followed Greta.

She walked softly but swiftly, keeping close to the wall. Thankfully, the carpet softened our footsteps. On one side of this corridor were full-length stained-glass windows and on the other side were doorways that led to the libraries and sitting rooms of the castle. I could smell the expensive cigars and velvet luxury as we walked by them. No one was in sight.

Greta kept moving forward, a finger on her lips, stepping softly, panning the area, like a young tracker on a mission. Katy and I followed silently, perplexed. We had no choice but to trust her right now. The noise had receded and we hadn't seen anyone else.

At the end of the corridor was a massive wooden door, which was where Greta seemed to be leading us. When we got to the door, I reached to open it, but it was locked. But Greta wasn't even looking at it. She opened a much smaller door nearby with a sign that said, *"Härentoilette,"* and stepped inside, motioning us to follow her.

Katy and I stepped in after her, wondering what rabbit hole she was taking us into. We were in one of the castle toilets and around us were the plushest stalls I'd ever seen in my life.

Greta walked up to the small window at the back, scrambled onto the sink to unlatch it and open it wide. We peered outside to the castle gardens. There was no one on this end of the grounds. Using her hands, Greta gestured for us to get out.

"Through the window?" Katy asked.

"But what about the others? Where are they?" I asked.

Greta shrugged her shoulders. She had no idea what we were saying. I looked at Katy. Before we could say anything else, Greta jumped out of the window.

"Wait!" I cried.

"Oh, my god, is she okay?" Katy asked.

"Komm häihin!" We heard Greta whisper urgently from outside. *"Ech Kommen!"*

We had no choice. I clambered out and Katy followed.

As soon as we were out, Greta made a motion to close the window. Katy pressed against it to make sure no one would notice it had been opened.

We were now facing the woods on the other end of the castle where Luc had joked earlier that werewolves slept.

From somewhere behind us on the castle grounds, we heard people shouting.

"Laft!" Greta said, pointing to the woods. I stared at her. She gave me a push and pointed at the woods again.

The voices were getting closer.

Greta looked furious that we weren't getting what she was saying. She stamped her foot down. Another push.

"Police!" I heard someone shout from around the corner.

"Laft!

Katy and I bolted toward the woods, without a glance back.

One ship drives east and another drives west
With the self-same winds that blow;
'Tis the set of the sails
And not the gales
That tells them the way to go.
Ella Wheeler Wilcox

Chapter Forty-eight

We stopped at the edge of the woods and ducked behind a massive oak tree.

Peeking from behind it, I saw the strangest sight.

Two police officers were running after a man we'd not seen before. Despite his girth and fancy shoes, he seemed to have a slight advantage on the officers. They disappeared around the corner, not even noticing the little girl in the Alice-in-Wonderland dress standing next to the castle doors.

When the men were gone, Greta turned away and walked around the building, but not before giving a cheeky grin and a wave in our direction.

Katy and I looked at each other, puzzled.

We trod carefully among the trees and found a small opening to sit in. Katy removed her heels and rotated her ankles before putting them back on again, wincing slightly. We'd dressed to cater to a royal party, not run into the woods. The canopy above us was teaming with sparrows, their songs filling the air. They didn't seem to notice the drama happening right under their beaks.

"How did they know we were here?" Katy asked.

I shook my head. "Can't be Fred's goons. These are cops. Did you hear the police sirens?"

She nodded. "And two shots," she said, looking at me with wide eyes. "I hope Tetyana didn't get into a gunfight."

"The police don't just shoot like that, do they? Unless she did something rash...." I paused, feeling a chill up my spine. "I hope she didn't pull out her gun when she saw them coming."

"Maybe this is all something to do with her, not us," Katy said thoughtfully. "We don't even know where she's been before, and her story's a bit strange."

She had a point. We knew nothing about Tetyana and the little we did know didn't fully line up.

"But why were the cops chasing that man just now?" I said. "What does he have to do with us?"

Katy shrugged her shoulders.

Something rustled among the trees. We turned our heads around.

Nothing.

"We've got to get back," I said. "We can't leave them back there."

"Poor Win," Katy said. "She's probably scared to death. Hope they're okay."

We got up, dusted our skirts and were ready to find our way back when we heard the sound. It was like a herd of wildebeest was stampeding our way.

"Run!" I yelled.

I grabbed Katy's arm and ran through the trees, pulling her with me.

"Stop!" someone shouted behind us. "Hey!"

We didn't look back. We kept running, zigzagging our way through the trees. I didn't know if they were still following us, because all I heard was my heart pounding inside me like an angry African drum. I was sure we'd outrun them when Katy's heel caught on something and she came crashing down with a cry.

"Katy!" I stopped and rushed back to her.

I knelt beside her. She clutched her foot and groaned. The sound of the others running came closer. I looked around desperately for a hiding spot. The best we could do was to get behind a large tree but I'd have to carry Katy now, and she wasn't a small girl.

"Asha!"

"Katy!"

I swiveled around to see Win and Luc appear from between the trees and come dashing toward us. Win threw her arms around me, nearly bowling me over. Luc plopped on the ground next to Katy, panting mad.

Everyone began to talk at once.

"Are you okay?"

"What happened?"

"Did you see the police?"

"Where's Tetyana?"

"Did Greta tell you—?"

"Wait!" I said, shushing everyone.

From the distance came the sound of a dog barking. We looked at each other in alarm.

"Police dogs?" I said.

"We have to move," Luc said scrambling up. "They've got guns."

"Katy, how are you doing?" I asked.

She massaged her foot. "Nothing major. Hurts a bit, but I can walk. I lost my shoe—"

Without a word, Win plunked a pair of red canvas shoes on Katy's lap. We stared at her as she rummaged around and brought out another pair and handed them to me.

"How did you—," I said, noticing Luc was carrying two of our bags as well.

"No time to explain," Luc said. "We gotta run."

"What about Tetyana?" I said, scrambling to put the shoes on.

We heard the barking again.

"We gotta go, guys," Luc said, giving a worried look in the direction of the castle. "Now!"

We got up and ran. We ran nonstop, dodging rocks, ducking under low-hanging branches, jumping over roots that jutted out of the forest floor, keeping an eye out for each other, making sure no one was left behind. We stopped a few times to catch our breath, but we kept running. We were deep in the woods now.

Fifteen minutes into our run, I felt a sharp pang on my right side.

I stopped and leaned against a tree, trying to catch my breath, waiting for the pain to pass.

"Asha!" Luc cried and stopped. Katy and Win stopped as well.

"Go ahead," I said, "I'll catch up. Go!"

All three stumbled toward me, panting loudly, and plunked themselves at my feet. I slipped to the ground next to them.

"Sorry, have a cramp," I said, trying to breathe through the sharp pangs. "You guys have to go."

No one spoke. Everyone was breathing like we'd run a mile. *But we had run a mile or more*, I thought, looking at the dark canopy behind us. *I can't believe we came through all that.*

"I need to stop too," Luc said.

"Me too," Win said.

Katy merely nodded, saving her breath.

"Do you have water in the bag?" I asked Win. She shook her head.

We leaned against the trees for a minute. We couldn't hear the dogs anymore. It must have been well past eight but there was still some light left from the midsummer's day. The forest was quiet but I could hear a river somewhere nearby.

We were sitting on a carpet of springy moss that had masked our running footsteps. The place looked peaceful, but I shivered. *Too peaceful.*

I wasn't sure if it was my imagination but the woods felt enchanted. Vines the size of a man's arm intertwined with tree branches, looking like prehistoric snakes crawling over the trees. The trees themselves seemed to huddle close together as if they were hiding things they didn't want us to see.

Then, in that quiet, a bird suddenly burst into song on a branch above us. I looked up to see a plain brown sparrow with his chest puffed out, like a miniature feathered Pavarotti.

Luc looked up to where the bird was perched, singing its little heart out. "Hey, can you guys climb up that?"

"Climb?" Katy asked.

"It'll be safer," Luc said. "And we can rest for a bit longer."

I looked at the low branches.

Win was already up and reaching for a branch. The bird flew away as soon as it heard the rustle of the leaves. "It's not hard," we heard Win say from above us, straddling a branch. She pointed at a knot on the tree. "Use that to step up."

Katy climbed up behind her, and I followed. We got three quarters of the way up where the branches were still broad enough to sit. Katy even found a spot to lean against. Luc wanted to go higher, but I didn't trust the smaller branches above. Dogs may still sniff us out, I thought, but at least we'd have cover from people coming this way.

"What happened to Tetyana?" I asked as soon as Luc and Win had settled in.

"We don't know," Luc said.

"Don't know?" Katy asked.

"We were in the kitchen with Greta when we heard the police sirens," Luc said, "Tetyana told us to get our bags and meet her at the cellar. She was going to get you and we were all going to come to the woods because we couldn't get to our van anymore."

"So we stuffed everything in our bags," Win said. "That's how I had your shoes."

Luc turned to Katy. "You still have the cash packet, right? We couldn't find it in your room."

She nodded, patting her chest. I'd vaguely noticed her breasts had enlarged considerably in the recent days, and now I knew why. She was keeping the money in her bra.

"We were ready to leave when Tetyana came running saying the building's full of cops and she couldn't get to you. So we asked Greta to find you," Luc said.

"We didn't understand what she was saying but she helped us," I said.

"I think she thought it's a big game," Win said.

"So how did you two get out?" Katy asked.

"We got to the cellar through the servants' quarters. Tetyana was with us," Luc said. "When we got to the end of the tunnel and opened the door to the parking lot, there was a cop standing right near the back door."

"Oh no," Katy said.

"We couldn't go back in. He'd already spotted us and was waving us over. That was when Tetyana pointed to the van and started yelling."

"She shouted something about a man and a gun or something like that," Win said.

"When the cop turned to look at the van, Tetyana told us to run to the woods," Luc said.

"So we ran," Win said.

"Then we heard the gunshot."

"Did she get shot?" I asked, my heart in my mouth.

"I looked back but she was still standing," Luc said. "So was the cop. They were both staring at our van. No idea what was going on."

Win shook her head. "It was hard to see because we were running."

"There was a second gunshot though," Katy said.

No one said a word.

"She's a fighter," I said, more to myself. "She's gonna be okay."

We sat quietly for a minute, trying to imagine where she was, what she was going through.

"I feel bad for leaving her," Win said finally.

"She knows what she's doing," I said. "Besides, she'd have got mad if you hadn't listened to her."

"Can we go back now?" Katy said. "We can't just sit here."

"If the cops got her," Luc said, "there's not much we can do right now."

I peered through the woods. It was dark, and we were in the thick of the forest. "I'm worried we'll get lost," I said. "It'll be better in the day."

"So we spend the night here?" Katy asked. "And tomorrow?"

"We've got to find Tetyana," I said.

"I'm dead thirsty," Win said. "Wish I'd brought some water."

"Me too," Katy said.

"You guys hear that?" Luc said, cocking his head. "That's not too far away."

"The river?" I asked. "Been thinking the same thing. Why don't we try to find it and think of our next steps there?"

Katy nodded. "At least we'll have water and maybe a place to sleep."

Win sat up gingerly and got ready to climb down. The rest of us followed her down.

We walked toward the sound of the river, deeper into the woods. We knew we were going in the right direction because the roar of the river got louder with every step.

There was some light from the rising moon, enough to see our general surroundings. The birds, settled in for the night, had gone quiet, and the woods seemed somber. *This is a forest of goblins and fairies,* I thought, stepping over a large root. *What if we get lost here? What if we die here?*

We walked in silence for five minutes, moving as quietly as we could. The adrenaline that had been pumping in our veins had depleted and our pace was slowing. From time to time, one of us stumbled on a stone or a root, so we started to walk abreast, holding on to each other.

The trees were thinning and the ground beneath us was changing from soft moss to brown dirt. A wind swept across us, blowing our hair and swaying tree branches. After a few minutes, we came to a thin line of trees, the demarcation between the forest behind us and whatever lay ahead.

We stepped through the tree line into an open area.

"Watch out," said Luc.

"Oh, my god," I said.

"It's the end of the world," Win whispered.

Chapter Forty-nine

Five feet in front of us was a deep ravine. If we'd run out of the woods without looking, we'd have rolled down the cliff.

We stood in silence at the edge, looking at the desolate gully below, feeling the wind whip around us menacingly. A dark river meandered below, the sound we'd been following. On the other side of the ravine was a forested hill, or at least it seemed to be in the dark. We huddled closer, shivering, the cold sapping the little energy we had left.

We were at a dead end.

At least we found water, I thought, looking down at the river below. To get to it, we'd have to scale down the sheer cliff wall. An impossible task. After surveying this landscape for a while, we began to move. It didn't matter which direction we took anymore because we didn't even know where we were.

I now knew why no one had bothered to come after us. They knew there was no way out of the forest. We'd have to return to the castle grounds or die in the woods.

We turned right and walk along the edge of the cliff. There were no clouds in the sky that night. Early stars twinkled above next to a nearly full moon. I wished I'd learned more about the skies so I'd know which direction we were heading.

"Look!" Win said, her sharp eyes noticing something. She walked up to a dip at the edge of the cliff. Then as if stepping into a void, she disappeared.

Katy and I gasped.

"Win!"

We ran up. She was standing on a ledge below the edge of the cliff. "They go all the way down," she said, pointing at the roughly hewn steps. Luc jumped down to join her.

I looked around nervously.

Where there were steps, there were sure to be people. But no one was around, except us. I climbed down to join them on the ledge, testing each step as I did. Here, the cliff jutted out in a gentle slope, and someone had cut these steps to form a path down. But in the dark, it was difficult to see how far they went, or whether they went anywhere at all.

The wind was stronger here. A sudden gust came. I grabbed on to Win to keep steady. She seemed fearless though, standing strong, peering into the abyss below, more curious than afraid. Luc was at the edge too, looking down.

"Hey, be careful," I said.

"That looks dangerous," I heard Katy call from above.

"Come on down," Luc said, motioning to her.

"Could be a dead end," she said.

"I'll check," Win said, letting go of my hand and bounding down the steps.

"Hey!" we all called out, but she disappeared into the darkness. "Win!"

Luc jumped down after her. We had no choice. I waited for Katy to join me and we climbed down after them, testing one step at a time, holding on to each other.

We caught up to the others twenty steps below. They were standing in front of a dark hole on the cliff wall. It was hard to see inside, but the entranceway was large enough to fit us all abreast.

"What's that?" Katy asked in a whisper.

"A cave," Luc whispered back, peering inside.

I could no longer see the bottom of the gully, but I knew it was a long way down. It was tempting to step inside this sheltered den, away from the wind and the threat of a fall.

"Do they have bears in Luxembourg?" Katy asked, vaporizing my temptation in an instant.

If we don't disturb a bear in there, I thought, we could very well bump into the police, waiting to capture us. I wasn't sure which I wanted the least. Another gust of wind blew, making us reel from the force. We stepped closer to the mouth of the cave.

We were almost inside.

"I can check first if you'd like," Luc said, with a grin. "If I don't come out, there's definitely a bear in there."

No one laughed.

"We can't go down any further," I said. "Especially in the dark. It's too dangerous."

"Maybe we can rest in here for a bit," Katy said.

We looked at each other and as a group, stepped inside the mouth of the cave. Shoulder to shoulder now, the four of us took another step forward.

We were in a mid-sized tunnel. We stood still for ten seconds, clutching each other's hands, to let our eyes adjust to the darkness. There was a yellow light coming from somewhere like someone had installed an incandescent bulb inside. We walked forward again, taking one step at a time. After twelve steps, we came to another doorway of sorts, an opening to something bigger.

We stared into the cool, open space. Almost fifty feet high above us was an opening from where the pale light was coming. It was a stream of moonlight, entering through the hole and lighting the entire cavern, like a chandelier from the heavens. We stayed at the entrance for a minute, spellbound by the sight.

Holding hands, we took another step forward. That was when something brushed by my ear.

I jumped. It flew by me again.

"Eeek!" I shrieked, flapping my arms.

The echo of my voice bounced off the walls. With a fluttering roar, more of these things flew out and circled the cave. It was like watching a real-life horror movie.

An electric torch turned on suddenly and pointed up. It was Luc. He'd remembered the torch he'd found at the castle caves and had been carrying with him all along.

"What are they?" I asked, ducking as another one got too close.

"Bats," Katy whispered.

"They don't hurt people," Luc said.

"How do you know that?" I asked.

He shrugged. "Read it somewhere."

"They're cute little things," Win said.

"Shh," Katy said. "Let them settle down and get back to their sleeping spots."

It took a whole minute for the bats to quieten down. A few still fluttered around, but none came close to us.

More cautiously now, and using Luc's torch, we started exploring. The cave was the size of a basketball court. Long icicles dripped down like alien candelabras from the ceiling, and stalagmites rose from the floor like strange sculptures. Other than these natural wonders and the large bat family hidden in the crevices, there was nothing else in the cave. Not a sign of a bear or castle guard or police officer anywhere.

We walked around the cave and returned to the entrance. Near the entrance, we noticed a low tunnel, the size of a large sewer pipe. I bent down and peeked, but saw nothing but a black hole. Luc shone his torch so we could get a better look. This was like an anteroom to the larger cave. The ledge outside was small; it had been a miracle none of us had fallen. The steps carved into the cliff face wound into the blackness below.

"We're not walking down in this darkness," I said.

"We can sleep in the cave or in here," Luc said, shining his torch around the entranceway.

"Or we can sleep outside and have bears eat us," Katy said. "If we don't fall over the edge first."

"I'm not sleeping with the bats," I said with a shiver. "I'll stay here. You guys can go inside."

"I don't care," Win said, plopping down on the ground. "I'm really tired. I can sleep right here."

After looking for the smoothest spot on the ground near the entranceway and double-checking for bat droppings, we lay down and huddled against each other for warmth. Though we were all hungry and thirsty, Luc fell asleep within seconds, snoring gently. Win was next, falling asleep with her head resting on Luc's arm.

Katy and I stayed awake, whispering to each other for a while, wondering about Tetyana, sharing our fears of what might come next and our disbelief in what had just happened. Then Katy too fell asleep. I stared into the lonely darkness of the cave, listening to any sound that might signal danger, but I heard only my friends' breathing.

It took me a long time to fall asleep, and when I did, I dreamed of being pulled by unseen forces through that low pipe tunnel. In my dream, I stumbled into an underground cave to see a tall vampire with bloodshot eyes and a red cape, waiting for me. Screeching bats fluttered around. A subterranean wind howled through the cave. Trembling, I yelled for help only to discover I'd lost my voice. The vampire smiled an evil smile and called out my name. His voice sounded suspiciously like Vlad's. He came closer and closer, calling my name louder and louder. I stood in place, petrified.

I woke with a shudder, drenched in sweat. My heart was pounding, and my mind was whirling.

That was when I saw the shadow of a face, inches from mine.

"Asha!"

I drew back screaming.

Chapter Fifty

I punched at the face but hit air.

"Get away from me!" I yelled.

Next to me, Win, Luc, and Katy jerked awake. I heard Katy scream. I felt Luc rummage in the dark for his torch, cursing. I threw another wild punch, protecting my head with the other hand, against what, I didn't know. Missed again.

"Asha!" someone scolded. "Stop it!"

Tetyana?

I stopped trying to pummel the air and peered through the darkness. Someone was kneeling in front of me.

Luc turned his torch directly on Tetyana's face.

"Tetyana!"

Everyone screamed and jumped on her. Inside the cave, the bats fluttered and screeched in annoyance at being disturbed again.

Tetyana looked like she'd crawled through a mud bath. Her hair was wet and pinned against her skull. Her face was covered with green tainted muck. But we didn't care. We held her tight.

"How did you get here?" I asked.

"Through the tunnel," she said, pointing behind her. "How did *you* get here?"

"Through the woods," Win said.

"What's on your face?" I asked.

"Mud," Tetyana said. I noticed she was supporting her right elbow with one hand.

"Are you hurt?" Katy asked, leaning forward.

"It's nothing," She shifted, grimacing. She looked at us. "How about you? Are you all okay?"

We nodded.

"We're good," Luc said.

"Just a roughed-up ankle for Katy when she fell, but otherwise okay," I said.

"I was so worried for you," Win said. "We heard gunshots, then I didn't see you anymore."

"That was the cop," Tetyana said. "He was shooting all over the place."

"Did he shoot at you?" I sat up and pointed at her elbow.

"This? No, just missed a step," she said.

"Tell us from the beginning," Katy said.

Tetyana let out a big sigh and wiped some gunk from her face.

"While you were upstairs at the dinner party," she said, looking at Katy and me, "we heard police sirens. So I asked Greta to warn you and told Win and Luc to get ready to move quickly. The van was out of bounds so we had to find another way."

"Through the woods," Win said.

She nodded. "We got through the tunnel to the parking lot, but when we got out, a cop was standing right outside. He was on his phone and didn't see us at first so he didn't know where we came from."

I nodded. I'd heard part of this story.

"But when he saw us he called out. I pretended someone was behind our van and pointed and shouted. The cop pulled out his gun and turned to the van—"

"That's when we ran to the woods," Luc said.

Tetyana nodded. "I didn't want him to see where you were running so I shot the nearest police car."

"Whoa!" Katy said.

"You shot a cop car?" I asked.

"Windshield for maximum effect. I was quick and my silencer was still on, so he didn't know where the bullet came from."

Her eyes were flinty.

"He turned around and shot at the van, thinking the shooter was there. While he was looking around confused, I slipped back into the cave. I heard him shoot again, just as I slipped in. I think that van's a goner now."

"But how did you get here?" Katy asked.

"Remember those catacombs?" she said. "I had to take my chances. I stumbled down those stairs and ran like hell. I ran through the tunnels hoping it'd take me somewhere. I was either going to get out or die trying."

"Oh, my god," Win said.

"It was wet and slippery in there and I couldn't see much. I fell halfway on some steps." She jerked her elbow at us. "That's how this happened."

"So that catacomb tunnel comes all the way here?" I asked.

"I ran till I hit a dead end. It was a cave, a big one like that one." She pointed at the cavern where the bats were now back asleep. "I heard someone yell. It was a girl's voice. It was faint but I was sure it came through that tunnel."

"That was me," I said in an embarrassed voice. "Bats freak me out."

"Glad they did. I couldn't go back the way I came, so I waited to see if I could hear anything else. Either way, your yell meant there were people out here and maybe there was a way out. As soon as I found the tunnel, I crawled through it."

"Good thing you did," Luc said.

"We need someone to look at your bruise," Katy said.

"Had worse and survived," Tetyana said with a shrug. Her eyes narrowed. "So how did you all get here?"

Between the four of us, interrupting and interjecting, we described our escape.

When we were done, Tetyana leaned back against the wall and closed her eyes. In the dim torchlight, she looked worn out like she'd just returned from the front lines of a battle. She opened her eyes after a few seconds.

"Hey, we can't sit here all night waiting for them to find us." She pointed at the entrance. "What's out there?"

"We're on the edge of a cliff," I said, shaking my head. "There are only two ways out. Back through the woods to the castle or down this straight cliff."

"Where's this river?"

"All the way down," Win said. "At the bottom of the cliff."

"What's past that?"

"Looks like a hill with a forest," Luc said. "Hard to say in the dark."

Tetyana asked us to describe the cliff in detail, including the ravine below. When we were done, she looked around us and said, "How do you all feel like a night hike?"

"It's dark outside," Win said.

"All I have is this tiny thing and the battery's running out," Luc said, waving his torch.

"You said the moon's out tonight," Tetyana said. "I've tracked through worse with gunfire and in the middle of the night with no moon. I'll find us a way down."

No one spoke.

"Trust me," she said. "The castle guards know these caves and they know the woods. It's only a matter of daylight before they and the police come looking. We need to start moving now."

"It's a death wish," Katy said.

"It's super dangerous," I said, feeling, all of a sudden, the warmth and safety of the bat-filled cave.

"You guys haven't seen dangerous," Tetyana said, sitting up.

"Tetyana, how do you know all this? What are you?" I said. "I mean—" I didn't know how to finish the sentence. At twenty-one, she was the oldest, but sometimes the things she said were too old, even for her.

"I'm a rebel soldier."

I stared at her. *What does that mean?*

"I didn't know that," Luc said. "I thought you were always a—" He stopped.

"A hooker?" she finished his question.

We looked away. That sounded far worse out loud.

"I was a primary school English teacher once," Tetyana said in a low voice, looking at the ground. "In another life. In another universe."

So that's why her English is so good, I thought.

"Why did you work for Zero and Vlad then?" Win asked, her voice innocent, curious.

"Because it's the fastest way to bail out my brother," Tetyana replied. Her face looked more haggard than ever.

"Your brother's in jail?" Katy asked.

"Why?" Win asked.

"Because he wanted freedom." Tetyana's voice had softened. "He was at the wrong place at the wrong time. Should never have let him come with me."

"Come where?" I asked in a whisper.

"To the battlegrounds to fight for independence, but in the end, the Russians captured us. They caught him and me." There was no emotion in her voice. It was like she was telling us what happened on her way to get groceries.

"They put me in the torture room. I don't know how many days I was there. The warden said he'd let my brother go if I brought him fifty thousand US dollars. He was the one who enjoyed hurting me the most. I didn't mind the physical pain, but I broke down when he told me he was going to kill my brother and described how in detail."

I stared at her through the thin light of Luc's torch, feeling like a thick black fog had suddenly enveloped us. It was getting hard to breathe in here.

"I promised to bring the money but I wanted him to show proof he wouldn't touch my brother. They asked the church in town to take him as kitchen help and gave instructions to shoot him if he tried to run away."

She stopped and swallowed.

"I'd do anything to save my brother's life."

She was quiet for a while. We all were.

When she spoke again, her voice had risen. Her eyes flashed like she was ready to hit someone, kill someone.

"My government doesn't give a fuck about its own people!"

Her anger grew as we watched in shock.

"I fought for my country and they abandoned us! I'm on my own now. That's why I worked that god-awful job. Do you think I had a choice?" She was shouting now. The bats in the cave next to us screeched as if trying to outdo her.

"That's why I want to go back. I've got to get Yevhen out. Alive. That's all I want."

I remembered Tetyana's keen interest in taking money in exchange for helping me get Katy and Win out of the London brothel. I'd thought she was money hungry and without a conscience. That conversation seemed like eons ago, but it had only been seven days.

"I'm so sorry. I didn't know," I whispered, struggling to find the right words. "I'm so sorry."

"You know what?" Tetyana sat up, cradling her injured elbow. "I wasn't even fighting because I was brave or wanted to do a noble thing. Do you know why I fought?" she shouted. "Do you?"

We shook our heads.

"Because those bastards came one night and shot my mother, right in front of us. She was the real fighter. She organized rallies.

They didn't like that, you see. So they killed her, just like that." Her voice broke.

Tears streamed down her cheeks, streaking through the mud on her face. I wanted to lean over, comfort her, put an arm on her shoulder, anything to make her feel better, but I sat hunched in my corner with a lump in my throat, watching her helplessly.

"Then they took Yevhen. He was only nineteen," Tetyana said, her lips quivering. "I shouldn't have let him come with me—"

And then, our strong and fearless Tetyana broke down.

This time, no one hesitated. We scrambled over and gathered in a circle around her. We held her as she sobbed.

Chapter Fifty-one

Tetyana led the way down the steps, holding the torch. Luc took the rear. They each carried a gun.

Win, Katy and I walked in the middle, holding on to each other.

Tetyana hadn't cried for long. As soon she had caught her breath and swallowed her sobs, she pushed us away. "No time for this," she said. "If we don't start now, we'll be in worse trouble."

She leaned over and took Luc's torch from his hands. We got up and followed her out of the cave. No one had any idea where we were going, only that we needed to get as far away from the castle as we could.

The steps in the rock face stopped a hundred feet below the cave. After that, there was only a crude path someone had slashed between the short bushes growing along the cliff wall. The cliff here wasn't as steep as I'd thought it was.

"Hunter's tracks," Luc said from behind us. "Probably come here to shoot boar."

The path was rough. We had to hold on to each other or the bushes for safety. I was grateful for the torchlight, but other than being a confidence booster, it did little else. Tetyana soon shut it off to rely on the moonlight to guide the way.

"We can see better this way," she said. "Our eyes will adjust to the darkness better. Also, someone could be on the lookout and see the light."

I shivered at the thought of anyone watching us meander down the cliff. I didn't have time to panic though because the trek required all my attention. Certain places were so steep, we had to get down on our bottoms and crawl down.

"Try not to think beyond your next step," Tetyana called out. "And always make sure the person behind is fine. That's all you need to focus on. I'll take care of the path ahead."

I wondered what we'd have done without her. Stayed in the cave till dawn and got caught, I thought. Tetyana knew what she was doing and sometimes even went ahead several steps and waited for us to catch up.

After an hour of nerve-racking climbing, we sat down to rest. Win said she was exhausted. So were the rest of us.

"We all need water," I said. "That would help."

"Not too far now," Tetyana said.

Yes, I could hear the rush of the river below us. After two minutes, we stood up again, eager to get to the water.

"I'm going to drink that whole river," I said. "Don't care how dirty it is, I'm gonna drink it."

"Probably the cleanest you'll ever drink," Luc said, from behind me. "It's spring water. Better than any fancy bottled water you'll find."

"True," I said. "It's not the Ganges in India, that's for sure."

"I'm going to have a dip in it," Katy said. "I stink like a dead cat with all that running and sleeping in caves."

"After we drink it, and after we dip in it, we gotta cross it," Tetyana said from up front.

"How are we going to do that?" Win asked.

"We'll find a way," she said.

When we finally got to the riverbank, we ran up. The water was cold, like it came from a fridge, except this water was the sweetest I'd ever tasted.

Tetyana cleaned the mud off her face and body, and the rest of us followed her in to dip into the water. It was too cold to stay in more than a few seconds at a time, but it felt cleansing, refreshing like it melted our sweat and fears away.

Then we rooted around the knapsacks to see what else Win and Luc had thrown in and changed into jeans and T-shirts, thanking them for having packed sensibly, even in those tense circumstances. It helped that we'd been carrying very little, anyway.

After that, we got to work.

Tetyana was right. She must have been a scout or trained as one when she was a soldier because in ten minutes, and in the dark, she'd calculated the narrowest area of the gully where logs had jammed into rocks and figured out how to get across.

We teamed together to haul five logs over, creating a slightly less treacherous path to the other side. Luc sacrificed his shirt for us to hang on to as we stepped across, one by one, guided by Tetyana.

By the time we got to the other side, my legs felt like scrambled eggs and Katy was barely holding herself up. Tetyana looked for a place behind a line of bushes above the river where we could get a few hours of sleep.

We went on a rotating night watch again, Luc for the first two hours, then me, then Tetyana. Katy and Win wanted slots as well, but Tetyana said they'd be on duty the next night, so they needed a full night's rest. Luc's hand watch, our only timekeeper, said it was one in the morning.

There wasn't much night left.

This time, I fell asleep the minute my head hit the ground, snuggled between Katy and Win. I went into a deep dreamless sleep and woke only when Luc gently shook my shoulder so I could take watch.

Before he went to sleep, he handed me the gun and gave me a quick how-to guide. I could barely take it all in. The weapon looked even more ominous under the moonlight. As soon as he curled up with the others, I put it on the ground next to me, too scared to touch it, in case I accidentally set it off and shot myself, or the others.

I settled myself on the hard ground next to the weapon, listening carefully, ears perking to every rustle of the leaves, alert to any change in the sound of the river that might signal an intruder. I was thankful for the moon and the stars above. There was something to look at, at least.

Tetyana had given strict instructions to wake her up if I saw or heard anything. So I strained my ears and eyes, and I waited. Though I was sitting between two thick bushes, it was chilly. Every once in a while I glanced behind me to see the group huddled together and wished for a bit of their collective warmth.

It's when you're alone in the dark that your mind wanders inward.

I sat cross-legged looking at the moonlit expanse in front of me, thinking of each of my friends. They looked so peaceful, I thought, yet, each and every one of them had gone through unspeakable horror at some point in their lives. Now, under the high Luxembourgian night sky, their faces looked so young, so fragile, I couldn't help but wonder how anyone could have looked at those same faces and inflicted pain on them. But they had, not once, but over and over again. How could anyone with a human heart take pleasure in hurting others like that?

Maybe not all humans have human hearts, I thought with a shiver. Aunty Shilpa used to say there is a devil-god, one of the many Hindu deities, who roams around stealing hearts, turning people into demons, and that was why people did bad things. But I had a hard time with that story. It was too easy.

When Zero trafficked Win, when Vlad raped that yellow-bloused girl in the warehouse, and when the man with the machine gun whacked her to death, no one else was to blame but themselves. When Tetyana decided not to kill Zero or Vlad at the Brussels house, she made that decision on her own. She could have easily taken their depraved lives and none of us would have blamed her.

So, no. I felt no sympathy for the monsters roaming this earth. If their hearts had turned to stone long ago, they were solely to blame.

I was the luckiest of our group. There had been times I'd come close, very close, to harm, but I'd always gotten away. I'd fought back and run. I'd taken wrong paths and I'd made my share of mistakes, but I'd always had options.

I cried when I heard Katy's story. She hadn't had a choice when she was raped at ten. She'd been just a little girl who never saw it coming from her own uncle. It was the same for little Win. Her own father, whom she should have been able to trust more than anyone else, sold her. *Sold her.*

I looked over at Tetyana sleeping at the edge of the group. I'd been wrong about her. *What would you do if you'd been captured by a military force and tortured, knowing your younger brother was locked up in a nearby cell, threatened with death?* I still didn't know Luc's story, but I knew it wasn't a happy one. I remembered the look on his face when he'd called Zero evil.

It was getting to the darkest and coolest part of the night. The moon was my only companion now. The stars had dimmed or gone away, maybe to hide from my dark ruminations.

I looked up at the moon, searching for the face of the man in the moon, but saw only dark splotches of alien craters.

All of a sudden, I felt alone. So alone. The chilly night was getting to me. I started to shiver uncontrollably. I was supposed to be keeping watch. I was supposed to have that gun in my hand and keep a sharp eye out. But all I felt were warm tears streaming down my cheeks.

I cried silently, shaking violently, without stopping for a very long time. It was like everything that had happened over the past few days, the past few months, the past several years, had finally caught up to me, as I sat alone in the middle of the night in a country I didn't know, on a continent I wasn't supposed to be on. I buried my head in my shirt so I wouldn't wake the others and cried and cried.

By the time I was supposed to wake Tetyana, I'd composed myself enough to keep watch on the surroundings. I was thankful when she took over because I badly wanted to close my tired eyes to the pain I was feeling.

Part NINE

If it were not for hope, the heart would break.
Greek Proverb

Chapter Fifty-two

The next morning dawned crisp and clear.

The first thing everyone noticed was the sheer cliff on the other side of the river.

"We climbed down that?" Win asked as we stood gaping at the steep incline in awe.

"I can't even see the steps from here," Luc said.

"Can't believe we did that," Katy said, shaking her head.

"How did you know which way to come down?" I asked Tetyana.

She shrugged. "Instincts. Just felt my way down. There's always clues around."

The sound of the river rushing below was comforting. I was starved but I didn't want to leave. I felt safe here but Tetyana had other plans.

"No one will think we came down that thing in the middle of the night and survived," I said.

"They'll focus on the forest and the tunnels before they try the cliff, won't they?" Luc asked. "Gives us a head start."

"That was a hunter's path we took last night," Tetyana said. "If the hunters can come down, so can the police and castle guards. And faster too. Time to head on."

We began our hike away from the river, slowly to start. Luc and Tetyana, who knew the region the best, scoured the area for berries and leaves we could chew on. It wasn't much, but it stopped our stomachs from growling. Tetyana had already made us drink as much water as we could from the river before leaving.

And we were off.

This time, we tracked up the hill following a stream, staying under the canopy of trees, Tetyana leading the way. And this time, our destination was as far as we could walk without crashing of thirst or hunger.

We took five hours to get up the hill.

"Wow," I said when we got to the top.

"It's beautiful," Katy said.

We stared at the scene below.

We were looking down on a tiny village set in a lush green valley. A church spire rose among the white buildings and a herd of cows grazed in a pasture nearby. The village looked like it had been land-scaped by a magic wand—a slice of heaven created on earth.

Standing at the top of the hill now, the memories of the day before seemed far away. I wanted to run down to the town and ask the first person I met if they had a place to eat, to sleep, to shower.

"We've got to be careful," Tetyana said as if reading my mind.

"Can we get some food though?" Win asked. "I'm starved."

Tetyana's military-trained eyes surveyed the area.

"Follow me," she said. "Stay close and tread lightly. There could be hunters from the village around here."

"What do we do when we get down?" Katy asked.

"We improvise," Tetyana said.

As we began our hike down, the view of the town disappeared.

My spirits rose. With every step, I felt like we were getting closer to freedom, and with every step, I felt a sliver of hope return. Though we still didn't know if Fred and his goons were running around look-ing for us and we didn't know if there'd be a police van at the foot of this hill, waiting to haul us away, I felt hopeful. I felt I was on my way back to my original journey, on my way to Goa, closer to reuniting with Preeti.

We climbed down in silence, watching our steps, making sure the person behind was still with us. As I walked, hearing the soft foot-steps of my companions, a shadow of sadness crossed my heart. Split-ting up was inevitable, and I didn't want us to break apart.

This is my family now. Why can't we all stay together?

I knew where Tetyana wanted to go.

Luc still thought Sicily was the best place to hang his hat.

Then, there was Win. *What will happen to her?* She couldn't go with Tetyana to rescue her brother as that would be too dangerous. She wouldn't want to come trekking with us to India, a country totally foreign to her. Would she want to go back to Laos? I wondered.

Will this hike be the last time we'll all be together?

We took three full hours to walk down the mountain and into the village. I had a feeling Tetyana had avoided open areas, opting for the longer but safer path where possible. Though we were all hungry and tired, the walk through the woods was almost pleasant.

A hare crossed our path at one point, and Luc spotted a deer and her fawn among the trees soon after. We stopped to watch them and they stopped to watch us; the mother twitching her ears, ready to spring away at a moment's notice. In the bright morning sun, the woods were no longer dark or forbidding. The sun had banished any feelings of foreboding remaining from the night before.

When we finally got down to the village, there wasn't a soul around.

Tetyana gathered us behind a large oak tree at the edge of the village.

"Luc," she said. "This is your show now. You need to take the lead. Find us food and a place to rent a car, okay? If you can find two cars, even better."

"I'll try," Luc said. "They'll know I'm a foreigner though."

"You speak German and French. That's better than anyone else. The rest of us will have to zip it," she said, drawing a line across her lips.

We nodded.

Tetyana looked at Katy. "Do we still have any euros?"

Katy dug into her bra and brought out some money. "Euros on the left and dollars on the right," she said, with a wonky smile.

"Give Luc all the euros we have," Tetyana said. "There won't be any exchange booths in this little place. And keep those dollars safe. We'll need them later."

Katy nodded and slipped the wad of remaining money back under her shirt.

"Okay, let's go see if we can find something to eat," Tetyana said, walking out to the open pasture.

The only noise we heard was cowbells. We found a dirt path that wound its way around the field toward the center of the village. We passed farms with quaint white houses and small red barns. From here, we could see the church in the middle of the village, its tiny spire holding a weather vane in the shape of a metallic rooster. It turned as we walked toward it.

Suddenly, a large border collie ran out from a farmhouse, its tail wagging, tongue hanging, and giving us a such an exuberant dog-smile that we had to stop. The dog jumped on Katy like she was a long-lost friend, making her laugh out loud, a sound I hadn't heard in so long. Win joined in, petting and playing. Even Tetyana smiled watching them.

"He's still a pup," Katy said, scratching behind his big furry ears.

"Fetch!" Win said, throwing a stick she'd found on the ground. The dog happily dashed off on his mission.

"Oh, oh," Tetyana said, straightening up. "Trouble at thirteen hundred hours."

"Straight ahead, to the right," Luc said, translating her military directions for the rest of us.

I looked over to see a middle-aged woman walking over from the farmhouse. She had a curious look on her face.

Luc hailed her as she got close.

"Gudde moien!" Good morning!

She didn't reply or smile but nodded her head in acknowledgment. The dog ran to her, then turned and ran back to us. *Look at all these strange people I found*, he seemed to say.

"*Wat fur ein niedlicher welpe*," Luc said.

"*Danke*," the woman replied. Thank you.

The dog jumped on Katy again. She laughed and said, "Get down, you silly pup."

The woman looked at her curiously.

"I love your dog," Katy said, forgetting about our no-talking rule.

The woman raised an eyebrow.

Luc spluttered and said something in German or in Luxembourgish. The woman frowned. Luc spoke rapidly. The woman looked over at us and asked a question. I heard the words *"Universitat Luxemburg"* from Luc. He talked while we waited, wondering, smiling politely. Finally, she nodded and pointed at the church.

"*Danke*," Luc said. "Okay, folks." He turned to us and spoke in English. "Let's move along now."

With a goodbye wave, we left the woman and the dog behind, the dog now distracted by a red robin perched on a fence. He ran after it, barking.

"Sorry guys," Katy whispered as soon as we were out of her earshot. "I forgot I wasn't supposed to talk."

"Don't beat yourself up," I said. "We seem to have done okay."

"What did she say?" Tetyana asked Luc.

"I told her we're international students and came to tour a castle," he said. "I told her we went on a hiking trip, then got lost in the woods and missed our coach back. That's why we're all so dirty."

"You weren't totally lying about visiting the castle," I said to Luc.

"She said there's a small hiking shop near the church where we can find a change in clothes. There's a restaurant too. She said to say she sent us."

We walked toward the center and sure enough, to the right of the church was a small hair salon, and to the left was a small mom-and-pop restaurant with a happy yellow awning.

"Oh, good," Win said. "Finally, real food."

Next to the salon was a dentist's office, a bakery, and a flower shop. This was the town's main street. We walked past the shops to find the hiking store the woman had mentioned.

It sold outdoor and hunting gear. The two teens behind the counter looked surprised when we trooped in until Luc talked to them, telling them the woman with the dog sent us. After that, they became the friendliest and most helpful shop assistants. Win and I found it hard to find our sizes, but we found cargo pants and T-shirts that didn't make it look like we'd spent the night in the woods.

We walked to the restaurant afterward, following the smell of home-cooked food. As we got closer, I realized how hungry I was. Luc opened the door for us. It was just after lunch, so only one other couple was seated inside, finishing their meal. They stared as we stepped inside.

Luc said a polite good afternoon to them and pulled out chairs for us like a local gentleman entertaining his foreign friends.

In a few minutes, a plump woman in glasses bustled out of the kitchen. She came over to our table, removed her glasses, and looked at us with a hand on her hip. *She doesn't look very friendly*, I thought.

"Vun wou kennst de?" she asked. "Where do you all come from?"

Luc pointed at himself and said in English, "Belgium."

He turned to Win. Taking the silent cue from him she said in a bright voice, "Thailand."

The woman's eyes moved around the table.

"The States," Katy said, with a smile.

"India," I said, not wanting to complicate things.

"Lithuania," Tetyana said, her face set in a half smile.

The woman seemed satisfied with our answers. After a longer chat with Luc, she said *"Wellkom,"* and went off to get the menus.

"What did you tell her?" Tetyana asked in a whisper.

"I didn't have to say anything. She knew we were coming," Luc said, keeping his voice low, just in case someone in the vicinity understood English. "The woman with the dog already phoned her. She said next time we go hiking in the woods to carry a phone. I told her we did, but couldn't get a signal. She said she was going to complain to the telephone company because tourists were always getting lost and one day someone was going to die in the woods if they didn't fix the problem."

"Oh, good," I said, partly relieved we were not getting any unwanted attention and partly guilty at lying to these kind people.

"Didn't she ask how we got here?" Katy asked.

"There's a large castle ruin nearby. It's a tourist attraction, so she thought we'd come to see that. I didn't disagree."

"Good work," Tetyana said. "Did you find out about a car?"

"She said there's no place to rent cars around here or call a taxi, but her cousin, who's got a van big enough to fit all of us, can take us to where we can get a bus to town. But we have to find him first. He's supposed to be on a nearby hill herding cows."

"It's a good start," Katy said.

I was glad we were all going to be together for a little longer. I didn't want to say goodbye just yet.

The food came, and we ate like we'd never seen food in our lives. When the woman inquired, Luc truthfully said it was the best meal we'd had in a long time. She walked away looking pleased with herself. When the bill came, we noticed she hadn't charged us for anything. It was a simple note that said, *"Eng secher Rees."*

"Have a safe journey home," Luc translated for us.

Everyone turned silent. Like me, I was sure everyone felt terrible for lying to our hostess. I felt like she'd just given us a warm hug to make up for all the bad people we'd met. For the first time in days, something warm and fuzzy stirred inside me. People aren't all that bad, I thought to myself.

We waited to thank the woman, but she only shook her head, patted Luc's back, and said *"wellkom,"* before returning to the kitchen with our empty plates.

We walked outside and huddled on a street bench to take stock of our plans.

"I don't like hanging around here for too long," Tetyana said. "The castle isn't that far away from here. Who's to say they won't come looking for us here?"

"The thing with a small town," Luc said, "is everyone knows we're here now."

"You think they called the police?" I asked.

Luc shook his head. "We've been good customers and nice to everyone. No reason for anyone to call or complain."

Tetyana nodded. "Okay, why don't you go find that farmer and his van. The rest of us probably shouldn't stand out here for everyone to see. We need to stay away in a quiet spot for an hour or two."

She looked around the street and pointed at the hair salon. "How does everyone feel about a haircut?"

"I could do with a trim," I said. "I probably look like a jungle girl."

"I'm not talking a trim, girls," Tetyana said, her eyes narrowing.

We looked at her puzzled.

"I'm talking a wholesale makeover."

Katy gasped. "But I love my hair."

"Do you want to make it easy for Fred or the police to find us?" Tetyana asked, with an eyebrow raised.

We remained quiet, contemplating this.

"Do I have to change my 'do as well?" Luc asked. I knew he was more vain about his looks than any of us were. This was going to be hardest for him.

"Yes, but later," Tetyana said. "You've got an important job to do right now. For now, go buy a hat and sunglasses at the hiking shop, then find the farmer."

Luc sighed in relief.

"And I'm going to get my short hair back," Tetyana said.

"No!" Win said. "Don't cut your hair."

"It's time I became myself again, hun," Tetyana said.

"Your hair's gorgeous just the way it is," Katy said.

"I'm a short-haired brunette who used to teach kids how to speak English in a little town near Kiev," Tetyana said, with a smile. "I know you don't believe me, but I'm not a redheaded vixen who likes to wear heels, like you."

Chapter Fifty-three

By the time we had our hair cut and colored by a team of friendly hairdressers, Luc was back.

The farmer had agreed to take us to the castle ruins, or "back to the ruins," as he put it.

It was only a twenty-minute drive. He left us at the foot of the hill near the parking lot. Nearby was a stop sign where buses came to pick up tourists and take them into the city. A group of Chinese tourists had overtaken the bus stop. It was nice we weren't alone but I worried we'd find space on any bus that came by.

We huddled in a corner, trying to figure out our next steps.

We could now pass as any cosmopolitan student group. Luc had switched his black bomber jacket and pants for an athletic suit with a hoodie and a baseball cap. Win was sporting a purple bob cut, which made her look like she'd come from sunny California.

Katy had her hair done up. She refused to color her hair but allowed them to trim and pin it up, making it look short, though we all warned her that meant a ton of work every morning. Mine was cut to the shoulders, layered and dyed a chestnut brown. It would take some time to get used to, but I was happy to be a step ahead of Fred and his goons.

"Next best step is Luxembourg City, for all of us, right?" I asked.

"Better if we can get into France directly," Luc said.

Tetyana was unusually quiet. She looked unusual as well, with her hair cropped short and colored brown.

"What do you think, Tetyana?" Katy asked.

She didn't say anything at first. When she looked up and spoke, her voice was solemn. "One step at a time. First, we need to get out of here safely."

"Hey." I looked over at Win who was standing quietly aside, her face scrunched up. "You all right?"

Tears were welling in her eyes. "I just want all of us to stay together," she said, wiping them away.

Katy pulled her in and hugged her.

A long coach pulled up to the bus stop cutting our conversation short and making the tourists twitter excitedly.

They gathered their bags, called out to each other, and swarmed the bus.

"We'll never find space in there," Katy said, shaking her head.

"That's a private coach," Luc said. "They won't take us, anyway. We need a city bus."

"What about hitching a ride in a car?" Tetyana said, looking at the parked cars. "We could try to get one of the tourists to take us."

"That means splitting up," Win said, her voice slightly high pitched. "We won't all fit in one car."

Nobody said anything.

We knew Tetyana was itching to return home, to find a way to rescue her brother, even though she still didn't have enough money to pay his captors.

"We'll need a van," Luc said.

"A bus is best, I guess," Katy said.

Just then, from the corner of my eyes, I saw an official-looking car with a bar of lights on top slowly turn into the parking lot.

Oh, no. Did they find us?

The coach driver who'd gotten out to load the tourists' bags in, jumped back in and started the engine. I didn't wait. I ran up to the door and leaped up the stairs.

"Excuse me, do you have space for five more?" I asked the driver.

"This is not a city bus," the driver said, with a thick German accent.

"We'll pay extra."

"I'm going to Luxembourg City."

"That's where we're going too," I said nodding.

I glanced behind me. Everyone was staring, wondering what I was up to. Behind them, the official car was inching its way slowly by the parked cars, as if checking for something.

"The city bus doesn't come for another hour," I said, turning to the driver with pleading eyes. "It'll be a huge help. Really, really huge."

The driver hesitated and looked at the woman sitting in a lone seat above him. She looked like a Chinese tour guide or translator.

"There's space at the back," the driver said to her.

"I'm okay if they pay," the Chinese woman said. "In cash."

"We'll pay," I said, nodding. "In cash. Not a problem."

The driver shrugged. "Okay, I'll drop you at the train station same as the rest of them."

"Thank you!" I turned around and signaled to the others to come over.

When everyone had jumped in, the driver closed the door and turned the bus to leave. Peeking out the window, I saw the car was still there, checking the parked cars. The decal on its door said "Parken." *Parking?* I breathed a sigh of relief. I'd worried for nothing, but at least we were getting out of here.

We walked in a single line to the back of the bus, surprising the throng of tourists as we did.

"You come with us?" one woman called out in English.

"Yes," Luc said.

"Welcome!" one of the others said.

"Thank you!" Win said.

"Sit here," said another, patting the seat next to her. "Join me."

"The driver said to go to the back," Katy said to her, with a smile. "But thanks!"

We found our seats at the very back, next to the smelly toilet. But our fellow bus riders were a curious bunch. Soon, one by one, they left their seats to inquire about us.

Through broken sentences, hand gestures and the use of electronic dictionaries, we soon learned they were retired teachers from Beijing, touring the world. They were mostly women and one quiet, shy man in the back who smiled and bowed his head every time one of us looked his way.

His female colleagues wanted to know everything about us: where we were from, why we were in Luxembourg and where we were going to college. It was hard to ignore them.

They were especially interested in Win and asked about her parents and what kind of company they were running in Bangkok. I think she said it was a clothing company, but I couldn't say for sure above the din. Everyone was talking all at once. I only hoped everyone was giving consistent answers.

Pretty soon a white-haired woman sitting in the row in front of us opened her purse and took out a silver flask. She held it high and said with a sly smile, "Party, girls?" That was when I knew we were going to be okay.

We all took sips, and I began to feel bad about lying to these people who were embracing us.

When the driver dropped us off, I felt like we were leaving good friends. They made us promise we'd come and visit them in China before they picked up their bags and shouted loud goodbyes to us.

We walked into the train station feeling a little lonely after that ride.

That day was the best we'd had from our entire stay in Europe. I remembered the woman with the dog, the restaurant owner who'd served us food on the house, and the farmer who'd stopped his work and went out of his way to drive us to the ruins for free. I remembered little Greta who'd befriended and helped us, in ways she didn't even understand.

The world wasn't that bad. There were good people everywhere, I thought. We just had to find them.

We found a bench to sit, while Luc and Katy pored over a large map of the station, looking for a currency exchange booth. I watched people walk back and forth around us and listened to the PA announcements in French, German and English. Once in a while, we felt the thundering of a train as it arrived at the station.

"Guys, look!" Win said.

I looked up to see her staring at a drop-down television nearby. It had shown train arrivals a minute ago, but it had switched to the news now. A picture of Baroness Agathe's castle appeared on the screen.

My heart leaped to my mouth. Tetyana scrambled up from her seat to get a better look.

The newscaster was speaking in German.

"Where's Luc?" I asked, looking around. Katy and him were walking back from the currency booth. I motioned to them to hurry over.

"What are they saying?" I asked when he got close.

We all stood in front of the screen, watching, trying to make sense of what was going on.

"Are they talking about us?" Tetyana asked.

The reporter spoke at length to the camera. He sounded very serious.

"You won't believe this," Luc said shaking his head, "you're just not gonna believe this."

"What?" Katy and I asked at the same time.

"The police didn't come for us."

"What the hell?" Tetyana said.

He lowered his voice. "Remember that list we put online?"

Everyone's faces cleared.

"I knew it!" Katy said. "I thought I saw Bob Halt at the dinner. He was on the list."

"That's why the police were chasing that man around the castle," I said.

Luc shushed us with his hands so he could listen.

To our shock, Monsieur Wilmar's face appeared on screen next.

"What's he saying?" I asked.

"He's saying a bunch of petty thieves stole from the castle kitchen on the same weekend."

We gasped.

"He's saying several vintage bottles of alcohol are missing from the cellar and that his mini kitchen was vandalized by a bunch of, er, ruffians."

"Are you serious?" Katy said.

"We never did that," Win said.

"Shh," Luc said. "Local police are now looking for culprits. Supposed to be a young team of, er—" He hesitated, giving me a cautious side glance. "Unskilled, foreign cooks."

"*What?* Unskilled?" I spluttered. "The twit! What else is he saying?"

"Er—he's saying that's what happens when you hire inept kitchen help with no, er, competency. He's saying the castle will change its policy to make sure they vet their caterers better in the future." Luc's voice trailed off. "Sounds like he's more scandalized by this than the arrests of johns."

"Monsieur Wilmar's such an ass—" I gritted my teeth.

"You should thank him." Luc nudged me with a grin. "They think it was a petty crime. This is good news."

"Yes, but there's no saying what will happen if they catch us for petty theft or otherwise," Tetyana said. "We can't sit around here."

I gave her a worried look.

"Where are your guns?" I whispered, remembering how she showed one to the kitchen staff that morning.

"Buried deep up the hill, while you all were asleep."

We stared at her.

"I was on watch last, remember? Don't worry. They're hidden well, deep in the ground, far from where we slept."

The news anchor had moved on to a different story. We turned away from the screen.

"Ok guys, here's what we found," Luc said, "next train with space for five is to Marseilles. It's the nonstop TGV. Leaves in ten minutes. What do you all think?"

"Marseilles sounds far away," Katy said nodding. "And that's a good thing."

"Yes, let's get out of here," I said.

"I'm coming with all of you," Win said.

Tetyana was silent for a second. We quietly waited for her to speak with worried looks on our faces.

"Sure, let's do it."

Everyone breathed a huge sigh of relief.

As soon as the ticket machine spat out our tickets, we grabbed them and ran to the platform.

It was a high-speed train that took us from Luxembourg City to the south coast of France, in less than seven hours. Tetyana gave us watch shifts so one of us would always be awake. Time passed quickly as we zoomed through the countryside so fast that everything outside became a blur of gray-green.

We pulled into Marseilles late at night.

From here, if we headed south, we'd hit Northern Africa. If we went east, we'd land in Sicily. And if we kept going thousands of miles southwest, we'd arrive in Goa, India.

Chapter Fifty-four

It didn't take long for Katy and me to buy tickets to Goa with a stopover in Mumbai.

We'd split up the cash, so we could each buy our tickets separately. That would avoid arousing suspicion in case anyone was looking for a ragtag international group of five young people trying to fly out of Marseilles all at once, we thought.

Luc was sure the Luxembourg police had our faces on the castle cameras. Though I hadn't seen security cameras back at the castle, I didn't disbelieve him. There had been some interesting modern contraptions hidden in the bowels of that ancient mansion, so I didn't want to make any assumptions.

Also, I didn't want to assume what the police in Brussels or London had on us either. I knew their focus would be the pimps and brothel owners, but they could have our photos, mine in particular, and I didn't want to take any chances.

As the train got close to the Marseilles Provence Airport, Luc had become more agitated, Tetyana more distant and Win more teary-eyed. We told her she could come with any of us, but she didn't want to decide. As far as she was concerned, we should all stay together, and she didn't care where that would be.

I worried about Win.

She was still a minor, but she'd more life experiences than many adults in this world. In fact, she'd spent a lifetime experiencing adults forcing things down her throat. The last thing any of us wanted to do was impose yet another decision on her. She had to think for herself and we had to respect whatever choice she made.

We promised to meet at the coffee shop next to the Air France ticket booth in an hour. By then, we'd each have made a decision and perhaps even bought a ticket.

That was an hour earlier.

Katy and I got to the coffee shop at the same time, and to my relief, she was sticking with our original plan. We grabbed a table and some tea and waited anxiously for the others to join us.

The coffee shop was next to a large open window. Outside, we could see people being dropped off, taxis coming and going. We sat silently watching the scene outside while we waited.

It surprised me that no one had questioned my stay in Europe. The ticket attendant flipped through my passport quickly and handed it back, apparently thinking it natural to have an Indian passport when returning to India. I realized then they'd be more interested in illegals coming into the country than leaving it.

Behind me, a lineup of travelers snaked through the terminal. Maybe she was in a hurry to process us all. Either way, I got my ticket and boarding passes all the way to Goa.

I switched from nervousness to excitement, knowing I'd see my cousin soon. *Finally!* I wondered how Preeti was doing, where she was, and whether she'd even recognize me after these years. I was fifteen when I left India and would be almost nineteen going back.

It was Win who arrived at the coffee shop next, with tears on her face. She looked nerve-wracked.

We watched her walk over, our hearts in our mouths.

"So what did you decide, sweetie?" Katy asked.

"I really want to go to Laos," she said, plunking herself on a chair between us.

My heart fell. I'd secretly hoped she'd come with us.

"But I don't know anyone there anymore," she said, wiping her tears with the tissue Katy handed to her. "So I'm gonna come with you. Is that okay?"

Katy and I stared at her for a second before we both grabbed her for a hug. I felt a sob come to my throat and swallowed quickly.

"I'm so happy you decided that," Katy said.

I got up to buy Win a cup of tea, feeling relieved. I'd have worried to death if she'd gone away on her own. We all would have.

"What about Luc and Tetyana?" she was asking Katy when I returned with her drink. "What do you think they'll do?"

"Everyone's got to do what they want to do," Katy said, looking down.

"Whatever happens, it doesn't mean we won't see each other again," I said. I knew though, if the others went their own way, I'd feel incomplete. We'd become close in such a short time. I crossed my fingers and looked around anxiously.

"There's Luc," Katy said.

We watched him approach us, knowing he'd have bought a ticket to Sicily. He'd been talking about it all the time.

Luc grabbed a chair and turned it around before sitting down and adjusting his cap. He looks smug, I thought.

"So?" Katy asked. "Don't keep us waiting."

"I hear Italy's beautiful this time of the year," I said, with a wry smile.

He put his ticket on the table and pushed it toward us. We leaned over to look.

"Hear Goa's nice too," he said.

"What?" Katy said, grabbing the ticket.

"You're going to Goa?" Win shrieked. "Me too!"

"Hey Win, why are you crying?" Luc said, reaching to wipe a tear from her cheek. She looked away, her face scrunching up.

"Should be happy, not sad," he said.

"I'm happy. That's why I'm crying," she said with a wonky smile.

"Love that color on you," Luc said, making a move to tussle her hair. Win ducked and blushed even more.

"Where's Tetyana?" I asked, looking around.

For the past fifteen minutes, I'd been trying to spot her in the lineups. When I first tried to look for her, I saw her at a free Internet terminal. *Checking that forum again,* I thought. *Wonder who she's looking for?*

After that, she'd disappeared. I'd scanned all the desks with flights going to Eastern Europe, but hadn't been able to see her, though she was easy to spot, even without the blazing red hair.

We waited an hour, getting more and more nervous.

The image of Tetyana clenching and unclenching her hands in the back of the white cargo van came to mind. I was the one clenching and unclenching my hands now. It had taken time to get to know Tetyana. I'd doubted her at the beginning, but now, I felt we couldn't move on without her. She put herself in the line of fire more than once to save us. Without her, we'd either be in jail or dead. She was a friend. She was family.

Luc and I went for a walkabout to see if we could find her but came up empty. I even checked all the washroom stalls. Our boarding time was now in twenty minutes and we didn't have much time.

"Do you think she's already gone?" Win asked anxiously.

"She'd never leave without saying goodbye," Katy said.

"Do you think she'll come with us?" Win asked.

No one spoke.

"She's got her brother to think about," I said finally. "That would be my priority if I were her too."

"There she is!" Win shouted out.

Yes, there she was, walking toward us, fast. Win jumped to her feet as Tetyana got closer. Something in her face told us all was not good.

"We're all going to Goa," Win said loudly, too loudly. "Can you come with us too?"

Tetyana didn't answer. She gave a small smile at Win, leaned over the table and whispered, "The police are coming."

Her voice was so calm it took us a second to realize what she'd said.

"What?" Katy said.

"Serious?" Luc asked.

Tetyana nodded. "This time, they're here for us."

"Oh no," Win said.

"When do you board?" Tetyana asked.

"In twenty minutes," I said. "Still got to get through security though."

"Here's what I want you to do," she spoke in her low voice.

We leaned toward her, ready to do anything she asked us.

"I want you all to get on that plane as discreetly as possible. If anyone asks, you were tourists here. Don't call any attention to yourself. Stay under the radar and stick together. And get out of here quickly."

We stared at her.

"Is that clear?"

"What about you?" Win asked.

Tetyana straightened up.

"Are you going back to Kiev?" I asked.

"Not to Kiev." She hesitated. "We don't have time to talk. You need to go now."

"Oh, my god!" Katy said, pointing out the window.

Two police vans pulled into the departure area, just outside the windows, near the taxi stand.

"Go! Now!" Tetyana pushed a piece of paper into my palm and squeezed my hand for a second before letting go. I stared at her. She stepped away and blew us a kiss. Then she turned around and disappeared into the crowd.

"This is the general boarding call for Flight Seven-Eight-Three."

That was our flight. We looked at each other. Tetyana had already vanished. The police were getting out of their van.

We didn't wait. We grabbed our bags and walked quickly toward security. I looked back once to see Tetyana's tall brunette head near the Russian airline desk.

I never even gave her a goodbye hug.

We were lucky the attendant at the gate noticed our flight time and pushed us roughly to the front of the line. "You're very late," she admonished us, before asking security to process us first. As soon as we got through the line, we ran toward our gate.

I saw Win wipe her face every few seconds. I felt like crying too, but couldn't. Not right then.

We were running along the third floor of the terminal which had glass windows on both sides. On one side were the parked planes, and on the other side were the vehicle departure and arrival areas.

"Hey!"

I looked back to see Luc had stopped and was staring out the window.

"What are you doing?" I asked.

"We don't have time!" Katy said.

Luc's face had gone white. Something was wrong. We ran up, crowded around him and looked below.

It was Tetyana. She was in handcuffs, getting ushered into one of the police vans.

Win gasped.

"Oh, no," Katy said.

My heart dropped. I wanted to run back to her. I turned around.

"Asha!" Katy grabbed my arm and stopped me. "No!"

"They'll haul all of us away," Luc said.

The police van pulled out and the blue light turned on. I watched as it sped away, without a siren.

The PA jerked me out of my trance. "This is the final boarding call for Flight Seven-Eight-Three."

We stared at each other.

"What do we do now?" Win whispered.

I opened my hand and uncrumpled the piece of paper Tetyana had passed to me.

"Phone number?" Katy asked, looking at the series of numbers hastily written on it.

"This is the final boarding call for Flight seven-eight-three. We're still missing four passengers. Please come immediately to gate seventy-five."

"We'll call her from Mumbai," I said, pushing the paper into my pocket.

We dashed toward our gate. The scowling attendants didn't waste time in rushing us through. Our seats were at the back of the plane. We stumbled into them, our faces flushed, our hearts pumping like mad.

"Please buckle up. We're already late for takeoff," a stewardess said in a crisp voice before walking away.

I sat back in my seat, feeling numb.

I was returning to India, flying back over the Mediterranean and Arabian Seas once again.

I wondered if I'd see Tetyana again. I'd abandoned Preeti and Aunty Shilpa and look what happened to them. All I had to trace Preeti was that letter she'd sent a year ago. I didn't even know if she was alive. Now, I'd abandoned Tetyana, at a time she needed help the most.

I put my head in my hands.

This was going to be a long flight.

—THE END –

Read the First Chapter of the Next Red Heeled Rebels Book Here.

Chapter One

"Oi!"

I swung around.

It's a cop.

"Halt, I said!" The man waved his arms like he was commanding an army.

No, it's an Indian immigration officer.

At least, that's what he looked like in the white uniform, peaked cap and gun hanging from his belt. If we hadn't been in an airport, I'd have thought he was a badly dressed, paunchy naval captain or something like that rather than someone who checked passports for a living.

He was marching toward us with a deep frown on his face.

My heart beat a tick faster.

What does he want? Does he know who we are?

I watched him stride up with a sinking feeling. I glanced at Luc but he wasn't looking my way. His face had gone a shade pale.

My gut screamed to turn and run. *But where would we run to?* We were in the international terminal of Mumbai's airport—a wide, open hall as big as a ballroom. There was no way we'd escape him. Plus, the man had a gun.

At least my friends were with me.

Katy, Luc, Win and I had just disembarked after an exhausting thirteen-hour flight from Marseilles. Other than a stopover in Amsterdam where we'd had a panic attack when we thought Win had been kidnapped again after she'd gone to the washroom without telling us, the journey had been uneventful.

We were bone tired. None of us had slept or ate or even talked on the plane. After what happened in France, all we could do was shift in our seats, struggling to come to terms with what we'd just done.

I'd only seen Tetyana's back for a moment before the French police whisked her into the police car. I'd wanted to run after her and scream at them to let her go, but Luc and Katy had grabbed me and pulled me away before I did something stupid.

We can't help her if we're all rotting in jail, they told me.

They were right. But all I could think of was how I'd abandoned a friend who'd been ready to kill for us.

How could we leave her like that?

When the plane finally landed in Mumbai, we stumbled down the staircase in a daze. India enveloped us in a steamy tropical fog that smelled vaguely of jet fuel and cow dung. I struggled to breathe.

Funny, I thought as I staggered across the hot tarmac that was threatening to burn my soles, *everything's so foreign*. India was my second home. Well, sort of. For three years of my childhood, anyway. *Have I been away that long?* It was a relief to get inside the air-conditioned terminal.

A few people stared as we shuffled in. We were a conspicuous crowd. Katy the redheaded Canadian, Luc the lanky French guy, Win the petite girl from Laos and me, the half-Indian woman.

Our plan had been to pretend to be clueless tourists and ask for visas on arrival. Luc had suggested Win hack into the Indian immigration system beforehand to get us all proper visas, but our departure had been so rushed, it hadn't been possible.

We'd been lucky so far.

Katy and Win had cleared customs with no questions asked.

The officer who took my Indian passport handed it back with a cursory glance. I'd forgotten to remove Preeti's letter tucked between the pages before passing it to him, but he hadn't even noticed. Luc was last in line. He was standing right behind me.

I surveyed the area.

Katy and Win were waiting for Luc and me under a sign that said *Baggage Retrieval*.

We had nothing to retrieve. We were each carrying our worldly possessions on our backs, in the small hiking backpacks bought in Luxembourg only a few days ago. We had our passports, a change of clothes, toiletries and a few bars of dark chocolate Luc had sweet-talked the first-class flight attendant into giving us.

We were on the run. This meant essentials only. And chocolates counted.

So far so good. No one had followed us. Nothing had seemed out of the blue.

Until now.

"I am talking to you!" The man in the white uniform stepped up to Luc and glared at him.

A second man in a white uniform was walking toward him with a long-snouted beagle on a leash.

This is not good.

"Me, sir?" Luc said, giving the officer an innocent look.

"Yes, I talk to you!"

What do they want from him? I was the one with a false visa and a passport made by someone who faked these things for a living. Everyone else had proper documents. If anyone was liable to get arrested by a customs officer anywhere in the world, it had to be me.

"*Merde!*" I heard Luc say under his breath. *Shit.*

"What's going on?" Katy mouthed silently at me. I shrugged.

"Did we tell you pass the gate?"

I turned around to see the officer standing five inches from Luc now, breathing heavily as if the exertion had been more than he could muster.

"I'm so sorry, Officer, but I thought we were done." Luc spread his hands. "Was there anything else?"

Respectful words. I noticed he emphasized his French accent, which usually charmed everyone he met. But this officer didn't seem impressed.

"Yes, there is very good reason," said the man, his face stern. "You know very well why we want to talk to you."

Luc's eyes flickered. He gave me a nervous sideways glance. My stomach sank. I hoped Luc hadn't brought any of his white stuff with him. *He couldn't have made that mistake, could he?*

The second officer with the dog was standing a few feet away, one hand on his hips, where he kept his gun.

"I will ask you again now," the first officer was saying, enunciating each word slowly. "Do you have anything to declare?"

Two local men stopped to look at the commotion. They smirked to see a foreigner in trouble. One whipped out his phone to take a video but bolted as soon as the second officer waved him away.

Thank god. The last thing we needed was our faces splashed on the Internet.

My heart raced. *I've got to do something. But what?*

"I'm, I'm clean," Luc stammered. "I'm really clean, sir. I have nothing to declare."

With a snort, the first officer reached over and yanked Luc by the shoulder.

"Hey!" Luc cried, pulling away. "What are you doing?"

I found my voice.

"Let him go!"

Ignoring me, the officer pulled a struggling Luc toward the back area, followed by his partner and the dog.

Motioning Katy and Win to stay right where they were, I rushed after them.

"What do you want with him?" I called out from behind.

The first officer gave a grunt.

"Where are you taking him?"

"Not your concern," he barked without even a glance at me.

"Yes, it is! You can't just arrest someone like that!"

He stopped and turned around, wringing Luc's shoulder as he did so. Luc grimaced in pain.

"Let my friend go!"

"Your friend is going to jail for very long time."

I stared at him in shock.

"And he knows exactly why."

Luc went limp and a look of resignation crossed his face.

I gave him a desperate look. "Luc—"

"Sorry, Asha."

Before I could say another word, the men hauled him through a doorway into a darkened corridor behind the customs desk.

The door slammed in front of my face.

The sign over the doorway said, "India Immigration Police. No Entry."

● ● ● ●

CONTINUE THE ADVENTURE...

Do you want to know what happens to Asha, Katy and the Red Heeled Rebels next? You'll find out in the third book of the series.

Asha is ready to cross oceans to hunt down her stolen cousin. But she doesn't know the terrifying stakes waiting for her on the other side...

The Girl Who Fought to Kill is a gritty tale of vengeance that will take you on a wild ride from the chaotic streets of Mumbai to the bustling city of Nairobi and to the dark lairs of human traffickers who ply their evil trade hidden in plain sight. And there will be revenge. Oh, yes. Sweet revenge.

Get The Girl Who Fought To Kill here: www.RedHeeledRebels.com[1]

---

1.   http://www.RedHeeledRebels.com

Your Gift

HAVE YOU READ THE PREQUEL story to the Red Heeled Rebels yet?

Read *The Girl Who Crossed the Line* to learn Asha's backstory and why her past haunts her.

Get your exclusive copy of the short story here: **www.RedHeele-dRebels.com**[2]

. . . .

---

2. http://www.RedHeeledRebels.com

The Red Heeled Rebels Series

• • • •

IN A WORLD WHERE JUSTICE no longer prevails, six iron-willed women rally together to seek vengeance on those who stole their humanity.

This is a story where the thrill of *Kill Bill* meets the wrath of *The Girl with the Dragon Tattoo.*

If you like gripping thrillers with flawed but gutsy heroines, vigilante action in exotic locales and twists that leave you at the edge of your seat, you'll love these books by multiple award-winning Canadian novelist, Tikiri Herath.

Pick up the Red Heeled Rebels books for a heart-pounding international adventure without having to get a passport or even buy an airline ticket!

• • • •

WHAT READERS ARE SAYING on Amazon and Goodreads:

- "Fast-paced and exciting!"

- "An exciting and thought-provoking book."

- "A wonderful story! I didn't want to leave the characters."

- "I couldn't put down this exciting road trip adventure with a powerful message."

- "Another award-worthy adventure novel that keeps you on the edge of your seat."

● "A heart-stopping adventure. I just couldn't put the book down till I finished reading it."

● "Kept me mesmerized and captivated with the rich descriptions which made me feel like I was actually inside the story."

● "This is a fantastic read that will have you traveling the globe. I absolutely loved this book. You won't be able to put it down!"

● "A real page turner and international thriller. Reminds me of why I've always loved to read. Because I can visit worlds and places I wouldn't ordinarily get to see."

To learn more about this addictive series, go to www.RedHeeledRebels.com[3]

• • • •

PREQUEL: THE GIRL WHO Crossed the Line

A reckless girl. A grave mistake. A fateful destiny.

All she wanted was to belong. Then, she committed an unforgivable crime...

• • • •

BOOK ONE: THE GIRL Who Ran Away

An estranged orphan. A treacherous plot. A perilous journey that could kill her.

She'd just survived a fiery car crash in the middle of nowhere. Both her parents are dead, but that's nothing compared to what she would face next...

---

3.   http://www.RedHeeledRebels.com

. . . .

BOOK TWO: THE GIRL Who Made Them Pay

A kidnapped friend. A forbidden house. A precarious journey to escape their captors.

They are fleeing a fate worse than death. They think they're finally safe in London, when one of them is snatched into a waiting black cab. And now, she will do anything to find her friend...

. . . .

BOOK THREE: THE GIRL Who Fought to Kill

A lost cousin. A heinous crime. An impossible rescue that risks it all.

She was ready to cross oceans to hunt down her stolen cousin. But she didn't know the terrifying stakes waiting for her on the other side that will test her resolve and courage...

. . . .

BOOK FOUR: THE GIRL Who Broke Free

A sweet sixteenth birthday banquet. A missing diplomat's daughter. A menacing family secret.

She thought she'd finally made it when she was invited to cater for the swankiest party in upscale Manhattan. But she didn't realize the birthday girl's family has other plans and the banquet is a ruse for something more perilous than she could ever imagine...

. . . .

BOOK FIVE: THE GIRL Who Knew Their Names

A glittering Hollywood gala. An actress with a dark vendetta. A cold-blooded murder among the stars.

She thought she'd snagged the most coveted catering job in Los Angeles, and a chance to meet A-list celebrities. But she didn't realize she was about to confront the most powerful predator in town on her first day...

• • • •

BOOK SIX: THE GIRL Who Never Forgot

A girl from the swamps. A family gripped by darkness. A killer on the loose at the Mardi gras.

She was invited to cater a lavish ball where New Orleans' blue-blooded families celebrated Mardi gras in style, away from the cacophony of common street parades. But she didn't realize a murderer was lurking in the shadows, waiting to frame her for their deed...

• • • •

AWARDS & PRAISE FOR The Red Heeled Rebels books:

- Grand Prize Award Finalist - 2019 Eric Hoffer Award, USA
- First Horizon Award Finalist - 2019 Eric Hoffer Award, USA
- Honorable Mention General Fiction - 2019 Eric Hoffer Award, USA
- Winner First-In-Category - 2019 Chanticleer Somerset Award, USA
- Semi-Finalist - 2020 Chanticleer Somerset Award, USA
- Winner in 2019 Readers' Favorite Book Awards, USA
- Winner of 2019 Silver Medal - Excellence E-Lit Award, USA
- Winner in Suspense Category - 2018 New York Big Book Award, USA
- Finalist in Suspense Category - 2018 & 2019 Silver Falchion Awards, USA
- Honorable Mention - 2018-19 Reader Views Literary Classics Award, USA
- Publisher's Weekly Booklife Prize – 2018, USA

Truth Is Harsher than Fiction

• There are an estimated 40.3 million slaves today. Compare this with the much less 12.5 million slaves bought over to the Americas between 1525-1866.

• 51% of globally trafficked victims are women, and 20% are young girls, to a total of 71% female slaves around the world. Some organizations have estimated this number to be as high as 80%.

• 99% of victims in the commercial sex industry are women and girls.

• Women and girls are trafficked for many purposes including forced marriage, pornography production, prostitution, forced labor, domestic work, and even forced begging.

• Sexual exploitation is estimated to be a $32 billion (yes, you read that right) industry.

• 76% of transactions for sex with underage girls are conducted online today.

. . . .

*2018 SOURCES:

Prajwala
International Labour Organisation
Human Rights First
United Nations Office of Drugs and Crime
The Root
Polaris Project
Force 4 Compassion

· · · ·

"Sometimes the story is the lie that exposes the truth."
~ Jason Silva

· · · ·

AS I RESEARCHED, PLANNED, and wrote these novels, I spoke with women and men from around the world, some of whom I'd never met before. They included women who are tirelessly fighting for equality and dignity in South Asia despite the push back and hostility from their own families and communities.

They included former military officers and peacekeepers who had been deployed to conflict zones and saw the heart-wrenching plight of children, but had neither the resources nor the permission to assist them.

Regardless of where they came from, they all shared with me their stories. They read mine. Most importantly, we discussed the difficult topics in these books frankly and without prejudice. I gained many insights through these chats, but one lesson I took away was there are good people everywhere.

These are the good people who do not apologize for harmful traditions nor tolerate cultural dogma. These are the good people who yearn to change age-old customs that subjugate our daughters and alienate our sons. These are the good people who desire to create a better world for all humanity, for now and for the future.

I was surprised to see how much of our world views we share, regardless of differences in gender, vocation, political views, sexual orientation, or nationality.

We all have more in common than not. And this gives me hope, hope for a wiser, kinder, open, and more connected global community that uplifts us all.

How would you like to write your own life story?

The Rebel Diva Self-Empowerment Series
www.RebelDivas.com[1]

The Rebel Diva books are life-changing practical guides that take you on an adventure of a lifetime. Uncover your purpose, your passions, and your talents to create a step-by-step masterplan to achieve your life goals.

You'll create a story in these Rebel Diva books and that story will be yours.

. . . .

WHAT READERS ARE SAYING:

- *"One of the most motivational and thought-provoking books I have ever read."*

- *"This book is phenomenal! This book is written for real people; no platitudes or empty promises."*

- *"A very inspirational read. This is highly recommended, especially if you're seeking to do and make a difference."*

- *"The author is teacher and cheerleader. She gives solid guidelines to help you figure out your goals and action plans, and she truly comes across as someone who cares."*

- *"This isn't just another self-help book—instead, this incredibly useful book includes a clear method and helpful ex-*

---

1.   http://www.rebeldivas.com/

ercises to help you uncover your dreams, passions and purpose."

- *"Very inspiring. Even though I am older, this book made me want to go after some of my dreams that I thought I was too old for. The book comes with a link that you can download a 100-page workbook. I plan on giving my daughter a copy too."*

- *"Proudly considering myself a Rebel Diva after taking this journey to self-discovery!"*

• • • •

SIGN UP TO GET YOUR exclusive Rebel Diva gift!

The Fear Buster is a short Rebel Diva workbook that shares three essential tools to help you overcome any fears or doubt and make both small and big decisions quickly. Go to the Rebel Diva site to get your personal copy as a gift.

www.RebelDivas.com/FearBuster[2]

---

2.   http://www.rebeldivas.com/FearBuster

Dedication

This book is dedicated to Dr Sunitha Krishnan and every other woman like her in India who has spent a lifetime working tirelessly for the rights of women and girls. They are true modern-day heroines, the wonder women of our era.

Acknowledgments

To my fantastic international team of beta readers who helped me through this adventure, who cheered me on as I toiled, and who gave me their frank feedback, thank you.

(In alphabetical order)

- Amanda L. Webster, USA
- Bill Joyce, USA
- Carolyn Pennett-Staresinic, Canada
- Cyndi Wannamaker, Canada
- Julia Di Bona, Canada
- Lindsey Nixie Albright, USA
- Mikaela Kate Hennessey, USA
- Nadia Brown, Canada
- Nadine Hutchinson, USA
- Otivbo Akhigbe, Nigeria
- Stan Myck, Counselor, Embassy of Luxembourg to the United States

· · · ·

TO MY AMAZING, TALENTED, superstar editor, Stephanie, thank you for coming on this literary journey with me and for helping make these books the best they can be.

· · · ·

TO ALL THE GENEROUS readers who take the time to review my novels and give their frank feedback, thank you. I owe you all a debt of gratitude and a glass of wine (or several) when you come to Vancouver next!

About the Author

Tikiri Herath is the multiple-award-winning Canadian author of the Red Heeled Rebels international thriller novels.

Born on a tropical island in the Indian Ocean, she grew up in Southern Africa, and has lived and worked in Southeast Asia, Europe, and North America.

She started her adult life as a lone immigrant girl, but went on to receive a bachelor's degree from the University of Victoria, British Columbia and a master's degree from the Solvay Business School in Brussels.

For fifteen years, she worked in risk management in the intelligence and defense sectors, including in the Canadian Federal Government and at NATO.

Tikiri's an adrenaline junkie who has rock climbed, bungee jumped, rode on the back of a motorcycle across Quebec, flown in an acrobatic airplane upside down, and parachuted solo.

But when she's not writing or plotting another thriller scene, you'll most probably find her baking in her kitchen with a glass of red wine in hand and jazz playing in the background.

To say hello and get free travel stories from around the world, go to www.TikiriHerath.com.[1]

---

1. http://www.TikiriHerath.com